OTHER BOOKS BY SUSAN FINLAY

The Outsiders Series:

In the Shadows (Book 1)

Where Secrets Reside (Book 2)

Winter Tears (Book 3)

The Forgotten Tomb (Book 4)

Project Chameleon Series:

Liars' Games

The Bavarian Woods Series:

Inherit the Past (Book 1)

Tanglewood Grotto (Book 2)

The Chambre Noir Series:

The Handyman

The Tangled Roots Series:

Breadcrumbs and Bombs

Look for more books coming soon, including the next books in her various series, and maybe a book or two in a young adult or middle grade series.

Breadcrumbs and Bombs

Breadcrumbs and Bombs

A Tangled Roots Historical Mystery

By

Susan Finlay

First Edition

Cover Design by Ken Dawson

Paperback ISBN-13:978-1981992508

Ebook ISBN-10:1981992502

Published in the USA

AUTHOR'S NOTE

Although this is a work of fiction, the historical figures and the war itself are real and I've tried to make this story as realistic as possible. I've read many nonfiction and fiction books about World War II and how it affected everyone, on all sides. I'm particularly interested in the lesser known stories of the ethnic Germans living in the former Sudetenland and their expulsion from their homeland at the end of the war.

My American father and one of his sisters worked on their family tree many years ago. On one side of the family, they were able to trace back to early 1800's. On the other side, they were able to trace back to the 1600's. My mother, who came from the former Sudetenland and Germany, was able to also provide some history for her family tree, but only back a couple generations. Years later, after she'd passed away, one of her brothers obtained some old WWII-era Identity Cards that his grandparents had carried. He made copies for me and for one of his sisters. From those, I was able to fill in some missing information from that side of my family's tree.

I tell you this, because I understand why people have an interest in genealogy. As I worked on this book, I got out those old records and photos and dug deeper around my family tree, in a similar way to what my protagonist does in this book. My historical research, and the story I wrote, helped me better understand what my German relatives may have endured.

CHAPTER ONE

Lucas Landry, June 2017, East Sacramento, California—

LUCAS LANDRY PULLED his Jeep into the driveway of his father's pale blue Victorian house. Sucking in a deep breath, he turned off the engine and sat there, brooding, staring at the house fraught with painful memories.

For five of his teen years, he'd lived with his family in this house his father had inherited, but when he'd left home for college ten years ago, he'd never looked back. Not once. Back then, he couldn't wait to move out of the house where his mother had died, where everything was a constant painful reminder of her suffering.

Leaving also meant he'd get away from his father's incessant complaining about the house. Lucas had once asked him, "You grew up in this house. Why did you move us here if you hated the house?" His reply: "Because I got it for free, that's why. I can suffer it because it doesn't cost me anything but what I spend on repairs and property taxes. Someday you'll understand."

Sitting in the car, hands still gripping the steering wheel like a life raft, he shook his head. *I'm not making that mistake.* Moments later Lucas's eyes were drawn to something shiny in the small window at the top of house above the second-story roofline, the window his mother had always called a decoy, whenever Lucas or one of his friends had asked about it. She'd shrug and tell them, "There's no attic. The design was just intended to make it look like it had an attic." Lucas had always thought it odd, but what did he know about old houses? Maybe she was right. Maybe houses were like people, not honest, never really showing their true colors, putting on façades and hiding their dirty secrets from the world.

So if there was no attic, what was shining in the window? He leaned forward to get a better look through the windshield. As it turned out, the 'something shiny' was only the sun hitting the glass at the right angle and it disappeared seconds later. Losing interest, his eyes wandered back to the wraparound veranda, complete with white railing, porch swing, and hanging pots of flowers, where he had hung out a lot as a teen. He realized his hands felt cold and clammy at the thought of going inside the house.

He didn't want the house, didn't want anything from the old man. Hell, his father certainly hadn't wanted anything to do with Lucas for the past five years, not even when Lucas made him a grandfather. He sighed and chided his reticence. It was just an old house. In today's real estate market—2017—in Northern California, Lucas knew he could easily sell it, provided his father hadn't let it deteriorate too much in the ten years since Lucas had gone off to college and started his own family. Only first he had to through all his father's belongings and figure out what to do with them. That was the hard part, the part he dreaded.

Guess I should get this over with.

Sighing again, he got out of the car and closed the door harder than he'd intended, making a loud smack sound, making him jump slightly. He looked around but nobody appeared to be watching. No nosy neighbors. *Okay, you need to calm down. Steel yourself and get the job done. Simple enough. A few hours and then you can call a realtor and never have to go back.* He pushed the lock button on his key fob and gave a backwards glance at the car as it beeped, before walking away. He did a double-take. Oh no, Bianca! She was sitting in the backseat, looking bewildered. Poor kid. He'd forgotten she was there. He pushed the button again unlocking the doors.

"Bianca, I'm sorry. I forgot I'd picked you up at daycare. Come on sweetie, let's get you out of that car seat." After unstrapping the buckle, he lifted her out of the seat, relocked the doors, and carried her down the sidewalk toward the front porch.

"Where are we going, Daddy?"

"To your grandpa's house."

"Yippee! I didn't know I had a grandpa."

Lucas didn't know how to respond. He let it go and continued walking.

The scent of flowers wafted in the air as Lucas stepped onto the bottom step. Taking a big whiff, he let the heady perfume fill his nostrils and somewhat ease his nerves. Memory of his grandmother's house—his mother's mother—came to mind. Her garden had smelled like this, back when Lucas was young, maybe four or five. Good memories there.

He reached the front door and rang the bell. *Crap! Why did I do that? Obviously nobody is home.*

After a moment gathering himself together, Lucas reached into his pant pocket and withdrew the door key, inserting it into the lock. As he opened the door, he froze, his mind's eye remembering his father standing there, refusing to let Lucas inside with his then one-week-old daughter, Bianca. *How could Dad turn his back on us? He wouldn't even look at the baby. She was adorable, dressed in a pink dress with ruffled bloomers and a bonnet, and wrapped in the softest lavender baby blanket. If he'd only looked at her . . . .*

Tears welled-up in Lucas's eyes. For some reason, he'd desperately wanted to share the joy of becoming a father with his father back then. But that would never happen. He shifted the now three-year-old Bianca in his arms.

He tried to step into the house, but his legs felt like anchors chaining him to the spot. He braced himself with one hand on the doorframe, his head drooping down, willing himself to forget the past. It doesn't matter anymore, he told himself.

After several moments and several deep cleansing breaths like he usually instructed his patients at the clinic to try when overwhelmed with emotion, he inched forward into the house and stood in the entryway, looking around in the house that used to be home.

It looked the same, at least for the most part. He wasn't sure if that was a good thing or not.

He walked over to the cream-colored brick fireplace and stared at the family photo sitting on top of the mantel, one of the few professional family photos they'd had taken. For a moment he was back in time, watching his mother hang their four Christmas stockings from the mantel their first year here. Lucas, Seth, and Dad were stringing garland along the front of the fireplace, giving the room a festive feel.

"Is that you, Daddy?" Bianca asked when Lucas picked up the frame.

"Yes, it is. And that's your grandma and grandpa."

"That's not my grandma!"

"Oh, sorry, let me explain. You're right. That's not Grandma, the one you see all the time. That grandma is mommy's mommy. The grandma and grandpa in this picture are my mommy and daddy. They aren't with us anymore. I'm sorry you never got to meet them, baby girl."

She nodded and stuck a finger in her mouth, then withdrew it and said, "Who is that?" pointing to his brother.

"That's my brother, Seth."

"Is he not with us anymore, too?"

Hmm, that was harder to answer. Seth was alive, as far as Lucas knew, but they had severed ties with each other four—or was it five?—years ago.

"I haven't seen Seth in a long time, sweetie. Maybe someday I will again." Was it wrong to tell a little white lie? He doubted he would ever see his brother again. That they didn't see eye-to-eye would have been an understatement, and one she wouldn't have understood if he'd said it. "I wish you could have met my mommy and daddy. Grandma would have loved you, little munchkin."

She looked at the photo again and then at Lucas and smiled her big beautiful smile. His little angel. So sweet and innocent.

Speaking of angels, in the photo his mother looked happy. The photo had been a Christmas present for the family and it was taken a few months before her diagnosis. Luke sighed. Six months after the diagnosis, the cancer took her. She didn't make it to a second Christmas here.

He set the frame back on the mantel and picked up the only other frame. In this one was a photo from his high school graduation, four and a half years after the family photo was taken. Just Lucas, Seth, and Dad. When Lucas was a kid, people often said he and his brother looked like their father. Yeah, right. Seth looked like him, but Lucas never saw any resemblance between himself and them. Sure, they all had the same blue eyes and brown hair, but his own hair was darker and always longish and with some waves and curls, while Dad—and Seth—had worn their hair extremely short. Dad had always kept his hair short, though, partially because of his time spent in the military. But whenever anyone asked him about it, he told them he didn't want to look like a girl with long curly hair. Lucas suspected Seth had copied him to win his approval.

Bianca didn't comment on that photo. Maybe she noticed the sadness.

Setting the photo back down, Lucas tried to push memories away. *Nothing to be gained by dwelling on the past.*

He strode to the kitchen, still carrying Bianca, and stopped in the doorway.

"Eeww, Daddy, something stinks."

"Yeah, I noticed." He put his free hand over his nose as he walked into the kitchen to check it out. Dirty dishes cluttered the counter top and sink. Trash was strewn all over the floor. Had his father turned into a slob toward the end?

Lucas's eyes searched for the trash can. It was beside one wall of cabinets, lying on its side and trash spilling out everywhere. That didn't explain how the trash got all the way across the room. And how did the can get knocked over? No ants or bugs or mice, that Lucas could see, which was a blessing considering it must have been that way for weeks. His father had been dead almost that long, having been found unconscious on the living room sofa by a concerned neighbor. An ambulance ride and a few hours in the hospital . . . and he was gone.

Lucas looked around, trying to decide what to do with Bianca while he cleaned up the mess. "Honey, I need you to sit here at the kitchen table for a few minutes, okay? Stay put."

After setting her down, he pulled the old garbage bag out of the trash can and tied it shut. Looking underneath the sink, he pulled out a box of trash bags and quickly filled it with the overflowing trash on the floor. Making an instant decision, he started dumping the dirty plates, silverware, dirty glasses, coffee mugs, and dried up food stuck on dishes and in the sink. No use trying to salvage the dishes. They were old and mostly scratched and chipped, anyway.

Once finished with that chore, he took Bianca by the hand and led her through the rest of the main floor—the living room, a small study, and a half bath. His wife Tawny had suggested he check out the house to see if anything in it was worth selling. She said she knew of a company that held estate sales for people. He'd actually wanted to just hire someone to come in and haul everything away that wasn't attached or that wouldn't go with the house when they sold it, but he'd listened to Tawny. She was always the voice of reason, when he was too emotionally involved to think clearly.

Well, the house itself was old but, now that he had bought his own house and knew a bit more about houses and the housing market, he recognized the Victorian charm and artisan details, like wainscoting, chair-rails, cherry wood stairs and railings, and large walk-in closets. The downstairs might have a few furnishings worth selling, but nothing great. A couple of antiques, he guessed.

He picked up Bianca and strode up the stairs. At the top, he glanced into his old bedroom. Small, mostly empty, except for a twin bed and a chest of drawers that had served their purpose but held no sentimental value. He continued on, passing Seth's old bedroom. Something darted across his path and he stumbled backwards. What the . . . hell was that? The mess in the kitchen sprang to mind. Oh God . . . a rat? Eeww. He gritted his teeth and tiptoed into the master bedroom, set Bianca on the bed, then bent down, and braced himself as he looked underneath the double bed. Two shiny green eyes with black slits looked back at him. A cat. Huh? Dad had a cat? Dad hated animals and would never let Lucas and Seth get a pet.

"Come here, kitty. I won't hurt you." He held out his hand, trying to coax the cat out. After a few moments, it crept toward him, and Lucas reached out and petted the animal.

"You must be really hungry. I'll get you something to eat, okay?"

That elicited some purrs.

Lucas stood up and said, "Come on."

The cat ran out from under the bed toward the door.

Bianca jumped up and stood on the bed clapping her hands. "Kitty. Can we keep it?"

Lucas grabbed her off the bed and followed the cat, without answering. The last thing they needed was a pet, especially now that he and Tawny were expecting their second child in five months.

The cat ran down the stairs and into the kitchen, where it turned and looked at him, as if saying, "Well, are you going to feed me?"

"Okay, if you live here, there must be cat food around here somewhere." He went into the walk-in pantry/storage room where his family had always kept food, cleaning supplies, etc. Here, the smell was even worse than in the kitchen. An overflowing cat litter box was stuck in the back corner of the panty and it stunk to high heaven. The floor was covered in cat pee and poop, too. Yuck! That certainly explained some things.

Finding a bag of dry cat food, he searched for and found the cat's food and water dishes and filled them both, then emptied the litter box into another trash bag and poured fresh litter in the pan from an open box of litter he found in the pantry.

While the cat chowed down, Lucas stroked her fur and was rewarded with more purrs.

Bianca tried to reach down and pet the cat, but the cat backed up, causing Bianca to pull her hand away. "She doesn't like me."

"She's scared, honey. Give her time to get to know you." Oh God, why did he say that? They weren't keeping the cat.

After the cat calmed, Lucas reached out and touched her collar and found a name tag. He turned it over. Hallie. "Hey there, Hallie. You're gonna be okay. I won't take you to the pound. Promise. We'll find you a home."

The cat of course paid no attention. She finished eating and drinking, licked her paws, then sauntered out of the room.

Bianca and Lucas followed her into the kitchen, Bianca finally getting to pet the cat, while Hallie groomed herself. "We're gonna be friends, Hallie," Bianca said.

"Stay there a minute, okay." Lucas went back into the storage room and cleaned up the floor the best he could. He would have to find or buy a bucket and mop later to really scrub down the floor, seeing as how he didn't see either in the supply room. The kitchen floor needs a good scrubbing, too, he thought as he walked back through the kitchen to the foyer.

"Okay, all done. Let's go back upstairs and look around."

He started to pick up Bianca, but she pulled back and said, "I'm three years old. I can do it myself. Grandma lets me at her house."

Should he let her? After Bianca fell down the bottom three steps one day and got a bruise on her cheek when Lucas was home alone with her, Tawny insisted they keep the baby gate at the top and bottom of the stairs. It didn't help that Tawny was already overprotective because Bianca had been a preemie and was small—dainty—for her age.

"Okay, but we'll take it slow going up. Stay close to me and let me know if you need help."

"Daddy, you're funny. I'm not a baby."

From the upstairs hallway, Lucas surveyed his brother's bedroom. A double bed with an antique headboard, frame, and footboard, a matching dresser, and chest of drawers filled the above average sized room. When they'd moved in to the house, Lucas had wanted this room—who wouldn't?—and explained that, as the oldest by three years, and being a teenager in middle school, he should get it. Dad had countered that his brother deserved the bigger room because he was an athlete and needed space for all his gear. Lucas had argued that being older should have some privilege. Seth and Dad had countered that Lucas should be happy that he wouldn't have the inconvenience of having to give up his room whenever they had guests staying with them. Hah, right. Lucas couldn't remember them ever having any house guests while he lived here. Returning to the present, he assessed the room. *Hmm, those pieces of furniture could be worth a bit of change.*

He turned on his heels and said, "Come on, Bianca." He strode to the entrance to his parents' room again, this time actually seeing it instead of hunting for an animal. Unbidden, he pictured his mother lying in the bed, thin and frail, waiting for the end to come.

He wanted to turn around and run down the stairs, but forced himself to hold fast. Glancing to one side, he spotted an antique dresser with another pair of photographs in frames sitting on top. It was an old-fashioned piece that, when he thought about it, was actually kinda half dressing table and half dresser. A large oval mirror was affixed in the center with a small armless cushioned chair perched in front of the mirror, creating the dressing table. Three large ornate dresser drawers sat on each side of the chair.

He walked over to it and picked up one of the photo frames.

"Can I see it?" Bianca asked.

He picked her up, and she touched the edge of the frame with her tiny fingers.

"Who is that baby?"

"That baby is me. That's my mommy holding me." His mother was beaming in the photo.

"You cute baby." She smiled, then placed her hands on both of his cheeks.

"Not as cute as you, munchkin. I'll have to show you your baby pictures when we get home."

She giggled. "I want to see."

In the second photo Lucas was a young boy, maybe eight or nine, standing on the shore of a nearby lake beside his father and Seth. Lucas was proudly showing off a fish he'd caught. His father stood beside him with his arms crossed, looking angry. Lucas remembered his father being angry at him for not catching more fish.

Turning away, he stared at the closet door. He supposed he would have to sell or donate his father's clothing.

Closing his eyes momentarily, Lucas tried to brace himself, unsure how he would feel about seeing his father's clothes. Then he opened his eyes and set Bianca down, not seeing anything that could hurt her if she looked around the bedroom.

He walked over and opened the closet door. His father's clothes somehow still carried the manly smell Lucas remembered. He struggled to keep memories at bay. *Best get this over with.* He reached in and began pulling hangers out, laying them and the attached clothes on the bed. He'd have to find some boxes to put them in. Maybe Tawny would know where he could get some. There might even still be some in their garage, leftover from when they moved into their house in Roseville last year.

What the hell? His mother's clothes were still in the closet, too, hidden in the recesses away from the doorway. Lucas had assumed his father had donated them to charity after her passing. Oh, man, he really didn't want to take her clothes out and get rid of them.

As he began removing them, tears threatened to come. He struggled, surprised at how strong his emotions were still, after all the years she'd been gone. Maybe that's why Dad never got rid of her clothes. Maybe his emotions wouldn't let him.

Once all the clothes were out of the closet, Lucas could found something he'd never seen before—a crack in the wall, but a crack that seemed artificially straight, behind where his mother's clothes had hung for all those years. He probed at the wall, thinking he'd have to get that patched up before selling it. As he pushed on one side, the wall moved, slightly outward. It was a hidden doorway. *Maybe an access door to plumbing.* Wait. He bit his lip. The master bathroom was on the other side of the room. *An attic?* Was there an attic in the house, after all? Was this the way up to the attic? He reached for the small indent, a tab-like space, and pulled it. The door opened into the closet, revealing stairs.

"Hello! Are you here, Luke?" Tawny yelled from downstairs.

"Mommy!" Bianca yelled. "Hi Mommy."

Lucas grinned, rushed out of the room, and stopped part way down the stairs, leaning on the railing and staring down to greet his wife, then turned, remembering Bianca. She was poised at the top of the stairs. He told her to sit there at the top, then after seeing her sit, he turned to his wife. "Hey, you. I'm so happy you could come. I found something interesting up here. Come on up."

"Okay." She kicked off her shoes, which she always did at home, and ran up the stairs, stopping and kissing him when she reached his steps.

"Careful you don't pull me down the stairs," he said with a chuckle.

"That would not be the sort of tumble I would think of." She grinned and kissed him again. "I didn't think I would get here before you left. Work was crazy, no pun intended, and I didn't finish with my last patient until half an hour ago. I'm happy you picked up Bianca already."

"It's nice spending extra time with her. Not every day I get off work three hours early, you know."

"This is a beautiful house," she said, turning around and surveying the stairwell and the upstairs and downstairs of the house from that perspective. "Are you sure you want to sell it?"

"I don't like this place. Too many bad memories."

"Good memories, too?"

He didn't respond. He felt a wave of something—he couldn't put his finger on it—hit him. Overwhelming sadness. His father was gone. Forever. His mother was gone. Forever. And he knew nothing about either of them. Not really. Nothing about their families' pasts. Nothing about who they really were as people. Why hadn't he ever pushed them to tell him and his brother about themselves and their heritage?

"Surely, you must have some good memories from living here."

He shrugged.

"Well, anyway, if you want, we could remodel and move in here."

He couldn't tell if his wife was joking or being serious.

"Uh, we have a house already, remember? And jobs near that house."

She shrugged. "I'm just saying. This house has been in your family for a while. And it's much bigger than ours. Did you forget that our family is growing? We have to sell one house, but nobody says it has to be this one. And as for jobs, we can get counseling jobs closer to this area, you know."

Uh oh, she's serious. "We could get a lot more money selling this place. Don't forget that."

She shook her head. "I know, but money isn't the most important thing."

He didn't respond. His choice had nothing to do with money. It had everything to do with his mother's pain, her death here, and with the way his father had treated his family. Was it any wonder that Seth had turned out the way he did?

"Anyway, what did you find?"

Thank God, she's letting it go. "Come on. I'll show you." After walking up a few steps, he added, "To be honest, I'm not sure what I found. You arrived before I got a chance to check it out."

At the top of the stairs, Tawny bent down and picked up a very patient Bianca, giving her a tight squeeze. "Did you have a good day at preschool?"

Bianca nodded.

In the master bedroom, Lucas closed the bedroom door and locked it so Bianca couldn't get out of the room, and then grabbed Tawny's free hand and pulled her into the closet.

"Wow, this is a good size closet. See, you're making my case for moving to this house."

Crap! She's still thinking about it. He pulled the knob again and reopened the door.

"Oh, my Gosh!" Tawny said, sounding more South African than usual. "It's a secret passage. To where?"

He chuckled, loving to see Tawny bubbling over like a little girl and letting her British accent from her childhood out. "The attic, I suspect. Come on. Let's find out."

They climbed the narrow stairs and landed in a large attic with wood floors, one small window, and loaded with junk—lots of junk—old toys, an old wooden cradle, several trunks, and various odds and ends, apparently having been used as a storage room over the past one hundred and fifty years.

"Wow! This is incredible. It's like a museum. I can't wait to see what's in those," she said, pointing at the old trunks and suitcases.

Oh crap! Lucas wasn't sure what he was expecting, but not the big mess he was seeing. He shook his head. Leave it to his wife to get excited about more work. That's what this was, no question about it. He walked around the attic, almost as big as the whole second floor of the house—well, not quite, but it seemed like it. The room was musty smelling, assailing his nostrils, and he noticed cobwebs and mouse droppings in a few places. *Good, that'll probably dampen Tawny's desire to move here.*

Six huge trunks took up residence along the length of one wall and a few more around the corner on another wall. At least that's what it looked like from where he stood. He couldn't see much detail as the lighting was too dim at the back of the room and the outside light coming in through one small window was waning as the sun set.

He looked around for a light switch. Where the hell was it? Then he noticed a pull-string hanging down from light bulbs on the angled rafters. Reaching up as high as he could, he was barely able to pull the string. *Good thing I'm six feet tall. Tawny certainly couldn't reach it.* The room lit up a bit more, with a yellowy glow.

Oh, hell! What had looked like six trunks was much more. Behind them and in the corner and part way up the next wall were row upon row of trunks and dozens of antique suitcases or valises, or whatever they were called, the kind he'd seen in old photos and on display in his university's history museum, dating back to WWI and WWII. Though the museum display of historical chests, trunks, and clothing held only minor interest for him, at the time he'd been enthralled by the black and white photographs. Stark, eerie.

He remembered wondering about his own family's history, back when he'd toured the museum with his classmates. His mother's family, he vaguely remembered his mother saying once, had originally come from Ireland, but had already immigrated to the U.S. before the first world war, or was it the second world war? He couldn't remember which. He had no idea where his father's family had been during wartime. All of Lucas's life, his father had been closed off about them, as if he . . . well, what, he couldn't come up with any good reason. Back when Lucas was sixteen and heard about the witness protection program, he'd even imagined his father being in that program. At least for a while that made him feel as though his father had a good reason to hide everything from them.

But later having learned that this house had been in the family for generations, Lucas gave up that fantasy. He also concluded that he wouldn't have had any family in Europe during wartime, unless they were U.S. soldiers sent over to fight.

Dismissing those thoughts, he pondered the antique trunks and suitcases now confronting him. The hinges and closing mechanisms on the ones he could see were ancient and very rusty, some tinged with green. *Copper.* Some had leather straps, all broken, long ago having lost their flexibility and strength.

He thought about how much of a struggle it must have been for someone to drag all those trunks and suitcases up the main house stairs, into the master bedroom's closet, and then up the narrow staircase to the attic. And to dispose of all this junk in order to sell the house and possibly convert the attic into another bedroom to market it as a fourth bedroom meant that he would now have to drag it all back down.

Ugh! Junk! How long had this stuff been up here, collecting dust and who-knows-what-else?

He swung around and studied the rest of the space. Along another wall were three old four-drawer metal file cabinets. Next to those he counted five rows of boxes and crates stacked up five high against the wall. "Three file cabinets and twenty-five boxes to look through," he said, groaning. A fleeting vision of opening the window and tossing out the boxes, contents and all, to crash down onto the lawn sounded appealing. Back to reality, he decided maybe a paper shredder could be brought up here to get rid of the stuff in the file cabinets at least.

He looked around, trying to decide where to begin this hopeless journey. Tawny beat him to it and was trying to open one of the trunks.

Lucas strode over and tried to open it, discovering that the lock was either locked or jammed. Seeing no other choice, he said, "I'll go downstairs to the storage shed and get some tools. I'll have to jimmy the lock."

Once he got the first two trunks open, Tawny brought Bianca up to the attic. Bianca was enthralled, wanting to peek into every crevice. Tawny spread out a blanket for her to sit on, and after dusting them off, gave her some toys she found in the corner of the attic. "I'm going to look through one of these trunks, if you don't mind," she stated to Lucas.

"Go for it," he said. He sighed and eased his butt down onto the floor, knees up and arms draped over them as he studied the task ahead of him. He glanced over at the boxes, thinking, *probably should have brought up a small step ladder, too.*

THE OLD TRUNKS and chests Lucas and Tawny had searched through so far, while not containing anything of monetary value, were filled with antique clothes that Lucas figured a history museum would love to get their hands on. Lacy evening gowns, casual dresses and skirts, silk blouses, white gloves, assorted hats and hat pins. This was a treasure-trove reminding him of the costumes in old movies he and Tawny sometimes watched. Some looked like they might have been worn by those doomed travelers on the Titanic. It was his choice what to do with them. Anyone interested in turn-of-the-century clothing from California would certainly want some of the stuff he'd found and he was sure an antiques dealer would pay money to get them. But he would personally rather see them go to a museum where they could be displayed and lots of people could enjoy seeing them.

They stopped looking through the trunks after a couple hours because they all needed dinner and needed to get home to put Bianca to bed.

By the time they got home, they were both bone tired and went to bed early. In the morning, Saturday, they rose early, ate a quick breakfast, dropped Bianca off at Tawny's mother's house, and then went back to his dad's house. *It's gonna be a long day,* Lucas thought as he turned into the driveway.

Lucas decided to look through one of the filing cabinets while Tawny continued with the trunks. Opening the first drawer, he rifled through the folders in front. Looked like old house papers. Hmm, maybe the deed to the house was in there? He made a mental note to check more closely, later. Then came folders for insurance policies (really old), medical bills (again really old), newspaper clippings, and other miscellaneous junk.

Near the back of the drawer was a really fat manila binder. He reached for it, wondering what could be in it. He had to pull hard to get it out from between the tight folders. Unraveling the tie that held it closed, he opened the binder and peeked inside. Photos! Tons of black and white photos, loose, turned every which way.

He carried the binder over to the folding card table he'd set up in the middle of the room, set it down, and plopped his butt onto one of the folding chairs.

Maybe he would see someone—relatives, maybe?—wearing some of the clothes he and Tawny had found in the trunks. That might make Tawny's suggestion of keeping some of the clothes more desirable, not that they would be considered family heirlooms, but at least feeling some connection might make a difference.

Dumping out the contents of the binder, he spread the photographs across the table and started turning them in the right direction and right side up to view them.

Kinda like starting work on a jigsaw puzzle. He leaned over to reach some of them better. After several minutes he scratched his head.

"Hey, Tawny, can you come over here for a minute? I need your opinion?"

"Sure." A few moments later, she stood looking over his shoulder. "Whatcha got here?"

"Damned if I know. Far as I can tell it's a bunch of photos of lots of different people from totally different time periods. Do you think someone was collecting photos of strangers, or what? My brain is boggled trying to figure this out."

Tawny began rearranging the photos into four groups, while Lucas watched.

"Ah, now I see what you're doing," he said. "You're way better at this stuff than I am. How many time periods do you think we have here?"

"At least three. These," she said, pointing to one group, "look like they were taken in this area, maybe in the mid to late 1800's. Photos weren't so common back in those days, which may be why there are only a few."

"Yeah, that makes sense."

"And do you see their clothes and the tools they're holding?"

"Oh, I didn't notice that. They look like miners."

She grinned. "Kinda like the seven dwarfs, huh?"

He chuckled.

"This second group," she said, "looks like they were taken around here, too, but later. I'm thinking early 1900's, possibly during the Great Depression."

Lucas gave her hand a squeeze and then pulled another chair over. "Sit. You're doing great, baby."

She glanced over her shoulder and grinned, then sat down. "You know, this group over here is the most interesting to me."

"Why's that?"

"They look foreign. Didn't you say your father's mother came from Ireland?"

19

"She maybe did, but I don't know when they came here. And that's not Ireland in the photos. Looks more like the Alps in some of them."

"Oh." She picked up one of the photos, one with a quaint house in the background, and turned it over. "It has writing on the back. It says Mutti und Vati, Altstadt, Sudetenland. Here's another with a bunch of kids. The back on it says: Christa, Fritz, and some other names I can't read. The handwriting is hard to decipher, and it's blurred in spots. Like it got wet."

"The Sudetenland? Wait. I remember learning about it in one of my German classes in college. It was part of Germany for a while during World War II. If I remember my history lessons, after the war the Sudetenland was split up and became part of the Czech Republic and . . . well, I don't remember the details. Anyway, the Sudeten Germans were expelled and sent back to Germany."

"Yeah, yeah, I vaguely remember learning something about it, too, in school. It wasn't covered in much detail," Tawny said, frowning, apparently trying to remember more.

Lucas squinted at the photos Tawny was holding. "What I'd like to know is who are those people and why would my father have their photos in his file cabinet?"

"You told me last night that your mother said the attic window was probably a façade. You think maybe she didn't know the attic existed."

"I don't know. Maybe my father didn't know about it, either. Maybe nobody told him when he inherited the house. Then again he might have known and didn't tell anyone else. It seems unlikely they never discovered the door in the closet."

She nodded. "All this stuff may have belonged to your grandparents or great-grandparents. That's kinda exciting, isn't it?"

"Maybe. For all we know, this stuff could be a part of a collection that one of my relatives bought in a yard sale. Who knows? We shouldn't assume these people in the photographs are my ancestors."

"Why not? I don't believe for one minute that someone collected this stuff and stored it for years if it didn't mean something to them. Your father never talked to you about his family, and now you have a chance to find out more about them. Who know, maybe something here will lead you to find descendent family members and meet them."

"Maybe you're right." Lucas looked at the rest of the photos in that group. Quite a few of them were of children, and some were of adults and were labeled Mutti and Vati or Mutter and Vater. Other photos showed a picturesque village with mountains in the distance. "See, here," he said, pointing to one photo. "I don't resemble any of these people."

Tawny said, "Lucas, looks don't mean a damn thing. Bianca looks more like me, with dark skin and dark eyes. She won't be seen as Caucasian, and you know that. Which means that even though you have dark hair and most of the people in the photos are blondes, that doesn't mean you aren't related to them. We can't tell their eye colors since the photos are in black and white, but even if we could, what difference would it make? You can be related to them, no matter how different you look from them."

"Yeah, I see your point," he yielded and tossed the photos onto the table.

"I sense a 'but' in that statement."

He held her gaze for a moment before looking away. "I just don't want to get my hopes up. My parents never told us anything about our ancestors. Maybe they didn't know anything. Or maybe they had a good reason to keep the past a secret."

"Don't you want to find out?"

He shrugged. He didn't want to tell her why he had misgivings. Sure, he wanted to know who he really was and where he came from. But, sometimes, you're better off not knowing. That's where sayings like be careful what you wish for, don't poke the bear, and the road to hell is paved with good intentions come from.

"Look here, some of them have somewhat curly hair like yours. With blonde hair, I would expect some of them have blue eyes, like yours."

"You're really reaching, aren't you? Let's face it, these are probably strangers and not relatives of mine."

She ignored that comment and continued examining photos. "Look at this last group of photos. These are from Germany, according to the writing on the backs of some of them. There are people's names, too, but I'm having trouble reading them. Ilse and Ursula, I think, are two of them. Hard to tell the rest."

Germany. Nazis. What if he was related to Nazis? Oh hell.

"Take a look at this one," she said, offering him a photo.

He took it and studied it. "Okay, so maybe this is another group of relatives. Or maybe they are people who met the Sudeten Germans later, when they got expelled from the Sudetenland, they went to this other town."

"Maybe. Did you come across any family tree type documents?"

"Nope. I haven't gotten very far yet."

"Keep digging," Tawny said. "This could be something big. Maybe we'll uncover your family's history—or, at the least, this house's history. Wouldn't it be exciting to find out how far back in your family tree this house could reach?"

"Probably not that long. I mean, if these people who lived in Germany during the war are part of my family tree, wouldn't that mean they didn't own this house for more than a couple generations?"

"There were photos of miners in the file, too."

"Yeah," Lucas said. "That makes me believe my original idea—that the photos were merely part of someone's collection."

"Oh, Lucas, stop being so closed-minded. You could come from a family of miners and a family of German immigrants. You already know your mother's family came from Ireland. Maybe you have ancestors who came here from other countries hoping to become rich. Who knows who you're related to?"

He closed his eyes as his mind spun, considering the myriad possibilities. This must be what it feels like to suddenly find out you're adopted and have no idea where your roots lie. That's how his father had left him. Rootless. Bound only to this old Victorian house. The only thing he knew for sure was that his family had at least two racists that he knew of. Wasn't it possible he came from a whole line of racists?

CHAPTER TWO

Christa Nagel, September 5, 1943, Altstadt, Sudetenland—

CHRISTA NAGEL DAWDLED after school on Friday afternoon in front of her family's house, an old stucco'd farmhouse her great-great-great-grandfather had built. The house, like most of the others in town, sat three feet back from the road and was two stories tall, with an attic at the top and red shingles on the roof. It had been passed down through the generations, most recently to her grandparents. But those grandparents had moved away to Germany almost ten years ago, when Christa was a baby. She didn't even remember them. She often wondered why they'd moved and why her family hadn't. *But then*, she thought, *maybe we stayed because we got their old house.* Her parents had installed indoor plumbing in the kitchen so that they had running water for the sink and had painted the house the palest of pale yellow seven years ago when Christa was three. Most buildings in town were white or off-white or beige. She guessed her parents wanted to stand out, but weren't ready to commit to a bold color. The paint was already peeling due to the harsh winters, but her parents weren't repainting. Their house wasn't the only one deteriorating. No one had the money to keep their houses in good shape. And like her family, most couldn't afford to add indoor toilets and bathtubs. They used an outhouse in the backyard and they bathed in a large tub that they set up in the middle of the kitchen. Only the village's wealthiest families had indoor bathrooms. She sighed. *Why can't we be wealthy?*

Her younger sister, Julia, standing on the front porch with their brothers standing on the steps below, turned her head and yelled to Christa, "Are you coming inside? Today is my birthday, remember? I turn eight."

"*Ja.* I am coming." She followed Julia and the boys, Fritz and Ernst, into the house, then smacked into the back of Julia, who had stopped in the foyer without warning.

"Why does Vati have a suitcase packed?" Julia asked.

Their father was standing in the parlor with a suitcase at his feet.

"He is going away on a business trip," Mutti said "He has gone on those before, remember?"

When had her farmer father ever gone on a business trip before? Christa wondered. In her ten years, she didn't remember him ever leaving home except to visit his parents in a nearby town, and when he did, he usually took one of the kids with him. Whenever he sold their vegetables or fruits, it was to the locals.

Hmm, maybe he is trying to sell some of our livestock. Maybe we need money and that's the only way to get more.

"Stay, Vati, please," Fritz, the youngest of the school-age kids said.

"*Ja*, stay home with us," Julia said, arms crossed and feet firmly planted, daring anyone to argue. "Today is my birthday. We have to celebrate. It is tradition."

"Do not worry, *meine liebling.* I am not leaving until the morning," Vati said. "We have a birthday celebration planned for tonight. Your mother is going to make a cake and a delicious meal."

Christa, too, folded her arms across her chest. No, he wasn't trying to sell livestock. He wouldn't pack a suitcase for that. He would only go away for a day. Something wasn't right. No, they weren't telling the truth. The younger kids might believe it, but not her.

"I need you to all do your chores quickly today, so we can work on making a special dinner for Julia's birthday," Mutti said. "Christa, I will expect you to help with the cooking."

Big surprise. I always help with the cooking. "All right, Mutti. I will be back inside after I feed the chickens." She rushed up the stairs and tossed her rucksack on her bed, then back down the stairs and out the side door to the yard where they kept their chickens.

She opened the pen's door and stepped inside, closing the door behind her to keep roaming chickens from escaping. Her family was lucky they still had chickens and still got fresh eggs. Most people in town didn't have any. Christa's mother often sold them or bartered with their extra eggs to get flour for making bread.

"Are you ready for your dinner?" Christa said to the chickens that were romping around her feet. "You will have to leave me some room to get through." She giggled, and pushed her way through the yard. Reaching the bin where they stored the grain, she opened the lid, took out a scoop full, and fed the hungry fowl.

Next, she went out back to their garden and pulled out four potatoes and four carrots. She hoped that would be enough for the soup she knew her mother would make for dinner. Before long, the weather would turn cool and their garden would end for the season. She was glad now that she and Mutti and Vati had stockpiled vegetables in their root cellar and canned their fruit in there, too. They would certainly need them later.

Most of their land and cattle and goats had been seized by the Wehrmacht, the German military, leaving them only a small patch of garden, two cows, and two goats—enough for their family, for now, anyway. She'd heard that in nearby towns, like the one where her other grandparents, Vati's parents, lived, the soldiers were taking all livestock and even confiscating produce grown by farmers.

It wasn't like they could go to the store and buy them. Not here, not during the war. She'd heard on the radio that in Germany and other European countries, every family got ration cards that allowed them certain foods, if those were available. Often, the foods were gone before the people standing in the long lines made it into the shops. Mutti had said that she feared rationing would begin here, too, and they needed to be prepared.

She entered the stube (parlor) and found her mother feeding the baby milk from her breast.

"I will bake the cake in a few minutes," Mutti said. "Will you get out the flour, eggs, and milk for me? Oh, and put the large pot on the stove and start cutting up the vegetables for our soup."

"All right, Mutti." Christa carried the potatoes and carrots into the kitchen and set them down on the counter top, then looked up at the assorted utensils, pots, and pans—dented, tarnished, and worn from years of service—that hung above the stove. In the afternoon light she could understand why her youngest sister was afraid of the massive black iron stove with its narrow chimney and wouldn't go near it, saying it was a monster that would eat her. Too much of listening to the Hansel and Gretel story Mutti read to them, Christa thought.

She shook her head, and pulled over the step-stool, climbed up, and pulled down the soup pot, filling it with water for the soup and setting it atop the stove. She also grabbed the tea kettle that was sitting on top of the stove and filled it with water. Looking at the pile of small logs stacked on the floor next to the stove, she decided her brothers would have to bring in more wood soon from the pile of wood their father had cut and stacked outside.

She walked over to the cupboards next to the stove. Her father had painted the cupboards a year ago, a pale blue, and added glass knobs on the outside, making the kitchen cheerier than it had been when they first moved in. She opened one of the doors and pulled out the burlap bag of flour and set it on the countertop for her mother.

Above the cupboards were two unpainted pine shelves holding jars of various sizes and shapes, jars that were filled with spices, oats, and salt. She picked up the salt and the pepper and set them on the stove top for seasoning the soup.

Mutti came into the kitchen and put on her apron, then broke open some eggs and began working on the cake while Christa sliced vegetables and dumped them into the soup pot. Working alongside Mutti made Christa smile. Alone time—just the two of them—meant a lot. Julia looked after the baby and gave their mother some time away from the baby and that, too, meant a lot.

After dinner, the family sat in the parlor, ate birthday cake, told ghost stories, and sang German folk songs until the youngest kids could barely keep their eyes open. Mutti and Vati put baby Andreas, four- year-old Giselle, seven-year-old Fritz, and eight-year-old Julia to bed and Vati said goodbye to them and told them he would be gone by the time they awoke.

Mutti and Vati instructed nine-year-old Ernst and ten-year-old Christa to come back downstairs with them.

"We need to talk to you about something," Mutti said.

Christa held her breath for a moment upon hearing that. She was right. They had lied to them.

Downstairs, Mutti sat in a chair and said, "Sit down, children."

They both sat stiffly on the sofa, side by side. Christa didn't look at her brother, but she knew he was nervous, too. His right knee was bouncing.

"Vati has been conscripted into the Wehrmacht. He has to report for duty in Hitler's army tomorrow."

Christa squinted her eyes at her parents. "Why? We are not Nazis, are we?"

"*Es macht nichts*," Mutti said. "They give the orders. We have to follow them. They do not care about our political beliefs."

Vati put his hand on Mutti's leg. "We have to be careful what we say. But your mother is right. Disregarding their Wehrmacht's orders can get you imprisoned or killed."

Ernst said, "I do not understand. We live in the Sudetenland, not in Germany. It is not our war."

"That is not entirely true," Vati said. "The Sudetenland and all of Czechoslovakia are part of Germany now. We heard the news on the radio of the Nazi takeover of the Czech government. They control the whole country."

Christa struggled to hold back her tears, for Vati's sake. "How . . . how long will he be gone?"

"We do not know," Vati answered.

"But why does he have to fight for Hitler?" Ernst asked. "I still do not understand. We do not live in Germany. None of us were born there. We are Sudetendeutsch."

Vati sighed out loud. "*Ja*, my family and your mother's family have lived in this land for several generations. We have never even been to Germany. But, as your mother said, it matters not. The Sudetenland is now part of the German Reich. Hitler claimed it in 1938. Even if they did not control Czechoslovakia, they control us."

"I heard about that in school," Christa said. She'd also heard that many of the Czechs living in Altstadt thought that all the Sudetendeutsch were Nazis or supported "*Der Führer*" and "Hitler's Army", and they didn't want them here anymore. If her father joined the army, wouldn't that confirm their beliefs?

Vati said, "We have been lucky so far that we have not been as affected as citizens inside Germany have been, but the war is expanding and we have been sucked in, too."

"You could be killed," Christa whispered. "Do not go. Please do not."

"I have no choice, *meine liebling*."

"What would happen if you refused to go?" Ernst asked.

"As I said, they would come for me and throw me in prison or shoot me dead. That would not help our family."

"You could go away or we could hide you," Ernst said.

"*Nein*," Vati said. "That would put all of you at risk. The Nazis kill resisters and they kill people who interfere. I have talked to other people and I have listened to the radio—both the Volksempfänger radio and the BBC broadcasts on our old radio. You must not tell anyone that we still have that old radio. It is against the law."

Christa knew about the Volksempfänger radio. The Nazis had delivered them to every German household, and her parents sat and listened to it in the evenings after the kids went to bed. She had overheard it sometimes when she came downstairs to go to the outhouse. She never got to hear much, but she'd overheard some women in town talking about that radio and they called it the "All Nazi, All the Time" radio. Christa hadn't known about another radio until now. She wanted to ask about it, but kept quiet.

Her eyes filled with tears. She'd heard stories, too, about people being dragged from their homes and shot. Not here in Altstadt, but in surrounding towns. Some Jewish families in Altstadt had disappeared, too. She'd seen with her own eyes soldiers taking a Jewish friend and her family away in a truck.

"I will write home whenever I can. I will survive. I am young and strong and determined to come home. You two, as the oldest, will need to help your mother around the house and help her take care of the younger kids. Promise me you will."

"Of course, Vati," they said in unison.

Mutti said, "We do not want your brothers and sisters to know. They are too young to understand yet."

Christa glanced at her brother and then they both nodded.

Their parents stood up in unison and announced that they all needed to get to sleep now. Vati had a long day ahead of him tomorrow and needed his rest.

Lying in bed, Christa tossed and turned. How was she supposed to sleep when her father was about to go into battle? She glanced over at her two sisters, each sound asleep in her own bed and wished she hadn't been old enough to understand what was happening in their lives. She lay there, trying to remember what she'd learned in school about *Die Wehrmacht*—the German military. It was comprised of Die Kriegsmarine (the navy), Die Luftwaffe (the air force), and Das Heer (the army). Which would Vati be in?

Then she thought about what Vati had said, that he had no choice about whether to go or stay. Her teacher had told the class that every officer, soldier, sailor, and airman now owed his duty, honor, and loyalty to *"Der Führer"*, that nasty little man who had come through their town and others, in a parade last year. How could anyone pledge their loyalty to him? Even at her age she could tell he was terrible for her people. Poor Vati.

The next morning, while Vati made final preparations for his departure, Mutti kept telling her, "Hold still. How do you expect me to braid your hair if you keep fidgeting?"

"But why do you worry about my hair on such an important day? Should we not be helping Vati get ready?"

"He does not need our help."

"What is he doing?" Ernst asked from his spot at the kitchen table.

"He is dressing in his uniform that was delivered here yesterday while you were in school," Mutti said, tying the first braid. "Now turn so I can fix the other braid."

Christa did as she was told. It was a ritual she was accustomed to but was harder to sit through this morning, because of her anxiety over her father. Normally, she enjoyed the feel of her mother's hands on her head; she supposed that was because, being the oldest of six children, it was the one moment of each day that she received her mother's individual attention. She sighed.

"I suspect I will have to cut off your hair soon," Mutti said. "It is getting dangerously long."

Christa closed her eyes. Here we go again. Her blonde plaits extended almost to her waist, and every week her mother told her that if it got long enough that she sat on the ends, she would chop it all off. She was afraid her hair would get caught in the washing machine wringer.

When her mother finished, Christa asked, "Did you make the roll on top of my head?" The other girls in her class wore their hair parted on one side and braided, same as Christa did, but recently added something new called a Center roll or a Victory roll, depending on who she asked. Christa had watched her best friend's mother do it. She took hold of a wedge of hair on the upper part of the longer side and wrapped it around a finger numerous times to form a roll, then pulled the finger out and pinned the hair in place on top of her daughter's head with bobbie pins. Then she braided the rest of the hair into two plaits as usual.

"Yes, I made it the way you wanted. Your father will be pleased with how nice you look when you see him off on his trip."

Christa didn't respond. She didn't want to say that it could be his last memory of her.

Twenty minutes later, Mutti, Christa, and Ernst stood outside on the porch, waiting with Vati. He was dressed in a gray military uniform and shiny black boots. At nearly six feet tall he looked impressive.

After five minutes of waiting, a large group of men from their village, all dressed the same and carrying one valise each, walked by their house, and Vati stepped in line with them. Most of the men's faces showed no pride. Only a few of the men's faces glowed with excitement. Christa's father appeared to be trying to keep his face blank, but she knew him well enough to see the sorrow in his eyes.

"Can we walk with them for a while?" Christa asked, turning to look at her mother.

"I guess that would be all right. But do not leave the village, and come straight back home. Your brothers and sisters will awake soon and will want their breakfast. Remember, you are not to mention the uniforms or soldiers."

Christa and Ernst walked alongside the men, some who were smiling and laughing and obviously excited to be fighting for their country. But Vati wasn't, and neither were some of the other men. When the group arrived at the next house to pick up another soldier, Vati waved at them to go home.

How could Mutti and Vati think they would keep this a secret from the younger kids? Most of the village's German men were leaving. Only the Czech men and the elderly men of both nationalities would stay. At least she figured the Czech men would stay, but she wasn't sure. The Sudetenland was part of the Reich now, as Vati had said, which she supposed could mean the Wehrmacht would conscript them, too. She would have to ask Mutti later.

How were the women supposed to take care of the farms, the stores, and their families? Life was hard enough for them already.

After the other kids were up, breakfast finished and morning chores done, Mutti sent Christa off with a basket of eggs to take to the shops in town. She was supposed to ask them if they would buy them or allow her to trade for fresh meat, canned meat, or whatever she could get. That's how it had to work right now. Mutti usually did the shopping, but with Vati gone, she couldn't do everything. Mutti told her that in Germany, people were starving and were using food ration cards to get food. That might happen here soon, if the war continued much longer.

She left the house carrying the basket and wearing a dark green dress, matching sweater, dark brown knee-high socks, and brown shoes.

The air was brisk but the sky was clear blue, promising a warm afternoon, as she strolled down their paved street, Blumegasse Straße, looking left and right at the rolling hills on either side of the town, nestled in the narrow valley. The hills were checkered with farm fields and woods. Now that the weather was changing, the fields were no longer green and lush. She hoped they would be able to grow vegetables in their garden for a few more weeks. Seemed like all she thought about lately was food.

Passing several more houses like theirs, all three-stories tall and built around the same time as theirs, about a century ago, she arrived at the intersection where she turned onto Bahnhofstrasse. On the corner sat the tiny German school where she and forty-one other school children spent their weekdays. Next door was the Catholic Church, with its tall copper domed spire, where her school teacher, the church's priest worked when he wasn't teaching. The village's cemetery sat nestled next door to the church.

On those few days when the priest was needed at the church to hold a funeral service, the whole class went with him and sat quietly in the pews.

The Czech school was bigger and was on the other end of Alstadt. Christa had never been inside it, but had heard from neighbors that two-thirds of the village's fourteen hundred residents were Czech and that's why their children had a bigger, nicer school.

Christa didn't mind, really. Her school was cozy and everyone knew everyone else, regardless what grade they were in.

Past the cemetery was the heart of the town with buildings made of concrete and stucco, most of them painted white with red pitched roofs—the bakery where they got Black Forest cherry tarts and fresh bread and rolls, the grocery shop, the post office, a Protestant church, the *Metzgerei*, or butcher shop, the bank, the *Drogerie*, or drugstore, and several other businesses that Christa had never been inside. All of the buildings butted up against each other. She liked to imagine them as tall Germans and Czechs standing together, arms linked at the elbow, and dancing a polka. When she thought about it for real, though, she figured they were butted against each other for support and to ward off the drafts during the cold and snowy winters.

Halfway down the block, she entered the *Metzgerei* and talked to the apron-clad Pani Korbelová.

"*Guten morgen*, Christa. Where is your mother today?"

"She stayed home with the younger children. I brought eggs." She held up her basket.

"Are you here for wurst today?"

"Yes. Do you have any left, Pani Korbelová?" Many of the locals would have called her Frau Korbelová even though she was Czech, since she was a married woman and they were called Frau in German. But Christa had been taught in school to be respectful of the Czechs and address them in their own language. That's why her teacher taught them the Czech language, as well as German. Some German parents didn't like that, especially now that the Sudetenland was part of Germany. Some had gone as far as to withdraw their children from the school. The teacher, distraught over the withdrawals, had told the class that it was even more important now to learn the Czech language and respect the people who lived around them. Wartime was a time when people found it hard to know who they could trust, and people needed to know they could count on their neighbors for help. It's a time to come together, he'd said.

"No, but I have *Braten*?" Pani Korbelová said. "Will that do?"

Christa smiled and nodded. "Do you need eggs? I can make a trade."

"I will give you eight *Braten*," Pani Korbelová said, eying Christa.

Christa bit her lip, wishing she'd paid more attention when she'd come here with Mutti a few times. "I . . . I guess that is all right."

After Pani Korbelová wrapped up eight Braten in paper and handed them to her, Christa handed over the basket of eggs and exited the shop. She had more than enough Braten for the whole family. Mutti would be happy.

She hurried home and burst into the house, handing her mother the paper wrapped package and telling her about the trade. "Pani Korbelová offered me eight Braten for the eggs. That is wonderful, is it not?"

"That is all you got? Eight Braten for two dozen eggs?"

"There were that many eggs? Are you sure?"

"Of course I am sure."

"But I got enough for all of us. Is that not good?"

"*Nein, nein*. Frau Korbelová," and she stressed the Frau, as if she was trying to insult the woman, "took you for a fool."

Christa felt her cheeks grow warm. "I . . . I am sorry. I thought it was a fair trade. I will do better next time."

"I will have to do the shopping myself. You will stay home

and take care of your brothers and sisters next Saturday."

Christa groaned inside. More time with her brothers and sisters was not what she wanted. Somehow she would have to show Mutti that she was responsible and could perform the shopping; anything to get outdoors and away from her rambunctious siblings. She loved them. But she had her limits.

Ilse Seidel, September 5, 1943, Memmingen, Germany—

ILSE SEIDEL EXITED the French doors at the back of her family's townhouse, a tall narrow house connected to others just like it, within the heart of the town's center, and walked along the paved walkway for a few feet to the edge of the *Stadtbach*, or town brook. Grabbing hold of the metal railing, she swung herself down to a sitting position, leaned forward and dangled her feet over the edge toward the water the way she always did, her hands and elbows resting on the railing for support. How peaceful it felt here, with tall half-timbered houses and businesses on either side of the narrow canal, shading the water from the sun and blocking out all signs of war. She could almost forget the closed up shops in the Markplatz, the damaged houses and businesses, and the rubble scattered everywhere. She could almost forget, but not really. Would the bombing ever stop? Would it stop before it destroyed their city? Memmingen was her city, the place where she was born. Would she die here, too? With each passing day it seemed more likely.

She crossed her legs and moved one hand to rest on her throat, swallowing the sadness. Her grandmother, Oma Seidel— her father's mother—was killed in a bombing a week ago in the nearby town of Biberach where she'd lived with her daughter's family. Oma's son-in-law, Markus, was fighting in the

Wehrmacht's army, as was her oldest grandson, Matthias. Only Oma's daughter, Karolina, and Karolina and Markus's youngest son, Hermann, remained in the house now.

Ilse's family only knew of her passing because Hermann, the same age as Ilse, had ridden his bicycle to Memmingen to tell them. Ilse hadn't spent a lot of time with Oma Seidel, but she loved her and missed her all the same.

Ilse's best friend was killed, too, right here in their town two days ago, her friend that she'd gone to school with since kindergarten. *Fifteen years old is too young to die.* She swiped at the tears accumulating in her eyes.

Death. No one should die from bombs. Certainly not civilians. What had they done to deserve getting their limbs torn from their bodies?

She'd heard that one of her neighbors had grieved over his wife's death from one of the bombings and, unable to deal with his grief, had thrown himself into the river further downstream from here and drowned.

Ilse would never do that. A bomb might get her, too. Who could say? But she would not willingly let the war destroy her or take her away from her family. Not unless her dying meant saving their lives. Sure, there were days when she wanted it all to end, but not that way.

"There you are," Johann said, causing her to jump, not hearing his approach. "Mutter told me to find you. She needs you to take our ration cards to the market before the lines get too long."

"*Ja.* I am coming." She grabbed hold of the railing with both hands and pulled herself upright.

She knew better than to ask why Johann couldn't go to the market. He was thirteen and had been recruited to join the junior branch of the *Jungvolk*, the youth program for ten-to-fourteen year olds. Mutter and Oma and Opa Fischer, Mutter's parents, had been discussing it for days, with Johann called into the parlor regularly to join in the discussions. He didn't want to join the program. Oma didn't want him to join, either. Opa thought he should go, because he'd heard that parents who refused to allow their children to join were subject to investigation by authorities. Mutter objected because she disagreed with Nazi ideologies, but she was torn because she'd also heard that students who didn't join were subjected to frequent taunts from teachers and fellow student, and could even be refused apprenticeships.

Ilse decided she wouldn't join the girls' version of the program. If they tried to recruit her, she would flat out refuse. Her brother had to make his own decision. With their father already fighting in the army, how could the authorities find fault if the children didn't want to join their youth programs? They couldn't.

"Mutter, I am ready to go to get our rations," Ilse said when she found her mother in the parlor.

"*Gut. Danke.* The ration cards are on the kitchen counter. Try to get something. It is still early enough that you might get a good place in line. Hurry, though."

"I will." She grabbed the ration cards and rushed out the front down and down the cobbled street to the Markplatz, a huge cobbled town square, onto which shops of all kinds and the town hall building faced. Already she saw the lines forming in front of the bakery, the butcher shop, and the other food shops. Which line should she start with?

The line for the butcher shop was longest, but still not too long. She might have a chance of getting a smoked ham before the shop ran out of meat. She took her spot in the line and gazed around her as she waited her turn, studying the people, the damaged buildings, and the soot covered walls.

Everyone she saw looked thin, way too thin, the same way her family did. An elderly woman was half bent over, her bones protruding, making her look like a hunchback.

A propaganda poster emphasizing the interdependence of German military and industrial capabilities caught Ilse's attention. Then, another poster with a young boy about Johann's age and a military officer, with the words '*Offiziere von morgen*' that made it appear *Hitler Jugend* could be easily transformed into army officers, jumped out at her, reminding her again of the Nazis' attempt to recruit her brother and other children.

Although it wasn't meant to, the second poster also reminded her of the people who had worn yellow stars on their clothing five years ago. The Wehrmacht soldiers had forced all of the Jews all over Europe to wear the yellow stars. Within a few months, those Jews had disappeared from Memmingen. She'd heard rumors that most Jews had disappeared from everywhere during the early part of the war. They'd been rounded up and put into trucks and taken away to ghettos or concentration camps.

Some of her classmates from primary school had been among those who were taken away. Five years ago their teacher had told the class that Jews were no longer allowed in their schools.

Johann had been especially upset one day when he'd tried to take some books to his best friend's house, since the friend couldn't come to school. Several scary soldiers had stopped him, all pointing rifles directly at him and telling him that he couldn't do that.

They were going to shoot her little brother. For taking books to a Jewish boy! How crazy was that!

Two days later, in the Markplatz in front of the Renaissance town hall building in the early evening, Nazi soldiers had built a big bonfire and were tossing books—hundreds of books—into the fire. Why? No one would tell her why?

Johann had begged his mother and grandparents to take his friend, Isaak, and his mother and sister in and hide them from the Nazis. They told him they couldn't do it. Said it was too dangerous. A few days later the three of them were gone.

Ilse wondered, for the first time, if her father had ever rounded up Jews or taken them to concentration camps. She thought maybe someday, when he returned, she would ask him. But, then, on second thought she wasn't sure she wanted to know.

She sighed and turned her attention to the line in front of her. After half an hour, she got a small ham and then rushed to the line for the bakery. By mid-afternoon, she returned home with a loaf of bread, the ham, a sack of flour, and five potatoes. Not much, but slightly more than she got last week. Those rations, supplemented with their carefully monitored stock of supplies in their cellar, would have to last the family of seven for a week. *Please, Gott, let this food get us through,* she prayed. Her family was getting too weak to keep going on like this.

Petr Jaroslav, September 5, 1943, Prague, Czechoslovakia—

PETR JAROSLAV DIPPED the clean cloth into water and then wiped his little sister's forehead. She smiled weakly at him, but then erupted into another coughing fit. He held her shoulder with one hand and gently rubbed her back until the coughing stopped, then helped her lie back down on her narrow bed. She was getting weaker with each passing day and the doctor who had come yesterday morning told the family to keep her as comfortable as they could. There was nothing to be done to save her. How was he supposed to watch his ten year old sister, his adorable little sister, die? It was just a month ago she'd celebrated her tenth birthday and had begged for a birthday cake. Their mother had baked a small cake with the little bit of flour she could scrape together, and each of the seven siblings in the family got a few bites of it. Mother refused to eat any of it, saying she'd made it only for the kids.

Tuberculosis. The doctor had told them he'd seen many patients with the disease. He said it happened in war time. There was nothing he could do to save her.

Tears flowed down his cheeks. He turned his head away from his sister and looked up to the ceiling. His sister's eyes were closed, but he didn't want to take the chance that she would open them and see his face, his weakness. It was acceptable when his mother and sisters cried. But he was supposed to be strong and brave and here he was, pain and sorrow clearly overwhelming him.

He had just joined the Czech resistance and would soon be expected to shoot Nazis, blow up Wehrmacht tanks, and fight hand to hand. His father had joined the group soon after the Germans had invaded Czechoslovakia. He'd fought them when they took over the Capitol city and evicted the government employees. Not that it had made a difference that anyone could see. But the group was growing. Petr's two older brothers, Antonin and Josef, had been in it for a couple years and they remained hopeful they would soon take their country back from the Germans.

Petr swiped at his wet face with his hands and sleeve to wipe away the tears. *Calm yourself. Cry tonight in your bed, not here where Vera might see you.*

No one had told Vera what was wrong with her. Their parents had made the kids swear they wouldn't tell her. She still hoped to get well and return to school. Was it right to keep it from her? He didn't know. At fifteen, he wasn't sure of much. Hell, he could die tomorrow in a bombing. Bombs were exploding every day, it seemed, here in Prague. And in another month, after short training, he might even be one of the people setting off a bomb. Antonin had told him about several of his recent missions. They seemed to be getting more dangerous every day.

From that perspective, maybe it didn't matter if one knew they were going to die, or when. Maybe he should just accept that his days were numbered the same way Vera's were. Maybe they would be together regardless.

He steeled himself to look back down at his sister. In her sleep, without the coughing fits, she looked peaceful. Happy, almost.

Standing up, he picked up the bowl of water and the cloth and wondered what he should do with them.

"Here, I will take those," his mother said. He hadn't heard her come into the room.

"Are you sure we cannot get another doctor to look at Vera?" he whispered. "I cannot stand—"

She put her finger to her lips, and motioned for him to follow her outside. In the hallway of their apartment building, she said, "Petr, it is too late. The doctor told me a few hours ago that she will not last until nightfall."

Petr pursed his lips and turned away to hide his eyes as they began to tear up again.

CHAPTER THREE

Lucas Landry, June 2017, Sacramento, California—

"I FOUND SOMETHING, Luke. Oh, this is interesting. It looks like a set of diaries," Tawny said. She held the little books up for Lucas to see. "They're all in German."

Lucas anxiously raked his fingers through his hair. This could be it. The clue that would tell him about the strangers in the photos. Did he really want to know? What if he really was related to Nazis? What if he had grandfathers or great-grandfathers who'd been high ranking officials in the Wehrmacht, the German military? Up until now he'd always assumed his ancestors were all American and Irish. He got up and walked over to Tawny, accepting the diary from her. "I guess we'll find out if I remember any of the German I studied in high school and college."

Sitting back down at the folding table, he started reading. His German was rusty but that wasn't his biggest problem. Reading the handwriting was difficult. Definitely a child's or teenager's handwriting and the letters were . . . well, old-fashioned. He'd seen some of this style of handwriting before when one of his

German professors had the class do some research projects and write papers. He'd had trouble then, too. He scratched his head, trying to remember some of that writing. After an hour, he was getting through the material, at least somewhat. At least he thought so.

"Oh, Luke, I found some old books. Some are in German. And one is a very old German-English dictionary. Would that help you?"

He sighed and rubbed at his eyes, bleary from the strain of trying to read the old handwriting. A dictionary could help, but what he really needed was a text about the old-style handwriting, if there was such a thing, or better yet, someone fluent in German who could translate it for him.

"Thanks." He looked over his shoulder, stuck his hand out, and she placed the book in his hand. He flipped through a few pages. *Hmm, definitely will help.*

He still didn't know who had written the diaries but definitely a school-age girl. She was describing her town and her school. Her life during a war. Second World War, he assumed, but he didn't see a date anywhere in the book.

An hour later, Tawny came over and rubbed his shoulders, his neck, kneading and easing tense muscles. "You should take a break." He didn't answer. "I can look in the kitchen and see if there's any coffee that I can make up. Your father has a coffee maker, right?"

"Oh, sorry. I was falling under your massage spell," he said, turning and smiling at her. "Yeah, I think I saw one on the kitchen counter top. Thanks, babe."

"You're welcome. I'll be back in a few minutes." She patted his shoulder, turned, and left.

Right after, Lucas heard something in the stairwell. *Hmm, maybe she couldn't find any coffee and is coming back to tell me.* When he turned to look, Hallie the cat padded up onto the attic floor from the stairs and sat down, her head and eyes shifting in slow motion from one end of the room to the other, obviously studying the intriguing new room and probably wondering how it got here without her knowing.

"What do you think, Hallie? Interesting?"

She meowed, then got up and walked around the room, sniffing and rubbing her body on everything.

Yep. Typical cat. Wants to stake her claim on the territory.

That made him think of Seth. He hadn't shown up the lawyer's office for the reading of their father's will. Dad had left the house and everything in it to Lucas. According to the lawyer, it was his family's tradition to leave the house to the eldest son, if there was a son, or the eldest daughter, if there wasn't a son. Did Seth know that? Did he not want to fight over it? Dad had left his car and boat to Seth, and he'd left money to both of them, split equally. Maybe that satisfied him.

 Footsteps on the stairs pulled him out of his thoughts.

"I have two hot coffees," Tawny said. "I see you have a visitor." She nodded to Hallie. "I found an unopened bag of potato chips in the pantry. I know, chips don't go with coffee, but I didn't find any cake—not fresh enough to eat, anyway, and I'm starving. Eating for two, now, you know."

He chuckled. At four months pregnant, she ate enough for three people. "Yeah, I tossed out a lot of stuff yesterday and I'm sure we'll have to toss more."

"I saw some food still in the pantry, that we don't need, but it's still edible. Maybe we can donate to one of those homeless shelters."

"Good idea."

Late in the afternoon, after a lunch break at McDonalds and a second snack break, Tawny said, "Oh, my Gosh, I found another set of diaries and some . . . well, I'm not sure what . . . maybe identity papers."

"Oh, yeah? Let me see." He reached around and took the offered books and papers. "I think you're right. I've seen some like these before in one of my college classes. People throughout Europe had to carry these at all times during WWII."

Some of the dates went back to the late 1800's. Interesting! Lucas spread them out on the table and tried to make sense out them. They showed birth dates, birth names, married names, parents' names, and he thought, town of residence. He could kind of piece together that he was looking at two families, though he couldn't be sure until he could draw a family tree chart. One thing he could tell already was that, so far, he didn't have papers for many family members, and none that linked to his family directly, at least not in an obvious way.

Oh well, that didn't help much. But it was interesting.

He picked up one of the diaries from the second batch. *Hmm, obviously written by someone else.* The handwriting was different, the names of the siblings were different, as was the setting. He set it aside for later, then stood up, stretched his legs, and yawned.

"I think I need to do some research before I read more of those diaries. Maybe if I know more about the war and the areas mentioned in those diaries, the diaries might be easier to read and make more sense to me."

"How are you going to research?"

"Internet at home, books in the library. Let's go home for now. We—or I if you don't want to—can come back tomorrow, or after work on Monday." As they made their way down the narrow stairs from the attic, he said, "You know, I might be able to meet with one of my old professors and get his or her opinion and advice about the identity papers."

"Good idea." Lucas turned and went back into the attic and came down moments later with a couple of the diaries and papers.

In the master bedroom, the cat rubbed up against Tawny's leg.

"What about the cat? We can't leave her here alone?"

"She'll be okay for a day or two alone. Guess we should make sure she has plenty of food and water, though, before we leave. Oh, and I should clean out the litter, too."

"I cleaned the litter box while the coffee was brewing."

"You shouldn't have. Pregnant women aren't supposed to handle litter boxes. Remember when our neighbor Maddie was pregnant and had to have her son clean the litter box?"

"I forgot. Do you think it might have harmed the baby?"

"One time? Probably not. Did you wash your hands good afterwards?"

"Don't you know me? Of course I washed my hands good." She hit him on the upper arm, jokingly.

"Yeah, my little neat-freak. How could I forget?"

MONDAY AFTER WORK, Lucas sat in Professor Joanna Meier's office discussing the diaries and papers Lucas had brought from the attic. Lucas had made an appointment with the professor early that morning, in between seeing patients. "Those are identity cards, right?"

"They are Ahnenpaß. That translates to 'family tree of Aryan descent'. So, yes, identity cards were required of all citizens during WWII."

"Of Aryan descent? Does that mean what I think it means?"

"Proof that family members are not Jewish."

Lucas ran his hand through his hair. "I guess that means they weren't sent to the concentration camps or the gas chambers, then?"

"Probably not." The professor put on her glasses.

"So they would have been safe."

"No, not necessarily, and especially considering that they were living in the Sudetenland. For most of the war, they were safer than in Germany, which was getting bombed left and right and was suffering severe food shortages. But near the end of the war, when the Soviets advanced into the region, they would not have been safe."

Lucas thought about the girl in the diary he'd been reading. "They might have left the country before then."

"Possibly. Though most Sudeten Germans didn't want to leave, even when they were told they had to."

"All Sudeten Germans had to leave?"

"Unless they were needed to work in certain jobs after the war. Those Germans were actually not allowed to leave." She hesitated a moment. "It's interesting that one of these people in the documents you brought in was of Czech background. I don't know if that meant her family didn't get expelled from the Sudetenland, but my guess is that they did because she was married to a German and they had children together."

"So, marriage to a German meant she was no longer Czech?"

"It's complicated, but that's probably how the government looked at it. It kind of worked that way regarding the Jewish people, too, during the war. As I understand it, even when a Catholic person married a Jewish person, the Reich considered any children born from the union to be Jewish. They were sent to concentration camps."

"Oh, wow, I didn't know that."

"If you need help translating the diaries, let me know," the professor said. "You can leave them with my assistant."

"Thanks. Guess I'll try to read them myself, first."

"A word of caution before you leave," Professor Meier said, eyeing him through bifocals sitting low on her nose. "If you find that these people are related to you, you might not be happy with what you find out. You might discover you're related to Nazi war criminals or to Czech Revolutionary Guards who tormented the Sudeten Germans. Either way, you may regret ever having researched your family tree." She hesitated a moment, then added, "I personally know someone who found out he was related to one of the top generals in the Nazi command. He was devastated and wished he hadn't found out."

Yeah, Lucas understood that. But he already knew he was related to a Neo-Nazi. He'd had to deal with the consequences of that already.

CHAPTER FOUR

Christa, February 10, 1944, Altstadt, Sudetenland—

FROM A BLOCK up the road Christa saw Mutti standing on the front porch, holding baby Andreas and obviously looking for her older children, Ernst, Julia, Fritz, and Christa, as they made their way home from school. Christa also saw Giselle all bundled up in her warm coat, playing with something, likely her doll, on the steps near Mutti. Is something wrong? Mutti rarely watched for them after school, and never when it was cold out. She didn't want the younger kids exposed to the cold air because they might get sick.

The other kids apparently saw her, too, because Fritz and Julia took off running toward the house. Moments after arriving on the porch, Fritz ran back and yelled out to Christa and Ernst, "Mutti got a letter from Vati. Come quick."

Christa started to run and tripped over something, landing face down in the snow, eliciting yelps of laughter from her brothers. *Esels* (donkeys), she thought. She pulled herself up and dusted off the snow from her face, coat, and leggings with her mittens, then ran the rest of the way home. Stepping onto the small porch, she turned her head and glared at both boys. They nudged each other, making goofy faces.

Christa shook her head. *Boys. Always acting like idiots.*

The children all followed Mutti into the house, gathering around her in the living room.

"It came half an hour ago," she said. "My hands are shaking so hard I can barely get the envelope open." Finally ripping it open, she withdrew a single sheet of paper. She read in silence, tears suddenly trickling down her cheeks, and she almost dropped the page.

Oh *Gott*, was it something bad? Why is Mutti crying? Is Vati all right? What's going on? Christa's heart was pounding. She glanced at her siblings who were twitching and murmuring, obviously also scared. They looked over at her, too. *I'm the oldest. I have to set a good example and not cry or act worried.* She placed her hands, which often betrayed her nerves, under her upper thighs to keep them still while she waited.

Oh Gott, how long do we have to wait?

Mutti finally looked up, cleared her throat, and then read aloud:

Dearest Hanna, Christa, Ernst, Fritz, Julia, Giselle, and Andreas,

I am safe. No need to worry. Sorry I could not write to you sooner. The commanders have trained me to work as a medic for my platoon and now we are in Holland, but I cannot give any details of our location, for security reasons. I can tell you that I help treat the wounded men and I have saved a few lives already in my short time here. I carry a pistol for protection, but I have not used it and hope not to have to use it. You can rest easy that I am not in combat. I have seen and treated many wounded. I won't describe the horrors I have witnessed, but rest assured I am all right and looking forward to my first leave. The commanders tell us we will get a three-day leave soon, but again, no details. Will write again when I can.

P.S. I have taken up writing poetry when I get time. Can you imagine—me a poet? It helps me cope. I will send some poems with my next letter, if you promise not to laugh at my silly attempts at creativity.

You loving husband and father,

Franz Nagel

Now Christa was crying, relieved, after fearing the worst. But Vati was all right! And he was writing poems. That's something she had been doing ever since the nuns at school taught them about poetry last year.

Two days later, during mathematics lessons, each grade level working on specific grade level assignments in their notebooks, the teacher clapped his hands together. Everyone looked up from their work, some grumbling at the interruption. "We must go into the church, children. I am sorry to disrupt your work, but I have a funeral. Please put your papers in your desks. It's cold out, so put on your coats and hats, and as usual, line up at the door."

Christa sighed. This had happened at least twice a week in the past few months, and while she didn't mind getting a break from work sometimes and escaping the classroom, she'd come to dread this particular kind of interruption. Usually, the deceased was an elderly man or woman who had succumbed to tuberculosis or pneumonia or had starved because the food supply in the town's shops had dwindled. Only the people who had farms or who had planned ahead by canning foods and storing them in their root cellars were eating sufficiently. Mutti sometimes took food to elderly neighbors, but she couldn't spare much. Not when she had seven mouths to feed.

In line, one of the boys said, "Herr Father Braun, who died?"

Their teacher said, "The father of Helga Schumann."

Everyone gasped.

"Oh *Gott!* That is why Helga is not in class today?" Julia said, clasping her hands on the opposite arms, as if she was freezing, even though they were still inside the warm classroom.

Father Braun nodded, not reprimanding her for saying Oh *Gott*. Maybe he agreed with her.

"Her father was a soldier, too," Julia said. "He left when my father did. Helga told me her father was in the same unit as Vati. Does that mean Vati is dead, too?"

"It doesn't mean your father died," Father Braun said. "He is probably safe."

Ernst said, "We got a letter from Vati two days ago. He is alive and safe. He said so."

Christa felt a chill run up and down her spine. That letter was written a month and a half ago. She'd seen the date on the letter and the postage mark on the envelope after Mutti passed the letter around for the children to hold. Anything could have happened to Vati since then.

The class entered the church in single file, silent, their hands folded in front of them as they walked down the main aisle. Christa couldn't believe how many people were here. Must be most of the town—well, most of the remaining town—including the Czechs.

Her eyes searched for Mutti. She hadn't mentioned Herr Schumann's death, but if she'd heard about it, she would come. She and Frau Schumann were friends, as were Helga and Julia.

There she was, holding Andreas and hugging Helga's mother, Frau Schumann. Giselle was standing beside Mutti, holding her doll with one hand and Mutti's skirt with the other,

her eyes glazed-over, probably not understanding what was happening.

Poor Helga. She was red-eyed, tears dripping down her face. *That could be me and my brothers and sisters*, Christa thought. *Please, Gott, do not take my father, too.*

Ilse Seidel, February 10, 1944, Memmingen, Germany—

"I AM GLAD those Jews are gone," Johann said as the family sat around the parlor in the evening listening to the Volksempfänger radio, and the announcer was talking about the round-up of the Jews.

Ilse gaped at her brother. "What is wrong with you? That is a terrible thing to say. Your best friend was one of the Jews rounded-up several years ago. You were devastated. Have you forgotten?"

"You are in the *Jungmädelbund*. Do they not teach you anything?" he countered.

She bit her tongue, knowing it was futile to argue with someone brainwashed by the Nazis. He had been forced to join the *Deutshes Jungvolk*, as she and her family had feared, and he'd practically gone crazy, raving that he refused to go. But when the soldiers had come to the door and escorted him, willing or not, to the *Jungvolk* meeting, he'd gone. For the first few weeks, he'd complained and told his family he hated it. But then something changed. He started making friends and hanging out with the other boys from the group.

A month later, the soldiers had come again, this time for her. She knew already resisting the command was futile. All she could do was go through the motions. She would never allow them to brainwash her. As part of the *Jungmädelbund*, the League of

German Girls, she sewed slippers for the military hospitals and repaired soldier's uniforms. Even Mutter and Oma helped with that. And why not? Not all of the men fighting in the war were Nazis and not all had gone to war willingly. Her father, maybe had gone willingly. She didn't ask. All she knew for sure is that he was one of the first to go from their town.

"I should speak to my commander," Johann said, "and tell them they need to do more in the *Jungmädelbund*."

"No. Please do not say anything," she said. "Please do not cause trouble for me."

"I won't," he said, but then added, "but you need to do your part for our country. It is a shame the girls do not get to go on the summer camping tours and cycling tours the boys get to go on. Maybe if you did, you would feel more committed."

She nodded, hoping he would let it drop and listen to the radio instead.

The Volksempfänger radio ("All Nazi, All the Time") droned on in the dark parlor, darkened not only by the single lamp in the room but also by the black-out shades on all the windows. The radio kept on about the latest triumphs of the Wehrmacht. It was hard enough listening to the propaganda, but now static was interfering so much, it was beginning to grate on Ilse's nerves. The Volksempfänger radio was the only radio Germans were legally allowed to listen to, but when Johann wasn't around, she and Mutter and Oma and Opa listened to the BBC radio Opa kept hidden under his bed.

Apparently the static grated on Opa's, too. He got up and smacked the radio and began fussing with the dial. Then the house rumbled, shaking the glass in the windows.

Ilse glanced up at the ceiling. Airplanes were near. She couldn't hear them, but she knew. She'd heard the rumbling many times before. Almost the moment she thought it, the air-raid siren blared so loudly her younger sister screamed and covered her ears with her hands.

Opa yelled, "Everyone to the bomb shelter, *schnell!*" As if any of them needed to be told. They'd done this too many times. But Ilse understood. He was the man of the house and it was his job to protect them. He didn't bother turning off the radio, just grabbed their coats from the coat rack near the front door and, after they quickly donned their shoes, handed the coats out and herded them out the door. "Run!"

All of their neighbors, everyone from the townhouses nearby, were outside already and running in the same direction— toward the bomb shelter beneath the Protestant church half a block away.

Mothers, some carrying babies, others holding children's hands, were running, obviously afraid to slow down because a bomb could drop anywhere at any time.

A loud droning caused everyone to look up at the sky. Dozens of fighters and bombers were flying directly overhead, probably headed for the town's airport. That airport had recently been taken over and turned into a military base, making the whole town a target, the allies trying to take out the airport to make it harder for the Luftwaffe to launch aircraft.

The sound of a bomb dropping was followed by a deafening explosion, perhaps on the next street over, but she couldn't tell in the darkness, the falling debris sending people into hysterics and running faster. While she was running, Ilse noted that the planes almost always came at night, most often after everyone had gone to bed.

Thick smoke filled the air, making her stumble, choking and coughing on the soot filled air. The explosion was so close.

Fearful, Ilse looked around for her younger sister. She spotted Mutter holding Ursula's hand and they were nearing the church. She scanned for her brothers and Oma and Opa. The boys were holding onto Oma, helping steady her as she ran.

But where was Opa? She turned around. He was behind her, maybe fifty feet, half stooped over. Was he hurt?

She rushed over to him. "Opa, are you hurt?"

"Just . . . hard . . . to catch . . . my breath," he said.

She wrapped her arm around his shoulder. "I will help you. We must hurry. More planes will come."

Together they worked their way through the crowd. She wasn't sure whether it was safer to walk close to the buildings or out in the middle of the street.

As they neared the doorway, it was jammed tight with people trying to push their way through. Apparently, the stairway down to the bomb shelter was also jammed with bodies.

"Keep moving!" someone yelled in front of her.

Another group of airplanes roared overhead, and Ilse heard explosions somewhere near the town. *The airport*, she suspected.

Finally, after worrying they would not get in, everyone struggled down into the tightly packed shelter. She and Opa searched for the rest of the family, eventually finding them sitting on top of some crates. They shuffled over on the crates as much as possible and made room for Ilse and Opa to sit, too. *It is going to be a long night*, Ilse thought.

The following morning, stiff and achy, Ilse walked out of the bomb shelter with her family, expecting to have to shade her eyes from the morning sun. But there wasn't any sun. Only dark winter clouds and smoke.

She covered her mouth with one hand, while carefully navigating over debris. Some buildings on this street appeared untouched, but many others had been ripped apart.

The front of her family's townhouse had four broken windows, but no other visible damage. Their home was sandwiched in between two other townhouses, and one of those had taken more damage, debris having crumbled down from part of a side wall, leaving a gap into the interior. *Guess we are lucky it is only windows. This time.* Somehow they would have to repair the windows, and quickly, because of the cold winter weather—they couldn't get glass, so they would probably have to find boards and nail them over the windows.

Before they got inside the house, snow began falling.

Petr Jaroslav, February 10, 1944, Olomouc, Czechoslovakia—

Early morning, before the rest of the family was up, Petr put on his heavy coat, picked up his rifle, and left the house, closing the door quietly behind him. No need to wake up everyone and definitely no need to tell them where he was going. Although only fifteen, his days of having to tell his parents what he was up to were long over. The war had seen to that. Not only was Petr now a soldier of sorts, but his father was one of the top men in the Resistance. He set most of the assignments and knew exactly where each of his men and women were going. Petr was going to meet with two new recruits and one experienced soldier, Ambroz Fejfar. The four would hike through the woods, avoiding the roads that would be watched by the gestapo. Their assignment was to plant bombs at a factory the Germans relied on to supply parts for their military planes. If they could destroy those, they were told, it would set-back the German campaign and give the allies the upper hand. That was the plan, anyway.

A few days after Petr's mother had revealed that it was too late to get treatment for his sister, Vera had died and the family had buried her in a cemetery in Prague. A month later, the family had packed up and left Prague. Their country needed resistance fighters in other regions. They needed to spread out and cover more ground. That had taken them to Olomouc, the sixth largest city in Czechoslovakia, and one of the largest in Moravia. They were in the eastern part of the country, which Petr hadn't thought he would like, but he actually found it to be pleasant, with rolling hills, forests, and lakes.

Petr, his older brothers Antonin and Josef, and their father, Olexa, were an integral part of the Resistance in Omolouca, but mostly Petr was given smaller assignments, like pick up allied paratroopers who dropped from airplanes in the dark and needed transportation to their assigned designations.

Today's job of planting bombs, though, was far more dangerous, Petr knew it was exciting, too. If all went as planned, he was going to kill some Nazis and make them pay for what they'd done to his brother's fiancé and her Jewish family. Jews. Why torment the Jews, just because they were a different religion? Made no sense. None. The Nazis had forced their way into that family's home, took the father out into the corridor and shot him in front of his wife. Then they dragged out all the women and children—not just Rebeka and her family—but everyone in their apartment house, past their father's dead body, onto the street where a truck was waiting. They'd loaded them all onto the truck, packed tightly like cigarettes in a pack, and drove them away. No one in town had seen them since. But Antonin had heard from a reliable source that the truckload of Jews had been taken to Theresienstadt Concentration Camp.

It wasn't the worst camp, from what Petr had heard. They didn't have gas chambers. *Yet.* Though they did sometimes load prisoners onto trucks and take them to camps in Poland, where they did have gas chambers. And sometimes they merely drove them out into the middle of the woods, made them get off the truck and line up, then shot them all dead.

Petr wasn't sure which was worse. All he knew was he wanted them to pay.

CHAPTER FIVE

Lucas Landry, June 2017, Sacramento, California—

"LUKE, WE CAN'T keep driving back and forth between our house and this house after work every day," Tawny complained, standing over the cat's food dish while the cat ate dinner. "It's too tiring. Why not bring the cat to our house?"

"It's not just about the cat. I still have to go through all of this stuff and get the house cleared out. I can't list it for sale until then. And though it would be easier, I can't just chuck all the stuff in the attic. I need to solve my family tree mystery. I need to make sense of what we've found."

They'd divided the attic into four sections and had been rearranging everything as they went along. One corner had been designated as the German section, where they set aside anything potentially related to the German connection. Another corner was for items that Lucas might need if he decided to research more ancestral connections, say the miners in the photos, for instance. Another corner was designated for stuff to sell; another for stuff going to the dump.

"Then let's move in here. It's bigger and better than our house. We can turn your old room into a nursery for the new baby. Bianca can have your brother's old room. This house would be perfect for us."

Uh huh. Here we go again. She'd been harping on him all week to move into this old house. Not gonna happen. She had no idea how miserable he'd been living here. His mother's illness. Her death. His father's rejection. No good memories. He'd seen horror movies set in old Victorian houses. Ghost stories. Well, this one might not have ghostly demons knocking on walls in the middle of the night, but it had its share of other kinds of ghosts.

"I like our house. We can add on another room, if we need it. And with the money I inherited—well it's not a lot, but it's enough to allow us to remodel both houses and sell both. The proceeds from selling two remodeled houses in California could add up to a good chunk of money. Then we could buy a brand new house in an up-and-coming neighborhood. We'd climb in status."

There, that oughta appeal to Tawny's desire to improve her family's social ranking. Her mother had brought her to the U.S. back when Tawny was a teenager, intent on making a better life for them both.

"No, no, no. I don't like new houses. They don't have any character or history. And, besides, money and status aren't everything."

Lucas tilted back on his heels, his mind reeling. "Uh . . . well, okay, we could just stay in our current house and use the money we make from selling this house to do some traveling. You've always wanted to travel."

She waved her finger at him, the way mothers do with their children. "Don't try to appeal to my desires. Yes, I would love to travel, but your argument doesn't work. The same could be said about doing it the other way—selling our current house. We

61

could remodel this house and turn it into something beautiful. It has good bones. Some modernizing without destroying its character would be perfect. I could bring mother over here. She has a keen sense of design. She could help."

Lucas groaned inwardly, then turned his attention to the mess they'd made in the kitchen. They'd picked up sandwiches at a deli on the way here and ate them at the kitchen table, feeding a few bites of lunchmeat to the cat, who had immediately snubbed her cat food. It was only after they'd finished their food that the cat had returned to her own dish.

Tawny pulled the full trash bag out of the trash can and took it outside to the bin, returning as Lucas was finishing straightening up the kitchen.

Lucas, trying to smooth things between them, said, "Look, we could have your mother come over and give us her ideas. We could fix up the place. That would make it more appealing to buyers and get us a better price. But I really don't think I would ever want to live here again. Once was enough."

This time she was the one who didn't respond; instead, turning her attention back to the cat.

"We need to come here every day, for now," Lucas said. "At least I do. You can stay home with Bianca. I appreciate all the help you've given, but I can finish up with looking through my father's belongings and the stuff in the attic. It should only take another week or so."

She still said nothing.

"After that, we can even take the cat to our house, if you want."

"Okay, then." Her words said okay, but he could see her dissatisfaction in the way she grabbed her carry-all bag and stuck her feet in her sandals.

They spent the rest of the evening working in the attic, with the cat sprawled out on a blanket near them, sleeping and purring. Lucas and Tawny barely spoke. *Definitely a chill in the air.* Tawny usually got her way, and she obviously wanted him to move their family into the house. *Not gonna happen, if I have any say about it.*

On the drive home, Tawny said, "Have you talked to your brother since your father passed away?"

His shoulders tensed. "I don't know where he is or how to reach him." Not that he'd tried in the past five years.

"Does he know that your father died?" She glanced over at Lucas.

"Yeah, according to the lawyer. Seth got Dad's car, some money, and a few other things, I guess."

"But not the house."

"What's that supposed to mean? Do you think I should give him half the money when we sell it?"

"I didn't say that. It's yours. You said that your father left it to you because you're the oldest and that's the family's tradition. Nothing wrong with that. I'm just wondering how your brother is feeling?"

"Why? You've never met him. You know nothing about him."

"Okaaayy. I didn't mean to upset you. I can't help if the psychologist in me comes out a bit."

Again silence and tension filled the air.

A few blocks from home, Lucas conceded, "I'll talk to the lawyer and see if he'll give me Seth's contact information. I guess we have some catching up to do. I could at least ask him if he wants any of Dad's personal items, like his clothes and tools and books."

"Thank you. Maybe you two can repair your relationship. You have a brother. That's more than some of us have."

Tawny had lost her brother ten years ago. He'd drowned in a boating accident.

Lucas reached over and held her hand. "Sorry to bring up sad memories," he said, knowing that it was Tawny that had actually broached that subject, but wanting peace between them.

Two days later, Lucas drove up to a small bungalow, verified the address, and parked alongside the curb. He sat for a few minutes, trying to prepare himself for visiting his neo-Nazi brother. Would he be a skin-head? Tattoos up and down his arms?

At the front door, he rang the bell and waited, barely breathing. At last, the door opened.

A young blue-eyed blonde woman stood there holding a blond baby boy. "Can I help you?"

"Uh, yeah, I mean I hope so. I'm looking for Seth Landry?"

"What do you want with him?"

"I'm Lucas. His brother. Just want to talk."

She raised an eyebrow, then turned to look over her shoulder. "Wait here." She closed the door.

He waited. Nothing. He glanced at his watch. Once. Twice. Five minutes gone. Was Seth avoiding him?

The door opened again. Seth stood directly in front of Lucas. At least two inches taller than Lucas now. *Wow, when did that happen?* He no longer had a crew cut. His hair was still shorter than Lucas's and slightly lighter brown. Looked good, clean, well-combed. *Not what I expected.*

"Hey, brother, how have you been?"

"Um, I'm doing fine, Seth. How about you?" *This is awkward. What do you say to a brother you fought with the last time you saw him?*

"Where are my manners? Come on in, if you have a few minutes." He stepped backward and held the door open wide.

Lucas glanced back at his car, then stepped into the house.

"Well, you kinda met my wife, already, Allison, uh, Ally. We have a son, Benny. He's turning one in a couple of weeks.

They're upstairs. Diaper change." A little girl with blonde pigtails walked over to Seth and grabbed hold of his jeans leg. "And this is our daughter, Skyler. She's three."

Lucas bent down and looked closely at the little girl. Big blue eyes. Blue eyes like his and Seth's. "Nice to meet you, Skyler. I have a little girl your age. She's your cousin."

The girl stuck a thumb in her mouth and leaned against her father' leg.

"She's real shy around strangers."

Lucas winced inside. God, he had a niece and nephew and he was a stranger to them. Tawny would give anything to have nieces and nephews, and here he'd turned his back on family.

Lucas straightened up and looked at his brother. "Sorry, Seth. I should have tried to patch things between us."

"Not your fault. I didn't contact you, either, man." He hesitated a moment, then added, "Wanna come in and sit awhile?"

"Sure." He followed Seth into the living room and looked around. Leather-looking brown sofa, not real leather Lucas could tell, and a matching loveseat and recliner. Toys scattered on the beige carpet. A well-used double stroller open and sitting near the foyer. A brick fireplace across from the sofa. An entertainment cabinet with a flat screen TV, about forty-five inches, sat next to the fireplace.

Lucas sat on the sofa, and Seth sat in the recliner.

Seth glanced at Lucas and started to stand. "I forgot to ask. Can I get you something to drink? A soda or cup of coffee?"

"No, I'm fine, thanks."

Seth nodded and sat back down.

"So, what have you been up to?" Lucas asked.

"You mean, am I still a neo-Nazi? That's what you want to know, right?"

"I . . . uh, well, yeah, but more than that. I really want to know more about your life. I mean, with Dad gone, it's just you and me."

"With Dad gone?" Seth said, an antagonistic tone in his voice. "Hell, he's been gone a lot longer than a few weeks, for me, at least. We stopped talking five years ago when he found out about my political beliefs."

"What? I thought you and he got along great. You were his All-star athlete son, his favorite son. You were his perfect chip off the old block son."

"Yeah, well, not according to him. When I told him about my feelings, he started screaming. Told me I was a disgrace. He said his family was German and some family members were Nazis and he hated them. Said they were a disgrace and he wanted nothing to do with them. Said that's why he left home right after he graduated high school."

"Until he inherited the house," Lucas said, again remembering his father's words about getting the house for free but not liking the house. Things were beginning to fall into place. "That's why he hated that house."

"Yeah," Seth said, "he took the house but locked away all memories of his family. He never once talked about them to us, did he?"

"Nope."

"He never told us about his family living in Germany. How was I supposed to know how he felt about the Nazis?"

Lucas was tempted to ask if it would have made any difference. Would Dad's hatred of the Nazis have kept Seth from becoming one? Maybe, maybe not, but he didn't want to get into an argument again so instead, he said, "Yeah, he wasn't much of a talker. At least not to us."

Seth nodded.

Lucas said. "Well, now I've got the house. My wife wants to live in it, but I'm having problems even considering it."

"Just because Dad complained about it, that doesn't mean it's not a good house. He complained about everything and everyone."

"So that's the way you remember him, too? I'm really surprised. I thought you and he were close."

"We may have been, when I was a kid. Not later, though."

"You never talked to him after your argument?"

"Never. You know how he was. Once he got something in his head—the idea that someone was dissing him or his beliefs— that was the end of the relationship."

"Yeah. Was that before or after I fought with him?"

"Around the same time, I think."

"So, let me get this straight. He didn't want anything to do with me because I was engaged to a black woman from South Africa. But when he discovered you were a neo-Nazi, he didn't want anything to do with you, either. You're prejudiced against black people, too, aren't you?"

Five years ago, Lucas had gone to talk to Seth about his engagement to Tawny. He'd told Seth he wanted to introduce him and Tawny to each other. He was sure they would get along. That's when Lucas discovered he didn't know his brother at all. Seth told him he didn't want to meet her. He'd seen photos of her on Lucas's Facebook page. He knew she was black. He tried to talk Lucas out of marrying her. He told him about his political beliefs, if that's what you could call them. They'd ended up in a big fight. One of them had thrown the first punch. He couldn't remember now, which one. That had led to further punching and a few bruises. Lucas went home to Tawny and told her he'd fought with his brother, but didn't tell her what the fight was about.

Seth said, "We want Americans to be a pure race, yes. But my beliefs are totally different from Dad's. You seem to think that if we're both racist, we're the same. It doesn't work like that."

Lucas didn't know how to respond. Obviously their little girls, cousins or not, would never get to become friends. Their wives would never meet, either.

"You know, Dad yelled at me once and told me I should go live in Germany with the other Nazis. He had a bug up his butt. Said that when he was a kid here, his classmates and neighbor kids gave him a hard time because of his German ancestry. Called him names. Painted swastikas on his fence. Apparently, he never got over that."

"Do you know how Dad found out about Tawny's race? I didn't tell him. He already knew before I got a chance to say anything."

"He saw the photos on your page, too. Like I did."

"But we weren't friends on Facebook."

"Actually, you were. We both were. I found out he used a neighbor's name to spy on both of us. Old man, Jonas Browning. Lived a couple houses down."

"Oh yeah, I remember Jonas. He used to take us out to his parents' farm for horseback rides. That was the best thing that happened when we were living here."

"That's him. I only found out when I talked to Jonas one day and mentioned something he'd posted. Jonas was baffled, rubbed his beard, and said he had never used Facebook. Didn't know how."

"How did you figure out it was Dad?"

"I asked him. It was a longshot, but I got to wondering how he knew about Tawny."

"Did he admit it, that he'd faked the account?" Lucas asked.

"Yeah."

Hmm, maybe, but it could just as easily be Seth lying.

Seth said, "I got to talking more with old Jonas. Do you know he knew our grandparents? He lived in that house next door to theirs for decades. He told me Dad has two sisters living in Santa Rosa."

"What? Are you sure?"

"He gave me their names, address, and phone number. They live together. I went to visit them once or twice."

"Can I get their information? I want to meet them."

"Sure. Be right back."

Lucas waited as Seth strode upstairs. A few minutes later, he heard Seth and Allison arguing. He couldn't make out their words, but recognized raised voices.

Footsteps on the stairs caused Lucas to turn around and look. It was Seth coming back down.

"Sorry about that," Seth said. "Allison wants me to get dinner started. She had a really crappy day and doesn't feel good."

"I hear ya. I should be going, anyway." He stood up and moved toward the door.

Seth followed and said, "Here's that information you asked for." He handed Lucas a piece of paper.

Stuffing it into his shirt pocket, Lucas said, "It was real nice talking with you, Seth. Hope to do it again, soon."

Seth nodded.

Lucas strode back to his car, and took the paper out of his pocket once he was seated and he saw Seth close the front door. Santa Rosa. That's where the aunts lived. Not too far from here. He could be there in an hour and a half.

He stopped at a gas station for gas and called Tawny on her cell phone to let her know where he was going.

Traffic was heavy, but he finally arrived at the address he had written down. A large Spanish-style mansion. At least it looked like a mansion to him. He parked on the street in front of the house, opened the wrought-iron gate, strode along the brick walkway to the front porch, and pressed the doorbell.

Moments later, a woman with pale blue eyes opened the door.

Lucas, for a moment, thought he was looking into his father's eyes.

"Yes, may I help you," she said with barely a hint of a German accent. So faint, in fact, that Lucas thought he might be imagining an accent. Her hair was gray and styled in a bob.

"I hope so. I'm looking for my aunts. I'm Lucas Landry."

She gasped and put her hand over her heart. "Oh, my goodness. I . . . oh, forgive me . . . please come in."

The foyer was massive—two stories tall—and tiled in a sienna-color. In the center of the hallway, beneath an elaborate Spanish-style chandelier, was a large diamond-shaped design in bright Mexican colors. It immediately gave off warmth and feelings of happiness.

He followed the woman into another room, the living room apparently, with one wall covered in floor-to-ceiling windows. The view of the ocean from up here on a hill was spectacular.

"Please sit. I will go find my sister." She motioned toward a pale beige real-leather sofa and left.

Lucas sat for a few minutes, then stood up and walked around the room, stopping in front of large bookcases lining another wall. Books of all kinds, some in Spanish and a few in German, filled the shelves. Some of them looked quite old.

"Do you know any foreign languages?" someone asked.

He swung around.

The woman had returned and with her was her sister, he guessed. The sister had short, curly hair streaked brown and gray. Her eyes were brown and she walked with a cane.

"I studied Spanish and German," he said, "although I'm a bit rusty. My pronunciation isn't great in either language."

"Good for you, that you learned other languages," the first woman said. "I forgot to introduce myself. I'm Anna Marshall, oldest sister of your father. This is my younger sister, Elsa Cartwright. Joseph is the youngest."

"Was the youngest," Elsa corrected. "We were shocked to hear of his passing. The attorney called us. What happened to him?"

"Yes, please tell us," Anna said, motioning for Lucas to sit. She and Elsa sat in the two recliners.

"He died of a drug over-dose," Lucas said.

"Drugs? Our brother was a drug addict? Do you mean heroin?" Elsa said.

"No. It was an opioid addiction. He was injured in battles over in Kuwait and Afghanistan years ago. He got hooked on the painkillers back then. It was an off and on battle for decades. I tried to help him. I'm a therapist in a mental health/drug abuse clinic. Some I can help, but he wouldn't listen."

Both women shook their heads.

"He died at home?" Elsa asked.

"Sort of. A neighbor came over to return something he'd borrowed and found Dad unconscious on the sofa. He called 9-1-1, and the paramedics took him to the hospital, but it was too late. The doctors couldn't save him."

"Stubborn as a mule, our brother was," Anna said. "He was stubborn from the day he was born."

"You shouldn't speak ill of the dead," Elsa chided. She glanced at her sister and added, "Anna has had her share of pain, but she's never liked taking pain meds. She'd never get hooked on them."

"I had back surgery last year," Anna said. "And now it's Elsa's turn for surgery. She's getting a hip replacement in a few weeks."

"Knock on wood that I make it through the surgery," Elsa said. "Almost didn't make it through my hysterectomy five years ago."

"Sucks getting older," Anna said. "But I guess we shouldn't complain. We've lived longer than our brother and we're still going. Every day is a blessing."

"You've got that right," Elsa said.

"Well, listen to us, going on. What brings you here, Lucas?" Anna asked. "We met your brother a couple of years ago, but he didn't tell us much about you."

"Sorry, but I didn't know either of you existed until today. Dad never talked about his family or about the past. I only found out when I went to visit Seth. He and I are reconnecting now, I guess. We hadn't spoken in years."

"We never did understand why Joe abandoned the family. He was a difficult child and a horrible teenager, rude to our parents, disrespectful, mouthy."

"They tried to reach out to him several times after he left home, but he wanted nothing to do with them or with us."

"So you never heard from him?"

"That's right," Anna said.

No one spoke for a few minutes. On a whim, Lucas said, "Did you know about the attic in your parents' house?"

The two women glanced at each other and then they both smiled.

"Goodness, I'd forgotten all about that; the secret attic we called it. Elsa and I would sneak up there and hide sometimes. Joe would search the house, looking for us. Then, at dinnertime we would come downstairs and pretend we'd been in the house all along and that we'd made ourselves invisible so we could spy on him."

Elsa chuckled. "I guess maybe we were a bit bad ourselves. I'd forgotten about that. We were the older ones. We should have looked out for our little brother more instead of taunting him."

"Well, he deserved it, sister," Anna said. "Before we started hiding in the attic, he would do rotten things to us. Remember how he would stain our clothes to get us in trouble with Mother and Father? And he would lock us out of the house, so that we couldn't finish our chores."

"Yes. I had forgotten that, too. He was always getting into trouble in school for spray-painting graffiti on lockers and stealing lunch money from kids. He would sometimes get into fights with other kids, too. Because of him, we all got called mean things. Nazis, German pigs, krauts."

"Are you sure that was because of my dad?"

"Definitely," Elsa said. "He would bully other students. Then, in retaliation, they would tease him about his heritage. Knowing that we were his sisters, we would hear it, too."

"Seth told me that Dad hated being German. Is that true?"

Anna said, "You have to remember, this was in the early to mid-sixties, during the Cold War. Not that long after World War II. Hatred of Germans was common practically everywhere for many years."

Elsa said, "Joe wanted more than anything to be the all-American boy, regardless what his genes said. He was born here in Sacramento. He'd never been to Germany. He had no interest in our native country. Anna and I were born in Biberach, Germany and didn't come to the U.S. until 1957. I was three years old and she was four-and-a-half. We'd lived here already for two years when Joe was born."

"Did your parents speak German at home after you moved here?"

"No. Well, not after the first year. From the start they insisted we learn English, and once we did they insisted we speak it always. That's why neither of us remembers much German. Not after all these years. We know we have relatives still living in Germany, but we can't communicate with them."

"Really? Do you have names and contact information?"

"Probably somewhere," Anna said. It would take us time to find it."

"Sister, Seth has it. Remember, we gave it to him when he visited us."

"Oh, that's right."

Lucas looked at the clock. "It's getting late. I should get back home. I have a wife and daughter waiting for me. They would love to meet you both sometime, if that's okay." The moment the words left his mouth, he wanted to pull them back in. What was he thinking? His aunts might be just as prejudiced as his father and brother.

"Of course it is," the aunts said in unison.

"Maybe we should get to know each better before we add them to our conversations," he said. "I have lots of questions about the family's history, stuff that would probably bore them."

"We'd be happy to talk with your more," Anna said. "But it might have to wait until after Elsa's surgery."

Lucas nodded. Not what he wanted to hear. Recovery from hip replacement surgery wasn't going to be a picnic, and could make them shun any visitors.

As they walked him to the door, he turned and said, "I have one quick question. What were your parents' names?"

CHAPTER SIX

Christa Nagel, April 20, 1944, Altstadt, Sudetenland—

THE WOODS LOOKED a bit spooky in this area, with the dense pine trees huddled together for warmth, barely leaving room for Christa, Ernst, Fritz, and Julia to walk through. But the dark woods also made for the best play. The foursome came here whenever they got the chance. With schools shut down by the Wehrmacht, there was more time for exploring, which Christa knew worried Mutti, but also gave Mutti some quiet time. Soon after the school closures had been announced, poor Mutti had almost pulled out her hair, stuck with a house full of kids, day in and day out. Christa worried about Mutti. Christa didn't know how Mutti coped with running the house, taking care of six kids, shopping, and making repairs on their clothing and the house. Christa hoped she would never have to be responsible for all of that. Of course the older kids helped with chores, but that still left an awful lot for Mutti. She sometimes sent them out here to collect small pieces of wood for their stove and fireplace. That was today's assignment, but she also told them they could play for a while, too, so that the baby and Giselle could nap. Maybe Mutti needed to nap, too.

"Hey, look over here," Fritz yelled. "I found something."

Christa was closest to him and got to him first, with Ernst fast on her heels. Julia was running toward them, carrying a large log, and Christa half expected her to trip over something and go flying. Somehow, Julia didn't trip, and Christa turned her attention to the item Fritz had found.

On the ground was a wadded up cloth. A big cloth, like a bed sheet. But why would someone bring a sheet out into the woods? She glanced around, looking for gypsies who might be camping here. No one here except her brothers and sister.

"What do you think it is?" Fritz asked.

Ernst bent down and prodded it with a stick, lifting an edge up and showing more of the material. Strings hung from it.

"Oh *Gott*," Christa said. "Is that a . . . a parachute?"

"That is what it looks like to me," Ernst said, bent at the waist, his upper body turned to look up at his siblings. "Do you know what this means?"

"A soldier landed very close to this spot," Christa said, glancing around for a possible landing place. "Over there, in the clearing." The clearing was maybe fifty feet from where she stood. "Question is, German or allied? And where is he? Is he wounded?"

Ernst dropped his stick and picked up the parachute with his bare hands, examining it closely. "Definitely allied. Must mean the Americans or Brits are moving in. What I do not know is if the German soldiers captured him."

"They might have seen the plane and they could be searching for him," Christa said. She had seen German soldiers around town for days, stopping people, forcing them to show their identity cards. Could this be why?

Julia said, "Should we look for him? Maybe he needs help."

"Why would he need help from kids?" Ernst said. "He must have jumped from a plane before it crashed. He is probably long gone from here."

"Would he not have taken his parachute with him?" Christa asked. She couldn't imagine him leaving that behind. That could give him away, when most likely he was trying to hide the fact that he'd landed here.

"Not necessarily," Ernst said. "Maybe he got spooked. He might have heard German soldiers in the woods and had to get away quickly."

Christa felt goose bumps on her arms, and not just from the cold air. That poor man may have been killed right here in this spot. She glanced down to see if she could see blood on any of the pine needles. She didn't see any here, but it could be anywhere, really. Finding his blood out here in the woods and the clearing would be like finding a needle in a haystack.

Fritz said, "You are probably right. If that is what happened, he might have dropped something, like a gun or food or something we could use."

Ernst gave him a lopsided grin. "Food? Really? You have food on the brain."

"It is possible," Fritz said in his defense. "He would have been carrying food rations in his rucksack, would he not?"

Christa and Ernst exchanged looks.

As the oldest, at eleven years old, Christa was in charge. What should she say? She took a deep breath and let it out. "All right. Let us finish gathering wood and if we happen to find anything else while we are at it, we will decide what to do with it. Then we go straight home."

"What about the parachute?" Fritz asked.

"Fold it up as small as you can and hide it under a bush or under a bunch of pine needles. When we are ready to leave—and that has to be soon—we will come back for it."

77

All four children rushed around, looking for wood to take home, carefully checking to make sure any wood they put into their rucksacks was free of bugs and worms, and searching for any signs of an airman or his supplies. Christa found a knife and flashlight near the place where they'd found the parachute. She stuck them in her rucksack along with wood she'd collected, and continued her search.

Hanna Nagel, April 20, 1944, Altstadt, Sudetenland—

WHAT WAS TAKING the kids so long? Hanna opened the front door for the tenth time, and stuck her head outside, looking in the direction the kids would be coming from. The sun was setting and it would soon be too dark for the kids to be tromping through the woods. What if they didn't come home? What was she supposed to do?

She went back to the kitchen and stirred the pot of soup. Giselle had been whining for an hour, wanting her dinner. Hanna had already fed the baby his milk. The table was set and the soup was ready. *The kids must be freezing,* she worried, looking out the window again. With the sun going down and the temperature rapidly dropping. She tried to remember if they'd worn their hats and gloves. She hadn't paid attention. What kind of mother was she? She wrung her hands and paced across the kitchen to the front door.

One more look.

She opened the door again and leaned out, holding her breath.

"Mutti! We are home," Julia yelled, running up the steps and hugging her, then pushing past her into the house.

Hanna started to go after her, then stopped and hugged each of the other kids as they entered the house. "I thought you got lost," she said, once everyone was safely in the house. "What kept you so long? Did something happen?"

"I am hungry," Fritz said, ignoring her question. "Are we going to eat dinner?"

Hanna opened her mouth to repeat her question, but all the kids were hurrying into the kitchen, away from her. She lifted her hands in a gesture of defeat, and shook her head. Part of her thought she should be angry and reprimand her children for scaring her so, but no real harm done, they were home now and safe. Well, as safe as they could be during a war. She followed them into the kitchen and scooped soup into their bowls.

After dinner, she and Christa washed and dried the dishes, while the boys unloaded the wood they had all collected in the woods and stacked it next to the stove.

When they sat down in the living room for their evening of reading and storytelling, Fritz said, "I found something exciting in the woods today."

Hanna looked at him, curious. "What did you find, my boy?"

"He found a parachute," Julia said.

"Hey, I wanted to tell her. That is not fair."

Julia said, "We all found it. It belongs to all of us. And so does the knife and flashlight Christa found."

Hanna gasped.

"What is wrong, Mutti?" Christa asked.

Hanna's heart was pounding and she felt dizzy. *Oh mein Gott!*

"Mutti, you look pale. Are you sick?"

With her hand clutching her chest, she said, "You did not bring those things into this house, did you? Please tell me you left them in the woods."

Fritz jumped up, his eyes moist and shiny, and his face red. "You are scaring me, Mutti. We . . . we brought them in our rucksacks. We were not stealing, or nuthin'. The soldier who dropped from the airplane lost them and we found them. Finders keepers, right?"

Hanna couldn't speak. She closed her eyes, remembering the news she'd heard on the BBC radio months ago, after the kids had gone to bed. Alone in the dark living room, she'd practically gone into convulsions listening to the horrific story. How could she tell her children what had happened to the people in Lidice?

It had happened less than two years ago, northwest of Altstadt. Not terribly far away. Hitler had ordered that all men over fifteen years of age in Lidice be executed. All of the women and children were taken away, supposedly deported. The village was set on fire and the remnant of every building was destroyed. Even the animals were slaughtered. Hanna shuddered, picturing the scene in her mind.

She'd tried to keep it from her children. They didn't need to know the depths to which their government had sunken, but they needed to know now.

She took a deep breath and said, "I must tell you something. Sit down and listen. What I'm about to tell you is horrible. Almost two years ago, the SS General of Police, Reinhard Heydrich, the Acting Reichsprotektor of Bohemia and Moravia, was assassinated by men who had parachuted into the country from Great Britain. The SS suspected the residents of the small village of Lidice had harboured local resistance and partisans and had aided the paratroopers."

Ernst and Christa, both wide-eyed, looked at each other. Mutti wondered what they were thinking, but continued. "According to the news on the radio, the SS killed all of the men there and took the women and children away. Then they destroyed the village. They erased all evidence that it had ever existed." She left out details that would scare them more, and which she couldn't bare to say out loud. According to the BBC news, the women and children weren't simply deported, as the Volksempfänger news claimed. They were imprisoned in concentration camps. Most adults in the Sudetenland had heard rumors about concentration camps where the SS was holding Jews, but until the Lidice massacre, many hadn't believed it.

Julia and Giselle cried, and Christa hugged them both.

Fritz yelled out and pulled at his own hair. "We didn't help any soldiers. I swear we didn't. We looked for the parachute man, but he was gone. Are the SS soldiers going to come for us? Are they going to wipe out our village, too?"

"Did anyone see you?" Mutti asked. "Think carefully."

Ernst said, "I do not think so."

"Where are the parachute and other things you found? Go and get them and bring them to me." She stood up and added wood to the fireplace to grow the fire.

When Fritz and Christa came back with the items, Mutti grabbed the folded parachute and tossed it into the flames. As it burned, she looked at the knife and flashlight lying on the floor. "I will bury these after you all go to bed. You must promise me never to go into those woods again."

Christa said, "But Mutti, even if we do not find things again . . . other things left by parachute soldiers, the SS might still blame someone in our village for helping the allies. We could still be . . . ."

She didn't finish her sentence, but Hanna understood and she didn't have a good answer. After several moments, she said, "We have no control over what others in our village do or what the SS thinks or does, but we must not be the ones to bring destruction. We must do everything we can to keep ourselves and our village safe. Do you understand?"

All of the children nodded.

"Good. Let us try to concentrate on a good book for now, and put this incident out of our minds."

Ilse Seidel, April 20, 1944, Memmingen, Germany—

JOHANN GRINNED EAR-TO-EAR as he stood in the front parlor wearing his new uniform, and Ilse wanted to smack him upside the head. He was starting in the training class for becoming a Wehrmacht soldier. He wasn't old enough to officially join the Hitler Youth, but the war had been going on for too long and the army was running low on soldiers. They needed every man or boy they could get. Ilse couldn't believe that her brother was actually eager to join the army. He bragged about how he was going to be trained the right way and then he could not only be a soldier but also move up in the ranks. He would make something of himself, he said. More likely, Ilse decided, he'd get himself killed. Johann was strong and smart, but he didn't know anything about war. For all his big talk, he was still an innocent boy. He was gullible and had allowed the Nazis to brainwash him.

Mutter went over to Johann and straightened his hat. "You look handsome in your uniform, Johann. But you must know I do not want you to join the army. Please, will you change your mind about going to the training class?"

"You know I cannot refuse to go. Even if I wanted to, which I do not. No one turns down an offer to join the Hitler Youth."

Oma began crying, and Opa put his arm around her shoulders.

Christa stood, wringing her hands together, in the middle of the parlor, halfway between her mother and Johann and her grandparents. Her younger brother, Robert, and her sister, Ursula, stood at the bottom of the stairs, watching, wide eyed.

Robert said, "I will not go. No one can force me to join any of the groups."

"You are too young," Johann said. "You are only eight. You have no idea what you are talking about. When you are old enough, you will change your mind."

Mutter said, "Let us pray the war does not last that long. I do not want to lose both of my sons."

Johann glared at her. "Thanks for the vote of confidence in my abilities. I am not stupid. I will not get myself killed."

"War does not only kill stupid people." With that said, Mutter turned on her heels and walked toward the stairs. Robert and Ursula moved out of her way, and she strode up the stairs without looking back.

Two weeks later, Johann came home, packed a bag, and announced that he was being sent to the front. The army needed new recruits, and his whole class had been called up. They were all required to report to Biberach for medical examinations and then from there they would head out.

Mutter fell apart when he broke the news, and she barely got herself back together enough to hug him and say goodbye. Ilse thought Mutter was already grieving for him, as if he'd died.

The family continued on after he left. In some ways, life was easier with one less mouth to feed, but it was harder, too, without a pair of strong hands for doing repairs around the house. Bombings were common and even though their house hadn't taken a direct hit, they always had indirect damage. And when one of the adjoining houses had incurred extensive damage, it was in the family's best interest to help with their repairs, too, because they counted on the heat and protection the adjoining walls afforded.

Two weeks after Johann departed, the family celebrated Ursula's twelfth birthday with the smallest of cakes—but at least it was a cake, Ilse had told her. She didn't tell her that she'd been saving small portions of flour for it for a month and that Oma had traded a piece of her jewelry for it. Ilse didn't know why someone wanted the jewelry, but figured it must be someone who had a contact who could help her trade it for something she needed. That's how it usually worked in Memmingen during the war.

Thomas Landry, April 20, 1944, San Francisco, California—

MUSIC PLAYED ON the radio in the living room of the Landry family's Victorian house. The DJ was playing the top ten songs, and Thomas was swaying to Bosame Mucho (Kiss Me Much) by Jimmy Dorsey while he swept the floor. With his mother, Rachel, working in a weapons factory while his father and older brother were fighting overseas, Thomas and Teresa had to help with the chores after school. He didn't mind, as long as he could crank up the radio while he worked. In truth, not minding was an understatement. He was at home, while most of his buddies had to work after school. All he had to do was babysit his younger sister—and she didn't require much effort, seeing as how she was shut up in her bedroom working on homework for at least an hour and then had to help him fix their dinner. Yeah, he had it pretty easy. Dusting, sweeping, laundry, grocery shopping, house repairs. All pretty basic stuff. What worried him was that he was almost finished with his junior year of high school, and then one more year to go. At graduation, he'd be eighteen and would be drafted into the army, unless he opted to voluntarily enlist like his brother and father did.

Up until two months ago, he hadn't wanted to be a soldier. Didn't like guns and certainly didn't want to kill anybody. But in letters from Pop and Ronald, they'd described what was happening to Jews; to their people. Then, in Ron's latest letter, he'd described the way the damned Nazis were rounding them up, putting them into concentration camps, and starving them. Ron had even said he'd heard rumors that they were being gassed to death or taken out in the woods and shot point-blank.

After reading that letter, Mom had cried and cried, dabbing at her eyes with a handkerchief, and finally announcing that she needed to go to the Synagogue to speak with the Rabbi. "Stay here with your brother," she said to Teresa, then glanced at Thomas. "I won't be long."

Ten year old Teresa had turned to Thomas, her eyes moist and face red, and asked, "What can Rabbi do about it? Can he help save the Jews in Germany? I'm scared. Are they going to get us, too, and take us away?"

Thomas hadn't told her that it wasn't only Jews in Germany that were being targeted, and wondered now if it was wrong to keep her in the dark. It was bad in Poland, Czechoslovakia, Hungary, France, and other European countries. Thomas had read the letter after Mom finished it. And neither of them had read the letter out loud or given it to Teresa. Mom had snapped the letter back from Thomas and taken it with her to show the Rabbi. Teresa only knew the parts that Mom had talked about.

He had patted Teresa's shoulder and said, "No, you're safe. The Germans aren't in the U.S., and our military won't let them come here. But as for your question about the Rabbi, he can't stop the Nazis. That's why Pop and Ron and I have to fight. I'm going to join in and stop the killing of innocents."

He turned up the music to drown out his worrisome thoughts.

CHAPTER SEVEN

Lucas Landry, July 2017, Sacramento, California—

"I STILL DON'T know how any of the people in the photos are connected to me," Lucas said. He and Tawny were again looking through the boxes and file cabinets in the attic. So far, neither of his grandparents' names had come up in the diaries.

After visiting Seth last week, he'd told Tawny about his brief visit and said while they had not resolved their issues yet, at least they were again on speaking terms for the moment. How could he tell her without hurting her feelings—or without pissing her off—that Seth was a racist and wouldn't even meet her or Bianca? Hell, he would be angry if her family had broken off ties with her because they didn't think he was good enough. Who wouldn't be? Best to keep that from her, at least for now.

He diverted further inquiry about Seth by telling Tawny about his two aunts, Anna and Elsa, that he'd found out about and had gone to meet very briefly in Santa Rosa. He said they seemed nice, talked a bit about his father, revealed his grandparents names were Tom and Emelie Landry, told her about Elsa's pending surgery, and had left telling them he would visit again when they were both feeling better.

His aunts didn't know anything about Tawny and Bianca. He'd wanted to tell them all about his family and show them pictures on his cell phone, but he hadn't. What if they were prejudiced, too, and would then refuse to answer questions about his family's history because he had a mixed-raced child? He needed answers, so he kept quiet about his family to keep the door open between them—at least until he knew more.

"Maybe you should concentrate on the other photos, then," Tawny said. "You know, the miners or farmers or whatever they were."

"I don't know. That would be harder, because those date further back. Besides, I'm not really into all that genealogy crap. That's more of a women's thing."

"Lucas Landry, I can't believe those words came out of your mouth. Shame on you! Men and women, both, are into genealogy. What a sexist thing to say."

Lucas felt his face grow hot with embarrassment. Being called sexist was the last thing he wanted. "Sorry. I . . . I guess I was trying to find a way out of doing all that research. I mean, digging around for family's roots is hard work, and what if I don't like what I find out? What if I find rotten potatoes, so to speak?"

He looked away, pretending to examine a box he'd already gone through.

"I would do it in a heartbeat—and don't say it's because I'm a woman. Knowing your family history helps you know more about yourself, about where you came from, and why you do the things you do. The more you know, the better. You know that from your psychology training."

"Yeah, I know." Seeing his father's eyes again in his aunt's eyes had stirred up mixed feelings in him. He would never see his father again, but those two women were a link to him and had awakened his sense of heritage. Back when he was in Grad school, he'd had to look into his family and write papers about his childhood. That had been tough, but he'd done it. This time, he had a chance to look further back—back into his father's and grandparents' lives.

Tawny said, "At least with those possible ancestors—the ones in the 1800's photos—we might be able to check public records here in Sacramento."

"Yeah, I guess that makes sense," Lucas said, looking at Tawny again. "I'd like to know more about them, for sure, though I'm thinking maybe they aren't related to me. I mean, those photos might have come with the house when my ancestors bought it and emigrated from Germany. Anyway, I think I may have a chance of getting information about my German relatives directly from my father's sisters. That's the best way I can think of to get answers. Unfortunately, they are getting up there in age and both have some health issues. I mean, they aren't that old, but Dad was younger and Mom was younger, and both of them are gone. I think I need to spend time with them now, before it's too late." His eyes teared up and he choked back tears that surfaced. *Wow, where did that emotion come from?*

"Aw, Luke. You must be hurting over the loss of your father. I should have been more sensitive, more comforting, and I've not really talked to you about your feelings."

"No, you've been great," he said, hoping he'd squashed the emotion enough that it wouldn't try to surface again while he was speaking. "You haven't pressed me to talk, and that's exactly what I need—not to be pressed, I mean. My father and I . . . well, you know, there's never been any love lost between us. It's just that with the aunts, I felt something, like they gave me a sense of family, maybe." He ran his hand through his hair. *Why can't I figure out what I'm trying to say?* "I guess maybe I have a sense

88

that we could be family. You know, that we might be more than just linked by blood. More than names on a family tree chart. Does that make sense?"

"You want to share your life with blood relatives. I get that."

He reached out and pulled her close, his chin resting on the top of her head. "No, it's not that. Not exactly. I mean, you and Bianca and our new baby—and your mom, too—are all the family I need."

She looked up into his eyes. "Of course we're your family. But I know it's more complicated than that. You need other ties, too, heritage to ground you. You need to know where you came from. It's important to find those links."

Roots. Back to that genealogy stuff. Maybe he did need roots for his family tree. *Huh.*

He reached over and kissed her. "I don't know what I would do without you. I sometimes think you know me better than I know myself."

"We need each other." She ruffled his hair. "It's funny how we came from completely different backgrounds and cultures, yet none of that mattered. We're family and we have each other. We share the same moral values and the same beliefs. Maybe some of that comes because we both studied psychology, do you think?"

"Yeah, probably what we learned in college influences us and we share that commonality, but it goes beyond that, too. We understand each other," Lucas said. As he held Tawny in his arms, though, his brother's face and words broke through Lucas's self-preserving armor: We want Americans to be a pure race, yes. But my beliefs are totally different from Dad's. You seem to think that if we're both racist, we're the same. It doesn't work like that.

Oh, God, I can't keep something like that from Tawny, but how can I tell her what kind of family I come from? And what if Seth is right and my family were Nazis?

"Maybe it's dumb to dig around in the past," Lucas whispered into Tawny's ear. "Don't they always say that you should let go of the past and live in the present, or something like that?"

Tawny pulled back and said, "Don't you dare wimp out. You need to do this. I'll help you as much as I can, but you might never get this chance again. Not after your aunts are gone. Use it."

He opened his mouth to speak, but what could he say? What reason could he give for stopping? Tell her what he feared? She would ask why, and then he would have to tell her.

"No one wants you to live in the past, but you should know what happened in the past. Didn't you ever see posters in your history class that said 'Those who don't study history are destined to repeat it', or something like that?" She smiled at him.

"Yeah, I remember that. You're right. I need to find out what my ancestors did."

THE NEXT MORNING, he called his aunts and was told Elsa was going in for surgery ahead of schedule in two days. An opening in the surgeons had come up. Lucas got the information, arranged for a day off from work, and agreed to meet them at the hospital.

He strode through the hospital's antiseptic-smelling corridors, trying but failing, to block out errant thoughts of people suffering in lonely rooms, some dying, and some waiting for word that an organ had finally been found.

Watching for signs that would lead him to the waiting room where he was supposed to meet Aunt Anna, he didn't notice, and almost collided with, an orderly pushing an empty gurney. "Sorry," Lucas said as he swerved out of the way, chastising himself under his breath.

A voice came over the loudspeaker, calling for a doctor, stat. A shiver raced down his spine and along with it came a memory he'd shoved to the back of his mind—the day the paramedics had arrived at a different hospital, rolling in a gurney with his father strapped to it.

Someone, he couldn't remember who, had called Lucas on his cell and told him to meet the paramedics at the hospital. He had actually been nearby and arrived right behind the emergency vehicle. He'd followed them into the emergency room and down a corridor, but was barred from going into the room where they were going to work on his father.

He'd sat for a long time in the waiting room, barely holding off tears and guilt. Why hadn't he tried harder to get his father into rehab? Good God, drug addiction treatment was his specialty. He should have been able to get through to his father. His father's addiction problems had gone on for years and probably subconsciously influenced Lucas's decision to specialize. For all the good that had done. Yeah, maybe Lucas helped other people, but what good was it when he couldn't help his own family?

Before Tawny could get there and offer her comfort and support, the doctors had spilled out of the room where they'd been working on his father, one of them walking over and calmly, quietly assuring Lucas they'd done everything within their power. His father was gone.

Shaking off the past, he finally found the right elevator and took it up to the floor where he was supposed to meet his Aunt Anna. He sat in the waiting room with her quietly for an hour, and then her daughters and Elsa's son and daughter, along with a bunch of kids and grandkids filled up the waiting room. Lucas became an outsider.

He was introduced to everyone, and they were all friendly enough, but he quickly realized it was too soon to be accepted into their circle. That's what he told himself, as he said goodbye to Anna.

"I'll keep in touch," he said, "and we'll get better acquainted later, when everyone is less stressed. Please call when Elsa gets out of surgery. I'll come visit her later when she's ready." Whether they would ever be close, he couldn't say. But it almost made him weep as he walked to the elevator comparing this family to his relationship with his father and brother.

Outside, the June air was warm and smelled of flowers from the garden beds in the parking lot. Flowers made the hospital look less intimidating, more inviting. Not everything that happens in a hospital comes out bad, he reminded himself. People get well, babies are delivered, and maybe Aunt Elsa will be okay.

Since he had the rest of the day off, he decided to stop back at Seth's house. With any luck, Seth would be at work and he could ask Allison if she could give him the contact information for their relatives in Germany.

When he rang the doorbell, it wasn't Allison who answered.

"Hey, brother, what are you doing here?" Seth said, "Didn't expect to see you again so soon, considering it was five years between the previous two visits. Know what I mean?"

Lucas nodded, looking over toward the house next door for a moment, trying to figure out how to answer.

"Yeah, I didn't expect to be coming by either, but I was on my way home from the hospital. One of the aunts is having surgery."

"Oh, sorry, I didn't know. But you didn't have to come by to tell me."

"No, well, that's not why I came. I was wondering if I could get contact information for our German relatives. Aunt Anna and Aunt Elsa told me they gave you a list."

"What the heck do you want that for? You aren't going to fly to Germany, are you?"

"Well, no, I . . . I hadn't really thought . . . ." He shrugged. "I might try calling or writing." Good grief, was he actually thinking he might go to Germany Was he really going to get in touch with strangers and try to make new family ties? His brother's question hit the nail on the head. What was he thinking? What was he feeling? Had he done so well with the new relatives he'd seen today?

CHAPTER EIGHT

Christa Nagel, July 18, 1944, Altstadt, Sudetenland—

CHRISTA WAS COLLECTING eggs in the chicken pen when Ernst opened the gate and strode inside. "What are you doing here?" she asked. "Are you going to help me clean the pen? Please say yes, or leave."

"Well, you are in a sour mood. What did I do to deserve your ire?"

She pushed loose strands of hair from her face with the back of a hand. "Sorry. You have done nothing wrong. It's just . . . nothing. I am just sad. Today is my birthday."

"Why are you sad? Eleven is a fine age." Ernst looked thoughtful. "You know, you should go put on your best dress and get Mutti to fix your hair. It is a mess, you know."

"Ha, and what best dress should I wear? I have so many to choose from."

"Wow. You really are in a sour mood. I know at least you have one good dress. Not everyone does. Mutti said that the Meiers down the road lost everything in the fire at their house last week. You see, it could be much worse."

Ernst was too easy-going. Nothing ever rattled him. Well, almost nothing. That parachute incident had, but nothing since then. If only she could see the bright side of their lives, she scolded herself. But tonight there would be no birthday cake, no party, and no celebration. In the past few months the Nazis had taken half their chickens, which of course meant half their eggs were also gone. That meant they had fewer items to barter with at the shops. Their ration cards gave them barely enough food to feed a family of four—and there were still seven of them, now that Vati was away. Even with the few vegetables they were able to grow in their small garden, those left to them after the soldiers came, they were starving. The food supplies in their root cellar were almost exhausted, and Mutti couldn't spare any flour to bake a cake. Their flour was needed for real food, like bread.

"We could make mud pies," Ernst said. "Cannot eat them, but we could have fun throwing them at each other."

"Don't you dare!" But she laughed. Ernst could make her laugh when no one else could. He ran out of the pen, slamming the door behind him, and glanced over his shoulder to see if she was coming.

She took off after him.

"Where are you going in such a hurry?"

Christa turned toward the deep male voice, stunned and unable to speak at first. "Vati? Oh Vati, you are home!" He was standing near the door to the main house. She ran to him and swung her arms tightly around his waist. "I am so happy to see you."

"I would not miss my oldest child's birthday, now would I?"

"But how? How could you get away? Are you not supposed to be fighting?"

"Not fighting. No. I am a medic and I should be helping people. But . . . I have an injury of my own. They sent me home, and if I am lucky I will not have to go back."

95

"That is wonderful, Vati. I mean that you can stay home, not that you are injured." As she looked at him, she couldn't help but wonder if he'd deliberately gotten hurt. How else could he be here right on her birthday?

"It is all right. I knew what you meant," he said, chuckling.

By now, Ernst was waiting to hug Vati. Within moments, Mutti and the other children had gathered outside and were eager to hug and kiss Vati, too.

"How badly are you hurt?" Mutti asked, looking up at him from their embrace.

"Just my leg. Shrapnel from an explosion pierced my thigh, but I was lucky and it did no permanent damage."

"Oh my poor Franz. They brought you back home on a truck, then?"

"Part of the way. I had to walk from my drop-off spot. The regiment was heading to another battleground."

Mutti made a tsk, tsk sound.

"Vati," Fritz said, "you really may not have to go back?"

"I do not know." Vati and Mutti exchanged glances. "It depends. Germany is losing the war. It could be over in weeks or months."

Christa stayed silent. Mutti had begun letting her and Ernst, as the oldest, listen to the BBC radio with her after the younger kids were in bed. She knew that the Russians were in Poland and pushing back the Wehrmacht ground soldiers. Altstadt was near the Polish border. What would happen when they reached the border with the Sudetenland? The Russians were said to be winning, and they were supposedly killing German civilians and raping the women and young girls. Would Vati be able to protect their family?

Breadcrumbs and Bombs

Ilse Seidel, July 18, 1944, Memmingen, Germany—

ILSE SHOOK HER younger siblings, Ursula and Robert, trying to wake them from their deep slumber. *How could anyone sleep through all the noise?* she wondered. The air-raid sirens blared outside like a banshee. Commonplace, these days, yes. Perhaps they had become so common that people could easily weave them into their dreams. But how could anyone not hear the fighters roaring directly overhead, shaking the house so loudly they sounded like they might land on top of their roof? "Wake up, both of you." Both kids were now rubbing their eyes, her brother rising up on one elbow and making a grumpy face, and her sister rolling over onto her side, away from Ilse. "I'm serious. We must hurry to the shelter. Don't you hear all that noise? Come. Grab your shoes and hurry. Mutter, Oma, and Opa will meet us at the shelter." Mutter, out of breath, had stumbled into Christa's bedroom moments earlier and told her to get the kids safely to the shelter. She would help her parents, both of whom were sick and not walking especially well. She would have her hands full.

All the loud footsteps running down the stairs was masked by the horrible noise overhead. A herd of elephants could have run down the stairs and no one would have heard.

Outside now, Ilse, Ursula, and Robert ran through the cobbled streets amongst their neighbors. The sky rumbled and crackled like a devilish thunderstorm and everyone froze, gazing up at the roiling sky. Tonight was different. This wasn't allied planes dropping bombs on the town or on the nearby airport. Tonight, both allied and German planes shared the heavens. What was happening? Ilse stared in anticipation, unable to look away.

Sharp cracks and explosive sounds filled the night air. Sparks flew from plane to plane. The sky was on fire, exploding into breathtaking displays, followed by gray and orange clouds of smoke.

"*Mein Gott!*" somewhat yelled. It was then that people began to panic and run again. Ilse realized that the planes being hit and plane debris would be crashing to the ground on top of them.

"Oh *Gott*! Run!" Ilse yelled to Ursula and Robert. "*Schnell!*" She reached out to grab them, but they were already racing toward the bomb shelter. She ran after them and only hesitated a moment, helping a fallen woman and her little boy get back up and moving.

Inside the shelter, Ilse couldn't see much. A few lanterns gave off yellowy light, but the people in the entrance were slow moving and blocked her view.

She bit her lip, not wanting to scream at them to keep moving so others could get inside. Maybe they were old, like Oma and Opa. For all she knew, they could be the ones holding up the line.

A man in line behind her yelled out for the people in front to move, and he didn't hesitate to yell obscenities.

Ilse cringed. Bad enough that everyone was scared. The line did, however, begin to move and she could now glimpse some people sitting around, huddling with their families, trying to comfort small children, and keep warm. Ilse suddenly realized it was frigid in here. With so many people packed in like sardines, one would think it would be warm in the shelter.

As she picked her way down a haphazard aisle, she put her hand over her mouth and nose. Oh, *mein Gott*, what was that horrid smell?

She glanced to her right and saw a man squatting and defecating in front of everyone. Whether he was scared and lost control, or just had to go too badly and hadn't gotten a chance, she didn't know. And didn't care to find out. *Just keep moving.*

What if her siblings didn't make it to the shelter? She was supposed to get them here safely, and they had gotten separated from her. What if Mutter had too much trouble dealing with Oma and Opa and they were still outside? What if an airplane fell—she couldn't finish that thought. *Keep moving.*

"Ilse, Ilse! Over here."

She turned to her left, following the sound of the voice. Ursula was standing on her toes, waving her arm wildly. Robert was beside her. Thank *Gott*!

She rushed over to them and hugged them both. "Have you seen Mutter?" she asked.

"*Ja*," Ursula said. "She and Oma and Opa are over there." She pointed. "They saw us but cannot get over here because of the crowd."

Ilse nodded, relieved. That was all right. They could see each other and know they were all safe. *For now.*

An hour and a half later, the all-clear signal chimed and the people began exiting the odorous shelter. As Ilse stepped outside, she covered her mouth and nose again, unsure which smell was worse, in there or out here. The night air was pungent, a mix of smoke, fuel, and something she couldn't quite put a finger on. Death, maybe. She grabbed hold of Ursula's hand on one side of her and Robert's hand on her other side. Together, they moved away from in front of the door and waited to the side for the rest of the family.

When they arrived home, Opa turned on a single lamp in the parlor, and they all flopped down, huddled close together for comfort and warmth.

Mutter said, "What happened? Some people said it was an air battle."

"We heard that, too," Ilse said. "It must have been, because the planes were attacking each other."

Opa left the room and returned with his BBC radio. He turned it on and adjusted the antenna to listen to the latest news.

Indeed, there had been an allied mission—an extensive strategic bombing campaign. Not only in Bavaria but in other parts of Germany and in other areas of Europe, as well. German fighters at the Memmingen Airdrome—the airport—had risen to attack the allied planes. Memmingen was on the news. The world news.

"Who won?" Robert asked. "They did not say."

Oma and Opa exchanged glances. Opa said, "Nobody won. I am sure there were casualties on both sides." He shut off the radio. "We go to bed now. We will see what tomorrow brings."

Petr Jaroslav, July 18, 1944, Olomouc, Czechoslovakia—

THERE WERE TIMES Petr Jaroslav wished he were a Jew. Then he would get inside a concentration and . . . and what? If he was a Jew, he wouldn't have weapons. He wouldn't have any choice and wouldn't be able to do a damned thing to help anybody else. Sometimes he heard people in town talk about the Jews and say they deserved what happened to them. "Look at them, meekly standing on the street with their suitcases, letting the gestapo prod them and poke them. Then they climb onto the trucks as if they are going on holiday. Surely they must know what is happening." A friend of the first speaker would pipe up and say, "They do not care. Or they are too stupid to fight back." It took all of Petr's strength not to jump into the conversation and give them a piece of his mind. What the hell were the Jews supposed to do? The gestapo had guns, assault rifles. They killed people right out in the open if they disobeyed. Would either of those two men fight back if they were in the Jews' position? No. No question there. Petr knew who the fighters were. He knew who the 'yes men' were, too.

Three days ago Petr's oldest brother, Antonin, had trekked all the way to Thereseienstadt to get his girlfriend Rebeka out. He did it against the strident advice of their father and all the other men who outranked him in the resistance. Antonin didn't care what anyone said. He was getting Rebeka out and nobody was going to stop him. Wasn't that the sort of thing they were all fighting for? Freedom?

At least he'd gone on his mission prepared. Armed to the teeth, from all accounts. Antonin didn't get inside. According to news that had reached the family by way of the grapevine, he had seen Rebeka standing in the yard. She didn't wave or acknowledge him. She couldn't, without drawing attention. The guards saw him, anyway. He was shot before he could finish cutting through the barbed wire fence.

Supposedly, Rebeka had gone into hysterics. The guards had grabbed her, took her and made her face the other prisoners, and then shot her dead, too.

First Vera. Now Antonin and Rebeka. He was losing his family, picked off one at a time.

CHAPTER NINE

Lucas Landry, July 2017, Sacramento, California—

"I DON'T KNOW what to do with the contact information for my German relatives," Lucas told Tawny. He'd thought about it off and on all afternoon. They'd finished eating dinner an hour ago and were now sitting on the sofa, with Bianca on Tawny's lap. "Seemed like a good idea to get it, you know, in case my aunts don't know enough about our family's history. They were pretty young when they left Germany and moved to the U.S." He hadn't told her who had given him the contact information, letting her assume that Aunt Anna had given it to him at the hospital.

"When do I get to meet your aunts? I know Elsa is in the hospital, but maybe I could meet Anna," Tawny said, reaching her hand into a bowl of popcorn.

Lucas opened his mouth to speak, but before he could get a word out, his cell phone rang.

"Oh, Lucas, I'm glad I could reach you."

"Hello, Aunt Anna, we were just talking about you. How did the operation go?"

Tawny raised an eyebrow, and Lucas remembered he hadn't told her he left before Elsa got out of surgery.

Anna didn't answer right away. Uh oh, that's not a good sign.

"Lucas, she . . . Elsa . . ."

Lucas held his breath, feeling a weight pressing down on his shoulders the way it had when the doctors had come out of the room where they'd been working on his father, solemn expressions on their faces. No. She couldn't be dead, too. It had only been a month since her brother had died.

"What happened?" he asked, closing his eyes, not wanting to hear bad news.

"The surgery went okay. The doctors don't know why, but believe she had a stroke afterwards, or maybe there was a bad reaction to the anesthesia. She's in a coma and might not . . . wake up." She broke down and sobbed.

He let her cry. Poor woman! When she quieted, he said, "Do you want me to come over? Are you at the hospital? I can be there in an hour." He glanced over at Tawny, a questioning look on her face.

"No, no, it's okay." He heard her blow her nose. "I'm staying here at the hospital tonight. My kids and Elsa's kids are here and there's no need for you to come. But you asked me to call and let you know. You've been nice to us and you're family now."

You're family now. Was he?

"Aunt Anna, is there anything I can do for you, or for the family? I'm really new to this and I want to—"

She cut him off, saying, "You don't need to do anything, Lucas. Just knowing you care helps. Get a good night's sleep, and maybe come by the hospital tomorrow, if you can. Tomorrow is Saturday, right?"

"That's right. I'll come by tomorrow."

"Thank you. Take care of your wife and child. Family's everything," she said, her voice cracking toward the end. "Elsa . . . would tell you that herself, if she could."

Lucas hung up the phone and closed his eyes. How was it that these two women he'd barely met had already become important to him? If Elsa died, he would be devastated, and it would not be from losing a resource for his research. And why didn't he feel as bad about his own father's passing? *Am I cold-hearted? Am I guilty of reverse prejudice?*

He opened his eyes and took in Tawny and Bianca. "I love you both," he said, and leaned toward them, taking them both in a giant hug.

"What happened to your Aunt? Elsa, right?"

"She made it through the surgery, but afterwards something went wrong. They don't know what happened, but she's in a coma."

"Oh my gosh! I'm so sorry, Luke."

"Daddy, is she going to die? I don't want her to die," Bianca asked, her big brown eyes looking up at him. She leaned toward him to give him a hug.

"Thank you, sweetie. We don't know yet." He patted Bianca on the head, and gave Tawny a questioning look.

She shrugged.

Neither of them had ever talked to Bianca about death, so Lucas didn't know why she would ask that question. Then it hit him. He had talked to her about his parents that day when he'd first gone to check out his father's house. He'd told her that they'd died.

"I'm going over to the hospital in the morning," Lucas said. "They don't need me there right now. Lots of family there, you know."

Tawny covered his hand with her own. "I hope she pulls through. You and Elsa have some catching up to do. I'm sorry you didn't find your aunts sooner."

Yeah, that was unfortunate. Then another thought occurred. *Why couldn't they could have found me? Seth found them and had told them about me. They might have even known about me before then. Did they not care?*

In the morning, Tawny was sick to her stomach and running a fever. Lucas went into Bianca's bed to check on her, since she hadn't run into their bedroom and pounced on the bed to wake them up like she usually did.

"How are you this morning, bug? Are you sleeping in?"

"My head hurts, Daddy. And my tummy feels yucky."

He reached down and felt her forehead. She was as hot as Tawny. "You stay in bed and I'll get you some medicine, okay?"

Back in their bedroom, he said, "Sorry to bother you, hun, but where do you keep the medicines? And do you have any children's cold medicine?"

"Oh no, don't tell me Bianca is sick, too."

He nodded.

"It's in the master bathroom in the medicine cabinet. Would you bring Bianca in here, please? We probably have the same thing. Might as well be sick together and keep each other company. You can bring me medicine, too, and a couple glasses of water."

"Okay. Be right back."

He returned to Bianca's bedroom. "Hey, bug, it's me again. Mommy is sick, too, and wants you to keep her company, if that's okay with you."

She held up her arms, and he picked her up, along with her teddy bear.

After setting her on the bed next to Tawny, he hurried downstairs to the kitchen, grabbed two glasses and filled them halfway with water, then picked up a box of tissues and climbed back up the stairs. He set the items on the nightstand closest to Tawny and left again to get the medicines.

"You're going to wear yourself out with all that running around," Tawny said when Lucas came back with the medicines.

"Do you want me to give the medicine to Bianca?"

Bianca sneezed three times in a row as if answering.

"Absolutely not," Tawny said. "You should leave this room and spray disinfectant in the hall bathroom and downstairs bathroom and the kitchen and anywhere else that we've been in the past day and go wash your hands. Then go visit your aunts in the hospital."

"I could be carrying germs. Don't want to expose them or their families. I'll call Aunt Anna and let her know what's going on. I can visit them another day."

"Shoo. Go spray, wash your hands, and then go to the hospital. After that, go to the other house and do more research. Keep yourself busy and let us sleep."

"But—"

"No buts. Go. I don't want to see your face around here until night, is that clear?"

"You're going to need food."

"Feed a cold, starve a fever. We both have fevers and won't be eating anything for a while. Go."

"What about the baby? Will your being sick with the flu affect the baby?"

"Don't worry about that. I'll call the doctor's office and ask, but I'm sure it will be fine. Go."

How could he not worry? Bianca had been two months premature. They didn't know why. They almost lost her.

"Lucas, just go. We'll be fine. Don't come back until nighttime. We need to rest and you need to stay away from us so you don't get sick."

He was halfway down the stairs, when he heard something. It sounded like, "Daddy", but he wasn't sure. He retraced his steps to the top of the staircase and said, "Did you say something?"

Bianca called out, "Daddy, can you bring me the kitty?"

"Your stuffed kitty?"

"No. The real one."

He sighed and looked over at Tawny, who nodded. The things a father did for his family. "Okay. I'll bring her over, if I can find her. She likes to hide, you know."

He left the bedroom and gently closed the door behind him. Downstairs, in the pantry, he found disinfecting spray and cleaned up the kitchen, the coffee table and sofa, and then the main floor bathroom and Bianca's bathroom. That done, he scrubbed his hands.

His watch read 9:30. It would take him an hour or hour and a half to get to the hospital, depending on traffic. He turned to run up the stairs and tell Tawny and Bianca he was leaving, but remembered what Tawny had said about not wanting to see his face until night. They were probably asleep, anyway.

He strode through the kitchen and out the door leading into the garage. As he got into his car to head over to the hospital in Santa Rosa, he pushed the garage door opener and watched in the rearview mirror as the overhead door lifted.

Busy day ahead. Oh, wait. The cat. Oh, crap.

All right. The wife and kid come first, he thought. He drove to Sacramento, put the litter box, supplies, cat dishes, and cat food in the back of his Jeep, and then went in search of Hallie. The search was easier than expected. She was sleeping on his Dad's bed. He scooped her up, locked the front door as he exited the house, and placed the cat loose in his car. Of course she meowed all the way to his house, periodically looking out each window and trying to climb over him twice.

Finally, he arrived home and did everything in reverse, starting with taking the cat into the house and letting her explore. When she finally made her way up the stairs and into the master bedroom, Bianca let out a loud cry of joy.

AT THE HOSPITAL, Lucasseco sat with Anna and her family. Nothing had changed overnight. Someone asked if he'd brought his family with him, and he explained that they were down with the flu.

"Sorry to hear that," his cousin Jacob said. "We'd love to meet them." He glanced at his mother. "Mom's hoping she might get to babysit your little girl, isn't that right, Mom?"

She nodded and dabbed at her eyes with a tissue. Then she went on and told them stories about when she and Elsa were little girls playing in their houses, both in Biberach, Germany, and Sacramento.

Everyone listened and nodded and laughed in the right places.

Jacob whispered in Lucas's ear, "We've all heard these stories dozens of times, but it makes her happy to remember the good old days."

"Does she ever talk about the war?"

"She wasn't born until after the war but, yeah, she sometimes talks about what it was like for her family during the post-war area. They all had a pretty tough time."

Lucas wanted to ask more, but didn't want to upset Anna by not listening to her.

In the early afternoon, some of the family left to get lunch.

Jacob said to his mother, "We need to grab a quick bite and then I'm taking you home to get some sleep. You hardly slept a wink last night. I'll drop you off back at my house, and then I'll go pick up the kids at their mother's house. We'll stop back by the house then and pick you up."

"But someone has to stay here in case Elsa regains consciousness."

Lucas was about to say he would stay, but Jacob said, "Her kids are staying here. They're eating in the cafeteria downstairs and have their cell phones with them. They'll be back up here in probably fifteen or twenty minutes."

"I'd rather stay," Anna said, refusing to budge.

"Absolutely not," Jacob said. "I can't have you not sleeping and then getting sick, too."

"Oh, I guess you're right." She grabbed her purse and tried to get up. Jacob had to take her hand and pull her up.

Lucas walked with them out to the parking lot.

Jacob said, "We'll call you later to give you an update. Mom has your phone number, right?"

"Yeah. Thanks."

Lucas watched Jacob and Anna stride across the lot and get into a shiny black Mercedes sports car. As they drove past him, he headed in the other direction to his ten year old blue Jeep.

He didn't really know anything about Anna's son. *Probably a doctor or lawyer, driving an expensive car like that.* But then again, maybe Jacob's father had been a CEO of some big company or something and was rolling in money. The house Anna and Elsa lived in was certainly expensive.

As he drove back toward Roseville, he randomly wondered why his mind automatically tried to put people into slots. He knew nothing about Jacob or about Anna's deceased husband. Hell, he barely knew anything about his own deceased father or his own brother. And yet, here he was guessing about these strangers.

He pulled into his driveway and went to push the button on the garage door opener. Uh oh. Crap, Tawny didn't want him coming home until night.

Well, maybe he should call her and see how they were feeling. They might need something. He shut off the engine, then took out his cell phone and called Tawny. "How are you feeling?"

"Tired. We've both been sleeping and yet I feel like a truck dragged me down a dirt road for hours and hours."

"Is there anything I can do?"

"Is that Daddy?" Bianca said in the background. "Hi Daddy," she shouted in the phone. "Thank you for bringing Hallie to us."

"Hi right back at you."

"Okay, baby, lay back down and try to sleep some more. Sorry about that. She's running a temperature of 101. She wants to get up, but as soon as she tries to get off the bed, she changes her mind. Says she feels dizzy and like she might throw up."

"Poor kid. And you, poor wife. Isn't there anything I can do?"

"No, I don't think so. Where are you?"

"Uh, in our driveway. I got distracted and was operating on auto-pilot, I guess. Are you sure there's nothing you need or nothing I can do?"

"That's really sweet, Luke. But all I really want to do is sleep. You go on over to your Dad's house and get some work done."

"Okay." He was about to say bye, then remembered something. "Did you call your doctor's office?"

"I did. They told me not to worry. Pregnant women get sick with colds and flu all the time."

Lucas said, "Oh good. Thanks for checking. All right, I guess I'll head over to Dad's. I figure I could tackle some of those crates we saw the other day. You know the ones that were hidden behind some suitcases."

"Oh, yeah, that should keep you busy. Let me know if you find anything good."

"I will."

Tawny said, "I forgot to ask. How is your Aunt Elsa?"

"No change."

He drove back to Sacramento, stopping for a quick lunch on his way. At the house, he didn't have to worry about checking on the cat, so he headed straight upstairs.

He switched on the light in the attic and then pulled one of the crates out of the corner to a brighter area. He picked up a crowbar he'd found in the garage back when he and Tawny had first started digging through the stuff up here and pried open the crate.

Oh wow, the crate was jam packed with stuff. He picked up and set aside a stack of old newspapers, began stacking old books—he stopped moving things—diaries! He picked up one and started reading. Huh? What language is that? Definitely not German. He'd studied Spanish in school—wasn't fluent but could read it. Definitely not Spanish, either. The sloppy handwriting didn't help matters.

Slavic. It had to be. And that made sense. Some of his ancestors had lived in the Sudetenland, which was part of Czechoslovakia. So it was possible that they had Czech family, too.

"Well, that's not going to help me," he said. He set the diary aside and picked up the next. German. He recognized the handwriting. He'd read other diaries by the same girl, Christa. Then he picked up another. Hmm, different writing, but again German. *Ah! Probably the same girl who wrote the second batch of diaries*

Tawny found the first day we were looking through boxes. He unloaded the rest of the books but found no more diaries.

Well, at least he had a few more to read through. That could help him. He'd have to find someone who could translate the Slavic one for him, but he could read the other two himself.

He set that crate aside and opened the next one.

On top he found a military uniform. German. Well-worn.

CHAPTER TEN

Christa Nagel, July-August 31, 1944, Altstadt, Sudetenland—

THE DAY AFTER Vati came home, Mutti strutted and clucked like a mother hen, caring for him as if he were her little boy. He wasn't allowed to do any lifting or work, according to her. His leg didn't really seem that bad to Christa. The other kids kept bugging him to show them his wound. Eventually, he'd given in and raised his pant leg. Giselle had been horrified and ran to Mutti, but Christa and the other kids had thought it wasn't any worse than the wound one of their cows had gotten last year when she tried to escape from the German soldiers who were rounding up all the livestock from the farms. "Vati, do you have to turn in your uniform?" she asked. They were sitting on the sofa, both of them reading books.

"That is a good question, little one, for which I have no answer. When they gave me permission to go home, I just kept my mouth shut and left. I did not want them to reconsider, which they might have if I had asked questions." He winked at her, and she smiled.

"I would not have asked, either. You were smart, Vati."

He patted her on the head.

"We do not have any livestock anymore," she said. "And the soldiers confiscated most of our land. I guess that means you are no longer a farmer."

He pursed his lips and nodded.

"What will you do?"

"Hmm. I may have to go to one of the bigger cities to find work. We will have to wait and see."

TWO WEEKS LATER, Vati took the train from Altstadt to another city. Christa didn't know which one. He returned in two days and announced to Mutti and the rest of the family that jobs there were hard to come by and he would have to travel again to a larger city with factories.

He made many trips, each time to a further city, each time coming home with no prospects, and each time looking more worn and concerned. On one of the trips, he managed to bring back some fruit that he'd picked in a field. That temporarily cheered Mutti up.

"I may have to wait until the war ends," he said after his latest trip, looking tired, but effecting a weak smile. "We can manage. The war is winding down, I know that for sure. Another year and it will be over."

Mutti said, "We may not be able to wait until then."

"Why is that?" he asked.

She wrung her hands together, opened her mouth to reply, but then hesitated. Finally, glancing at Christa and Ernst, she said. "We are expecting another baby."

Vati said, "Are you sure, Hanna?"

"I have gone through six pregnancies. I know the signs. If I am correct, the baby will be due in the spring."

Vati struggled to keep his face blank. Christa could see the effort. But without hesitating, he pulled Mutti into his arms and kissed the top of her head. "You are a wonderful mother. This baby will be lucky to have you."

"You . . . you are not upset?" she asked, her dark brown eyes looking up into blue-gray ones.

"*Nein, nein*, we will manage. I will go to Prague tomorrow. Surely I will find a job there."

Another baby? Christa groaned inside. More diapers to change and to wash? Washing was Christa's job. Didn't she have any say in the matter? And what did they need with another baby? Weren't the six kids they already had good enough for Mutti and Vati? *Mein Gott*, they can barely feed the family as it is. How are they going to feed another?

VATI RETURNED HOME after his trip to Prague, this time smiling, his face bubbling with excitement. "I got a job, Hanna. I will have to live in Prague during the week in a boarding house near the factory. But it's a job. I will make enough money to pay room and board and still be able to send money home for the family." Christa watched and listened, unsure if she was happy or sad. His leaving would be difficult on the whole family.

Mutti pulled away from his embrace. "*Nein*. You cannot leave us," she cried. "Do you not know how much we missed you all those months you were away? How can you leave us again?"

Christa looked back and forth between her parents.

"I thought you would be happy," Vati said. "Is this not what you wanted?"

"*Nein*. Not if it means you will not be here with us. We are a family. We stay together."

He sighed, ran his hand through his hair, and said, "You knew I was going on these trips to find work? Did you not understand that I would have to live wherever I could find work?"

"I thought I could cope with it. We managed without you before. But now that it is happening, the thought of you leaving us again is unbearable."

"Because of the baby you are expecting?"

"*Nein*." She swatted at his hand. "I have had enough babies. I know what to expect. It is not that."

"You want me to turn down the job?"

"*Ja*."

"You are sure? This is not because of female hormones spiraling?"

Huh? What did that mean? Christa glanced at Ernst. He shrugged.

"*Ja*, I am sure," Mutti said.

"Then I will go to the town hall in the morning. I can use a pay phone there. I will call them." He hesitated, looking at each of the children's faces and Mutti's face. "It will not be easy feeding all of us, but I want to make you happy. I will stay."

"*Danke*." She pulled him close and kissed him, with all of the kids watching.

Fritz and Julia snickered, and Giselle pulled on Mutti's skirt.

Christa felt her heart twist. Of course she wanted the family together and happy, and she certainly didn't want Vati to live away from them, but wasn't there any other way? Why couldn't they all go with him?

Two weeks later, a knock on the front door startled them all during dinner. Mutti and Vati exchanged glances. Christa didn't like the sound of that knock, and she was pretty sure her parents didn't, either.

Mutti started to get up, but Vati put his hand on her shoulder.

"I will see who is there. Wait here."

Hearing a loud male voice and then Vati's voice, Mutti and the rest of the family, except for the baby who was strapped in a high chair, rose from the table and peeked around the corner.

Mutti gasped.

Two uniformed soldiers stood there, both high-ranking officers, Christa guessed, based on their uniforms and medals.

Mutti stepped forward. "What is happening?"

"Frau Nagel?"

She nodded.

"Your husband has been recalled to the front," one of the officers said. "We are short-handed, and as he is recovered from his injury, he is deemed fit to return."

Christa couldn't believe what she was hearing. Tears dripped down her face. She turned and ran up the stairs.

Ilse Seidel, July-August 31, 1944, Memmingen, Germany—

THE TOWN OF Memmingen was over-run with German soldiers, everywhere Ilse looked on her way to the market. Seeing their guns made her shiver. Some of the soldiers didn't look any older than her brother, Johann. Were their families far away, worrying about their safety the way Mutter, Oma, and Opa worried about Johann? Had any of these soldiers lost friends or comrades in the air battle last night? Some of the men smiled and waved to her, as if they were classmates seeing each other again after the summer break. But she doubted any of them were from this area. School had been on break now for almost a year, and she rarely saw any of her former classmates around town. Most of the teachers were gone. Some were Jewish and had been 'relocated to the ghettos'. Then she'd heard the news on the BBC radio that said the Jews were moved into concentration camps. She couldn't believe they would do that. Other teachers had been conscripted. Students had been forced into the youth groups and didn't have time to waste on school, the government told them. She would give anything to go back to school and have a normal life again.

At the marketplace, every shop or booth she stopped at had run out of food. The clerk at the butcher shop leaned forward and whispered, "All the food is going to the soldiers. The gestapo demanded we give them all the good cuts of meat. Hardly anything was leftover. What there was got snapped up within five minutes of our shop opening. I have heard the same thing happened at the other shops."

"What are we supposed to do? We will starve."

The clerk glanced toward the window. Ilse followed her eyes. Two soldiers stood on the sidewalk directly in front of the butcher shop, smoking cigarettes, their rifles hanging off their shoulders. One of them turned and glared at the woman as if he could hear her, which of course he couldn't, but it gave Ilse chills.

"They do not care if we starve," the woman said. "Why are they fighting? If all of the citizens die, why does it matter if the country has more land, more power, more anything?"

Ilse didn't respond. She knew that any talk against the country or against the Wehrmacht could get a person executed on the spot. No trial. The woman took a big risk talking about this to her, but it could also be a set-up. She'd heard of people engaging or encouraging that kind of talk to entrap people. Why? Because it got them special privileges or made them important to the soldiers. Trust no one. That's what Oma, Opa, and Mutter told Ilse and Ursula and Robert. They were right.

The only food she was able to get today was a few potatoes and an equal number of onions. Not even one meal worth of food. She lumbered home and handed the basket to her mother.

"*Mein Gott*! I cannot make enough soup for all of us with that."

Ilse said, "I could go to the forest and see if I can find mushrooms. Or maybe apples or berries."

Oma said, "*Nein*. The soldiers are searching the woods. The woods are too dangerous."

"I know an area that has wild trees with bean pods. Johann and I found some beans there last year. I think it is in a different area than where the soldiers have been searching. Besides, the soldiers are back in town now. They are all over the place and they did not bother me."

No one said anything, so Ilse picked up her now empty basket and left before anyone could stop her.

An hour later she found the bean trees she'd talked about and was thrilled to find perfect-looking bean pods on them. Why hadn't she thought of this place sooner? They could have been eating beans for months.

When she'd filled her basket to the top, she started back toward home, walking back through tall grass that waved in the warm breeze. Something darted across her path. She froze in fear, her heart nearly leaping out of her chest. *Breathe*, she told herself. Once her heart slowed back to a reasonable pace, she stared at the creature standing less than fifty feet away. *A fox! Oh, my goodness*. She'd never seen one up close like this before. The fox had frozen and seemed to be waiting to see if she'd noticed it. Suddenly the fox took off, running into a thick expanse of pine trees to her right, the pine forest with walnut trees mixed in, the forest she had forgotten about. This was the forest she and her best friend had played in sometimes when they were kids. Back then, she and her friend had been fearless and the forest had seemed inviting. Now her friend was dead, killed in one of those early bombings. Now the forest appeared dark and gloomy, the tall trees being close together, standing like sentinels, guarding their territory and warning people to stay out.

Dark. The perfect place to find mushrooms, she thought. She edged toward the trees and, sure enough, she spotted mushrooms. Mushrooms for their soup. She rushed forward and bent down to check them. Vater had taught her how to tell the difference between safe mushrooms and poisonous mushrooms. She bit her lip, studying them, then smiled. These were edible. She picked a dozen and had to readjust the contents of her basket to fit them in.

She stood up straight, and as she did, she heard something. The fox? It had seemed afraid of her, but might she be the one in danger? Would a fox attack a person?

Standing as still as she could, she listened. Nothing. Then she heard it again.

A moan? Was the fox caught in a trap? It was forbidden for people to catch, kill, or eat wildlife. That was a Nazi rule. But that didn't mean someone hadn't gotten desperate and set traps to catch wild animals. If it was caught, what would she do? What should she do? Her family needed food. But she'd looked into the fox's eyes.

She crept toward the moaning. A man. A uniformed man. Fear stabbed her, and she stumbled backwards.

"Help me," he said, seeing her. In English! She'd studied English in school, never expecting to need it, but it was a required course.

"What happened?" she asked.

He pointed up toward the sky.

Mein Gott! The air attack last night. "Did your plane get shot down?"

He nodded.

"How . . . how did you survive?" She glanced around and didn't see an airplane or pieces of one, nor a parachute.

"I jumped with a parachute. It is here," he said. "Underneath me. I was afraid it would attract attention, so I hid it."

"Where are you hurt?" She squatted down to get a closer look at the man.

He turned slightly, moaning again, and showed her his side. A bloody mess of a wound covered his side. Then he pointed to his left leg.

She gasped, then involuntarily turned her head away. "I am sorry. You need medical attention."

He pulled on her sleeve as she started to get up. "Please, you can't tell anyone I'm here. I'll be taken prisoner, or worse. Let me die alone. It's better this way."

"I am not going to let you die!" She tried to get up again, but he bent forward and reached up, grabbing her arm.

"You would be making my life unbearable if you tell someone. Please. Don't." He moaned again and put his hand over his bleeding wound.

She sat down beside him. "How did you get these wounds, if you landed with a parachute?"

"I landed in the trees. A branch or two must have jabbed me in the ribs and leg. I wasn't shot, if that's what you're thinking."

"If you were not shot, then I can clean the wounds and try to bandage them. I do not think you will die."

"You'd do that? Aren't you worried what will happen to you or your family if you're caught helping the enemy?"

"I do not consider you the enemy. The allies are our saviors, if you can stop this war."

He studied her face, without comment.

She felt her face grow warm under his gaze. He looked to be around her age. Maybe a couple years older. Dark hair, blue eyes,

121

muscular. She looked away again, this time because she didn't want him to see that she was intrigued.

"I should go and get water. There is a stream nearby." She didn't wait for him to answer. A few minutes later she returned with her apron soaking wet. It would have to do.

After cleaning his wounds, she wrapped strips of his shirt, which he'd removed, around his middle section and around his left thigh and tied them. "Where is your airplane, or what is left of it?"

"On the other side of the woods. I was lucky that the wind carried me away from the wreckage. I'm sure I would have been captured if it hadn't. I fell among the trees and stayed there, figuring the trees would help hide me."

"Are you English or American?"

"American."

"I have never met an American before. How old are you?"

"Nineteen. And you?"

"Seventeen. Well, almost. My birthday is next month."

"Ah. You're my brother's age."

Neither of them spoke for a few minutes.

"I should go home. My family is waiting for me. Do you have anything to eat?"

"A few rations in my pack."

"I will try to bring you something tomorrow."

"Please don't put yourself at risk for me. I'm grateful for what you've already done. Cleaning and bandaging my wounds. I'll rest up and be on my way."

"You cannot walk. Not yet. Stay here and I will come back. I promise."

She hurried back home, but when she got close to town slowed her pace, not wanting anyone to get suspicious. She nodded to people—including soldiers—and carefully made her way back to her family's townhome.

Mutter said, "What took you so long? I was worried sick something had happened to you."

"Sorry, Mutter. I found these." She held up her basket full of bean pods and fresh mushrooms.

Mutter smiled with delight and grabbed the basket from her hands. "Come help me add these to the soup. I started cooking it a few minutes ago."

While they worked on the dinner preparations, Ilse said, "There are more bean pods and mushrooms out there. I will go back again tomorrow and get more. There may be berries around, too." She smiled inwardly. She'd done it. She'd provided a plausible excuse for leaving the house again and going into the woods. If she brought back only the amounts of food they needed each day, she could continue the trips for days or maybe weeks, without Mutter getting suspicious.

"Good. But be careful. The soldiers may still be searching the area. I wouldn't want you to get caught by some of them. I've heard stories of soldiers attacking innocent girls and women."

"I will be careful." As the evening wore on, though, she couldn't shake the thought that she might not be safe. Someone in town might see her leaving each day, get suspicious, and follow her. That could lead to death for her and for the airman.

Each day she varied her route. One day, as she was bringing food for him, she came across an abandoned house in a wooded area, apparently abandoned because it had been damaged by one of the bombs dropped over the past couple years. She decided to take the airman, Ronald, there, but he wasn't able to walk that distance yet. Finally, at the end of two weeks, seeing that his wounds seemed to be healing fairly well, as far as she could tell, she went to him to tell him about her plan to move him. When she got there, though, he was sick, probably a cold or the flu. He was shivering and obviously running a fever.

She laid next to him for a while so he could get some warmth from her body. Later that night, she sneaked out of the house in the cold night air and took a blanket to him. She realized, though, that he desperately needed better protection from the elements if he was going to have a chance to get well. The next day, leaning on her, he walked to the shack. After digging through remaining cabinets, she was able to find a flashlight, another blanket, and some towels he could use as pillows, creating a bed for him there. The problem now was finding food in this new area to take back to her family so she could keep up the pretense.

Thomas Landry, July-Sept., 1944, San Francisco, California—

TOM LANDRY, HIS mother, and sister sat around the living room listening to the news on the radio. According to the news announcer, the war was almost over, Germany was losing. They all cheered and clapped, laughing and toasting with their coffee mugs. "Maybe Pop and Ron can come home soon," Tom said. "Wouldn't that be grand? No more terrible news, no more fear that something bad might happen to them." He glanced at his sister and then looked at his mother. She was smiling, but tears were rolling down her cheeks. Tom stood, walked over and hugged his mother, with his sister soon joining them.

He knew his mother waited anxiously every day for the mail to come, hoping for good news, and dreading bad. Every time someone rang the doorbell, she peeked out the lacy curtains on the front window to see who was standing on the veranda. He wasn't sure if she would open the door if someone official looking from the military was standing there.

A few weeks later, when the doorbell rang, his mom rushed to the window, pulled back the curtain, and screamed. Tom felt his stomach twist in a knot of fear. He glanced at Teresa. Her face was white.

Mother turned, ran, and flung open the front door and wrapped her arms around someone.

Tom and Teresa ran over to see who it was.

"Daddy!" Teresa yelled, pushing her way into the hug.

Tom stood back, waiting. When the kissing and hugging broke apart, he too rushed over and hugged his father. "Glad you're home, Pop. I've really missed you."

"Missed you too, son," he responded, tousling his son's hair.

"Are you home permanently?" Mom asked, her gaze locking onto Pop.

He didn't answer right away, instead looking down at the floor, his foot moving slightly. "I . . . they let me come home on leave. I'll have to go back in a couple of weeks."

Mom looked broken for a moment, but then smiled. "Well, at least you're home," Mom said, smiling and pulling his arm to get him to come inside. He didn't budge.

He looked at her, frowning, and said, "They let me come home because Ron is missing in action. There was an organized air attack. His unit was part of a mission to take out the air base near Memmingen, Germany. The Germans apparently got a tip and they had their planes in the air when our guys got there."

"Did they kill him or capture them?" Mom asked, shaking.

"No one seems to know."

How could this happen? Tom wondered. On the news all they heard was that the allies were winning the war and that it would be over soon. Real soon. Like months maybe. *It's not fair.* Ron had to make it home.

Tom felt his knees get weak, and knew he needed to sit down. He found the nearest chair, a few feet from the entrance and sat on the edge of it, his mind reeling. Mom and Pop and Teresa sat on the sofa, talking. Tom heard Teresa tell Pop that when she grew up she was going to become a nurse and heal wounded soldiers. Tom swore to himself that he would join the army as soon as he graduated high school, regardless of what became of his brother and regardless of the war's progress. He'd be eighteen then and would be old enough. No one could stop him.

CHAPTER ELEVEN

Lucas Landry, July 2017, Sacramento, California—

LUCAS LEFT THE Slavic diary with a professor at his former university. He was recommended to Lucas by his German professor, the one with whom he'd talked about the identity cards he'd found. The man had told Lucas he would translate the diary when he had some free time. Said it would probably take awhile, but didn't elaborate. What did awhile mean? A few weeks? A few months? After leaving the university, feeling dissatisfied, Lucas stopped at Tawny's clinic. She was on lunch break and he was picking her up to go out for a quick bite.

He pulled up to the curb and waited. Whenever he picked her up for lunch, he usually found her waiting for him right there by the door. Only not today. He glanced at his watch. Right on time.

While he waited, he thought about the past week. Tawny and Bianca had recovered from the flu within a few days, and he hadn't gotten sick, big thumbs up. His Aunt Elsa had regained consciousness and although she was still in the hospital, she was probably going to be all right, according to her doctors. Another thumbs up. Not a bad week.

He turned on the radio and tuned in to his favorite classic rock station, rolling down the window to get some fresh air while he waited and listened. His favorite oldie came on and he turned up the volume a notch, not too loud, but loud enough to make him smile and imagine he and Tawny were at a party, dancing the way they had back when they first started dating.

Five minutes passed. Maybe she forgot? He turned off the radio and pulled out his cell phone to give her a quick call. Ah, there she was, exiting the building and striding toward the car. He put his phone away.

She opened the door and slammed it. Hard enough to rattle his teeth.

"Uh, I'm happy to see you, too," he said, wondering what had made her angry.

"Oh, sorry. It's not you. I'm just . . . just livid."

Did he dare ask why?

"I didn't get the promotion. The supervisor called me into his office. Do you know what he told me?"

"That you didn't get the promotion?"

"Shut up. You could be a bit supportive."

He bit his lip. Shoulda seen that coming. Okay, let's try this again.

"Tell me what happened, Tawny. I didn't mean to be unfeeling."

"He told me that one of my patients had complained about me. The jerk—the patient—had apparently called me all kinds of names, the kind of racial slur names that could start a fight, you know what I'm talking about?"

Lucas nodded, his mind meanwhile dredging up his brother.

"The patient doesn't want to see me anymore because I'm black. Can you believe that? What the hell difference does my race make?"

"It shouldn't make any difference. Are you sure there wasn't more to it than that? I mean some patients and therapists don't click. It doesn't mean anything. We're all different and sometimes we can open up more with some people than with others."

She turned and faced him, her eyes fierce. "Don't you think I know that? I've been doing this as long as you have, you know."

Whoa, that wasn't normal for Tawny. "Okay, okay. Don't bite my head off. I'm trying to help."

"You're right," Tawny said, her tone less sharp. "I'm sorry. It's just that I don't like this. Not one bit."

She crossed her arms and turned her head to look out the passenger side window.

Leaning toward her, Lucas said, "Tawny, sweetie, tell me what's going on. Did you have a bad session with this patient?"

"No, I only saw the guy once, a couple months ago. Maybe less. I'd have to check the date. He was friendly. We had a good session, actually. He told me he loved my accent. He's got issues that I could have helped him with, none of which have to do with race. He made a couple appointments after that, but canceled each one. Then, wham! I get called into the supervisor's office about the promotion and get this bullshit."

"Oh, wow. That really sucks. It's not fun when a patient is rude or argumentative or tells you he doesn't like something about you or your methods. But acting like everything is fine and then running to the boss behind your back is worse, in my opinion."

Tawny said, "If the patient had told me, I could have talked to him, maybe we could have resolved the issue, or at least referred him to another therapist. Now, the supervisor won't let me talk to the patient. There's nothing I can do."

"I agree. I'd rather someone be honest with me up front. I can see why you're upset. It almost sounds like the patient planned this." He hesitated, glanced out the windshield a moment, then said, "Are you sure the boss didn't make it up as an excuse for why he didn't give you the promotion?"

"I can't answer that. Like I said, I never spoke to the patient again, so I have to assume he went to a different counselor. But how the hell would I know? No one included me in the conversation."

"Well, either way, don't let it get you down. You are a great counselor. You deserved that promotion, and one day you will get it. You might have to change jobs after the baby comes, but you'll get the job you want. I'm sure of it."

Tawny sat for a few moments. "Thank you, Luke. You are the best husband a girl could have. I don't know what I'd do without you." She reached over and hugged him. "I'm going to try to put this out of my mind. There's plenty of patients out there and plenty of jobs in this field. I don't need that guy."

Lucas didn't understand why her boss would wait until now to say something about a complaint. He wanted to ask more, but figured it was better to let it drop for now. She was feeling better, and he didn't want to spoil that.

"Ready for lunch?" he asked.

"Yes. Take me somewhere good. I want to pig out." She patted her still small but growing belly. "The baby is hungry, too."

Lunch was good. Tawny actually laughed and talked, but she seemed worried, he could tell by the wrinkles in her forehead. She always got those when she had a bad headache or was stressed. Based on her conversation with her supervisor, Lucas was pretty sure that remained the culprit.

After dropping her back at her work, he went back to his work and met with a group of patients in drug-rehab. The patients kept his focus, distracted him from personal thoughts, but on his way home from work that evening, his thoughts returned to Tawny and her problem patient.

If she was that upset about a patient not wanting to work with her because she was black, how would she react if she found out about his father and brother rejecting her?

That begged another scary question. She was upset because the patient hadn't been honest with her and hadn't told her to her face. Because he hadn't, she couldn't talk to the guy and try to resolve their differences. Lucas hadn't been honest with her, either. Would she push him away if she found out?

He pulled into the driveway of their home and rested his forehead on the steering wheel. Why hadn't he told her the truth five years ago, back when his father was still alive and she could have tried talking to the guy? Maybe they could have come to some resolution.

Yeah, right. It was totally different with Dad. Dad wouldn't have given an inch. He was that prejudiced!

CHAPTER TWELVE

Christa Nagel, September 1, 1944, Altstadt, Sudetenland

CHRISTA NAGEL WASHED clothes and bedding in the wash tub set-up in the root cellar. It was by far her most hated chore. The only good that came from it was not having to change diapers, wipe snotty noses, or break up squabbles. Some days, she wished she were an only child. Most of the time, she figured that if Mutti and Vati could have only one child, they wouldn't pick her. She was the oldest and could do the most chores, but she wasn't a cherubic baby or a sweet little boy or girl, just a gangly, ugly eleven year old girl. In the spring, there would be even more competition. She could never compete with a brand new baby. She knew it was wrong, but sometimes she wished a bomb would drop and destroy her family's home and all the kids, except her. *Gott will probably smite me for thinking something so horrible.* She vowed to go to Church tomorrow and go to the confessional, if the priest was still in town. How wrong was it that she hadn't been there in months and didn't even know if the priest was still there?

That night, she tossed and turned in bed. She conceded she didn't really want her brothers and sisters dead. But what if *Gott* had been listening to her thoughts and took them from her? She cried and prayed. *Please don't take them. I didn't mean it. I love my family. If you have to take someone, take me.*

In the morning, she put away the laundry and then trudged through chilly streets to the church to speak with the priest and give her confession. Hardly anyone was outside, but whether it was because of the cold air or because of the soldiers stationed here, she didn't know. She kept her head bent down most of the time to avoid eye contact with the soldiers. No one wanted to be noticed by them or to be questioned. Once inside, she immediately headed for the confessional.

"Will *Gott* take my brothers and sisters?" she asked the priest sitting behind a grating. He couldn't really see her, but she knew he would recognize her voice from school. "I didn't really mean it."

"It was a moment of weakness, my child. *Gott* understands."

Hanna Nagel, Dec. 24, 1944-Feb. 1945, Altstadt, Sudetenland—

HANNA NAGEL RUMMAGED through the root cellar, looking for something she could prepare for dinner for the children. They were all getting too thin; any thinner and they would be just pale skin stretched across protruding bone. How was she supposed to eat enough for herself and a growing baby inside her? This was very bad. Pregnancy was a time when a woman needed to eat extra food, and nutritious food at that, not watery soup and a few meager scraps of potato. And she worried so often about Christa. At eleven years old she looked more boy shaped than girl shaped. How would she grow up and attract a husband if she didn't get enough food to enable her body to develop into a woman's body? Ernst was a worry, too. He kept growing taller, like a beansprout, for the life of her she couldn't see how, but his weight lagged so far behind. At ten years old he was tall. Not as tall as a man, but tall for his age. Hanna would never have thought anything of his height, except that her neighbor's boy, only a few months older than Ernst and the same height, had been grabbed and conscripted into the army. The frantic mother had produced papers showing he wasn't old enough. It mattered not. They did whatever they wanted and made their own rules. Since that day, a month ago now, Hanna kept Ernst hidden from the officials so the same wouldn't happen to him.

The baby inside her suddenly kicked hard. Hanna put her hand protectively over her belly. She should not bring another baby into this world. Not at this horrific time. But *Gott* had given her this precious life and she would protect the baby, no matter how difficult the circumstance. That's what mothers did. If her baby had already been born, she would give up her portion of dinner to feed her baby or any of the other kids. But she couldn't do that while the baby was still inside her. He or she needed the nourishment only she could provide.

She sighed and headed back up the stairs to the stube, then ambled down the hall and out the side door of the farmhouse. She didn't want to kill another of their chickens, but what else could she do?

Christa looked up when Hanna entered the chicken pen. It was clear from the look in the girl's eyes that she suspected something. Hanna rarely entered the chicken pen. Only Christa and Ernst, and occasionally Fritz, did.

"Christa, I need you to get a big bucket of water from the well."

"You are going to cook one of my chickens, are you not?" she accused.

There it was, out in the open. Hanna had hoped to take the chicken without Christa seeing, but it was too late. Christa was too clever for her own good.

"Sorry, Christa, but you know we have to eat. Today is Christmas Eve and we need our Christmas dinner. These chickens will all be eaten by the Nazis sooner or later, if we do not eat them first. It is only a matter of time before they come back for the rest of our animals."

"Please do not cook it. Please, Mutti."

"There is no other option. How many do we have left?"

"Six." Christa rushed over to the chickens and stood in front of them, as if forming a shield. "They give us eggs. If we eat the chickens, we will not have eggs to eat or to trade."

"No one is trading for them, anymore. They do not have anything to trade. Nothing we can eat."

"But we can eat the eggs."

"We are only going to kill one chicken right now. That will give us time to look for other options." Christa frowned. "I will let you pick the chicken, if that helps."

"It does not help!" she screamed. "Could you pick which one of your children to kill?" With that she ran crying out of the pen and into the house, slamming the door behind her.

Oh mein Gott. Hanna inched toward the chickens and studied them. In her mind she began seeing them as her kids. The roundish little one—that was baby Andreas, almost two years old. The light colored one that always followed the mother hen until it had died—that one was Giselle; the tall one—oh, that was Ernst, no question. By the time she'd studied all six, she knew she couldn't do it, either.

Resigned, she picked up all the eggs she could find and placed them in the basket they kept near the coop. With that done, she turned and strode out of the pen, through the front gate, and down the street. Time to pay a visit to the wealthy Czechs on the hillside. Maybe they would have food to trade for her eggs.

Half an hour later she returned with a basket of sausages. Those would make a fine Christmas dinner. When she entered the house, the kids were sitting in the living room, their faces tear-streaked.

"We do not want to eat one of our chickens," Giselle said. "We will not do it." She stood up and crossed her arms.

"Well, then, it is a good thing I got some sausages from one of the locals," Hanna said.

The kids jumped ups and shouted with glee.

Ja, it was the right thing to do, Hanna thought. *Chickens will come another day, but Christmas is not the right time for it.*

THE NEXT TWO months went by slowly. In January, Hanna encountered a large group of ragged-looking ethnic Germans on foot on her way back from town with the family's rations. The Germans stopped her and begged for food—anything for their starving children. She talked to the mother and found out they'd been living in a small town, similar to Altstadt, but in Poland. They were running away because the Red Army had taken over their town, raping women and even young girls, including one of the woman's daughters.

Hanna surveyed the children. The oldest, apparently the girl who'd been raped, couldn't have been more a year or two older than Christa. Hanna shivered.

Studying the tormented faces, and seeing her own children in them, she reached into her bag and pulled out a loaf of bread, broke it in half, and handed it to the mother. The mother hugged her and then broke the bread into small portions and handed them to her starving family. Hanna cried the rest of the way home.

Another time, when she picked up their rations, a clerk handed her a leaflet about the slaughter of Sudeten Germans in Poland. That poor family had been only one of many.

In spite of near starvation, Hanna's belly was growing. Her strength, however, was dwindling, but she was still alive and still protecting her children. They mostly had to huddle together at night to keep warm. At night Hanna shared her bed with three kids, and the other three kids huddled together in another bed. There wasn't fuel anymore for heat. Not in their house and not anywhere in Altstadt. Everyone was past complaining, near freezing.

The baby wasn't kicking as much now as it had two months ago. That worried her, but she couldn't see a doctor about it. The doctor had been taken away. He was desperately needed elsewhere, the Nazis had said. The doctor's wife confided in Hanna and others that she was certain he'd been taken to one of the concentration camps to treat prisoners who worked outside the camp in factories on day trips. Said the Nazi's couldn't let those needed prisoners die.

As for everyone else—the regular citizens—they could die for all the Nazis cared.

But Hanna's immediate problem was the baby in her belly. What would happen when the baby came? She would have to somehow find a midwife and figure out how to pay her. Hanna had pushed out six babies, but none by herself. She couldn't afford to pay a midwife, but she couldn't afford to attempt it herself and die in the process. What would her kids do without a mother or a father around to protect them?

This morning, she had stayed in bed as long as possible, for the warmth provided by the kids and the blankets. None of them needed to get up early, as it was snowy and cold outside and they wouldn't be doing outside chores. The kids sleeping in the next room appeared to be sleeping in as well. They were too quiet for it to be otherwise.

A series of loud booms in the distance brought her out of her thoughts. She carefully got out of bed and padded over to her bedroom window, lifting the corner of the blackout curtain to peek outside. Smoky black-gray winter clouds, swirling, thick, monstrous-looking, threatened to dump more moisture onto the already thick layer of snow. Her eyes moved to an eastern section of foothills hugging the mountains surrounding the town. Her heart sank. Dark specks in the white snow blanketing one of the hills resolved into ant-sized soldiers—fighting near a bare ridge. German soldiers trying to hold back the Red Army. It had to be. She knew it was the Red Army because she'd been hearing news reports for days on the radio. They'd been in Poland for some time and were reported to be nearing the Sudetenland border. They'd obviously reached it. A feeling of foreboding crept through her body, and she gripped the edge of the window frame to keep from collapsing under her heavy pregnancy weight.

Mein Gott! If the Russians win, they could be here in town within days. Weeks at most. And then they would be doomed.

Ilse Seidel, September-October 1944, Memmingen, Germany—

ILSE SEIDEL THANKFULLY found berries near the dilapidated house where Ron was hiding. Each day she picked a basket full and took part of them to Ron and the rest of them home to her family. She was able to sneak bread out of the house every couple of days and occasionally a potato or carrot. She feared it wouldn't be enough to keep the American nourished.

The only saving grace was that he was laid-up and not burning many calories.

Ilse was worried. Ron's cold or flu should have cleared up by now, but if anything it seemed worse. Months earlier, a neighbor had died from untreated pneumonia. Ron exhibited the same symptoms. Ilse knew Ron probably needed medicine or he would end up like that neighbor.

Ilse found a doctor in town and went to beg for medicine. "It is for my brother," she lied. "Our mother sent me."

The elderly doctor gave her a questioning look, but said nothing. Ilse was relieved he didn't ask her to bring her brother in for examination. The doctor was giving medicines to the poor and needy, working out of a derelict building.

"Better to use up the medicine I have here, before the military confiscates it," he said, smiling and winking as he handed her a bottle of pills. She said she couldn't pay him, but he only shrugged and replied, "I am Jewish—one of the few Jews who was not captured."

Why he entrusted her with his secret she couldn't say. Perhaps because he suspected she had her own secret to keep. It had taken her some work to find out about the doctor in hiding, because it was difficult to penetrate the underground in Memmingen.

A week and a half after Ron finished his course of antibiotics, he was sitting up and smiling when Ilse entered the shack.

"You look like a new person," Ilse said. "The medicine seems to have worked miracles on you."

"Sure did." He was interrupted by a coughing fit, but his chest was no longer rattling with the cough, and the fit was much briefer than before. "Guess I'm not quite ready to run a marathon just yet." He looked pensive for a moment, then said,

"I hope you won't stop coming to see me because I'm well now."

"Definitely not. I do worry, though, that you are in danger. I have seen fewer soldiers in town. But they could just be in the area patrolling the countryside now. Nowhere is safe."

"I know. I will need to leave very soon. I need to find a way to contact my unit or at least the U.S. military. If I'm lucky, they can steer me to a place where they can pick me up."

She nodded, not wanting to encourage him to leave. He must, of course, leave. She just wasn't ready for it. After almost three months of caring for her wounded and sick airman, what would she do once he was gone? She'd enjoyed their long talks. Even when he was sick, he would talk, or preferably listen to her talk, according to him.

Her American soldier was in danger here, but he'd be in worse danger if he was on the move in this hostile territory, without anyone guiding him. He had not one but two targets on his head. He was in a soldier in the U.S. military. He was also a Jew.

It had taken him a month or more to admit to her his faith. She could understand his wariness. When she hadn't pulled away, instead asked him questions about religion in general, it had led to a discussion about the Nazis and the disappearance of the Jews from the German towns. He'd told her what he knew.

He told her the Germans, her own people, had begun rounding up the Jews, but not to move them to their own communities as the Nazis told everyone. They'd been taken to concentration camps, or 'death camps' as some referred to them. When she asked what that meant, he hesitated, his color fading. Eventually, he shared with her the open pits he'd seen, filled with the remains of Jews of all ages, including mothers, children, and even babies dumped there to rot.

She'd heard rumors in town, whispers in the dark air raid bunkers, and of course she'd heard something about that on the BBC radio. Hearing it firsthand from someone who'd actually seen the pits filled her with anger and hatred for the Nazis.

She stood and caught a glimpse of white flakes through the window and walked over to get a closer look.

"What's going on?" Ron asked, fear in his eyes.

"Snowflakes. The first I have actually seen falling this season. I know there are several inches of snow on the ground," she quickly added, "but that fell overnight, while everyone was sleeping."

He stood up then, wobbly from not walking much in the past few months. She rushed over, put her around him, and helped him over to the window.

The door suddenly clattered open and a rush of frigid air entered. But the chill Ilse felt rising up her spine wasn't from the chilly air, but fear from her brother standing in the doorway, his rifle aimed at them. She gasped, feeling a bit faint. No one said a word for several seconds. Desperately thinking what to say, she opened her mouth, faltered, then blurted out, "I . . . how did you find me?" Then it hit her. He must have spotted her and followed. Her footsteps in the snow would have made it easy. "I thought you were deployed to Poland. Your last letter said you were in Poland."

"I wrote that letter months ago," Johann said. "I was sent here to Memmingen to help patrol."

"How long have you been here? Why did you not come to the house and tell us?"

"I should be asking the questions," he said. "Who is this man and why are you helping him?"

She took a deep breath and let it out. "Will you please put your weapon away, brother?" She hoped Ron would pick up on the word brother and realize who Johann was. Ron understood German.

Johann lowered his rifle and stood with his legs apart, totally blocking the escape route. "Tell me who he is."

Before Ilse could reply, Ron said, "I'm a wounded airman. I was in a four-engine bomber plane with a crew of ten that got shot down. I was one of only two who were able to jump out with a parachute. I got injured coming down in a thick copse of trees, but not badly. The other guy got hit with a piece of debris from the airplane on his way down. He didn't survive. When I was able, I searched for him and buried his remains."

Ilse had heard about what happened, of course. She tensed, waiting for her brother's reaction.

"That was months ago," Johann said. Turning his head to Ilse, he accused, "You have been helping him all this time?"

Ilse nodded, biting her lip, expecting Johann to point his rifle again.

"I should turn you both in," he said. "You know that. They will kill you. No questions asked."

"Please do not. Johann, if you care anything about me, you will forget what you have seen and heard here."

He didn't answer.

Was he thinking about letting them go? Was he going to turn them in? Would he shoot and kill Ron? Ilse had never been particularly religious, but she began to say a silent prayer.

"I cannot turn my own sister in to my commanding officers. I could not live with myself." He turned his attention to Ron, who had backed away and leaned against one wall of the shack, near the window, giving Johann a perfect target. "You will leave here by the end of the week. My unit will be searching this area next week. If they find you, they will shoot you."

"That is three days from now," Ilse said. She turned to Ron. "Will you be able to walk out of here by then?"

"Yes. Before your brother arrived, I already knew it was time to leave here. I've been readying myself."

"Good," Johann said. "Ilse, you must never tell anyone about the airman. Do you understand? I cannot protect you if you are caught helping or even suspected of helping the enemy."

"I understand. Thank you, Johann."

He turned on his heels and left them alone.

Ilse rushed over to Ron and squeezed him. "I am sorry. I tried to be careful and make sure no one was following me. I did not know my brother was in Memmingen."

"It's all right. I—we—knew I had to leave. This just confirms it. It's just lucky it was your brother that found us. I'll leave in the morning, before dawn."

Ron packed his few belongings into his pack and set it near the door, ready to leave at a moment's notice. Then he walked over and pulled Ilse into an embrace. "I will miss you more than you could possibly imagine," he whispered in her ear. "When I fell from an airplane, I fell into a dream and met the most beautiful princess I have ever seen. Have I told you that before?"

"You have."

"It's true. You saved my life and showed that people can be good and kind, regardless of their faith or their nationality. We come from different cultures, but we are people, all the same. I love you."

"I love you, too." She had never said those words out loud to anyone, not even her parents.

"You should get home soon. Your family will be expecting you and will worry if you don't come home by dinner time."

She shook her head and looked up into his eyes. "This is our last day together. I am going to make it last as long as possible and make it the best day we have ever shared so you will not forget me."

"Ilse, no. You must go."

"You cannot send me away like that. Come. Let us lie down and cuddle and talk. I am staying the night, or at least until almost dark. Mutter will be angry, but also relieved when I get home. She will not punish me."

"But I can't guarantee I won't . . . ."

"Won't what? Kiss me? Make love to me? I am counting on it."

Hours later, when she finally pulled herself away from his arms and dressed to leave, Ron pulled her back and held her, whispering, "I will find you again when the war is over. We'll be together. I promise."

"I will wait for you." With that, she gave him one last kiss and slipped out the door.

The next morning, early, she left the house while the family was still sleeping. As she'd suspected, Mutter had reprimanded her when she got home, but soon let it drop. Mutter probably suspected Ilse was seeing someone, but she didn't ask and Ilse was not going to volunteer any information.

She'd make up her mind before she fell asleep last night, that she had to see Ron one more time before it was too late. She walked in the semi-darkness through town and then into the woods, past a meadow, and was in sight of the dilapidated house.

But others were there. She froze in the moonlight. Her heart raced with anxiety. Who were those men? Over her initial shock, she crept closer, careful to stay behind tall bushes.

She stopped within hearing distance, and peeked out. Johann. And two other men in German army uniforms. His commanding officers?

They had hold of Ron and were shoving him and then they forced him to stand up straight.

Johann held up his rifle and pointed it at Ron. Before Ilse had a chance to react and try to stop him, Johann shot Ron in the chest. Ron keeled over, still as a rock.

Ilse gasped, falling to her knees in shock. She put her hand over her mouth to keep from screaming and drawing attention to herself. She would have called out to make Johann stop, if she'd had the chance. Screaming now would be futile and would only get her killed, too. Johann didn't care. He would kill her himself and not bat an eye.

Johann had promised he wouldn't turn Ron in. He had told him he had three days. Only a half day, a single night, had passed. Could his commanding officers have found out and left Johann no choice? She wanted to give him the benefit of the doubt.

Watching him smiling and helping the officers drag Ron's body back across the meadow, towards the trees and, probably to town, she couldn't believe what had happened. She stared at the trail in the snow, filled with blotches of red staining the snow, like breadcrumbs dropped along a trail to lead someone to some hideous rendezvous.

She buried her face in her hands, sobbing silently. Ron was gone. She would never see him again. He'd promised her they would be together when this horrid war was over. Johann had ruined everything.

Later—she didn't know how long she'd sat in the snow— she pulled herself upright and willed her legs to carry her back home.

On the walk that seemed to take forever, all she could think about was the fact that her brother had betrayed her. He was as dead to her as Ron was.

CHAPTER THIRTEEN

Lucas Landry, August 2017, Sacramento, California—

LUCAS READ THE translated Slavic Diary, making notes to add to his other notes on his computer. While interesting, it didn't fit with the prior information he'd collected. Who was this person and why was his diary stored in a box in his family's attic? It didn't make any sense. Unless it wasn't really a diary. Perhaps it was part of some would-be writer's novel. Or maybe it was a diary that an ancestor had found and kept. Hmm, maybe confiscated? What if the guy, a resistance fighter, according to the diary, was captured by the Nazis and tortured or put into a concentration camp. If that was the case, did it mean one of his ancestors was a Nazi?

Lucas puzzled over the mystery, but decided it was late and this was not about to be solved right now. He rubbed his temples, saved the notes he'd made on his computer, and closed the file. After switching off the lamp, he climbed the stairs and carefully opened the bedroom door. Tawny was sound asleep, snoring softly. She'd gone to bed an hour ago, complaining of fatigue, which was to be expected in her sixth month of pregnancy.

He kicked off his slippers and slipped into bed, careful not to disturb her. He wanted to sleep, but it seemed his made had a difference of opinion. After time, he glanced at his bedside clock, glowing green on his nightstand. Almost midnight. He'd been in bed for nearly an hour and was still wide awake. Big mistake working on family history stuff right before bed. He should have known better by now.

He rolled over, now face to face with his wife. She made little gurgle sounds, which normally wouldn't bother him, but tonight made him edgy. He rolled back over. What seemed like ten minutes more passed, but his clock showed it had been three minutes. Good thing tomorrow was Saturday and he didn't have to get up early and go to work.

Silently, Lucas pulled back his covers and slipped out of bed, donned his slippers, and padded back down the stairs.

After pouring himself a glass of cold water from the faucet, he walked over, sat down at his desk, and turned his computer back on and rubbed the stubble on his chin, waiting for the computer to boot up. He opened three files, minimized them, then opened a blank document and stared at the screen. Somehow he needed to create a family tree, pulling together all the information collected so far, including pieces from the *Ahnenpaß* forms, or identity cards as he called them, that which he'd gleaned from his aunts and cousins, from the various diaries and from the papers and photos he'd found in the filing cabinets. That was all good stuff. Problem was he didn't know where the people in those fit into the family tree, assuming they were even connected to his family. Not an easy task.

Okay, start with the identity cards.

He picked up the folder that held copies of identity cards and their translations, and began listing them. As he typed, he realized one of the maiden names was Slavic. She came from Moravia. Ah hah! Maybe that was how the young man who wrote the Slavic diary fit into the puzzle. He put an asterisk next to her name to remind him to look into it further.

He recorded birthdates and locations beside the names.

His list grew, but didn't visualize how they connected. *Okay, this isn't working.*

He leaned back to think, hands clasped behind his head. What could he do to make the links clearer?

Okay, what about drawing them onto a piece of paper, the way family trees were usually drawn? *A bit old school,* he thought, *but it doesn't really need to be on the computer, at least not for now. That might work.*

Lucas began writing a man's name & birthdate. Below that he filled in the man's wife's name, then her maiden name, and birthdate. He made a short vertical line below that and then entered their children's names and birthdates. It spread out from there.

Okay, he could do this.

An hour and a half later, with several do-overs laying in a pile on the floor, and three pieces of paper taped together, he had a sloppy but visual family tree. He wasn't entirely sure about the spelling of some of the names, because they had been handwritten in old-German style, but it was good enough, he'd done the best he could.

The birthdates actually went much further back than he'd realized—the earliest being in the year 1801. *How cool is that!* Furthermore, it looked like he had both sides of . . . well, probably his great-grandparents' trees, he guessed, for a couple generations. *Wow. Now I'm getting somewhere.*

But as he studied the list, his enthusiasm for his endeavor quickly waned. The tree, as drawn, ended abruptly. If the latest generation listed was his great-grandparents, what about his parents—Tom and Emelie Landry. And what about the Nagel family and the Seidel family he'd read about? Where were their records and how did they fit together with the others?

Argh! He stuck his drawing into the folder with the identity card copies, then closed the computer files and shut down his computer.

Tomorrow. He'd go back to the house and finish looking through the boxes. If that didn't get him the answers he needed, he'd . . . he'd what? Go to Germany and talk to his German relatives? Right, assuming they were really related. For all he knew right now, his father and aunts might not even be related to any of these folks. The attic history might precede his family ownership of the house. Lucas knew from talking to his aunt Elsa and Anna that his ancestors were from Germany, but precious little more.

His shoulders slumped as he climbed the stairs. This damned research was like trying to herd ducks! It was like Hansel and Gretel's dropping breadcrumbs through a forest, with birds picking up pieces and leaving big gaps in the trail.

Crap!

The next morning, Saturday, Tawny took Bianca to a swimming class at the recreation center, after which they would go shopping for baby things with Tawny's mother, Lani. That left Lucas free to go to the house and sift through more junk in the attic.

On his knees, Lucas reached out and opened one of the few unopened boxes and started poking around. Good grief, more stuff from Germany. Including more diaries, a small box with handwritten poems, and . . . eureka, letters from Franz Nagel. That would be . . . he scratched his head trying to remember where he'd heard the name. Yes!

Vati. Christa's father. The paper was old and wrinkled and the ink faded. God, this was a letter he'd sent to his family while he was in the army.

Lucas sat down hard on his butt, preparing to translate the letter. How cool was this? He'd read in Christa's diary about the letter, and now he was holding it in his hand.

He thought about the incomplete family tree diagram he'd made last night and thumped his own forehead. *Dummy! Why didn't I list the Nagel family, the Seidel family, and the Landry family on separate pages? If I have the names and relationships and approximate dates listed, won't it be easier to fill in the missing links when I get them? Now I have to do the tree yet again,* he fumed.

Reluctantly, he set aside the letter and the other diaries he'd just now found and continued digging through the box. Each of the last three boxes he rummaged through had produced some interesting clues that might help. When he finished looking through the last box, he felt an immediate emptiness inside, as if he'd lost a good friend.

After a few moments, it subsided. It was like watching a treasured TV series' finale and you knew that was it. The feeling of enjoying every show, but suddenly knowing it was over and you would never again have the joy of watching a brand new episode unfold before your eyes.

Lucas pulled himself up off the floor, which was a challenge, considering how long he'd been sitting like a pretzel. He re-stacked the boxes, still feeling slightly depressed.

Lucas stretched and yawned, then looked at his watch. Lunch time. He looked around for a bag or small box he could use to house his new stack of research material. *Ah, there in the corner, a box we emptied last week.* It was one of those metal chest kinds of boxes that had held some old tools—the kinds that might have been used for building the cabinets in the house. Not great, but it would do. He and Tawny had moved others into the garage, where they might set up a workshop of sorts, if they kept the house. He hated to admit it, but he was warming to the idea.

He placed the documents, books, etc. into the metal box, latched it closed, and then carried it down the stairs, closing the door to the attic behind him.

No sense making it easier to find the attic should anyone break into the house, right? He'd heard from a couple neighbors that there had been a few burglaries in the neighborhood over the past month, and an empty house was always a good target. That's another reason he and Tawny tried to come here almost every day, if possible, giving the impression that the house wasn't abandoned.

In the kitchen he opened the refrigerator and took out the lunch he'd packed, along with a can of soda, and set his food, drink, and the metal box on the kitchen table.

Time to get to work. His stomach growled loudly. *Nah, eat first, then work.* After eating his turkey sandwich and guzzling the last of his soda, Lucas opened the lid of the box and looked inside. What to tackle first?

Hmm. How about the handwritten poetry? He pulled out the envelope containing the poetry and skimmed through them, reading bits and pieces. Love poems. Poems about family. Poems about the war, written from the point of view of a soldier. Having a sudden thought, he dug around in the box, looking for the letter from Vati, pulled it out, and compared the handwriting. Huh, Vati wrote poetry. *Okay. Now we're getting somewhere.*

He wrote poems during the war and the poems were here in America, meaning Vati either survived, and brought the poems back to his family, or he didn't survive, and the poems were found among his belongings and returned to them at the end of the war. Hmm, not much help.

Okay. Let's try one of the diaries. He sure hoped these were continuations of the diaries he'd already read. He started reading a diary written by Christa.

Half an hour into it, his face was wet with tears. He'd known about the Red Army incursion and the wild expulsions of ethnic Germans, but this . . . Christa's description of atrocities committed was beyond comprehension. He set the diary aside to finish later, needing to calm himself. Rummaging through the other diaries, he found more from Christa and again placed them into what he surmised was chronological order. Planning to take them home to read tomorrow, he rubber-banded them together.

He found more diaries from Ilse, that he'd set aside earlier. He gathered them up, too, again placed them in chronological order, and started reading the first one.

Forty minutes later, he practically fell off his chair. A Landry. Ron Landry was an American airman shot down in Memmingen, Germany. Ilse and Ron. Oh, my God! Finally a connection.

He set the diary down, open, and leaned back in his chair. Anna and Elsa had told him his grandparents' names were Tom and Emelie. How the hell were they related? Did Ilse and Ron have a baby? Could that be Tom? He quickly did the math in his head. No, the dates didn't add up.

Okay, he rubbed his forehead. Gonna have to talk to Aunt Anna and Aunt Elsa. Maybe they can explain.

He sat quietly, thinking again about Christa's diary. He felt a chill run down his spine. The expulsion of the Germans from their homes was too similar to what was currently happening in various parts of the world. Guess people just don't learn from the mistakes of the past.

Glancing at the clock, he saw that it was late enough for Tawny and Bianca to be home. He stuffed everything back into the metal box, locked up the house, turning on the porch light to make the house lived in, and headed back home.

CHAPTER FOURTEEN

Christa Nagel, March, 1945, Altstadt, Sudetenland—

"I AM SCARED, Mutti," Christa said. "The soldiers—the fighting—it is getting too close to our town. What happens when they get here?" Two weeks ago, a few families with cars had packed their belongings, filled extra petrol tanks, and left town. Most of the remaining cars in town now, parked on the streets or in garages, were unable to go anywhere because petrol was no longer available. That made leaving almost impossible, except for those wealthy enough to afford train tickets and bribes for their families. Walking was out of the question, being unsafe; not to mention being much too far. A while back Mutti had confided in Christa that she kept money hidden in the house and said she thought she had enough to buy them transportation. Current rumor, however, now claimed trains were no long an option—at least not for Germans in the Sudetenland. There was supposedly a new forbidding Germans from public transportation. No one seemed to know what would happen to a German who tried to leave by train. That's why Mutti had wanted to go to the train station to check it out. Yesterday, a neighbor from a few houses away had confided in Mutti that she planned to take her kids south to where her sister lived and would take the train in the morning.

Mutti had stood at the front window, lifting the blackout curtain and peeking out so she could see when Irmgard and her children walked past. When she saw them carrying their suitcases, she and Christa had left their house and joined the small family on their walk.

Mutti and Christa stood now in front of the train station, watching, waiting to see if anyone was actually getting on the train, or if they might get arrested. Mutti was wringing her hands together. This was the make or break moment. They would find out if their family, too, could leave Altstadt by passenger train. There was no other way.

A train whistle blew, and everyone held their breaths. The train pulled into the station, black smoke puffing from the engine, brakes screeching, boiler hissing, and a bell clanging.

Irmgard went up to the conductor and spoke. Christa and Mutti saw them, but were too far away to hear their conversation, especially with the hissing of the train.

When Irmgard raised her voice, Christa's ears picked up a few words: soldiers, wrong, stuck. Irmgard swung around suddenly, gathered her four children together, then walked back toward Mutti and Christa.

Irmgard paused a few feet away, looked at Mutti, and shook her head, tears streaming down her face.

Mutti rushed to her and hugged her, then said, "What did they say?"

"Germans are forbidden from taking the trains. No public transportation for us." She walked away, sniffling, carrying a suitcase and holding her youngest son's hand, heading back to their home.

Mutti stood frozen in place, watching them fade into the distance.

"We are doomed," Christa proclaimed heavily. "I cannot believe we are stuck here. We should have left last week." But last week, Giselle and Andreas had been sick with bad coughs and fever. They wouldn't have been allowed on the train. Before that, Mutti had cramping and bleeding and was afraid she was going to lose the baby. It was always something.

"Do not talk that way," Mutti said. "We must keep hope, for the children's sakes. They are counting on us to keep their spirits up."

"Sorry, Mutti. You are right. But what are we to do?"

"We stock up on firewood and kindling. Then we board up our windows and doors, and make it look like the house is abandoned, that's what. We prepare a room in the house for the chickens and bring them inside. They'll continue laying eggs for us. We won't starve. You'll see."

Chickens in the house? Had Mutti gone mad? A month ago she'd wanted to kill all the chickens and eat them. She was scratching for grains of hope that didn't exist.

As they walked along the cobblestone streets, Christa tried to keep her eyes on the road in front of her, but they were drawn to the hillside to the east. She didn't need binoculars to see the soldiers, the tanks and the rising smoke from their campfires.

"Mutti, the soldiers will see the smoke coming out of our chimney. They will know someone lives there, will they not?"

Mutti didn't answer right away.

"We must keep the fire burning low," she said, finally. "We all sleep in the living room together, near the fire for warmth."

Christa considered her words. "If people think the house is empty, might they try to break in and steal our things, or try to move in?"

"Why must you always think of the worst?" she snapped.

155

"I am sorry, Mutti. I will do better. I promise." Christa still worried, but kept it to herself.

As they turned the corner onto their street," Christa changed the subject. "What will we do when it's time for the baby to come?"

"I found someone who will help with the delivery. She lives near here, close to the train station. Frau Bauermann."

"I know her. She is my friend, Claudia's, mother."

"*Ja*. Frau Bauermann is expecting a baby, too. When her time comes, I will go to her home and help her deliver. We help each other and won't cost either of us anything."

Christa felt a weight lift off her shoulders. She'd been worried that Mutti might be on her own and might need her to help. She wanted to help, but feared she would fail and would end in catastrophe.

"When it is time, I will find her Frau Bauermann and bring her to our house," Christa said. "I know which house she lives in."

Mutti patted her shoulder. "Thank you, Christa. I knew I could count on you."

At home, Mutti plopped onto the sofa and lifted her swollen legs, resting them on the coffee table. "I need to get this swelling down before I can work."

"Is there anything I can do to get started on the work?" Christa asked.

"What work?" Ernst asked, standing in the center of the room, holding three year old Andreas.

"You and Fritz chop more wood and bring it into this room. Stack up as much as you can beside the fireplace.

"Can I help?" Julia asked. Christa hadn't noticed her sitting in the chair in the corner of the room.

"*Ja*. You can gather up small kindling and put it in another pile in here.

"Do you want me to begin preparing a place for the chickens?" Christa asked.

"*Ja*. Start bringing in some straw and the nesting boxes and set them in the attic. I will help you in a few minutes."

"We are going to have chickens in the attic?" Giselle asked, her eyes bright.

"For a while," Mutti said, closing her eyes. Her face looked far too pale. Christa had noticed her mother slowing down on their walk home. What if the cramping and bleeding started again?

By evening, Christa, the boys, and Mutti had nailed boards across the windows from the inside, since they didn't have a ladder tall enough to reach the upper windows and working inside was easier, anyway. They'd taken down the blackout curtains now that they didn't need them and set them in a corner of the room.

Mutti had started to nail shut the back door, but Christa stopped her, saying they needed one not nailed. How could she run to the Bauermann's house when the time came to deliver the baby? What's more, how else would they get to the outhouse in the backyard or to town to get their rations? Mutti smacked herself on her forehead and then told them to leave the back door un-nailed, but locked.

They'd eaten eggs for dinner, again, along with hard bread, and fried potatoes. Afterwards, they brought all of their bedding downstairs and created a giant bed of pillows to sleep on, covering it with all the blankets they owned. With a low fire going in the fireplace, and the bed on the floor, it felt as if they were camping out in the woods. It reminded her of Vati, who used to take them on hiking trips up the hills into the highest part where they could look across the whole area and see their town and the people, looking like ants in an ant farm. They would build a campfire from scratch, roast their dinner, and sit around singing folk songs until they fell asleep in their makeshift beds.

Tonight, with the soft glow from the fire, one small lamp lit, and no drafts from the windows, the house felt cozier and warmer than ever. Why hadn't they done this sooner?

"Can I sleep in the attic with the chickens?" Fritz asked.

"Me too," Giselle chimed in.

"*Nein*. We stay together, here," Mutti said.

"But the chickens are probably scared in their new surroundings," Fritz said. "We can keep them calm."

"Those chickens are probably thrilled to be inside where it is warmer. You can check on them first thing in the morning."

Throughout the night, the older kids had taken turns adding pieces of wood to the fire. Before they'd gone to sleep, Mutti handed each of the older kids a flashlight with fresh batteries. That way, they wouldn't have to turn on the lamp and wake everyone up, if they needed to go to the bathroom in the middle of the night or add wood to the fire.

Christa rolled over and bumped into someone. She couldn't remember who was sleeping beside her and it was too dark to see unless she flipped on her flashlight. And why bother?

She rolled back over and heard snoring. Someone passed gas, too, and she waved her hand to chase away the smell. *Mein Gott*, she was wide awake now and couldn't get back sleep. Was it morning yet? How were they supposed to tell what time of day it was? Usually, even with blackout curtains, slivers of light would find their way through, around the edges or where two pieces of fabric didn't meet exactly. With the wood blocking the windows, nothing got through.

Other family members were ranging around. It wasn't only her. *That must mean it is morning, right?* She eased her way out of the jumble of bodies, careful not to step on anyone. As she neared the staircase, feeling her way in the dark, someone knocked into her and she almost fell.

Who the heck was that? Then she heard footsteps running up the stairs. Fritz, she assumed. She took off running. At the top of the main staircase, they squeezed into the same space, tightly rubbing shoulder against shoulder.

"Me first," Fritz cried out.

"*Nein*. Getting the eggs is my job."

"All right." He conceded, stepped aside, letting Christa go past first.

She rushed up the smaller staircase to the attic and opened the door. Startled, the chickens squawked and clucked and the sound of flapping wings filled the air. She couldn't see much in the darkness, but could certainly smell them. Light from outside peeked through in a couple spots, through spaces between the boards, but it was still dark. She certainly couldn't hunt for eggs. Where was the string to turn on the overhead light? She tried to move forward and reach up for the string, and almost stepped on a chicken. It let out a loud screech and went crazy flapping its wings.

"The chickens are loose in here, and I forgot my flashlight downstairs."

Fritz didn't say anything. A minute or two later, Christa heard a loud thunk sound and then Fritz yelled out in pain. *Oh no! He must have fallen on the stairs.*

She left the attic, closing the door behind her so the chickens couldn't get out. Then she rushed down the stairs.

Half way down the second flight, she bumped into Fritz, half sitting on the stairs. "Are you all right?"

"I . . . I think so. I twisted my ankle."

"Can you stand?"

She grabbed his shoulder and pulled him upright.

"Ouch!" he yelled.

"What happened?"

"I tried to put my weight on my sore foot."

"You are too big for me to carry, but I will help you down the stairs. Lean on me."

Mutti made Fritz lie down and the sofa and then bandaged his ankle. Once Fritz was comfortable, Christa carried her flashlight back upstairs and quickly found the string, turning on the light. Better. She checked on the chickens, fed them, and then looked for eggs. Finding only two this morning, she decided that was because their routine had been disrupted and the chickens weren't even sure of what time of day it was. She would talk to Mutti about removing the boards from the attic window.

By the end of the week, Fritz was feeling better and was able to hobble around, but Mutti insisted he rest to give his ankle a chance to heal.

That night, while the family listened to the radio and the younger kids played with toys on the floor, Mutti complained again of cramps and ferocious pain, unlike when she'd been pregnant with her other babies. She kept holding one hand behind her, firmly pressed to her back, and she couldn't get comfortable no matter what position she was in.

Julia brought in a wet towel and put it on Mutti's forehead the way Mutti always did when someone was sick.

"Should I get Frau Bauermann?" Christa asked, standing over the chair where Mutti sat moaning in pain and holding her belly.

"Ja. Something is wrong. It is too early for the baby."

Andreas and Giselle started to cry, and Julia comforted them as best she could.

Christa grabbed her flashlight and made her way through the semi-dark house to the backdoor. As she opened the door, Ernst held it open and went out with her.

"You should stay home with, Mutti," she said. "If something happens, the others will be scared and will not know what to do."

"And you think I would be better? The sight of blood makes me dizzy. I would be useless. At least out here I might be able to help you get through town without being accosted. Girls should not walk around the town alone in the dark."

He made a good point. They'd heard stories of girls and women being attacked or questioned by the gestapo or soldiers—sometimes it was hard to tell which—here and in surrounding towns. Not so much during daylight, but after dark, anything could happen.

They hurried along the cobblestone street, guided by their flashlights and the moon.

At the Bauermanns's house, Christa knocked, bent over slightly, trying to catch her breath. The cold night air and their brisk pace had made it difficult to breathe for a moment.

Claudia answered the door, a look of surprise on her face when she saw her old friend. Since school had ended, they rarely saw each other.

"Christa! Hello. I have missed you. Why is it we never get to visit with each other, when we have nothing else to do?" Her eyes widened suddenly and she stopped talking.

Christa, wondering why, turned her head. Of course. Claudia had noticed Ernst standing on the porch behind her and apparently realized this wasn't a social visit.

"Sorry to come here so late," Christa said.

"What is wrong? It is not safe to be out after dark," she said, her eyes darting into the darkness. "The curfew. Have you heard something on the news? Is that why you are here with your brother?"

161

Claudia's mother came into view behind her daughter, drying her hands on a dish towel. "Christa, what happened? Is it your mother?"

"It is Mutti. She is in labor, maybe. We do not know for sure. There might be something wrong with the baby. She is in pain."

"I will get some supplies. Come inside and warm up a minute while I get ready." As she dropped the dish towel, Christa saw Frau Bauermann's belly and remembered she was pregnant, too, obviously not as far along as Mutti, but maybe four or five months. Claudia's father hadn't come back from the war. He'd gone away the same time as Vati.

The walk back to their farmhouse was slower paced, because Frau Bauermann couldn't keep up. Christa and Ernst walked slightly ahead, each carrying some supplies, both watching for gestapo and any signs of danger. Christa looked over her shoulder periodically to make sure Frau Bauermann was still coming. A few times, Christa slowed down, allowing the *frau* to catch up.

As Christa and Ernst led her around toward the back of the house, she asked, "Why are your windows boarded up and why are we going into the backyard?"

Ernst explained what Mutti had insisted on. The *frau* made a clicking sound with her mouth. What it meant, Christa didn't know, but she suspected the *frau* didn't agree with that action.

They found Mutti lying on the sofa, with all the kids leaning over her, worried looks in their eyes, and Mutti moaning.

Frau Bauermann shooed the kids away.

Ernst, white faced, said, "Come with me. We will go upstairs and visit with the chickens. How does that sound?"

"But Mutti . . . is she going to be all right?" Giselle said.

"She is in good hands now. Frau Bauermann has promised to help her."

Ernst pick up three year old Andreas and then took hold of Giselle's hand. Glancing over his shoulder, he said, "Will somebody hold my flashlight? It's in my back pocket."

"I will get it," Fritz said.

As soon as they were out of sight, Frau Bauermann examined Mutti. "Well, I can already see the baby's head." She glanced around the room. "What are those pieces of cloth? Over there, near the window?"

Christa said, "Our old blackout curtains."

"Good. Bring them over and set them on the floor next to the sofa. We will move your mother onto those."

Christa did as instructed.

"All right, now help me. Get hold of her feet. I'll take her arms."

Once they moved Mutti, Frau Bauermann had Mutti spread her legs wide. Then the *frau* used the wet towel Julia had used earlier and wiped Mutti's brow. She began talking Mutti through the delivery process, telling her when to push, cautioning her when not to push, and then when to push again. Mutti kept groaning and crying out with each push, making Christa hold her breath, worrying.

"Get me a large bowl," the *frau* said. "I must break the sack when the baby comes out. The bowl will capture the amniotic fluid and keep it from getting over everything. After it fills the bowl, you must dump the water and bring the bowl back. I'll need it for the after-birth."

Christa didn't know what that meant, but she sensed she need to hurry. She dashed to the kitchen and searched the cabinets. Finally, she found the bowl she was looking for. The giant bowl they used for potatoes.

When she returned to the living room, the *frau* said, "*Ja,* good. You will help me. Hold your mother's hands while she gives a big push."

Christa rushed forward and set the bowl down beside the *frau*. Then she grabbed her mother's hands and felt the pressure of her mother's exertion.

After several minutes, the *frau* was pulling out the baby. "Almost there," she said, smiling at Christa and Mutti. "Keep pushing. Oh, Hanna," the *frau* suddenly proclaimed, "it looks like you have another son." Seconds later, the baby let out a loud cry.

Christa released her mother's hands and leaned over toward Frau Bauermann and the baby.

Mutti wiped tears from her eyes. "Is he all right? Nothing wrong? He is early. Does he need to go to the hospital?"

"I am not a doctor," the *frau* said, "but he looks normal to me, and I have had my share of babies. He is small and thin. But he will grow. I will clean him up and then we take care of the after-birth."

"Oh, thank *Gott*. I do not know what I would have done without you, Hilda. You saved my life and probably my baby's life. I owe you."

Color already seemed to be returning to Mutti's face as Christa looked on, feeling relief wash over her for her mother and her new brother.

"*Nein*. Do not worry one bit. You will get to repay me when it is my turn."

"I will be happy to help you deliver your child. Let us hope the war is over by then and our children can play together and become the best of friends.

"*Ja*. We will make sure they do."

Frau Bauermann got to work and finished what she needed to do, then cleaned the baby and wrapped him in a baby blanket she had brought with her. She turned to Christa and said, "You may bring your brothers and sisters down now to meet their new brother."

Christa darted up the stairs and burst into the attic. "The baby is here! Come see."

The children all rushed down to the living room and then stopped a few feet away from the sofa, where their mother was now resting, holding the baby lying on her chest.

"It is all right," Mutti said, smiling. "Come meet your new brother."

The children rushed over and crowded around mother and baby.

Christa looked around and saw that while she'd been upstairs, Frau Bauermann had straightened up the room, removing evidence of what had occurred. But Christa would never forget the fear and excitement of witnessing the birth right there in their own house.

"Well, I am no longer needed here," the *frau* stated, smiling. "I should be getting home to my family."

"We will walk you home," Ernst said. "Right, Christa?"

"Of course," Christa said. "You will be all right while we are gone, Mutti?"

"*Ja, ja*, I am fine. Be careful."

"We will," Christa and Ernst said in unison.

The following day, Mutti sent Christa to the Bauermanns' house to deliver a basket of eggs, as a thank you. The family was delighted to get the extra food and, as they didn't live on a farm or own chickens, they rarely ate fresh eggs.

"Tell your mother thank you from us," Frau Bauermann said, as Christa and Ernst were leaving. "She did not need to send those. She will be helping me soon enough with my delivery." She smiled and waved and added, "See you again in a few months. Or sooner. I will try to stop by next week to see how your mother and the new baby are doing."

A week later Christa couldn't stop sobbing, a waterfall of tears from falling from her face. Mutti, too, was crying and shaking. Their whole family sat in the Catholic Church's pews, listening to the priest talk about the Bauermann family. Poor Claudia. That poor unborn baby, too. What did they—or any of them—do to deserve this? A bomb had dropped on their house five days after Mutti's baby boy was born, killing everyone.

Why *Gott*? Why did you take them? Christa wasn't sure she wanted to ever step foot in a church again.

Ilse Seidel, March 1945, Memmingen, Germany—

ILSE AWOKE IN a sweat. Not from warmth in the cold house. She'd had the same nightmare again. Why did she keep reliving the day she'd watched her brother shoot and kill Ron? Month after month. And reliving that following morning when she'd walked into the market square to get the family's rations and saw Ron's body hanging from rafters in the middle of the square. She'd struggled not to scream and run to him. Was it any wonder she kept having the horrid nightmare? Night after night. Each morning at the breakfast table, Mutter stared at her, asking why she had dark shadows under her eyes. She had told her she was having trouble sleeping, blaming it on the bombing and the war ruining their lives. At first Mutter seemed to believe her, but Ilse knew she suspected something else. Ilse had suddenly stopped going to the woods and meadows searching for food. She stayed home most days, sitting on the edge of the wall behind their townhouse, her feet dangling over the edge above the river below, never reaching the water because the wall was too high.

She climbed out of bed and donned her loosest fitting dress, which now fit snuggly around the waist. How much longer could she hide the bulge that looked so odd on her rail-thin body? It was only a matter of time before Mutter took her aside and questioned her, not about the shadows under her eyes, but about the baby growing inside her.

Ilse had thought about her situation for months; ever since she'd realized a life was growing inside her. It was doubtful Mutter—her ever so proper mother—would forgive her for getting herself into this predicament: becoming an unwed mother and bringing disgrace to the family. She sighed. How disappointed Mutter would be if she ever found out.

Of course, her situation was much more complicated and precarious than worrying about what her mother would think. Ilse had helped the enemy—an American, no less. People got executed for that. To top it off, there was another equally if not more frightening factor. Her baby would be half-Jewish. If anyone found out who the father was, she and the baby could be taken to a concentration camp, unless the war ended now.

She pulled on her father's sweater, which she'd taken to wearing this winter, when the family could no longer get fuel for heating the house. At least the bulky sweater helped hide her secret. For now.

Ilse strode down the stairs and found the family already gathered around the kitchen table, eating bread and drinking water. She took her seat, avoiding their eyes, and chewed her bread slowly, savoring every bite and every crumb. She'd thought before that she was starving, but now, with two humans to feed, she couldn't get enough.

"I saw Johann yesterday," Ursula said. "He dropped off a package of uniforms that need mending."

Ilse stared down at her empty plate. *Don't say his name in my presence,* she wanted to scream, but how could she without explaining why she hated him. The day after he'd killed Ron, he had come to the house to let the family know he was temporarily stationed at the air base near Memmingen. She'd greeted him, as required, then made an excuse to go to the market. That, of course, was when she first saw the body hanging there for everyone to see. Someone in the square had said the Nazis put it there as a reminder to the locals. From that day onward, Ilse felt eyes on her, and on everyone walking the streets in their town. The Nazis were trying to figure out who had helped the airman. At least Johann had kept his word that he wouldn't betray her. Small consolation.

Mutter said, "Oma and I will get started on the mending this morning. Ursula, I need you to work on our laundry. Robert, please see what you can do about the pipes in the kitchen. We seem to have another leak." Robert had been learning about plumbing by interning with a local plumber. Although he was young, Robert had shown an interest at the right time, when he was in the repair shop to pick up parts for another project a few months ago. He'd apparently asked the right questions, and the owner of the shop had been impressed.

"I will get to work on it right away, Mutter," he said.

"Ilse, you are not looking well this morning," Mutter said. "You should go back upstairs and rest today. I worry about you."

"I am fine. Today is market day and I need to get our rations. I might even go to the woods to look for mushrooms. The fresh air and exercise would be good for me, *ja?*"

"I suppose, but I do not like the idea of you going alone. Not these days."

"I will be fine."

A loud pounding on the front door drew everyone's attention.

"I do not like the sound of that," Opa said. He pushed his chair back and stood up, then strode into the foyer.

He let out a loud moan sound, and everyone jumped up from their seats.

Mutter and Oma were first to reach him.

"What happened?" Oma said.

"An officer gave me this." He held out an envelope, which he'd opened, and the short letter that he'd removed.

Oma read it and covered her mouth with her free hand, and gave Mutter the items.

"Mein Gott! Oh, my Bernhard.*"* Mutter shrieked. *"Nein*! *Nein.* It cannot be true." Mutter crumpled to the floor.

Ilse's heart dropped as if a lead weight were pulling it to the ocean floor, knowing without words what the letter was about.

"What is it?" Ursula said, seemingly not understanding, but how could she not? Robert's face was ashen. He knew.

Opa said, "Your father. He was killed in action in Russia. The army does not know when or even if his body will be returned to us."

Over the next hour many tears were shed, everyone hugging and comforting each other in the way that only a loving family could. Many memories and recollections were spoken, others, unspoken, but felt.

After a time, Oma said, "Someone needs to get word to his sister in Biberach."

"I will go," Ilse volunteered.

"How? How will you get there? The trains are off-limits now."

"The same way cousin Hermann did when Vater's mother was killed. Remember, he rode his bicycle here. I can ride Vater's bicycle. I will be back in a few days."

"I do not like that. It is too dangerous, especially for a young woman," Mutter said. "I just lost your father, I am not going to lose you, too."

"I am going. I need to get away and have a change in scenery. Do you not you see? It has been too much, seeing all the destruction. Now Vater is gone, and we are all grieving. I need to

169

get away for a few days to think and to grieve in my own way. And Aunt Karolina needs to know about her brother."

Mutter stared as if she thought Ilse had lost her mind. Her mouth a tight, straight line.

Opa said, "Let her go, Maria. It will be good for her. The fresh air. The exercise. Like she said earlier."

Ilse could tell Mutter was going to object to Opa, then paused, seemed to calm herself, then replied, "All right. Fine. But take a knife with you, for protection."

Ilse nodded, turned and walked away to collect a few things.

CHAPTER FIFTEEN

Lucas Landry, August 2017, Sacramento, California—

AT HIS AUNTS' house, Lucas parked his Jeep and picked up the zippered folder he'd set on the front passenger seat. He'd brought a few documents from the attic, as well as the family tree drawings and a list of questions he'd prepared. The aunts were expecting him. He wasn't sure, though, if they knew what they were getting themselves into when they'd agreed to talk to him about family history. For that matter, he wasn't sure what he was getting himself into, but the diaries from both girls were tearing at his heart, making him eager to know how they were connected to him, and know what had happened to the girls and their families. They all had lived in such awful times. Had any of them survived?

He strode to the front door, looking at the enormous door a moment, then pushed the doorbell.

After what seemed like several minutes, making him wonder if they had changed their minds about seeing him, the door opened.

Aunt Anna smiled, clapped her hands together, and said, "Ah, my dear Lucas. We were so delighted when you called and wanted to get together. Come in, come in. Elsa has baked a scrumptious coffee cake and has a fresh pot of coffee made. She's waiting for us in the sitting room."

Lucas hugged Anna, then followed her in. Seeing Aunt Elsa already seated on a leather recliner in the sitting room, he walked over, bent down, and gave her a hug as well. "You look great, Aunt Elsa."

"Thank you." She beamed up at him. "It's been a long road to recovery, but I'm too tough of an old bird to let a hip replacement and stroke keep me down. Well, guess I've been lucky, too. The stroke wasn't near as bad as it could have been."

Lucas smiled, not sure what to say next, sitting down on the sofa across from her.

"I made us some coffee cake. You do eat sweets, don't you?"

He nodded and smiled, patting the small bulge in his mid-section.

"You never know these days, with all the new-fangled diets people are always trying," she said.

Lucas said, "Don't have to worry about me. I'll eat anything someone puts on my plate. Well, almost anything. I draw the line at Brussels sprouts."

Anna laughed. "I can't stand those disgusting things, either." She sat down next to Lucas.

"Shame on you both for not wanting to eat your vegetables," Elsa said, but she was smiling as she sat forward and cut pieces of the cake sitting on the coffee table and handed each of them the plates.

The cake smelled delicious, making Lucas's mouth water. *If this tastes as good as it smells, I may just move in.*

Anna poured three cups of coffee from a silver urn, and handed them out. "Help yourself to milk and sugar. If there's anything else you need, let me know and I'll get it."

Lucas added a spoonful of sugar to his coffee, stirred it, and set the cup on a coaster next to the cake on a side table before reseating himself. The room quieted as they sipped coffee and ate cake. When Lucas finished his, he said, "Aunt Elsa, that was the best coffee cake I've ever eaten."

"I used an old German recipe," Elsa said, beaming. "You would not believe the amazing cakes and torts and pastries they make over there, in Germany. Austria and France, too."

"Oh, yes, and Italy," Anna said. "My late husband and I spent a couple weeks in Italy every year during his retirement. We stayed in lovely places and ate the most scrumptious desserts you can imagine."

"Well, I've never been to Italy. Not so far, anyway. But I've been all over other parts of Europe," Elsa said.

Lucas saw an opportunity and jumped on it. "Have either of you ever been to the former Sudetenland?"

Anna and Elsa exchanged looks.

Elsa said, "I went there with my husband once. We were actually in Prague, Czechoslovakia on a business trip. My husband's business. I just tagged along."

"It's Czech Republic," Anna said.

"I know that," Elsa snapped. "But back then it was Czechoslovakia. Are you going to let me finish my story?"

"Go ahead." Anna stared down at her coffee, adding more sugar and stirring it, and continuing to stir it.

What was that about? Lucas wondered.

"As I was saying, I was tagging along and sightseeing on my own in Prague, but then I got to thinking about stories I'd read in the diary up in the attic. Do you remember, Anna?"

"Yes. When we were little, we would sometimes go up there and dig around in the boxes and trunks. One day, we found a diary written by a girl around our ages and we started reading. Back then, we still remembered enough of the German language."

"Papa found out and banned us from going up there anymore," Elsa said. "I don't know why. We weren't doing anything bad."

"Well, we did kind of make a mess, sister."

Lucas said, "Did my father know about the attic and the diaries?"

"No, I don't think so," Anna said. "He was outside every time he got a chance. Baseball, football, fishing, anything that he could do outside."

"Hmm, this may sound strange. Was it just that he liked being outdoors and doing sporting things, or did he want to be away from the house and the family?"

Again the sisters glanced at each other.

"I don't really know," Elsa said, looking somber. "I never did understand Joe. He was a loner, and yet he liked team sports. Never made any sense to me."

Lucas thought about that. Maybe his father felt like an outsider, and his wanting to be on a team stemmed from his desire to be a part of something, to belong.

"So, you remember the diaries about the girl in the Sudetenland, Aunt Elsa?"

"Oh, yes, I forgot what we were talking about. Getting old is no fun, I tell you. Well, anyway, I asked my husband, Howard, if we could make a day trip to the town mentioned in that diary. He couldn't because he had more meetings and wouldn't have any free time before we had to go back to the states, but he told me I could take a train there and look around on my own."

"So did you?"

"Yes, it took me a day to figure out the Czech name for the town. They—the Czechs—had changed the town names from German to Czech after the war ended, you know. Well, anyway, I found a train that would take me to the train station in that little town. Oh dear, I can't remember the name now. I got off and spent a few hours walking around, trying to talk to people, but most of them didn't speak English. It was sad that the town had lost at least a third of its population after the expulsion, and it never really recovered."

"Wow, that's interesting," Lucas said. "Maybe someday I can visit there, too."

Anna said, "Wouldn't it be lovely if we could all travel to Europe together? Maybe when Elsa is completely healed."

"Maybe. My wife's pregnant and, like Aunt Elsa, won't be able to travel for a while."

No one spoke for a few moments.

Elsa cut three more slices of cake and placed them on each of their plates.

Lucas took a bite, then asked, "Why do we have Christa's and Ilse's diaries in the attic? Are we related to either of those girls?"

"Ilse? Who is she? We didn't see any of her diaries," Anna said, glancing over at Elsa. "We didn't, did we?"

"I don't remember them."

"Oh, sorry, you mentioned Christa's diaries, so I assumed you'd also read one of Ilse's. I found the first ones in the same box."

"The first ones? You mean there were more?" Elsa said.

"Yeah. I found numerous diaries in different places, different boxes. I've read most of them. Still have a few more to read."

"Well, now you've got me interested," Elsa said.

"I can bring you some, if you want to read them."

"That would be just lovely," Elsa said. "Oh, I'm afraid we don't remember much of our German, but I suppose we could brush up on the language first. I'm sure it will come back."

"Both girls, I think, were Catholic. I was wondering if there might be church records showing the family names, birth dates, that sort of thing."

"Oh, I seem to remember in Christa's diary, the one we read, it mentioned a Catholic church and school," Anna said. "Hmm."

"What?" Lucas said. "Why 'hmm'?"

Anna said, "Interesting that she was Catholic."

Lucas leaned forward. "Why?"

Elsa chimed in, "Well, if she's related to us—and we don't really know if she is or isn't—that would be unusual."

Anna said, "You see, we're Jewish."

Lucas's mouth dropped open, his mind struggling to grasp this revelation. How long he sat there dumbfounded, he couldn't say.

"Are you all right?" Anna said. "You look as if you've seen a ghost."

"Oh . . . uh, yeah. I guess just surprised. I mean, my father never took us to Temple or a church of any kind. Mom's funeral was held in a protestant church, but she never went to church, either, that I remember. He never even talked about religion. I had no idea he was raised Jewish."

"That is odd," Elsa said. "One of our grandfathers was a Rabbi."

With that announcement, his mind was truly blown away.

"Lucas, you look pale. Are you all right?"

Lucas couldn't speak. *Holy cow! My brother, a neo-Nazi who wants to rid the world of Jews, has Jewish ancestry. He's not Aryan, like he believes he is. He's gonna flip out if he finds out. Now that's true karma.* He shook his head, trying to clear it.

Anna shook his hand, drawing him back to reality.

"Uh, no, I guess I'm really not. I wonder if I really knew my father. It's sad, because I have so many questions for him and I'll never get a chance to ask him. You know what I mean?"

"We do," the aunts said in unison.

Anna said, "I sometimes wish I could go back in time to ask our parents and grandparents questions, too. We just don't think about important questions and about heritage while our family is still around. Then later it is too late. We assume we have plenty of time. But we don't."

CHAPTER SIXTEEN

Christa Nagel, April, 1945, Altstadt, Sudetenland—

UPSTAIRS IN THE attic of their farmhouse, Christa and Mutti stood looking out the uncovered window at the mountains in the distance. The boys, Ernst and Fritz, had removed the wood covers from the two attic windows—one east-facing and one west-facing—and put back up the blackout curtains that had been stuffed into a corner. This morning, shortly after breakfast, Christa had carefully pulled back one of the curtains so she and Mutti could get a birds-eye-view of the war scene. It had been a week since they'd last looked. The sky had a blue-gray-purple cast to it, somewhat hazy, that on a peaceful day, Christa might consider pretty. Where were the ant-size soldiers? They weren't at the top of the hillside, anymore. She held her breath, praying. *Please let them be gone from here.* Slowly her gaze moved over the hill and mountain areas. She gasped, hearing her mother muffle a cry. *Oh Gott!* The soldiers weren't gone. There they were, further down the hillside and distinctly larger now. The fighting was definitely getting closer to their home. "What are we going to do now, Mutti? They could be here in a matter of days."

Mutti was visibly shaking, wringing her hands together in a way that she always did when she was extremely anxious. She turned and walked over to the west-facing window and pulled back the curtain.

Christa followed. *Gott nein!* Christa gasped again. Soldiers were fighting on the hills on this side, too. For the first time. Her family was surrounded, with no way out. They—her whole family—could be wiped out, as Frau Bauermann's had. Maybe today. Maybe tomorrow. Christa had heard of people taking their own lives because of what was happening. Last week, she'd gone into town to get their rations and heard that the Meier family had all taken pills. Their elderly next door neighbor had gone to their house to check on them, and found all four bodies. Mutti would never do that. She wouldn't commit suicide. It went against her religion. But Christa knew she could.

Mutti left the attic distraught, leaving Christa behind to feed the chickens and gather the eggs. The chickens seemed to have adjusted to indoor life and were producing their normal yield of eggs.

Last week, on her trip into town, Christa had managed to trade some eggs for a bag of flour. The week before that she'd traded for a bag of oats. She'd surprised herself that she was learning how to barter and concluded she wasn't half bad at it.

When Christa came downstairs with the fresh eggs and put them away in the kitchen, Mutti gathered the older kids together, instructing them to pack some of their belongings into boxes or other small containers. When the task was completed, they buried some of them in the ground closest to the house, where the ground wasn't frozen; others they hid in the root cellar or under floor boards. Money and jewels Mutti sewed into the lining of their coats and clothes, wherever possible.

"What do you think will happen?" Ernst asked.

"I have heard that Russian soldiers go into homes and take whatever they want. Sometimes, the soldiers confiscate the homes. I do not know what will happen, but we take what precautions we can. If we are lucky, we may not lose everything."

The rest of the day, and the next day, the family stayed together in the living room, reading quietly, or playing games, or eating. They rarely even sat at the kitchen table anymore. They no longer listened to the radio. Christa had tried to turn it on once. Ernst had, too. But Mutti said no. She didn't want to hear the news.

Baby Dirk let out a loud wail, waking up from his nap. Mutti picked him up and cooed to him. It was obvious from the way he moved his head and his little fists that he was hungry. Mutti pulled open the front of her dress and fed the one month old. Christa watched, feeling oddly tender toward him and her mother. She'd always felt jealous of the attention her siblings, especially the babies, got from Mutti. It was different now. Maybe because she'd helped with his birth, or maybe her family just felt a little more precious to her now.

"Mutti," Giselle said, "can we go outside and play tomorrow. Ernst said it is getting warmer out, and it has been too long since we got to play outdoors. Please. Can we?"

"*Nein!* You are not to go outside, except to go to the outhouse."

Giselle's eyes filled with tears and her mouth wobbled.

"Come, Giselle," Christa said. "Mutti is right. It is not safe out there, but we can play inside. How about a game of hide-and-go-seek? Are you up for that?"

Giselle's mouth curved up, and she nodded, brushing away her tears with the back of her hand.

"Me, too," Andreas chimed in. "I can hide good."

"All right. We can all play. Except for Mutti and Dirk, of course."

Mutti smiled and nodded, then slightly mouthed, "*Danke.*"

Christa felt a wave of love wash over her.

That evening, loud blasts and the roar of heavy equipment woke the baby, making him cry. Mutti woke and tried to quiet him.

Christa took her flashlight and ran up the two flights of stairs and into the attic. She closed the door to the attic, turned off her flashlight, and peeked between the curtain panels.

Tanks. Army trucks. Bright lights. Blinding lights. Soldiers and guns. The street in front of their house, and the neighboring streets were cluttered with military. Russians! The Red Army had taken their town.

Christa felt as if she couldn't breathe. She grabbed hold of the window ledge to keep herself from collapsing. Oh, *Gott*! She had to go warn Mutti and the kids.

She turned away from the window and found her way in the dark to the door without tripping over a chicken, not wanting to turn on the flashlight and risk someone on the ground seeing it.

Downstairs, she rushed to her family and whispered, "Mutti, they are here. The Russians."

Mutti let out a quiet moan. Ernst's face blanched in the pale light from the fireplace and the lamp.

The fire.

Christa rushed to the fireplace and threw water from the bucket beside it onto the fire to put it out. She remembered her conversation with Mutti from more than a month ago. What if someone sees the smoke from our chimney?

Maybe Mutti had been right about soldiers thinking the house had been abandoned. Maybe they would leave their house alone.

When the fire was out, Ernst switched off the lamp. Everyone stayed quiet, huddling together in their blankets, some crying quietly.

Eventually, they fell asleep, Christa could tell, because she heard snoring. Lots of snoring. Somehow she managed to sleep a bit, too. She must have, because she felt someone kick her mildly in the stomach, waking her up. She rubbed her eyes, wondering what time it was.

A flashlight lay on top of a cabinet in the foyer, shining a small amount of light in the kitchen. From that light, Christa could see Mutti pacing across the open space between the living room and kitchen, carrying baby Dirk and bouncing him ever so slightly.

Christa carefully inched her way out of the tangle of blankets and legs, and walked over to Mutti. "What time is it?" she asked.

Mutti said, "I think it is early morning. I heard noises outside. Engines and voices."

Christa shivered. "Do you want me to hold the baby for a while?"

Mutti handed him over to Christa. "Thank you, *meine liebling*. My arms were getting sore."

A few minutes later, someone pounded hard on the front door. Then shouted in Russian.

The children all woke up and Mutti rushed over to them and whispered, begging them to keep quiet.

Pounding again. More shouting.

And then the baby started crying—more like screaming. Christa desperately tried to quiet him. She put her hand over his mouth. Nothing worked.

Mutti ran over and took him from Christa. She couldn't quiet him, either.

Then something hard hit the door. Not someone's hands. It sounded like a bulldozer. Or an ax.

The wooden door cracked. Cracked again. And again. Three big Russian soldiers burst through the door.

Mutti handed the baby back to Christa, and said, "Go to the children. Try to calm them."

The soldiers grabbed Mutti and threw her to the floor. One of them ripped her dress and then undid his pants, while the other soldiers held her pinned down.

Mutti screamed and screamed as the men assaulted her, one by one.

Christa felt her chest would burst, shaking, raging inside, but all she could do was hug the children tightly to her as they all cried and watched, helpless to do anything to protect Mutti.

Finally, the Russians left and Christa handed the baby to Ernst and then rushed over to Mutti, laying still, curled in a pile.

"Mutti, are you . . . can you hear me?" Christa wasn't sure if Mutti was alive. *Oh Gott, please let her be alive.* Tears streaked down her cheeks as she bent down and listened for any sign of life. There, she was breathing, wasn't she? Christa gently shook Mutti's shoulder, not wanting to hurt her any more than she'd already been hurt, but wanting to shake her to get her to open her eyes. "Can you talk? What can I do to help?"

Julia ran over and said, "I will get a bowl and some water and towels. We can clean her up."

Fritz said, "We should move her onto the sofa."

Christa grabbed Mutti by the arms. Fritz took her feet.

"Let me help," Ernst said. "I am the strongest."

"Where is the baby?" Christa said.

"In his cradle."

Together, the three of them got Mutti to the sofa. Christa carefully rubbed a damp cloth over her forehead, cleaned her as best she could, and covered her with several blankets. Christa was terrified. Over all their ministrations, Mutti remained mute, unmoving. There was nothing more she knew to do.

Christa added dry wood to the fireplace and got another fire started. No need to keep the fire low now.

Over the next few days, Mutti slowly animated and began to recover, seeming more embarrassed and ashamed than anything else.

Ernst and Fritz rebuilt the front door as well as they could. They had used some of the wood they'd nailed to the upstairs window to do it.

Christa left the house only once, to get food. She heard from shopkeepers that women all over town—the German women, not the Czech women, had been raped by the Russians. Elderly men were beaten. So far, only the children had escaped attack.

Two days later, the Russians pulled out of town.

Everyone gingerly breathed a sigh of relief, that is until the Czech army and paramilitary pulled into town on a surprisingly warm spring day.

Within an hour of their arrival, a loud knock came again. Mutti started toward the door, but Ernst nudged her away. "I'll get it."

The Czech soldier at the door spoke loudly enough that the whole family could hear him. "Every German in town must meet in front of the town hall in fifteen minutes. Pack only what you can carry. If you don't show up, we will drag you out and shoot you."

He walked away and Ernst slammed the door shut.

The family ran around, frantically trying to decide what to take. As they carried their suitcases down the stairs, Christa remembered the chickens in the attic. She turned and looked up to the door leading to the attic. Mutti saw her.

"We have to take the chickens," Christa said.

"*Nein*. Leave them," Mutti said.

"But what will become of them? No one knows they are in the attic. They will starve. We should at least set them free. Give them a chance to survive."

"Or to be eaten," Mutti said. "I am sorry, Christa, they do not stand a chance, and we both know it. It does not matter."

Christa's eyes filled with tears. She couldn't make a big fuss, because that would upset the other children.

Mutti relented. "All right. We carry them outside and let them go. Maybe they get away and find a way to survive. That is the best we can do for them."

"*Danke*, Mutti."

They carried their suitcases to the foyer, then went back upstairs to the attic. Fritz went with them, and each carried down two chickens and set them free in the backyard.

"Goodbye. Take care of yourselves," Christa said.

Fritz and Mutti stood nearby, both with tears in their eyes.

Ilse Seidel, March 1945, Memmingen, Germany—

ILSE PULLED VATER'S bicycle up the cellar stairs and brushed off layers of dust. Why hadn't anyone used it all this time? She checked it over. Everything seemed in working order, except the tires were low. She went back down to the cellar and grabbed her father's air-pump, filling the limp tires with air. Leaving the bicycle and pump in the foyer, she went upstairs to her room and packed a few clothes and toiletries in a knapsack. Downstairs she pulled on her coat, affixed the pump to her knapsack, then strapped the affair over her back.

When she turned to go, Mutter, Oma, and Opa were standing near the foyer, watching her.

Mutter said, "Take care of yourself and watch out for soldiers who may mean you harm. If you cannot do it—cannot make the long ride—come back home. We will find another way to get a message to your Aunt Karolina. Curriers deliver messages all the time."

"Do not worry, Mutter. I will be fine. I have ridden to Biberach before. Vater loaned me his bicycle and I rode there with my best friend." Her voice caught unexpectedly. Her father and her best friend were both gone now. "I am strong. I have survived more than five years of war. I can do this."

Oma and Opa walked over and hugged Ilse, one on either side of her, and kissed her on the cheeks. Opa handed her a cloth bag and whispered, "Snacks for your trip."

Mutter seemed to grow rigid, her face stern. Had she seen him give her the bag with food? Mutter was always strict with her food portions, trying to stretch their rations as much as possible.

Ilse walked over to her and gave her a quick hug, careful to keep her protruding stomach away. Should she give the bag to Mutter? Would Opa be upset if she did? The baby kicked ever so slightly. No, she would keep the extra food. She and the baby needed it.

"How long will you be gone?" Mutter asked.

"I was thinking about that last night," Ilse said. "Perhaps a week. I guess it depends on Aunt Karolina. If Uncle Markus and the boys are still away, fighting, she might need some help around the house. I assume that Hermann is a soldier, too. He is my age."

Mutter nodded, probably thinking about Vater and Johann.

"You are lucky you have Oma, Opa, Ursula, and Robert to help you. Can you imagine trying to do everything yourself? And would you not be frightened?"

"*Ja*. You are right. Maybe time with your aunt will be good for both of you."

Ilse turned away and grabbed hold of the bicycle before she changed her mind—or more likely Mutter changed her mind about letting her go.

Oma handed her a knit hat, which Ilse slipped on. "Thank you, Oma."

"I made it for you last night with yarn from an old sweater. I hope it keeps you warm on that long ride, dear."

"It is lovely. And I am sure it will." She opened the front door and rolled the bicycle out and down the four concrete steps to the sidewalk.

"Goodbye, Ilse," Oma said.

Ilse looked over her shoulder and waved at all three of them. While they watched, she mounted the bicycle and began pedaling toward the town square, then rode through the Ulmer Tor, the north gate leading out of Memmingen. She was finally on her way. The cool wind in her face felt fresh and invigorating. For the first time since the war began, she felt free.

Several military trucks passed by, most going south towards Memmingen, or more likely to the air base outside of town. A few traveled north. Some of the soldiers waved at her or whistled.

She stopped a couple of times on her way, once to rest and check her directions and another time to rest again and eat an apple and a chunk of bread, the snacks Opa had packed for her. She ate every last bite, thankful for the nourishment for herself and the baby, but also felt guilty for the food she had, in effect, taken from the mouths of her siblings.

At last, in late afternoon, she arrived in Biberach and had to weave her way through a line of military vehicles. There weren't as many here as in Memmingen, as far as she could tell, but they were grouped together more.

Finding her aunt's house turned out to be much harder and took much longer than expected. It had been a long time since she had been to visit and her parents always knew the way. She couldn't remember precisely how to get to her street and, unfortunately, landmarks she'd expected to use were gone or unrecognizable, having been damaged or destroyed in the war.

Finally arriving, she walked her bicycle up the steps of the porch to the front door, leaned it against the wall, and rang the doorbell.

No answer.

The sun was beginning to set. Looking around the neighborhood, Ilse realized that the street seemed completely deserted. She felt a wave of panic rise up in her throat. Aunt Karolina didn't know she was coming. The family hadn't heard from her, not since the bombing that had killed Vater's mother.

What if Aunt Karolina wasn't here? Maybe she moved away. Or was taken away, or she could be dead. If no one was here, Ilse would be stranded in a strange town alone—at night.

She pushed the doorbell again. And again. *Please be home. Please.*

"Are you looking for someone?"

Ilse swung around to see who was talking. An elderly man with a cane stood on the sidewalk a few feet away. "Uh, *ja*, I am looking for my aunt. She lives here."

"She is in a poor way," he said. "I live over there, two houses down. Frau Wagner got word three days ago that her husband and oldest son were killed in action. Her younger son, Hermann, was home with her, on leave, at the time, but then he got recalled."

"Oh, *mein Gott*! Do you know where she is?"

"She is in there," he said, nodding toward the house. "Been holed up in there since Hermann left. I tried visiting her this morning. She would not answer the door."

"Will you help me get inside? She could be . . . ." She let her words trail, not wanting to say what she was thinking. Aunt Karolina wouldn't kill herself, would she?

188

"I guess that is better than calling the gestapo. One of my other neighbors wanted to do that two hours ago, but decided she did not want to call attention to our street." He shrugged. "Makes me wonder what that neighbor is hiding, but it is none of my concern."

Ilse nodded. "Should we go around to the backdoor?"

"Out of sight of the soldiers, aye?"

"Something like that."

Between the two of them, they were able to pick the lock on the backdoor and get inside.

Ilse turned on lamps as she walked through the house, looking for her aunt. The house was disorganized, but not dirty. On the kitchen table, Ilse found a letter, the letter telling Aunt Karolina about the deaths of her husband and son. The ink was blurred in numerous places, she suspected from tears soaking the paper.

"I do not see her, do you?" she asked the man.

"*Nein*. Maybe check the bedroom?"

Ilse climbed the stairs, feeling the burn in her legs from her long bicycle ride. Her muscles had atrophied from lack of proper nutrition, and she was paying the price for that.

In the first bedroom they checked, they found her aunt sprawled out on the bed, one arm dangling over the edge. "Aunt Karolina, are you all right?" she said, rushing to her side. "Aunt Karolina?" She shook her.

Slowly, her aunt's eyes opened. They were bloodshot, with puffy bags underneath. From crying? Ilse could understand that.

"Who are you?" She raised herself up on one elbow and opened her eyes. They quickly opened wider. "Ilse? Ilse Seidel? Is that you?"

"*Ja*. It is me. Are you all right?"

She shook her head. "My life is in tatters, beyond repair." She sat upright and looked past Ilse. "Herr Hefner. What are you doing here?"

"Helping your niece. She tried ringing the bell, but there was no answer. We were worried and came in through the back."

Aunt Karolina sighed, then said, "I never asked anyone for help."

Ilse looked at Herr Hefner. She didn't know how to respond or what to do. She'd come here to let Karolina know that her brother had died. How could she possibly tell her that now, after the poor woman had just lost her husband and son and had her other son leave for the war?

Herr Hefner reached out and took hold of Karolina's hand. "Let us go downstairs and listen to some music. Do you still have your husband's record albums? He would want you to listen to them and think about the good days."

Karolina stared at him for some time, then got up, slowly, as if her bones ached. "I suppose you are right. I have not listened to music in ages."

Ilse followed the two of them down the stairs. Her baby kicked twice, reassuring her that it was still alive, which she'd worried about since she'd felt nothing from the baby during the long bicycle ride. She touched her belly, but with the coat and sweater on, she doubted the baby could feel her touch.

Downstairs, she took off her coat and knapsack and laid them on a bench in the foyer. Karolina was putting a record on the record player.

Ilse stood, watching, unsure whether she should go into the living room and make herself comfortable, or wait to be invited. Karolina finally turned around and noticed Ilse.

"Come on, child. Join us and listen to the most beautiful music there is."

Mozart played on the record player as Ilse sat down on a chair and closed her eyes. She hadn't heard music in years, and listening now, and resting her tired body, she felt like she could melt into the furniture.

She must have dozed off, because the music had stopped and she didn't remember listening to the whole concerto. Karolina was putting another record on, and Herr Hefner was gone.

"Did your friend go home?" Ilse asked.

"*Ja*. He is old and said he needed to get to bed. You were sleeping pretty good yourself. Did you ride a bicycle here?"

"I did. It was tiring, but it felt good, too."

"Why did you come here? Did you hear about Markus and Mathias?"

"I did. I am so sorry for your loss, Aunt Karolina." Ilse felt guilty for not telling her why she'd really come, but at least it wasn't a complete lie. She did hear about the loss, just from Herr Hefner. "Is there anything I can do to help you? Do you need help planning their funerals?"

"There will be no funerals." Her aunt's features darkened. "Not right now, anyway. I might never get their bodies."

She shouldn't have asked that question. *How thoughtless of me.* She should have remembered that's the same thing that happened with Vater. And now she was upsetting her aunt all over again.

"We can still have a memorial service for them. I can help you arrange that if you would like."

"*Nein*. Who would come? Most of the men and boys are away. The women are busy worrying about their men and how to feed and protect their young. *Nein*. It is not the time. Maybe later."

"What can I do? Do you want me to go home? I would really like to stay for a while." She hesitated, looking at her aunt, and wondering if she could trust her. "I . . . had a loss, myself, a few months ago. My boyfriend was killed. I am carrying his child and no one knows. You are the first person I have told."

Karolina didn't respond right away, and Ilse worried she'd throw her out on the street.

"You can stay here with me," she said, finally. "Tell your mother that I need help. Tell her I am too upset about losing my son and husband, and that now with Hermann away, too, I cannot manage on my own. She will let you stay. Then you can hide the pregnancy. They will never know."

Ilse was stunned. Did her aunt really mean that? Could that really work?

"You would do that for me? You will help me?"

"What else do I have?" Karolina said. "I am all alone in this big, empty house."

Ilse got up and went to her aunt, kneeled beside her, and took hold of her hands. "I promise not to be a burden. I will get a job and help pay for supplies and utilities. I will help cook and clean and do the laundry."

Karolina chuckled. "You do not have to sell me, child. I am happy to have you here. We will be good for each other."

CHAPTER SEVENTEEN

Lucas Landry, August 2017, Sacramento, California—

LUCAS PULLED HIS Jeep into the garage. Tawny wasn't home yet, but that was okay, because he really needed to take another look at his papers and see if he'd missed something. Oh, God, he felt more confused than ever about his family's past. The identity cards he'd found in the attic all showed that the people in his family—assuming that's what they really were—were of Aryan race. That made sense and that agreed with his belief. If they'd been Jewish, they would have been taken to concentration camps or killed straightaway. None of that happened, as far as he could tell from the diaries he'd read so far. That being the case, it must have been his American side of the family that was Jewish, assuming his grandfather was American, which he didn't have confirmation of, yet. Tom Landry. The name certainly sounded American, although the man could have changed it when he immigrated, if he immigrated and hadn't grown up in Germany. But if he was American, how did he end up living in Germany and marrying a German woman? The wife must have been German, right? That's what Anna and Elsa had said. They, the aunts, and their parents, had spoken German in their home in Germany, and they still had German relatives over there. Crap. Why the hell didn't Tom Landry write a diary?

In the house, Lucas set down the folder on his desk and pulled out the papers. He found the family tree drawings and spread them out. Okay, one of the missing pieces was the Landry section. Maybe if he drew up that section of tree, using the data his aunts had given him, it would start to fill in the puzzle. It couldn't hurt, right? Well, with the way it had been going, maybe it could. *Oh well, moving forward.*

He grabbed a piece of blank paper from the printer tray and started writing his great-grandparents' names on the Landry side: William and Rachel Landry. Below their names, their children: Ron, Teresa, and Tom, Tom's wife, Emelie, and Teresa's husband, Arthur. He didn't know any of their birthdates yet. He wrote Jewish beside their names with a question mark. He drew three vertical lines and started filling in the rest of the family data, going forward. Their children's names and birthdates, their spouses names, and then drew more vertical lines, listing their children, their spouses, their children's children, and on down the line.

He sat back and studied the pages as a whole. Okay, this was all well and good, but what he was still missing was linkage between all the families—between the Nagels, the Seidels, and the Landrys. He scratched his head.

If he couldn't find the answers here, he might have to fly to Germany and look there. *Crap!* That's where most of their documentation would hopefully be, if it wasn't destroyed during the war. And maybe if he could talk to some of those supposed German 'relatives' over there, they might give him what he needed. But he couldn't very well take vacation now. He needed to save his vacation for when the baby came. Besides that, Tawny couldn't travel in the last couple months of pregnancy, and he couldn't leave her alone for a couple of weeks while he gallivanted around Europe.

No. He couldn't go. Not now. Maybe not this year.

The garage door opened. Lucas quickly stuffed all his papers back into the zippered folder and stood up.

"You're home," Tawny said, walking in the door. "I thought we would get here before you."

Bianca ran across the room and threw her arms around Lucas's legs. "Daddy, daddy, I got to swim today. It was really, really, really fun." She looked up at him, smiling.

He reached down and scooped her up in his arms. "I'm proud of you, munchkin, for learning to swim at such a young age. Would you believe I didn't learn how until I was a grown up?"

"Daddy, you're kidding me." Bianca punched him on the chest and smiled.

"I am not kidding. I was afraid of the water. But you are fearless, my little munchkin."

She laughed, and he set her back down. She took off running up the stairs. In the last couple of months, she'd become an expert on stair climbing and descending.

Lucas strode over to the entry and hugged Tawny. "Did you have fun shopping with your mom?"

"Oh, indeed. The best. I have a car full of baby stuff, which I don't want to unload until tomorrow. I'm beat."

"What other baby stuff did we need? I thought we mostly had everything left over from when Bianca was a baby."

"Mostly we did. We got a double stroller."

He pulled back from her and stared. "Is there something you haven't told me?"

"No. Not twins. At least not that I know. But with a double stroller, Bianca can ride, too. She gets tired easily. And Mom says it will help her bond with the new baby."

Yeah, sounds like hogwash to me. He didn't tell her that.

"We got more baby clothes. The baby is a boy, so we needed boy things. And some of Bianca's baby clothes were pretty stained and didn't survive."

She took off her shoes and tossed them on the floor near the front door, instead of setting them on the shoe rack.

And women say men are sloppy.

"That doesn't sound like a car full of stuff," Lucas said.

"Oh, well, there's more. Newborn diapers, bottles, sterilizing equipment, a really nice dresser/changing table combo. And a few toys and clothes for Bianca."

Again, Lucas stared.

"Don't worry. I didn't break the bank. Mom paid for most of the stuff. She said she intends to spoil her grandchildren. They're her only grandchildren. What could I do? I couldn't say no."

"It's okay, I guess. I mean, we could afford it even if she didn't pay for most of it. I just hope the kids won't get too spoiled."

Tawny said, "They won't. How was your day? Did you get a lot of work done at your father's house?"

He filled her in on what he'd found and on his visit with his aunts. He left out the part about them being Jewish. Not that she would have a problem with it. She wouldn't. But it would likely have opened a can of worms—the dozens of questions kind.

"Are you going to go to Germany and meet with some of your relatives?" Tawny asked.

"Huh? How could I do that? No, I figure I can maybe try calling some of them. I might go on Ancestry.com, too. You know they advertise that on TV. Could help me with my search. Could be fun, too." Oh, God, he couldn't believe he was saying that. He was working on his genealogy. Wouldn't Dad roll over in his grave?

"You should go to Germany. You have a passport. Remember, we got passports last year when we were thinking of going with Mom to Mexico for a trip? Why not take a quick trip to Europe? Like you said, we have the money."

"Well, yeah, but I need to save up my vacation days for when the baby comes."

"They have something called 'family leave' now. You can use that after the birth. Use your vacation days for your research."

"No, think I'll wait. Maybe we can go there as a family next year. I've got enough notes now. It can rest awhile." There was that word again—awhile. He shook his head.

They let the conversation drop, and Tawny said, "I'll get started making us something for dinner. We had tacos and burritos at the mall. Are sandwiches okay?"

"Yeah. Make two for me, though. Those really big sandwiches you make with like three inches of lunchmeat."

"Okay little piggy, you got it," she teased.

"Hey, I'm not a little piggy, just a piggy," he teased back, glancing into his study on his way to the kitchen, remembering the drawings waiting for him in his zippered folder. They were calling out to him. Waiting for answers he didn't have. His neck and shoulders tensed up again, threatening to give him a pounding headache. *I don't need this kind of tension in my life. That's it. No more of this digging into the past.* He would put all thought about his ancestry, his Jewish roots, and his troubled family relationships aside and get back to living his life. Who needed to dwell in the past? Not him.

The following week, on Thursday afternoon, he received a phone call from the head boss. She wanted to see him in her office in half an hour. *Uh oh.* As he walked down the long hall to her office, his stomach clenched. What was wrong? Had he made a mistake or pissed off a patient?

He knocked on the closed door, waited a moment, then opened the door.

"Oh, Lucas, there you are. Come in and sit," Lucy Bryant said. Lucy was in her mid-fifties, tallish, with brown hair, brown eyes, and big rimmed eyeglasses. Not particularly threatening or scary looking, but she exuded an air of authority that said, don't disobey me. Lucas rarely had contact with her. She was his supervisor's supervisor. The person that nobody wanted calling them into her office. *Like getting called to the principal's office*, he thought.

"You're probably wondering why I asked you to come here," she said.

He nodded. *That was an understatement. Wondering? More like thinking I'm going in front of a firing squad.*

"The company is in the process of opening new clinics. Have you heard anything about it?" She leaned back in her chair and gazed at him. Like the supreme psychologist talking to a patient or potential patient, looking as if she were a mind-reader. Apparently she wasn't, because if she was, she would know how terrified everyone was of her. Or perhaps she did know.

"Uh, I remember hearing something about that in a staff meeting at the end of last year, I believe."

"That's right." She smiled. "We're very proud that our clinics are doing well. That's why we're opening three more, one in Chino, one in Redding, and one closer to here. In Sacramento."

He didn't respond, wondering where she was going with this. Seeing his left knee was bouncing nervously, he intentionally stopped it. He hoped she hadn't noticed.

She handed him a piece of paper with the addresses of the new clinics and maps showing their locations.

The Sacramento location was only a few blocks from his father's house.

"We are hiring for all three clinics, and since many of the employees will be recent graduates doing internships, we need experienced therapists there, too, therapists who can serve as supervisors for the interns."

Lucas's heart rate quickened. Was this what he thought, was she promoting him?

"We've looked at employee records from several of our clinics, and spoken to each of their supervisors. You're one of the employees we would like to send to either Chino or Sacramento to work with the new interns. For you we were thinking Sacramento. Would that interest you?"

He took a deep breath, trying not to let her see, then slowly let it out, nodding. "Yes, it would. I would, of course, have to talk this over with my wife. She works in a clinic here in Roseville."

What would Tawny say? Of course she would be happy for him, but she'd recently been passed up for a promotion at the clinic where she worked. He hoped it wouldn't reopen that wound.

"The clinic won't open until mid-October and we won't bring employees there until the beginning of October. As an incentive," she said, "you would get four weeks paid vacation, leading up to your October first start date."

Now his heart was thumping. Was this some kind of message? He didn't want to move into the house, did he? If he lived there, he would have to confront the nagging mystery of his family's past and the haunting memories of his parents.

But a promotion and a chance to give Tawny what she wanted? How could he say no to that?

"That sounds great," he said. "Uh, may I enquire about the salary?"

"Of course. With the added responsibility of being a supervisor, you would get a bump of ten thousand dollars a year."

That clinched it. He would live with the house. "Okay. Can I give my wife a call and discuss it with her?" As if he didn't know what she would say. Still, she would want him to include her in the decision. He would want to be included, if the shoe was on the other foot. That's what being partners meant.

"Certainly. Can you get back to me with your answer by the end of the day?"

"Will do, and thank you."

He hurried out of the office, back down the hall, and into his own tiny office. As he closed the door, he did a little dance, unable to contain himself any longer. Calming down, he sank down into his chair, and picked up the phone.

"Of course you should take the promotion," Tawny said, after he told her about the conversation in Lucy Bryant's office. "Do you know what this means? We can move into your father's house and you can go on your trip to Germany."

"I, uh," he said, scratching his head. "Yeah, I know. That's what you really want, right?"

"It's serendipitous," she said, her voice almost cooing. "Don't you see? We're meant to live there. I'll have time off after the baby is born. I can look around for a job closer to home while I'm on maternity leave. And you, mister, can go on that trip to Germany. Hang up the phone. Call Lucy Bryant and tell her you accept the job in Sacramento. Then call a travel agent and buy your plane ticket."

Lucas chuckled. "I guess you've made up my mind."

"Am I being too bossy? You can tell me if I am."

"No. Not too bossy. Just the right amount of bossy."

Breadcrumbs and Bombs

Tawny Landry, Sacramento, California, August 2017—

TAWNY SMILED SO wide she thought her face might crack. *Yay! We're going to move into the Victorian house and my amazing husband is getting a good promotion that he deserves! What more could I ask for? Bianca will be excited, too.* She chuckled to herself and went to pick up the phone again and dial her mother's number to give her the good news. But as she started to dial, she thought about the nursery they'd just finished painting in their house. Now they would have to paint it again in the new house. The thought of moving all their furniture and belongings pained her, too. They would definitely have to hire someone to do the moving. While Lucas was strong and capable, she couldn't lift anything heavy right now, not in her condition. Lucas was always stubborn when it came to hiring help for work around the house, but surely he would see the need in this situation.

She smiled again, picturing them in the new house. They could use Lucas's old bedroom for the baby, and paint it the same pale blue they'd painted the nursery in their house. Bianca would be thrilled to get to re-do her bedroom. And she would be getting a bigger bedroom.

Best of all, Tawny had a great excuse to look for another job. She could get away from Ed Ballantine. The jerk. She would have filed a sexual harassment lawsuit, if she didn't have to tell Lucas. Knowing Lucas, he'd probably punch her supervisor out if he knew he'd propositioned her. This had happened twice, first a few months ago, and then again shortly before telling her she wasn't getting the promotion. Both times, he used the line that she could play around all she wanted, because being pregnant already, she didn't have to worry about getting pregnant with some other guy's baby. Just thinking about it made her want to punch him herself. Jerk, jerk, jerk.

And that supposed complaint from one of her patients about her being black, she suspected, had been a ruse. Something to lower her self-confidence, make her afraid of losing her job, make her more pliable. Sure the patient could have said something about her race. Plenty of people were biased. But she had no control over being black and had only seen him the one visit. But that didn't mean her boss hadn't used it. Either way, the jerk had tried to play her.

Her phone buzzed. She picked it up. Her next client was here. She stood up, and went out to the waiting room to greet her patient.

CHAPTER EIGHTEEN

Christa Nagel, April-May 1945, Altstadt, Sudetenland—

CHRISTA FOLLOWED HER mother and siblings to the gathering place in front of Altstadt's town hall. Most people present were wearing their winter coats, as well as either winter hats or heavy scarves wrapped around their heads and necks, like Mutti. The women and girls wore dresses or skirts with blouses, and long socks or stockings. The boys and the elderly men wore long pants. Although it was springtime, snow could still fall, and no one knew where they were going or what the conditions might be, and they wanted to be prepared.

Christa held her three year old brother, Andreas, and carried a suitcase with his clothes and her own. Mutti held baby Dirk and carried a larger suitcase. The other kids each carried a small suitcase with their own clothes. Christa remembered that Mutti had sewn money and jewelry into the lining of their coats and some of their clothes over the past few weeks, expecting that if they were forced to leave, they could take a few valuables with them. She was right. The Czech soldiers were opening suitcases, tossing belongings on the ground, and confiscating anything valuable. People were crying and desperately re-stuffing their remaining things back inside their suitcases. One soldier hit an elderly woman in the stomach with the end of his rifle when she tried to keep him from taking her suitcase.

Some of their Czech neighbors were standing on the sidewalks, watching, some with their arms folded and one hand resting at their throat. Expressions blank. What were they thinking? That they might be next? Did any of them feel bad about what was happening to their neighbors?

Christa doubted the soldiers would be rounding up the Czechs. On the walk to the gathering place, people had talked, saying they heard on the radio that Germans were not welcome in the CSR any more. They didn't belong here. Months ago she'd heard on the radio that their country, and other countries in the region, like Poland and Hungary were going to expel the Germans when the war ended. But the war hadn't ended yet. Either way, the Czechs and Poles and Hungarians would be safe. She felt sure of that.

"Line up over there," a Czech soldier said, pointing straight ahead. "We leave in five minutes. Take only what you can carry."

Christa helped Mutti herd the other children along. "What do you think they are going to do with us?" Christa whispered to Mutti.

Mutti opened her mouth to answer, but a soldier walked over and told them to be quiet.

Christa surveyed the line of Germans she'd known her whole life. Children from school, their mothers, their grandparents, elderly people without family in town, shopkeepers, and—wait, where was their priest? She looked up and down the line. He wasn't there. What did that mean? She wanted to ask someone, but who would know?

Numerous bystanders—all of them Czechs—rushed over and started yelling obscenities at the Germans. Some spat at their feet. One of them was a man Christa recognized from the bank where her parents had an account.

Guards at the front of the line began leading them away from town; not toward the train station as Christa had expected. Guards on either side of the line and at the rear shouted at everyone to move, to follow their leaders.

A memory of Jews being taken from their homes, suitcases in hand, and put into trucks, sprang to Christa's mind. She remembered, too, that she'd later heard they'd been taken to concentration camps. Many were supposedly killed in gas chambers. Was this revenge? Would the same thing happen to them?

She shivered, even though the sun was out and it was a warm spring day. *We had nothing to do with what happened to the Jews. Don't they understand that?*

As they walked on and on and on, Christa's belly ached from hunger and her legs hurt from exertion. She'd been mostly hidden away in their farmhouse for months and unused to physical activity beyond short trips into town to obtain their rations.

Children of all ages sobbed or cried out, complaining they couldn't walk anymore. Elderly people moaned. Mutti, still recovering from her attack and suffering from massive bruises, stumbled and moaned in pain. The sounds of suffering became an eternal nightmare and Christa wanted to place her hands over her ears to block it, but how could she when her hands were full? And then people began to crumple and fall to the ground. Tears welled up in Christa's eyes. It was all too much.

"Please stop," Christa yelled out to the guards. "We need rest."

A young guard, maybe eighteen or nineteen, she guessed came over and said something in Czech.

Christa was too tired to work out the translation.

He spoke again, this time in German. "You must keep quiet. They will not stop until it is time to make camp. Do not draw attention to yourself. You will only get yourself killed."

She opened her mouth to speak, but Mutti put her hand on her arm to stop her. *Huh? Mutti was carrying the baby and a suitcase. How could she touch my arm?* Christa really looked at her mother, and then looked at the line of people. Mutti had set down her suitcase and people were walking around it. "Take my smaller suitcase, Mutti, and I will carry your bigger one," Christa said, knowing she was stronger and could carry it easier than Mutti could.

Mutti nodded and took the small suitcase from Christa.

Christa hurried back to retrieve the larger and heavier suitcase. Then she struggled to get back to her family, weaving in and out of the line, and finally reached them. Poor Giselle was at the back of their family group, looking as if she might collapse at any moment. Christa wanted to pick her up, but she already had her hands full.

Ernst glanced over his shoulder. Then, without speaking, he slowed down, and when he was even with Giselle, he reached down with one arm and scooped her up. She wrapped her arm around his neck and buried her face against his body, whimpering.

Christa smiled slightly at Ernst, thanking him the only way she could since they weren't supposed to speak.

As the sky grew dark, the soldiers finally stopped.

Christa looked ahead to see what was happening. They'd stopped alongside a large barn. She wasn't sure whether to be relieved or worried. Was this their final destination? Would they be herded inside and slaughtered like pigs going to a butcher?

"We camp here tonight," one of the soldiers proclaimed. He was gray-haired and fat. How could anyone be fat during the war? Most people were starving. "Everyone can relieve themselves and then settle into the barn for dinner and sleep."

Christa quickly rushed behind a bush, set Andreas and the suitcase down, and took care of business. Then she helped Andreas do the same. When they were ready, they found the rest of the family, and together they entered the barn.

The familiar aroma of cows and manure hit Christa, making her suddenly homesick for their farm—not as it had become but as it had been before the war, back when the family had cows and pigs and goats. Gazing around the barn, she realized it was empty except for dirty straw strewn all over the floors and bales of hay stacked up in messy piles. Had prisoners or soldiers or resistance fighters camped here before them?

That brought up a different question. She wasn't sure what to call their group of German civilians. Were they prisoners or refugees or something else?

Someone, an elderly man she didn't recognize, pulled bales down and started breaking them apart for people to use as bedding. Soon, others followed suit.

In a while, guards came in and handed them each a bowl of soup and a small chunk of bread.

Christa's mouth watered, until she stirred her soup and found that it was mostly dirty looking water with a few pieces of potatoes. *Mein Gott!* Still, she ate it. The bread was better, but awfully dry.

After eating, her family huddled together, as they'd been doing for the last few weeks, and settled in to sleep. Cold night wind, seeping through the gaps in the barn's boards, made Christa and her siblings and mother shiver. She was sure glad they'd worn their winter coats and hats. The snoring, crying, and moaning from all around her kept Christa awake for what seemed like hours, until she finally drifted off.

The next morning, before they headed out again, many people, including Christa and her family, took clothing out of their suitcases and put on as many of their extra clothes as they could—layer upon layer—so that they could leave the suitcases behind. Anything they couldn't wear stayed in the barn.

The days and nights of walking blended. Walk, break for a meager lunch, walk again, terrible dinner, sleep, walk again. Day in and day out.

Whenever someone fell down or refused to walk, the guards would beat them. As if they thought that would somehow make them walk better, faster. How stupid. Didn't the guards have feelings? Couldn't they see that the women, children, and elderly weren't able to keep up the pace that the physically fit soldiers could?

Christa wanted to scream at them, to tell them they couldn't treat people that way, but then she would remember what the young guard had told her on their first day: Don't draw attention to yourself.

Ernst did say something one day and got hit in the stomach for it. The meanest guard had rushed over and pointed his gun at Ernst's head. Mutti, carrying baby Dirk, had pleaded with him not to kill her boy.

The guard lowered his gun and gave Ernst a warning. He would not let Ernst get away with it again.

Sometimes, someone tried to escape from the 'column' as the guards called it. Christa had no idea why they called it that. The escapees were always caught, then shot by one of the guards. No escape attempt went unpunished. No escapee lived. Ever. Not from their column, anyway. Christa now knew what to call them: prisoners.

Once in a while guards allowed them to forage for potatoes or carrots or beets growing in a farmer's field. The farmers, it seemed, had left—maybe on a forced march like theirs, or maybe on their own. No one knew. But they took advantage and everyone picked whatever they could dig up to be confiscated and cooked for dinner. For that, the guards didn't complain. Some days they came across bushes with wild berries, and everyone went into a picking frenzy, including the guards. Those episodes told Christa the guards were hungry, too.

Even with the extra food, everyone grew thinner and thinner as the days went by. It helped slightly when other groups from other towns, along with their guards, joined them, doubling and tripling the size of their column, but also bringing more supplies and food.

Some people simply dropped dead during the walk. Instead of helping to bury the dead or even letting the prisoners bury their own family members, the guards just dragged the bodies over to the side of the road or trail and yelled at everyone to keep walking. No time for goodbyes or for grieving.

Occasionally, someone went to sleep at night and never awakened. Christa decided if she had to die on this trip that was how she wanted to go.

Unfortunately, she woke up every morning, day after day, week after week, wondering if the walking would ever end.

Petr Jaroslav, April-May 1945, Sudetenland—

PETR JAROSLAV WATCHED his group leader, Ivan Stransky, beat an elderly woman who had stopped walking simply because she needed to urinate, unable to hold it in any longer. Ivan had screamed at her to get moving. She'd cried and attempted to explain that she didn't have a choice, but Ivan hit her in the stomach with the butt of his rifle. Now she was bent over in pain, but Ivan screamed at her again. Watching as urine ran down the wretched woman's legs, Ivan then pummeled her in her face with his fists until she fell, bleeding, on the ground. An elderly man intervened, lifting her up, and began walking her back to the group.

Petr thought of his own grandmother, realizing she probably would have done the same thing if she'd been here. Petr decided Ivan was an ass. Old people's bladders don't work as well as a younger person's does. What was wrong with him? Petr hated the Germans, as much as Ivan and all the other guards did. But he conceded that these particular Germans—women, children, and old people—didn't look much like Nazi sympathizers. If anything, they looked much like his own family.

Family. The thought threatened to overcome him. *Dear God, why did I have to think of my family?* They were all dead. Antonin had been killed attempting to rescue his girlfriend from a concentration camp. Josef was killed fighting in the Resistance. Vera died from Tuberculosis. Kamila, Milena, Gabriel, as well as their mother, Jolanta, were all killed in their home by a bomb. Petr remembered rushing home from a Resistance meeting immediately after the bombing, finding Kamila and Jolanta dead under rubble, but Milena and Gabriel were still alive. Both died in his arms minutes later. Only his father might still be alive, somewhere. Petr didn't know. As far as Petr knew, his father had dropped off the face of the earth.

It was an effort every day for him to keep memories of his family locked away in the back of his mind. He needed those memories pushed far back, away from his conscious mind, because when they surfaced, he couldn't function, couldn't focus on his job. Right now, he needed to stay clear and focused. As decreed by the President, his job was to eliminate the Germans, expel them all, get them out of the CSR (Czech-Slovak Republic) and return it to the way it should have been—pure and untainted by foreign blood.

Of course, there'd been more, too. The Germans—all of them—needed to be punished for what they'd done, whether or not they'd been involved.

Most of Petr's comrades had no problem punishing them. Petr hadn't expected to have a problem, either. He'd killed his share of Germans, just not usually civilians.

Late at nights, the guards would take turns staying awake, watching for signs of the Red Army. The Russians had continued moving westward and were still fighting the German army, who wouldn't give up and admit they were losing the war. The war should have ended months ago, but the damned Germans couldn't admit defeat.

Constant gun battles and bombings made it difficult on everyone—Russians soldiers, German soldiers, German expellees, Czech soldiers, and Czech civilians. No one was safe, and the odd thing was that they weren't safe from either side. Russians were attacking and raping the German expellees, even those under Czech guards. If the Czech guards and their prisoners were in the wrong place at the wrong time, they could all be killed by bombs from either the German enemy or from Russian friendly bombings. Most times it just seemed like insane chaos.

How or when the war would finally end he couldn't say, but he knew for sure which side would win. Everyone had known for months now that the Germans were losing. It was only a matter of time. He just prayed it would be a very short time.

Over the weeks, several refugee columns had merged, bringing ethnic German civilians from small towns scattered over the area. When they met up, usually by accident, the guards would exchange what little they knew. The soldiers in charge would then decide whether to join up or go on separately. More often than not, they merged, and why not? There was safety in numbers. There were more mouths to feed, but having more guards and more weapons meant they could defend themselves if any German soldiers or Russians threatened them.

Petr sighed, sitting by a fire in the evening, finishing the few bites he had left from his dinner of bread and soup. At least the soup the guards got had more potatoes than the soup the prisoners got, but not much more. Tonight, the woods were quiet except for the chirping of crickets and other insects. What would tomorrow bring? No one knew, except pain and hunger. Those were a given.

The next day, the Russian and Germany armies were battling it out in a nearby town. The sound of gunfire and bombs was incessant and deafening. The bombs sent thick black smoke into the sky, warning the guards where they needed to stay away from. Twice, the guards had to hide with their column in abandoned buildings because the fighting became too close for comfort.

After the second occurrence, Ivan gave the all-clear and moved their large column out again, heading toward the next town, one that supposedly—according to Intel they'd received from the Czech militia—was free of armies.

The Intel was wrong. Two hours later gunshots rang out from amongst the trees to their right, and the guards quickly herded the prisoners towards the far side of the road. This time, though, the shots were coming straight at the guards and the prisoners.

The guards returned fire, not sure who they were fighting. And then Petr saw three men in German uniforms, coming at him. He shot and killed the first, then the second. The third soldier had gotten off several more rounds while Petr had dealt with the first two soldiers. As he turned to take on the third soldier, he saw the enemy's gun aimed directly at him. Before he could react, the soldier went down, another guard taking the shot. Petr wiped his brow and realized his hand was shaking. That was too close. Good to know someone had his backside.

Hearing no more gunfire, he continued to scan the area, while four guards searched the woods on foot and the remaining guards kept watch on the prisoners. He wasn't even sure at this point how many guards there were in their column.

"Help us! Please," someone yelled from behind.

Petr turned and looked toward the voice.

One of the women in the column was kneeling on the ground, holding onto her young son. She looked up at Petr with pleading eyes. "He has been shot. Please help us."

He'd watched that particular family, day after day, struggling along like all the others. He didn't know their names.

One of the guards, a brusque guy who always rubbed him the wrong way, rushed over and pointed his rifle at the boy.

"No. Do not shoot him," Petr shouted. He rushed over and moved the other guard aside. "Where is your son wounded?" he said in German.

"His leg," the woman said.

"I am trained in first aid," Petr stated. "I will examine the wound and see if I can help. I cannot promise anything."

The woman nodded, her eyes pleading. Her other children gathered around, leaning down and crying. Petr recognized the oldest girl, pretty girl with long blonde braids. He'd talked to her on the first day and cautioned her to not get noticed. She looked to be around the age his sister Vera would have been if she'd lived.

He lifted the boy's pant leg, wiped the blood away with a cloth from his pack, and studied the wound. "Looks like the bullet went straight through." He looked around the ground and found the bloody bullet.

"What does that mean?" the woman asked.

"I am going to use alcohol on the wound to disinfect it and then I will bandage it. He is lucky. Damned lucky. He will have difficulty walking for a while, but he will live."

The woman cried and said, "Thank you."

"What is your name?" Petr asked the boy while he was working on his leg.

"Fritz. Fritz Nagel."

Ilse Seidel, April-May 1945, Memmingen, Germany—

AFTER ILSE SPOKE with her aunt the night of her arrival in Biberach, she sent word to her parents via a messenger her aunt had told her about, that she was going to stay with her aunt for a while. She told them about Aunt Karolina's husband and oldest son being killed, and her younger son being recalled to the war. Ilse also told them that she didn't want to further crush her aunt by telling her about Vater. She would give her time to recover, first. The following week, she received a return message, saying that she should stay as long as Karolina needed her. But they also had sad news. Johann had been killed, also, in the war. She tried to cry for her brother, but tears wouldn't come. He got what was coming to him. Was it wrong for her to feel that way? She didn't know.

She and Aunt Karolina had stayed home for those first few weeks after her arrival, talking, getting to know each other. Ilse felt closer to Aunt Karolina now, than she did to her own mother.

After the message from her parents, Ilse felt free to take a job. She and Aunt Karolina had stumbled across a bulletin board with an advertisement that the local orphanage needed help. They'd both gone there right away and interviewed. The nun in charge told them they'd been overwhelmed with the number of orphans they were getting. Sudeten Germans were arriving every day in Germany, and especially here in Bavaria, and with them came many orphaned babies and children.

Ilse loved working with the kids, as did her aunt. They played with the children, read to them, and sometimes sang songs with them. As an added benefit for Ilse, they also interviewed prospective parents to find homes for the orphan children. Her decision about whether to keep her baby or find a home for the baby or them both loomed over her like a dark thundercloud. The time for that decision was quickly approaching.

In mid-May, an entire company of Americans soldiers thundered in and took over the town of Biberach. From Christa's vantage point at a window inside the orphanage, it was not a hostile takeover, but seemed a joyous event. She, and the other employees, the nuns, and the older children ran outside to watch as the parade of vehicles approached. People lined the streets, cheering and waving at the American soldiers. The war was finally over.

On that momentous day, Ilse felt a flood of emotions. She no longer had to fear repercussions for having helped an American airman—at least not from the Americans in control of their town. She might not even need to worry anymore about the danger to a half-Jewish baby. But she wasn't going to let her guard down. Not yet. She'd learned, quite well, that you couldn't count on anyone or anything. She wanted to say 'except for family', but her brother had made even that statement impossible.

A couple weeks later into the occupation, someone knocked on the front door in the early evening, while dinner was cooking on the stove and music was playing on the record player.

Ilse wiped her hands on a dish towel and went to the door. When she saw her mother standing there, she couldn't believe her eyes. Her mother's gaze went down to Ilse's bulging stomach, and Ilse wanted to turn and run away, but stood frozen in place.

"So this is why you did not come home," she spat. "You did not want to tell us you were carrying a bastard."

"I . . . I am sorry, Mutter. I wanted to spare you the shame."

"You will put that bastard up for adoption. I do not ever want to see it. Your grandparents will never know about it. Do I make myself clear?"

Ilse nodded, not knowing what else to do.

Mutter pushed her way into the house. In the foyer, she stood gazing at the living room, taking in the fireplace, the music, and the quietness. "You are living an easy life here, I see. Another reason you did not come home."

"Not easy," Karolina said, standing up and turning to face her sister-in-law. "Ilse and I both have jobs. We work hard and help other people. Shame on you for judging us."

Mutter's mouth gaped open. Then she chided, "She has not sent any money back to the family."

Ilse walked over to the kitchen table and returned with an envelope addressed to her mother. "I was going to mail this tomorrow."

Mutter opened the envelope and pulled out a letter and cash. As she read the letter, tears began streaming down her cheeks.

Ilse wrapped her arms around her mother. "I am sorry, Mutter. I wanted to tell you in person about the baby, but I was scared."

Mutter patted her arm. "I am sorry, too, sorry I snapped at you. Everything has been so miserable, and I . . . I should be happy the war has ended, but nothing has changed for us. We still have nothing. Not enough food. No income, no husband."

"I know. That is why I am trying to help out any way that I can. I give a small portion to Aunt Karolina for allowing me to stay here. I keep a small portion. The rest goes to you and the family."

Mutter smiled meekly. "Thank you, dear."

Karolina said, "How did you get here, Maria? You did not ride a bicycle, did you?"

"The trains are running again. Even so, I will not be able to visit often, because we have little money for train fares. But it had been too long since I saw Ilse and I had to make sure she was safe."

The image of Mutter riding a bicycle made Ilse smile.

"When do you go back? Will you stay a few days? You can stay here. We have room. We are getting ready to eat dinner."

"Oh, well, I need to get back home tomorrow, to the children, but it would be lovely to stay here overnight and visit."

Ilse said, "Let me hang up your coat. Sit in the parlor and rest. We will have dinner ready in a few minutes."

After a dinner of roasted chicken—the first chicken they'd eaten in two years—with potatoes and carrots, they sat in the living room, feeling stuffed, and talked, really talked. Ilse told her mother about Ron, about his airplane getting shot down, and about his injury and pneumonia. She even told her about Ron getting shot by the Nazis, though she didn't say Johann was involved. Her mother had suffered enough. The only other thing she left out was that Ron was Jewish. She didn't know why she held it back, precisely—after all, she'd told Karolina—but maybe it had something to do with Johann's betrayal, she thought.

The next day, Saturday, both had the day off from work, and they were getting along so well, Mutter decided to stay one more night. They walked around town, stopped at a café and each ordered coffee and a piece of cake. The first cake any of them had eaten in years. It seemed that with the Americans' arrival came food and businesses.

By the time Mutter left Biberach on Sunday afternoon, Ilse was sad to see her go. They'd talked more in the past day than they had in years, it seemed. Why did it have to take so long to get to really understand each other?

Over the week that followed, the town grew livelier and the people happier. It wasn't that everything suddenly changed with the war over. It didn't. The streets were still congested with military vehicles and soldiers, but with American vehicles and American soldiers. They didn't threaten, didn't rob, didn't rape or beat anyone down.

The rest, having slightly more food and business, helped, too.

On Friday, after work, Ilse and Karolina walked home together, as usual, taking the same route and around the same time. Today, however, Ilse spotted a tall dark-haired man in an American military uniform. He was standing on a corner watching them as they crossed the street, coming his way. For a second, she thought he was Ron and her heart quickened. Oh, if only it had been him. She would have run into his arms and not cared what anyone thought.

He smiled and removed his hat when they walked past.

When they arrived at the house, Karolina said, "What is this?"

Ilse watched as she pulled off an envelope taped to the front door. She ripped it open, reading the notice inside, and sighed.

"What is it? Is it bad news again?"

"Hmm. Not sure. The government has assigned two families to live here with us. Sudeten Germans. The letter says that all houses with extra living space will be required to share their homes temporarily, until the Sudeten Germans can be assimilated into Bavaria."

Breadcrumbs and Bombs

"Does the government know I am staying here with you?" Ilse asked.

"*Ja.* The letter mentions you. But it does not matter. It is a four bedroom house, plenty of room for more people. It says two additional families are coming, taking one bedroom per family."

"That is all right with you?"

Karolina shrugged. "I guess we will not get lonely."

CHAPTER NINETEEN

Lucas Landry, September 2017, Sacramento, California—

LUCAS SLIPPED HIS boarding pass into his carry-on bag and made his way to the security gate of the airport, stepping to the end of the line. His heart raced with excitement as he perused the crowded airport. People were rushing in all directions, pulling suitcases on wheels, holding hands of their small children, and kissing loved ones goodbye. A voice over the loud speaker called for someone—a Reginald Baker—to meet his party at gate G4. The line was slowly inching close to the security gate, where people frantically emptied pockets, removed belts and shoes, and placed their carry-ons onto the x-ray scanner belt.

It was really happening. In fifteen hours, give or take, he would be landing at the Munich airport, where someone name Milo Jaroslav would meet him. From there, they would take a train south to Biberach. Lucas recognized the name Jaroslav from some of the diaries, but no one had told him yet how the Jaroslav family was connected with the Landry family. *Guess I'll find out.* He took a deep breath and stepped forward as the line moved again.

"Boarding pass and identification," a security officer finally said, holding his hand out.

"Oh, yeah, got it here," Lucas said. *Crap, why did I stick it in my carry-on bag?* He fumbled with compartments for a moment and finally unzipped the side pocket, pulled out the boarding pass, and handed it to the officer.

"Identification and passport."

"Uh . . . ." He waved his hands, sighed, and opened the zippered compartment again to retrieve his passport. Then he reached into his pant pocket and pulled out his wallet, slipped out his driver's license, and handed both items to the officer, who looked bored out of his mind.

The guy checked everything over and handed it back, motioning for him to move forward. A uniformed woman instructed him to take his laptop out its bag, place both items, along with his carry-on bag onto the conveyor, then remove his shoes, wallet, keys, etc. and place them into a plastic bin. As the person in front of him exited the metal detector, the same woman motioned him to walk into the metal detector, told him to lift his arms and stand on a particular location. A moment later security motioned him to move forward, patted him down, and ran a hand held device over his person, then directed him to move forward, where he retrieved his things. Quickly refilling his pockets and grabbing his things to keep the line moving, Lucas spotted a bench, sat down, fastened his belt, and put on shoes. *Note to self: next time weare slip-on shoes. Did I forget anything?*

He followed directions, and when he reached the assigned gate, he checked the nearby departures and arrivals board. So far, it showed his flight was on schedule, which meant he had at least an extra hour to eat lunch.

He browsed around, stopping briefly to look at books and magazines at a gift shop and purchased one novel. Several restaurants had their menus posted outside. *Wowzer. Which leg do they want?* Finally he found a little pizza joint that had 'affordable' prices, meaning they were only priced about four dollars higher than anywhere outside of the airport. He ordered a personal pan and drink, waited about ten minutes, then picked up his pizza and looked for a table. The tables available were either four-person table or two-person tables. He sighed, sitting down at the smaller variety, which was still too big for one person. He sighed again. He was excited about the trip, but thought of leaving Tawny and Bianca at home weighed on him. How was he was going to get through two whole weeks without them?

As he munched on overcooked, underachieving pizza, he tried to picture the cool places he would see and the photographs he would take and post on his Facebook page. Tawny had been excited for him, insisting he take lots and lots of photos and post them as soon as he could. "That way," she'd said, "it will feel like we aren't far apart."

After a lunch only memorable through indigestion, he headed back to his assigned gate and sat reading for half an hour. Several people who'd been sitting around him got up and left. What was going on? He grabbed his bags, pulling the carry-on on its wheels and slinging the laptop bag strap over his shoulder, and went to the electric board. "Good grief!" he said out loud. The airline had moved his flight to a different gate, due to a flight delay at this particular gate and hadn't bothered to announce it.

Some other passengers noticed his reaction, got up and flocked over, looking at the board as he left. He looked back and noticed them all rushing down the corridor behind him, looking for the correct gate.

When his plane finally arrived and boarding began, Lucas felt like a young boy waiting to go to Disneyland. Theme parks had been exciting and fun when he was younger, but now, an overseas flight—well, he couldn't imagine anything more enticing.

He and Tawny had talked about one day flying to South Africa, where she'd lived as a little girl. At the time, he hadn't been all that enthusiastic. Now that he was researching his family tree, Tawny told him a couple days ago that she wanted to research hers, too, and wanted to go to South Africa and do some of that research in person, the way he was doing.

He'd found himself getting excited about the prospect. Not bouncing off the walls excited, but intrigued. Why? He wasn't sure, but he suspected the whole task of researching his history had morphed into something exciting for them both. It had developed into something that they could share with each other and their children, something that would stay with them forever.

On the airplane, he found his seat, stuffed his carry-on bag and laptop bag into the overhead compartment, and sat down. When the flight attendant came around and told him to fasten his seat belt because the plane would be departing soon, he felt a bit lightheaded.

A short time later, the plane began to taxi and the pilot greeted the passengers and told them about the flight.

Oh God! This is really happening. Lucas's palms started sweating and his heart was pounding. Was this fear-of-flying? He'd heard about it, but since he'd never flown before, how could he have known he had it?

Soon after the pilot told the attendants to prepare for take-off, Lucas was pushed back into his seat and the plane accelerated down the runway. When the plane tilted upward and the engine noise escalated, he gripped both arm rests so tightly that the middle-aged woman seated next to him said, "It's okay. Once we get up to cruising altitude it won't be bad. This your first time flying?"

"Yeah."

"My advice, have a couple drinks and sleep through as much of it as you can. That's what I do."

"Thanks." Somehow, the woman's words had distracted him long enough that the plane was now flying more level and the noise had quieted. His heart rate returned to normal, and he attempted to relax.

Soon he decided that the flight was a piece of cake—except that it became way too long and his legs cramped from sitting squeezed into matchbox-sized chair spacing. Because he'd gotten a good deal on the airfare, he accepted the punishment. But he already dreaded the return flight and the take-off. That part he didn't like one little bit.

Finally bored enough to doze midway through the flight, his dreams were filled with childhood memories, in particular, two family road trips, one to Carlsbad Caverns and another to Yellowstone. Those had been great times. In his dreams the two separate trips had morphed into one another, clear and in living color, as if the trip was happening now, and not ten or fifteen years ago. Yet waking now, he realized he'd somehow forgotten about, or pushed to the back of his mind, those good times they'd shared.

He figured the memories had surfaced now because he was on another big trip. Different from those childhood trips, but all were major adventures for him.

He wiped the sleep from his eyes and tried finding something to watch on the personal media screen in front of him.

He tried watching a comedy movie, but instead of laughing, somehow it made him sad. It was about a family with two young boys. Why was he missing his parents now? After all this time. That made him wonder how much his fight with his father five years ago had colored his current views of his father, turning his father into some kind of monster that didn't actually exist.

But Seth had told Lucas he didn't like their father either, that he had negative memories, too. Seth had also had a big fight with Dad. Anger again might also have discolored his views. Lucas decided to think on that another time. Now was the time for his adventure to start.

After disembarking the plane, he followed the crowd—it wasn't like there was any choice to be made. Packed in the middle of a throng of passengers from various flights, he walked along until there were signs ahead, and booths. Ah. This was where he had to show his passport and visa.

After having his passport checked, he followed everyone down to baggage claim and retrieved his suitcase. At the exit, standing near the door, a young man was holding up a sign: Lucas Landry.

Lucas strode over to the man, uncertain whether he should trust a stranger holding a sign with his name on it. Before deciding, the young man looked at him and inquired in German, "Are you Lucas Landry? I'm Milo Jaroslav."

"Uh . . . " Lucas stumbled. With the long flight, time change, and sporadic sleep, he was having trouble thinking of the German words to respond. After a few seconds, his mind cleared and the German words came back to him.

"Uh, yes, I'm Lucas. Nice to meet you. Thank you for doing this, uh, meeting me and helping me out, I mean."

"I'm happy to help." The man smiled. "Are you ready?"

"Yes."

Milo lifted Lucas's suitcase and hurried out the automatic doors, Lucas struggling to keep up his pace.

Milo looked over his shoulder and said, "The next train leaves in fifteen minutes. If we hurry, we can catch it. That train will take us to the main station where we'll board another train to Biberach. The first ride is short. The second is long."

225

They arrived at the gate for the train, Lucas out of breath, and Milo said, pointing, "Ah, here it comes."

Lucas shuffled onto the train a few minutes later and plopped onto a seat. *Ah, relief.* Who would have thought that after sitting on an airplane for more than a dozen hours, he'd be happy to sit again? *Let's chalk it up to jet lag,* he thought.

He gazed around the train compartment. Impressive. Rather luxurious for a train. Nice seats. Clean. Restrooms at the end of each section. Wow. The train left the station, accelerating at a good clip, but it didn't set his body into turmoil the way the airplane had initially. The gentle sway as the train marched actually lulled him half to sleep.

The rest of the journey went by in a blur, literally. Disembark one train. Take escalators. Slog up or down multiple staircases. He felt disoriented, not able to keep track. Good thing Milo knew where to go. Board another train. Hunt for seats. This train was too crowded. People were actually speaking German all around him. All the train billboards and information were in German. *Looks like I'm in Germany. Wow!*

Scenery he'd longed to see, whizzed by blurry, sleep-deprived eyes. He'd expected to talk with Milo while on the train, but they weren't able to find seats together on the crowded train. That was okay. It gave him a chance to sleep a little. It wasn't until they were almost to Biberach, according to the electronic screen inside the train, that Milo was able to sit next to Lucas, people having left at earlier stops.

By the time they arrived at their destination, Lucas's legs were really stiff and sore.

"My father is picking us up here at the station and taking us to my great-grandmother's house," Milo said. "She invited you to stay there. Change of plans. I hope you don't mind."

"No, that's okay." He tried to remember what Milo had told him about his family. "Wait, who is your great-grandmother? Did you tell me her name? Sorry, I'm not altogether with it. Jet lag."

Milo chuckled. "I know all about jet lag. You're not an experienced traveler, are you?"

"Definitely not."

Tawny Landry, Sacramento, California, September 2017—

"MOMMY, WHAT'S WRONG?" Bianca asked, looking up at Tawny, concern in her eyes. She leaned in toward her mother and patted her cheek. "Are you sick, Mommy?"

They were sitting together on the sofa, watching cartoons and snacking on popcorn. Tawny had been trying to remain still and not make a big deal out of pain that was probably nothing more than Braxton-Hicks contractions. Normal pains. They had to be, right? It was too early for the baby. Besides, her water hadn't broken and she wasn't having any spotting or any severe pains.

"Oh, it's nothing, sweetie. Mommy's just having a few little . . . twinges. The baby is probably adjusting himself and trying to get comfortable. You know, how you and I wiggle around and bump each other when we fall asleep here on the sofa." She tickled Bianca, making her giggle.

"Maybe we should lay down and see if he gets more comfortable," Bianca said after she stopped giggling.

"You know, that's a good idea. Let's try it."

Bianca stood up to allow Tawny to lie down. After Tawny was comfortable, Bianca shook her head. "Mommy, that's not going to work. Your tummy is too fat. I'll lay down on the other end."

Tawny laughed. "Are you calling me fat?"

Bianca gave her a big grin, showing her baby teeth were filling in nicely.

"Okay, just for that, you better watch out. My feet are bigger than yours and they can kick."

Bianca pulled her legs up close to her chin, and said, "Hey, where's my popcorn?"

Tawny handed her the bowl.

After putting Bianca to bed two hours later, she laid back down on the sofa, stretching out, then picked up the phone and called her mother, Lindelani. They talked for a couple minutes about what they'd each done during the day.

"Is something bothering, sweetie? You sound tired. Are you missing Luke?" Lani asked.

"Well, yes, I'm missing him. He's only been gone a couple days, but I already miss him a lot. I didn't think it would be this hard."

"The time will fly by. And you know, they always say that absence makes the heart grow fonder. Or . . . I don't know. Something like that."

Tawny chuckled. "You're right. It's just that I've been . . . well, I don't want to alarm you. Please tell me you'll stay calm."

"All right. I'll try. What's going on?"

Tawny squirmed and bit her lip for a second as another pain came. When it had passed, she said, "I've been having pain and cramps off and on all day. Nothing terrible. And before you ask, no, the cramps aren't spaced evenly and don't seem like labor pains."

"Did you call your obstetrician?"

"No. It's Sunday."

"Medical clinics have doctors who are on-call. All medical clinics do. Especially obstetricians."

"I know that. It's just that I don't want to make a big deal out of it. It's probably nothing."

"Well, it was worrying you enough that you called me."

Tawny closed her eyes. "That's different. You're my mother. I can tell you anything, can't I?"

"Of course. And I will tell you to call your obstetrician and your husband."

"Oh, no, no," she spouted, eyes wide open, feeling like a dragon spitting fire. "I'm not calling Lucas unless I absolutely must. This trip is too important. I'm not going to ruin it for him."

"Fine. I do get that. But at least call your doctor. Most likely she'll have you go in for a quick exam to make sure everything is okay, then send you home and tell you to rest and stay off your feet as much as possible."

"Okay. I call her in the morning if the symptoms are still there."

CHAPTER TWENTY

Christa Nagel, April-May 1945, Sudetenland—

WHEN THE GUARDS yelled out for everyone to stop, Christa looked around and listened for what could be happening, but she saw nothing special. No gun shots. No other column joining them. No bombed out vehicles blocking the road. Nothing. They never stopped without a reason. That hadn't happened before, not once in the last four or five weeks they'd been walking. Of course, she wasn't counting the first few days, before the prisoners had learned what happened to anyone who created a scene or disrupted the walk in any way. Those first days, a young child had cried and cried, getting on everyone's nerves. The girl's mother had desperately tried to console her daughter, but nothing worked. The mother told the guards that she needed to change the baby's diaper. A nasty guard, one already hated by everyone, Christa felt sure, walked over and shot the girl in the head and dumped her limp body on the side of the road. The message being that anyone who kept the procession from moving would be either beaten or killed. Sometimes both. If they didn't hate him before, they sure did after that. Something was about to happen. She set Andreas down on the ground and shook her arms to get the circulation going better. Whenever she'd carried him or Giselle for any length of time, she'd felt guilty for being thankful they were so thin and underweight for their ages. Would she go to hell for her bad thoughts?

While they were stopped, people used the opportunity to relieve themselves in the bushes alongside the road instead of out in the open, but the guards stood by, watching them like vultures. Christa wondered if she would ever get used to prying eyes.

People sat down on the street or alongside it in the dirt, closing their eyes and trying to catch a few moments of sleep. Mothers changed their babies' diapers or tried to breastfeed them. Children didn't run and play as they would have back at home. Their energy had long since evaporated.

After a while, the sound of heavy vehicles approaching made everyone jump. The guards held their weapons up, pointing toward the sound, but when the trucks arrived and they saw who was driving, they lowered their weapons. The engines stopped, the drivers got out, and the guards and drivers greeted each other in Czech.

Christa remembered some of the Czech language she'd learned in school. Their guards had been expecting the trucks. This was a pre-arranged rendezvous.

"On the trucks. *Schnell!* No dawdling," the guard in charge said in German, mispronouncing words, whether deliberately or not, she couldn't tell. His name was Ivan. Every time she heard someone say his name, she thought of Ivan the Terrible from her history lessons, although this particular Ivan wasn't Russian. He was Czech.

Directly in front of Christa and her family, a young woman—undoubtedly the prettiest in the column—asked one of the guards with whom she'd become somewhat chummy, at least

231

as far as anyone could under the circumstances, "Where are they taking us?"

"To an internment camp," he said. "Theresienstadt."

Christa gasped. She'd heard of the place. A concentration camp.

The woman said, "We're going to be in there with the Jews?"

"No. They've been released. Those that survived, anyway. Move along." He shoved her forward and walked down the line, barking orders at them all.

Once he was out of earshot, Christa whispered to Mutti, "Did you hear what he said about where they're taking us."

"*Ja.* I do not want to walk anymore, but that place . . . it is too horrible to image what they will do to us there."

"Move it," another guard said. "Get up into the truck. Now."

Mutti, Christa, and Ernst lifted the younger kids up and then climbed up, themselves. The truck was nearly full. Three more people were shoved up into the truck and then boards were put in place to keep anyone from getting out. The guards routed other people onto the next truck.

They were all crowded together in the truck and no one could move. Julia held baby Dirk. The rest of the kids had to stand. No choice. Christa, Mutti, and Ernst couldn't pick them up in the tight space. Everyone stunk. Fortunately, the fresh air coming in around them as the vehicle moved toward their final destination made some of the stink fly away.

Finally, the truck jerked to a stop. Christa couldn't see the camp and wasn't sure if they'd reached the camp or not.

After several minutes, guards came and opened up the back of the truck, yelling for them to get out and line up.

Line up. Oh *Gott*, were they going to execute them? She'd seen them do that once when a small group of prisoners had tried to escape. They'd captured them, first, then lined them up and fired.

Petr Jaroslav, June-July 1945, Sudetenland—

SO THIS WAS the famous Theresienstadt. Earlier in the war the gestapo or the Wehrmacht, Petr wasn't sure which, had evacuated the whole population of this small walled town in North Bohemia, along the Ohře River. They'd converted the once peaceful town into a ghetto, as they called it, for some forty thousand Jews, if Petr could believe what he'd been told. He didn't have a reason to not believe it. Theresienstadt had been the concentration camp where Antonin and Rebeka had been killed by Nazis. The horrendous place where tens of thousands of Jews had been held and treated like dirt. Worse than dirt. It might not have been an extermination camp. He didn't know for sure. But he knew that many thousands had died here—of starvation, appalling conditions, or diseases. Thousands of others had been transferred from here to Auschwitz and other extermination camps. Theresienstadt had, from all accounts he'd heard, been a holding tank. It was also the place that the Nazis had tried to tell the world was a good place, because they'd come under scrutiny when rumors of death camps had circulated. In an effort to stop the rumors, the Nazis had allowed British reporters inside, once, to see how wonderful it was. All fake. They'd only shown the reporters a small section of the 'town' with dressed up prisoners, simulating a regular town life. The photos printed in the newspaper article were meant to deceive the public. Petr had no doubt the reporters had believed what they saw and what they'd written, but Petr and everyone else in his inner circle certainly didn't.

He followed the column of ragged, and some almost skeletal, Germans and the rest of the guards inside the gate and then through another gate—an archway with a sign that read 'Arbeit Macht Frei', which he translated in his head as 'Work makes (one) free'.

He stopped inside and waited with the other guards from his unit. The newly arrived guards, he'd been told prior to taking this assignment, would live here in guards' quarters and work wherever they were assigned. For how long, he didn't know.

Rows and rows of buildings—barracks, he assumed— sat to one side. In one area, he could actually see the remnants of the original town.

"You," the officer in charge said to Petr, "you'll be working in the children's section. Find yourself a bunk in the guards' quarters while the prisoners are being processed. After you're changed into your new uniform and settled in, report to me and I'll take you to the children's section."

Petr nodded and followed some of the other guards from his unit who had been given similar instructions.

Hours later, after all the newly arrived Germans had been processed, the guards were shown to their various sections. Along the way, Petr passed by one section that he was told held prisoners of war and political prisoners. Glancing into that section, he noted that they all had shaved heads and wore ragged convict uniforms, obviously worn by previous prisoners. Like the Jews, according to his sources. Obviously payback.

Petr held his nose later on that evening, as he entered the children's section. Here, many of the children had runny noses, were barefoot, and stank to high heaven. Most still wore their own clothes and didn't have shaved heads. Many of the kids here had been in his column, arriving earlier in the day, and he felt a strange sense of needing to protect them.

"Where are your mothers?" he asked in German.

"We do not know," a girl of about five years of age said. Her face was smudged with tears mixed with dirt.

A toddler Petr recognized was curled up on a bunk, surrounded by a boy and girl who were unrelated to him, but were trying to comfort him, all the same.

Numerous children he didn't recognize stared at him, eyes wide with terror.

Further back, in the corner, huddled together on a narrow cot, he spotted more children from his column. The young girl he'd spoken to on the first day, along with her brothers and sisters, including the boy who had been shot in the leg. Fritz, something or other.

But where was the baby and their mother?

He strode over to them. "Where is the rest of your family? Do you know where they have been taken?"

The oldest girl said, "Mutti and the baby are gone. We do not know what happened. We are scared. Do you think . . . do you think something bad has happened to them?"

Something about the mournful look in their eyes once again reminded him of his siblings. *Don't get involved. Do your job and remember they are Germans.*

He turned and walked away, looking around the rest of the quarters on his way outside. Standing for a few moments in the fresh night air, he took a deep breath and sighed. How can anyone stand it in there? The stink, the haunted faces of defenseless children, the feeling of pain permeating the air, pain from countless people who'd been trapped there over the years. Jews, war criminals, resistance fighters, and now ethnic German civilians, mostly women, children, and elderly.

Bile rose up in his throat.

He rushed back to the guards' section and lit a cigarette, wishing he hadn't taken this job. Had he really thought that seeing this place in person would help him get over Antonin and Rebeka's deaths? How could he have been so stupid?

Screams permeated the air, and he ran toward them, wondering what was happening. And where were the rest of the guards? Didn't anyone hear the screams?

He arrived at a women's barracks and yanked open the door. The screams were deafening. He rushed forward to help.

Guards were raping women. Beating them. One poor woman was trying to fight off three guards.

Petr rushed toward them to intervene, but a burly guard yanked him back. "You cannot help them. Keep your nose out of it. If you want a turn, you will have to wait. If you want to stop it, you had best get yourself outta here. You cannot do anything."

Cannot do anything? No one was going to help these women? He ran his hand through his dirty hair. The women were German. He got it. To the guards they deserved what they got, but it was wrong. He and his father and brothers had fought in the Resistance because they wanted to stop the evil that the Nazi party had brought to their country and to the world.

But revenge on women who hadn't been soldiers? That made no sense. How could repeating the atrocities of the German army make Petr's comrades any better?

He turned and slumped back through the barracks, embarrassed to look at the women who were crying and trying to hide, afraid for their lives or for their families. A baby cried, and then another.

Raising his eyes and searching the faces, he spotted several women with babies, including the mother of the children he'd spoken to earlier.

They shouldn't be here. Where was the commanding officer?

It took Petr an hour to find the commanding officer. When he did, he said, "Excuse me, sir, I am new here and not trying to cause trouble, but I noticed women with babies in the women's sections. I would like to transfer them to the children's section, where I work."

"Why is that?"

"The babies. They are children. They should be with the others. But also, the women are mothers and they can help take care of all the children."

"Makes no difference to me," he said, waving his hand. "Move them, if you want."

"Thank you, sir."

Petr didn't wait around for the commander to change his mind. He hurried back to get the women and babies, and hoped he wasn't too late.

With the other guards distracted by their nighttime activities, Petr had no trouble rounding up the women with babies, whispering to them that he would take them to the children's section where they would be safer. He hoped they would.

One woman, who didn't have a baby, reached out and grabbed his sleeve. "Please let me go with you. My children are in the children's section."

He remembered seeing her in his column with three little girls. They'd joined from another column a few weeks ago. "All right."

They slipped out quietly and he led the small group of five women and four babies to the children's section.

A guard stationed there stared at him as if he'd lost his mind, but the women and children went wild with cries of joy, hugging each other and kissing.

OVER THE NEXT two months, Petr found out that after the war ended, the Czech 'Revolutionary Guard' (known as the RG) had arrested soldiers from the German Wehrmacht who were marching through this area, some on their way back home, and had imprisoned them here, too. He didn't have any access to the area where they were kept and didn't witness what happened to them, but he had heard they were taken out of the camp daily for strenuous manual labor.

Petr, himself, witnessed guards beating elderly men and women, making children dance for them until they couldn't even stand up any longer, burning women with cigarette butts, bullying women and children and threatening them, slapping them, beating them with boards, calling them names.

Even the supervisors were sadists, who seemed to take pleasure in tormenting the internees. Shouting at them. Beating them because they tried to sit down or lie down or because they lost their balance and fell.

It was too much for Petr to bear watching, but he sometimes forced himself to watch. Although there was nothing he could do about it, he needed to remember clearly so he could someday tell about the horrors that had come to these people, the same as they had come to the Jews.

Shame overwhelmed him some nights.

Killing soldiers during war, killing to protect yourself or a loved one, beating someone because they had personally done something awful and needed to be punished—those were things he'd done and hadn't felt guilty about. Maybe he would pay for what he'd done. Maybe he already had; his family had all been taken from him.

What his comrades were doing was wrong, and he was pathetic for doing nothing about it, beyond keeping watch over the women and children in his section, as well as he could without drawing too much attention. There was only so much he could do.

He tried to tell himself that he was doing his best. It didn't always help.

The worse came one day in early July. He'd finished his dinner and was on his way to the children's section with the few bits of food he'd managed to hide away for the internees. As he neared the barracks, he heard screams. He rushed inside and found a guard attacking the girl, Christa. Her mother was crying and beating the guard, trying to pull him off her daughter, but she wasn't strong enough to do him any damage. The guard was obviously intent on raping the young girl, though he hadn't managed it yet.

Petr grabbed hold of him, pulled him off her, then stabbed him in the chest.

The mother thanked him profusely and held her shaking daughter in her arms. The girl, barely twelve years old, was all right, but now he was faced with a dilemma. How could he explain that he'd killed one of his comrades? His peers wouldn't see him as heroic. They would take him out and shoot him.

One of the other mothers suggested he tell no one. "Let them think the bastard ran off," she said. "Bury him in the ground between this barracks and the next, where no one will notice."

"That is right," another mother said. "We will help you."

That was his best option. He found a shovel and made haste digging the grave. All of the mothers helped him drag the body outside and dump it into the ground. None of them spoke of the incident. They were in it together, and they would carry the memory to their graves.

At the end of July he got word that most of the people who'd been brought in with his column would be loaded onto a train headed into Germany the following day.

After thinking about it overnight, he went to the commander's office first thing in the morning and requested to be assigned as a guard on that train.

Later that morning, he packed his few provisions into his pack and went to the staging area, waiting for the guards who were bringing the Germans out.

Soon they were all walking together, like before, this time to the train station in the next town. The train was waiting for them when they arrived.

The guards squeezed as many people as they could into each cattle car. Petr could see that the cars were overfilled and that hardly anyone could move. No one would have packed that many cattle into those cars. What made them think it was all right to do that to humans? His claustrophobia would drive him insane if he had to ride like that. My God, he hoped it wouldn't take weeks to reach their destination. At the dinner table in the guards' quarters at the camp the night before, the men had laughed when they talked about nearly every train losing a good portion of its German 'swine' passengers during the trip. That's part of what had kept him awake half the night, trying to figure out what he should do.

He reminded himself, as he slid one of the doors closed and locked it, that he was going with them and would do his best to make sure the guards didn't kill them. As for the rest of the danger, all he could do for the Germans in his care, was pray they would have the strength and endurance to make the trip. The car he and the other guards rode in wasn't great, but at least the men could lie down on beds of straw and cover themselves with warm blankets. He felt guilty, as he envisioned the prisoners in the cars behind him, suffering and maybe even dying.

Breadcrumbs and Bombs

Ilse Seidel, June-July 1945, Memmingen, Germany—

"HE IS THE most beautiful baby I have ever seen," Ilse said, touching her son's peach-fuzzy head. She'd given birth an hour ago, and the midwife, Ulla Stumpf, one of the Sudeten Germans staying at the house with Ilse and Karolina, had brought the baby to her, wrapped in a soft blue blanket. Aunt Karolina was seated next to her bed and leaning over to peek at the baby. "I know I should not hold him," Ilse said. "The nuns cautioned me not to get attached. It makes it harder for a mother to give her baby up for adoption if she holds it and gets attached. But I had to see him."

"Of course. It is only natural for a mother to want to hold her baby, even if it is only once," Aunt Karolina said. "You have a right. And that baby should get a chance to feel his mother's arms around him. He has heard your voice and grown used to use all these months."

Ilse nodded, tears flowing down her cheeks and onto the baby's head. All of a sudden she couldn't trust her voice.

Aunt Karolina squeezed her hand. "Have you found a family to adopt him?" she asked, her voice barely above a whisper. She pulled the blanket away from the baby's face slightly. "He is beautiful. Truly beautiful. Anyone would be thrilled to have such a precious baby. Anyone who could afford it, I mean."

"I talked to a couple who live in Augsburg. They are interested. I think they will take him. I will need to call them and let them know he is here."

Aunt Karolina didn't respond.

Ilse turned in her direction, wondering why she'd gone quiet.

"I have thought a lot about you and the baby," she said finally. "You are sure you want to adopt him out?"

"I am. I wish with all my heart I could keep him. That would be selfish of me. I do not have a husband and I cannot do that to him or to my family. You heard my mother."

Karolina nodded. "There might be another solution. What if I adopted him?" She sat up straight suddenly, as if waiting for Ilse to soak in what she'd said.

Ilse studied her face. In a few short months Karolina had become a second mother to Ilse. She trusted her implicitly. Was she offering this option because she thought it was something Ilse wanted, or was it because she wanted the baby?

Karolina said, "Forgive me if I have put you in an awkward position. I do not mean to pressure you. If you would rather let that couple adopt him, I will understand. I no longer have a husband, either, and it is doubtful I will remarry or have other children. I am forty years old. Is that too old to raise a baby?"

"You never said anything before about adopting. I am surprised, is all."

"You will move on with your life now, and the Sudeten Germans will not be staying at the house forever. Ulla and Birgit are looking for their own place, you know. The Kauffmans might stay for a while. At their advanced ages, they might be better off staying here until they can find their family. What I am trying to say is that I will be a lonely widow and I long for someone to love and care for. My oldest son—well, you know he is gone—and I have not heard about Hermann yet."

"You really want to adopt the baby?"

"With all my heart."

Ilse reached out her hand, and Karolina took it. "Then it is settled," Ilse said. "And to answer your question, *nein*, I do not think forty is too old to raise a baby. You have years of experience, a good head, and compassion."

"I have enough money, too," she said. "I will be able to support the baby. I only took the job at the orphanage because I wanted to help others, and it was good for me to get out and among people."

"I know. It has been good for both of us. We have both lost loved ones. Helping all those babies and children and the families who adopted them is something we can both be proud of, too."

"*Ja*, and it helps atone for our mistakes."

Tears trickled down Ilse's face. "I hope you are right. I still feel guilty for what happened to Ron."

"We all have regrets. It comes with living."

Someone knocked on the door and peeked her head around the corner. "Is it all right if I come in?" Birgit said. "Mutti told me she delivered your baby this afternoon while I was in school. I was so hoping to be here for the birth."

"Come in, Birgit. Shall we tell her the good news?" Ilse said, looking at Karolina.

Aunt Karolina nodded.

"My aunt is going to adopt him."

"That is exciting. I can babysit for you, whenever you need. I am old enough."

Karolina said, "*Ja*. I could use some help with him sometimes."

"Will you have to quit your job?" Ilse said.

"I do not think so. There is no reason I cannot take him with me. And I do not think the job will last long term. We are not getting as many children now, which is a good thing."

Ilse nodded. She'd already decided she would look for another job after the baby came. Something in a café or a shop. Away from the children and the constant reminders of what she was giving up. Away from the reminders of the war and the losses.

A few weeks later, she began work in a café that catered to the American soldiers. She enjoyed the job and got surprisingly good tips from the men. But they, too, were a reminder that she was finding harder and harder to live with.

One day after work, a month after she'd given birth, Ilse sat in the living room with the elderly couple, Gretel and Otto Kauffman, waiting for her aunt to get home with the baby. When Karolina walked in and Ilse heard the baby gurgling and cooing, she rushed over and picked him up from his stroller, hugging him tightly and wanting to kiss him all over his head.

What am I doing? She held him at arm's length and gazed into his beautiful blue eyes so much like his father's eyes and she knew then that she was getting too attached. It was time for her to move on. She needed to go away and let Karolina and baby Julian become mother and son, before it became impossible for her to leave.

At the end of the work week, after she'd given notice and worked her last day at the café, Ilse carried her suitcase downstairs and said her goodbyes.

"You do not have to do this," Aunt Karolina said. "We are family and you can stay here and be part of Julian's life."

"I cannot stay. It is not fair to any of us, if I stay. It is time for me to go and start living my life." She wiped a tear away. "I know you will raise him well."

"You can come and visit us any time you want," Karolina said. "You will always be welcome here. Do not forget it, and do not forget us."

"I will never forget. Thank you, Aunt Karolina. I owe you more than I can ever repay."

"You have repaid me a thousand times, with this precious gift." She held Julian on her hip and pinched his cheek gently.

Ilse hugged them both, then opened the door, picked up her suitcase, and left, walking down the sidewalk toward the train station. She was going home to her family in Memmingen.

CHAPTER TWENTY-ONE

Lucas Landry, September 2017, Biberach, Germany—

LUCAS BACKED AWAY from his bedroom window in Ilse Jaroslav's house and hustled downstairs to breakfast, knowing from the daily routine they'd followed all week, there would be delicious coffee, a torte, boiled eggs, real butter, and the best German bread in the world.

"Ah, you are up," Ilse said, ambling toward him with a platter of fresh bread in her hand. "Did you sleep well?"

"Sure did. Mmm, everything looks and smells great." He poured a cup of coffee, which also had become routine. It had taken him a couple days to adjust to the reality of meeting Ilse Seidel and to discovering that she had married Petr, the writer of the Slavic diaries he'd found in the attic. He was still waiting to broach the subject of how she'd met Petr. All week, family members had shuttled him all over the countryside for sightseeing and meeting people. He'd loved all of that, but it had left him precious little time to sit and really talk with the one person he longed to talk to. Ilse.

"You must eat quickly. Milo and his father will be picking you up in fifteen minutes to take you down to Memmingen. You'll like it, I'm sure."

"You aren't going with us?" Lucas asked, disappointed that yet another opportunity to talk would be lost.

"*Nein.* My arthritis is acting up. At my age, I spend most days around home. I am no good for traveling anymore. I would only slow you men down."

"I'm sorry you cannot come with, but I understand. I hope you feel better soon."

He studied her slightly wrinkled face with faded blue eyes and a pleasant grandmotherly smile. She wore her silver hair in a bun, kept a slender physique, and had a decent amount of energy. At eighty-nine years old she still looked pretty spry, he thought. She'd kept up with the five younger people when they'd all gone sightseeing together here in Biberach three days ago. *Not too shabby for almost ninety.*

"I could stay here today," Lucas said. "It would give us a chance to talk more. Get to know each other better. And I have so many questions that I haven't had a chance to ask."

"*Nein.* You should go to Memmingen. People waiting to meet you there. You will get far more answers you are looking for there than you will from me."

Lucas frowned, still anxious to ask questions, but the doorbell rang, and Ilse rose and left to answer the door. Sitting alone in the kitchen he thought about the people he'd met—mostly Ilse's kids and grandkids—when he first arrived here. They had taken him to visit many people, supposedly all related to Lucas in one way or another and in ways that caused his head to reel. It didn't help that many of the people here spoke a Bavarian dialect difficult for non-native-speakers to understand.

He'd tried making notes in his little pocket notepad, hoping to update his family tree drawings and details on his laptop in the evenings before he went to bed. That was not to be. By the time he got to his bedroom each night, he was wiped-out. They walked every day, thousands of steps according to his Fitbit, seeming like half of those were either up or down stairs to various trains and subways or up or down stairs in some castle, museum, city wall, you name it, they had climbed it. Good grief, how could anyone in this country become overweight, he'd wondered at first. But after eating some of the best food he'd ever tasted, meal after meal, every day, he revised the thought. Oh, and let's not forget the beer, a national treasure in itself. Generously served with almost every meal.

Ilse's grandson, Milo, and his father, Jacob, strode into the kitchen, Jacob bellowing as usual, *"Guten morgen,* Lucas." He walked over and patted Lucas on the back. "We've come to take you to Memmingen. Are you ready?"

Lucas nodded as he chewed his last bite of buttered bread and chugged the rest of his coffee. When he'd swallowed his bread and coffee, he said, "Just need to grab my jacket and notebook from upstairs. I'll be back in a minute."

In his room he searched for his cell phone. *Ah, there it is on the desk where I set it down. God, I hope I remembered to charge it.* Taking more than three hundred photos in the first week, he had given his phone camera a real workout.

"You might want to bring an overnight bag," Jacob yelled from downstairs. "Mutter says she thinks you'll want to stay a couple of days in Memmingen."

"All right," he yelled out. Hmm. *What's so special in Memmingen?* The place wasn't even in any of his Germany tour guide books, though it did sound somehow familiar. The cities he'd seen so far were large, with subways, fast trains, modern businesses, yet held onto their old-time charm: replete with medieval castles, palaces, baroque churches with tall spires or onion domes, and wattle-and-daub houses and half-timbered houses. Why go to a small town that had none of these things? Almost the moment he thought that, he remembered. It was the city where Ilse had grown up and where her parents had lived. And that's where U.S. combat planes had gotten into a major battle with German fighter planes above the city and the airport. Now he was excited.

As he came down the stairs and stopped in the kitchen, Lucas said, "I'm looking forward to seeing Memmingen. I've heard a bit about it in some old diaries I read. Ilse, are you sure you don't want to come with us? We'll have fun and talk about the old days."

She smiled. "Well, *ja*, perhaps it might be fun. As long as I can limit my walking. Let me quickly pull a few things together into my overnight bag. I will not be more than ten minutes. Is that okay, Milo?"

"Of course, Mutter. We're in no rush. I'm driving instead of taking the train so there is no time schedule to follow."

Lucas smiled, happy that Ilse was coming along. Based on her reaction, he gathered she really did want to come but had held back because she'd been worried she would be slowing them down. What a sweet woman.

Tawny Landry, Sacramento, California, September 2017—

"YOU HAVE TO call Lucas," Tawny's mother, Lani, said. She was sitting beside Tawny's hospital bed, holding Bianca on her lap to keep her from running around the room and making noise.

"I can't do that to him," Tawny said. "He's only been in Germany a little over a week. It would ruin everything."

"He should have a choice. You don't really think he would forgive himself if you have this baby without him, do you?"

"Now you're being overly dramatic, Mom. I'm not having it without him. I called his aunts. They'll come here when it's time for the baby, and one of them will film the delivery. The aunt said she's done it before, with her grandchildren. The other aunt said she'd sit with Bianca in the waiting room. Lucas will be able to see the whole birth, whether he's here or not."

"It's not the same, and you know it. Why do you always have to be so damned stubborn?"

"Don't talk to me that way, especially not in front of Bianca." Another cramp made her wince. *Stay in there a few days longer, little one. Please, for Mommy's and Daddy's sakes.*

Lani picked up Tawny's cell phone from the nightstand. "Call him. At least let him know what's going on. It's the right thing to do, and you know it."

She grabbed the phone out of her mother's hand. "Oh, all right."

The phone rang several times before Lucas answered.

"Oh, hi, sweetie," he said before she could say anything. "I've been meaning to call you. How are you and Bianca doing?"

"We're okay. Bianca is sitting on Mom's lap right now." She hesitated, wondering how to tell him without making him flip out. "How is your trip going? I love all the photos. Seems like you've been very busy."

Her mother mouthed the words: "You're stalling. Tell him."

Tawny waved her hand at her mother, then turned her back to her.

"Yeah, been super busy. I'm in Memmingen. Been here two days. I have so much to tell you. But I guess I'd rather tell you in person, when I can see your reaction."

She didn't respond.

"Are you sure you're okay?"

"Uh, well, not exactly. Before you freak out, listen, okay. I'm in the hospital. The doctor admitted me just as a precaution. I might be in labor. Been having cramps off and on for almost a week now, only now they've gotten stronger."

"You're in labor? Oh, my God! I'll be there on the next flight out of Munich. Hang in there."

"No. Listen to me. You don't have to cut your trip short. I've been through this before. I know what to expect. Besides, I might not even be in labor. It's still early."

"Yeah, well, Bianca came early, too. Remember?"

"Of course I remember, I was kinda there," she snapped, not really meaning to sound so snotty. "I'm sorry. I guess I'm a bit cranky."

"That's understandable," Lucas said. "I would be, too. I'm coming home. I hope I can get there before the baby comes. I'll have to go back to Biberach, get my things, then take the train to Munich. From there, I'll catch a flight. I'll make the reservation as soon as I can figure out timing."

"Lucas, no. Please don't ruin your trip," Tawny said. "I can manage here. As I said, I might not even be in labor yet. You could come home and then have to sit around waiting another few weeks for the baby to get here."

"Calm down. Rest. Follow your doctor's orders. I'll be there as soon as I can. No argument. It's my turn to be bossy."

She sighed and mumbled half under her breath, "All right, but don't blame your ruined trip on me. I didn't want to call and make you feel like you had to come home. Mom made me call."

"I know," Lucas said.

His voice sounded almost cheerful. *What the hell was with that?*

"Tawny, I don't blame you. I'm excited about our baby coming. Can't wait to see him! See you soon."

She hung up the phone and closed her eyes. This wasn't the way it was supposed to happen. She'd imagined a leisurely Fall day—on the exact date the baby was due—and then her water breaking and her realizing she was in labor. She and Lucas would drop off Bianca at Mom's house, and they would arrive at the hospital, where after a few hours of labor, with Lucas as her coach, she would deliver their baby.

She gnashed her teeth, pain gripping her again. *Think about the phone call, not the pain.* Lucas sounded okay. Happy even. So why did she feel guilty? *Seems like I can't do anything right these days. Can't even carry a baby to full-term. What the hell is wrong with me?*

"What did he say?" Her mother asked. "Is he coming home?"

She sighed, gritted her teeth, and turned around to face her mother.

"Daddy's coming home?" Bianca said, her big brown eyes filled with anticipation.

All the anger suddenly left her body. How could anyone stay angry when looking into that little girl's eyes? Tawny looked at Bianca's grandmother, too. Nothing but concern and love in Lani's eyes.

"I'm sorry for being so grumpy," Tawny said. "He's coming home as soon as he can. I'm not sure he'll get here in time for the birth, though. I think I should call his aunts again."

CHAPTER TWENTY-TWO

Christa Nagel, July 1945, Sudetenland—

THE TRAIN CAME to a stop, brakes screeching like a banshee, Christa covering her ears with her hands to muffle the sound. Her skin itched, as if something was crawling all over her body, but no amount of scratching helped. If anything, it somehow made it worse. Someone began a coughing fit on the other side of the car. Christa was sitting on the floor with her family, her legs folded under her body, in a most uncomfortable position. At least she no longer had to stand all the time. Everyone could sit in here, just not lie down. That they had room to sit almost brought her to tears again. Every few days the train stopped for restocking, and who knew what else. The doors would be opened and the dead bodies would be removed and discarded like so much garbage. So far, no one in her family had died, but it could happen. Frau Engelmann and her little girl had both died two days ago.

When the bodies were removed, an extra few feet of space would be gained. The only good thing that came with the stops, was that guards would bring them bread and water. Horrible tasting, but sustenance, all the same.

The doors now opened and she shielded her eyes from the bright sunlight, wondering who else had died, who else would be tossed out of their car.

"Time to get off the train," someone proclaimed. She couldn't see his face because of the bright sun, but she recognized the voice. Petr. Their Petr, as they'd come to think of him. Theirs because he had spent time with them in the internment camp, bringing them all extra pieces of bread, when he could, and talking with them, telling stories to the children, and giving them a modicum of hope.

Christa tried to pry her numb legs out from under her body. Pain coursed through her knees and legs. Her limbs had turned into pretzels after days of being crammed into this tight space. She finally peeled them out from under her and stretched them. When the pain eased and she thought they were steady enough to support her weight, she stood up and tested them. Wobbly, but she didn't fall over. Reaching down, she pulled Mutti's arm, helping her stand, amid a field of moans and groans. Christa wasn't sure how many of those were coming from her mother and how many were coming from the other people in the car. Between Christa, Mutti, and Ernst, they got all the children up, handing them one at a time down to Petr.

Once everyone had jumped, slid, or had been helped down from that cattle car, Petr left to go to attend to the next car in line behind them. Christa watched him for a few minutes, feeling as though they'd lost their lifeline. They were on their own.

"What do we do now?" Mutti asked. "Are we in Germany?"

"I do not know," Christa said. She gazed around the crowded train station and finally spotted a sign. They were indeed in Germany. The sign listed several other train stops: Bayreuth, Hof, Erlangen, Würzburg, and Nürnberg. All were city names she recognized from her geography lessons in school. The air smelled different here in the bigger city. More fumes from cars and trucks. No chickens. No cows. No manure. She missed the smell of farms and open land.

Several soldiers started yelling and rushing around, pointing guns and shooing them back onto the train.

Panic ensued and the Sudeten Germans frantically climbed back onto the train. Christa wasn't sure which car was theirs. It didn't matter.

A few minutes later, Petr appeared, helping the children and elderly mount the cattle car, and said, "The authorities refuse accept the train here. We must leave." With that, he closed the door.

The train car lurched, then started up again, the engine blowing its whistle loudly.

Christa attempted to sleep, but her mind wouldn't allow it. It seemed nobody wanted them. All those months in the internment camp, she'd tried to tell herself that it was only the Czechs in the CSR, the Czech-Slovak Republic, who didn't want them. The Germans would accept them, if they ever got that far. But now? They were outsiders. Worse than outsiders, they were dirt, homes for lice and fleas. Christa worried they might continue riding on the train until each of them died. Even if they did find a German city that would accept them, then what? Where would they go? They had no home anymore, they had nothing. How would they survive?

The train chugged along forever, it seemed. Between the wooden slats, Christa could catch glimpses of green grass and now could smell manure and farm animals. At least something felt like home.

At last the train's brakes screeched again, announcing another arrival. After several minutes, she expected the doors to open as they had earlier, but nothing happened.

Time passed, but how much time, she had no way of knowing. All she knew was that it was getting dark outside.

No one said a word, probably because they were all straining to hear something from outside to give them an idea of what was happening.

Finally the doors opened and there was Petr. She could see him clearly in the shadows of the sunset.

Petr said, "This city decided to accept the train. You can get out now. Everyone must go into the building and get processed. After that, you will be free to go wherever you want."

"Processed?" Mutti asked. "What does that mean?"

"I am not sure," Petr said. "That is what we were told."

They all exited the car as they had the last time. Christa searched for station signs as she had previously done. The sign she saw this time listed different train stops: Regensberg, Ingolstadt, Landshut, München, and Augsburg. These were Bavarian cities she recognized from her geography lessons in school. And at least here it smelled more like home. She took a deep breath, and quickly blew it out, then rushed to catch up with her family. Guards were herding them away from the train platform, up a steep flight of stairs, across a bridge that went over the train tracks, and then into an enormous building.

Inside, the noise was deafening. People everywhere, talking, and music playing a song Christa didn't recognize. Everyone had to line up and wait their turn, not knowing would happen here.

When it was the Nagel family's turn, Mutti gave the clerk each person's name and handed over ragged identity cards. The man didn't give them back to her, and she started shaking, tears threatening to come.

"We need our papers back," she said, her voice cracking.

"Not here," he said. "Later. Move forward."

After that, guards separated them into two groups, male and female. One guard took the males away; another guard took

Mutti, Christa, Julia, and Giselle to another room. They were told to undress and go to the showers. Christa felt panic rise up in her throat. This was like when they'd arrived in Theresienstadt. Not exactly the same, but too similar.

Arguing or refusing would do them no good, Christa knew. They'd been taught well in the internment camp and that would forever stay with them.

She and the rest of the females obeyed.

When they were clean, they were sent naked to a 'health station' where someone sprayed them with something which they called DDT. "It won't harm you," the woman in guard uniform said. "We must ensure you don't bring any diseases or insects into our country."

Another person shuttled them to an area where they were allowed to pick out something to wear, including coats and jackets. That task took time, because Christa had to not only find something for herself and get dressed, but also had to help Giselle, while Mutti helped Julia.

When they all dressed, Christa felt new again, almost like a new foal being born. She wore a flowered dress, long socks, a pair of black shoes, and a coat. They were directed to leave the area, and they returned to the main lobby, where they waited for the boys. Ernst had taken the baby with him, while Fritz had agreed to care for Andreas.

It took them a while, but finally Christa spotted the four boys, heading toward Christa and Mutti.

"You look human again," Ernst said to Christa, poking her in the side, a smile appearing on his face.

"You do, too," she said.

They waited, soon noticing others with new clothes beginning to leave the building. Mutti led them outside into the cool night air, then suddenly screamed.

"What is wrong?" Christa asked.

"Our clothes. Our coats. They have our money and jewels sewn inside." Mutti hurried back into the building to where they'd started earlier, the kids all following her as if they were tied together by a rope. Christa didn't dare get separated from her in this huge crowd.

Mutti tried to go back through the line to get to the shower area, with all the kids tagging along, but a guard stopped her. She tried to tell him she needed her old clothes, but he told her that wasn't possible.

"But we have no money now," Mutti said. "How are we to live?"

"Each person will get a small stipend and fresh identity cards," the man said. "Over there, you must finish your registration before you leave. Someone will also help you with resettlement."

Mutti's tension, visible in the tight creases on her forehead, seemed to disappear suddenly. "Oh, *danke*. *Danke*. I thought we were finished already. I guess we missed that section." She turned around and looked in the direction the man had pointed. "I do not see where we are to go, do you?"

"Over there," Christa said. "See that sign and the long line of people?"

"*Ja. Danke.*"

They hurried over to the line and secured their spots, waiting for their turns. Finally, they stood in front of a table with boxes of papers and a woman wearing a suit and eyeglasses.

"Names."

Mutti gave her their names."

"It'll be a few minutes," the woman said. She reached over to the boxes and began looking through the papers, until she pulled out seven papers. She folded each paper and handed them to Mutti.

Mutti thanked her, and waited.

"Can I help you with something else?"

"*Ja*. The man at the first station told us we would each get fresh identity cards and money, and that someone would help us with resettlement."

"You have the identity cards. I just gave them to you. Oh, wait, you are right, I forgot the money. Just a moment." She got up and went to a desk behind her and talked to another woman. The other woman gave her some envelopes, and the woman in the suit returned.

"Here you are," she said, handing the envelopes to Mutti. "A small amount per person to help get you started.

Mutti opened each of the envelopes and counted the cash and the number of envelopes. "*Danke*. We are very grateful."

The woman nodded.

Christa said, "What about someone to help us with resettlement?"

"I'm sorry, but we are overwhelmed by the number of refugees coming in. We don't have enough people to help everyone at this time. Perhaps if you can come back in a week or two . . . ."

She didn't finish, but looked at the next people in line, clearly dismissing Christa's family.

They walked outside, Christa wondering where they would go. Mutti led them back over the bridge toward the train station. On the train platform, Christa spied the train schedule. That's when Christa saw the name of the city they were in: Fürth im Wald.

She told Mutti the name. "Do you know the city?" Christa asked.

Mutti shook her head.

"Where should we go? And do we have enough money to take a train?"

"I do not know what we should do."

Someone lurched into Mutti and yanked off her coat, running away with it and with their money and identity cards. Mutti screamed and tried to run after the thief but tripped and fell.

Christa rushed over to help her mother. By the time she reached her, Mutti was getting up, motioning for Christa to catch the thief. She rushed up the stairs, her breath coming in ragged waves, but kept going. The man was elderly, she was sure. She'd caught a brief look at him.

At the top of the stairs, she stopped a moment to assess which way he'd gone. There—he was trying to cross a bridge, but a string of trucks and cars and people blocked the route.

She rushed forward and crashed into him, both of them tumbling onto the ground.

Someone came up behind her and bent down. "Are you all right, Christa?"

She looked over her shoulder. "Petr. I am happy to see you. This man stole Mutti's coat and our money and papers."

Petr reached down and grabbed the man, motioning for Christa to stand. He turned the man over, and Christa grabbed the coat and checked the pockets. She pulled out the papers and the envelopes, making sure the money was inside, and nodded to Petr.

Petr yanked the man up and shoved him into the crowd.

"Where is your family?" he asked, rubbing his hands together, blowing on them to warm them up. That's when she realized how chilly it was getting outside.

"Back at the train station," she said. "We have no idea where to go or what to do."

"Take me to them and then we can talk, *ja?*"

She nodded and led him back down the stairs to the train platform.

259

Petr Jaroslav, July 1945, Germany—

"WHERE DID YOU live before you moved to the Sudetenland," Petr asked Hanna. They were seated on a bench on the train platform. The children were all standing with hands in their coat pockets, trying to stay warm.

"*Nein*, we always lived in the Sudetenland," Hanna said. "I was born there. My husband was, too. And my parents and grandparents, and his. I came from another small town near Altstadt, where we lived before the expulsion."

"You mean you have never lived in Germany?"

"That is right."

"I thought . . . never mind. Your whole family is ethnic German, but lived in my country."

"Actually, my mother's family was not German at all. They were Czech."

"Really? Then that makes you half Czech. Why did you get expelled?"

"I am married to a German. Was it not that way when the Jews were rounded up? If an Aryan person was married to a Jew, that person was taken away, too, isn't that right?"

"I believe so," Petr said, his brain trying to make sense of it all. "Have you ever even been to Germany before?"

"*Nein*."

"You do not have any relatives here?"

She didn't answer right away.

He glanced at her, wondering what was going on.

"I may have family here," she said. "My parents and my sister and her family moved to Bavaria twelve or thirteen years ago. I have lost count. It has been years since I have heard from them." She shrugged her shoulders, continuing, "They may have been killed during the war, for all I know."

"That is good, Hanna. That you may have family here, I mean. They could be the answer. Where do they live? Do you have an address?"

She shrugged again. "I have nothing, because the soldiers took everything from us. All I have is what is in my head, and I have been trying to remember where my relatives went. I know it was somewhere near Augsburg."

"All right, that is a start. I will check the train schedule and find out when the next train to Augsburg leaves." He strode over to the ticket counter and made inquiries. After obtaining the train schedule he said, "Do you have a map I can buy? A map of Bavaria?"

The man pulled one out from behind him and handed it to Petr, who then paid him.

Petr returned to the bench. "The next passenger train to Augsburg leaves in the morning. We should go someplace warm where we can rest until then."

"Where can we go?" Fritz asked, his teeth chattering.

"Perhaps the building where you got registered," Petr said. "We should check there first, *ja?*"

Hanna nodded.

They had to fight their way through throngs of immigrants departing the government building, but they finally made it. Inside, they found many people sitting on the floor, or lying down, apparently all with the same idea.

Petr, Hanna, and the kids assumed places near one another and soon were fast asleep.

In the morning, Petr opened his map, studying it. The train journey would take a while, but it seemed like Augsburg was a much larger city than Fürth. It made sense to go in that direction.

Hanna glanced over his shoulder.

"Do you think you might recognize the name of the city where you have relatives, if you saw it on the map?"

"Possibly."

He placed the map on her lap. "We are here," he said, pointing to Fürth im Wald, "and here is Augsburg. Look around and see if any names jump out at you."

After several minutes, she said, "Here, this one. Memmingen."

Petr grinned. "That is very good. We will try there, first. It is a bit further, but could save us some time, if we find them there."

"We? You are going with us?" she asked.

He hesitated, unsure of when he'd made his decision and whether it was the right one.

"I will unless you would rather I did not."

"Why? Why would you go with us? What about your job back in the Sudetenland?"

"I have no family left in the CSR." He ran his hand through his hair, trying to stall while he searched for the right words. "I was a Resistance fighter during the war. I thought I knew who the enemy was and who the allies were. Now, I am confused and I am appalled at what my own countrymen have done to the ethnic Germans. I may be the only Czech person who feels that way, or at least one of the few, and that makes me an outsider. There is no reason for me to go back."

"What do you want from us?" Hanna said, wringing her hands together. "Some kind of payment for your help?"

"Certainly not," Petr said, feeling a bit hurt. Again he hesitated as he tried to put his thoughts together. "I never expected to say this. I do not believe revenge against a whole race or religion or nation because of what some in that nation did, is good. People should be judged on what they themselves do, and not on what their countrymen have done. Does that make sense?"

"*Ja*. I feel the same."

Petr took a deep breath, and let it out. "None of this is easy for me. I am a bit of a loner, I guess. But I have come to know your family and see a lot of my family in yours. That makes me feel responsible. I just want to help you."

Hanna looked at him, tears forming, then looked away and wept, burying her face in her hands, her shoulders shaking.

"What is wrong, Mutti?" Christa asked, leaning forward to touch her mother's shoulder.

"Nothing, little one," she said, lifting her head. "I am just grateful that someone is showing us such overwhelming kindness, is all. It has been far too long since anyone has been this good to us."

Ilse Seidel, July 1945, Memmingen, Germany—

SOMEONE KNOCKED ON the front door. Mutter said, "Will you get that, Ilse? I cannot imagine who it could be, coming at dinnertime." Ilse left the kitchen and shook her head, smiling, remembering the day Mutter had arrived, unannounced and at dinnertime, in Biberach. She wiped her hands on her apron and opened the door. "Uh, hello, how can I help you?"

"Is . . . is this the Seidel household?" a woman asked. Something about her seemed vaguely familiar, though Ilse had no idea why.

"*Ja*." Ilse glanced behind the woman and took in a group of waifs and a teenage boy, all standing on the steps or on the sidewalk at the bottom of the stairs.

"I am Hanna Nagel, Maria Seidel's sister. Is . . . is she here, or our parents, Klauss and Anna Fischer?"

Relatives? It couldn't be, could it, after all this time? Ilse put her hand on her neck, feeling her muscle throb under her thumb. "Uh, a moment, I will get them." She closed the door without thinking, turned, and rushed into the kitchen, then braced her back against a wall.

"What is wrong, Ilse? You look like you have seen a ghost."

"The knock at the door. She says she is your sister. From the Sudetenland."

Mutter dropped the rolling pin onto the floor and grabbed hold of the counter top's edge for support. "Are you sure?"

"I thought she looked vaguely familiar but did not know why. But I think it is her. The brown eyes. She looks like you and Oma."

Mutter took off running to the front door, pulled it open, looked, then pulled her sister into a tight hug. "I thought you were dead. How did you get here?"

"It is a long, horrible story. I will tell you about it, if you really want to know, but it will churn your stomach."

"Is that ... Hanna?" Oma said, pushing her way past Ilse. "Oh, *mein Gott*. Oh, *mein Gott* it is you. Oh ...my darling girl, I have ... been so worried," Oma began sobbing, tears streaming down her face.

"Mutter," Hanna said, flinging herself into Oma's arms.

Opa, Robert, and Ursula came bounding down the stairs. "What's going on?" Ursula asked, getting to the door first.

Mutter made the introductions. Then she stuck her head outside and gasped. "Who are all these people?"

"My family, and the young man who helped us while we were in the internment camp and later, when we arrived in Germany. He's our friend."

264

Mutter held the door open, and said, "Come inside. All of you." She motioned with her hand for her own family to move aside and let the newcomers inside. "Please sit."

"Ilse, please run to the shops and see if you can get more food for your aunt's family," Mutter said. "We do not have enough dinner for all of us." She pulled out some money from her skirt pocket and handed it to Ilse.

"That is not necessary," Aunt Hanna said. "We ate on the train on our way here. Please, don't go to any trouble."

It felt strange thinking of Hanna as an aunt. Ilse had never met her before, at least not that she remembered.

"Nonsense. That was probably hours ago," Mutter said. "Besides, you all look like skin and bones. We will get more food. It is not so hard these days. New shipments of food come in regularly now."

"*Danke*," Aunt Hanna said. She introduced her family to everyone before Ilse left. "And this is Petr Jaroslav. He is a Czech Resistance fighter who rescued us many times when we were prisoners at Theresienstadt."

"That is a concentration camp," Opa said. "What were you doing there?"

"They turned it into an internment camp for refugees—us ethnic Germans who were being expelled after the war."

"*Mein Gott*," Opa said. "I have heard terrible things about that place."

Oma walked over to Petr and took hold of his hands, looking into his eyes. She said something to him in her native Czech, and he smiled and answered her in Czech. She patted him on the cheek, smiled, and walked back over to stand next to Opa.

"Go now, Ilse," Mutter said. "See if you can find something that we can make quickly."

"All right." She headed for the door, and reached out to open it.

"Do you mind if I go with you?"

She turned toward the voice. It was Petr. She gave him a half smile and nodded. Together, they strolled down the street and into the Markplatz.

"This is a beautiful city," Petr said. "Much destruction, but amazingly, many of the buildings look unscathed."

"It is the loveliest part of town, and the most popular, too. I still remember how it looked before the war, back before the bombs. You might not know it, but this—what you are seeing now—is after months of clean-up. Workers are now starting to rebuild the crumbled buildings," Ilse said.

"You would not believe the devastation in Prague. This," he said, waving his arms, "is bad, but nothing compared to there. There is nothing left to rebuild in some places. My family's former home, our whole neighborhood—gone."

"I am sorry. I didn't realize your land was bombed heavily, too."

Some of Memmingen's old town had been destroyed during the bombing raids. Ilse had read in the newspaper that Memmingen's air raid alarm had gone off more than four hundred time in the last year of a half of the war. The last major bombing on April 9th, 1945, had levelled most of the southern part of town, even though the German air base in that area was no longer operable.

Even after the Americans had arrived, it had taken time to begin repairs. Looting and chaos ensued for weeks.

"Do you think I did the right thing, bringing your aunt and her children to Memmingen?" Petr asked. "I worry that it will be a hardship for your family."

"They have no other place to go, do they?"

He shook his head.

"Then you did the right thing." How they would ever fit all those people into their house, she didn't know, but she was happy to have their family here. It also helped, Ilse confessed to herself, that they'd brought this fine looking man, one who didn't wear either a German or American uniform to remind her of all she'd lost.

Petr stayed in the family's cellar for a few days. He kept insisting that he didn't want to be a burden, but everyone shushed him and said that he was welcome. They owed him a great debt.

Over the next few weeks, Christa, Ernst, Fritz, and Julia began going to school with Robert and Ursula, and seemed to be settling in well. Ilse rarely got to see them, because she worked full time in an office in a newspaper company.

Within the first couple of days of their arrival, Ilse had advised Petr, who had decided he wanted to stay in Memmingen, about a help wanted ad that had recently gone into the newspaper. The factory desperately needed workers.

Petr had interviewed and got the job, a good job, according to him. She also found him a small apartment down the street from the factory, because he said he couldn't stay at her family's house much longer. The house, including the cellar, he laughed, was ready to burst at the seams.

Petr told her that the apartment was perfect—walking distance to work and modern—well, more modern than any building he'd ever lived in.

Ilse was also pleased with the arrangement. Working at an office only a few doors down from the factory, soon led to her and Petr eating lunch and spending time together every day.

It was too soon in their relationship except for daydreams, but she hoped one day to share the apartment with Petr and move out of her family's house. She still hadn't told Petr about Ron and about her baby. Maybe someday, if they stayed together, she would open up about those past wounds. She might even take him to Biberach and let him meet her aunt and Julian.

For now, she was glad that life in Germany was returning to normal and her family, what was left of it, was together. Well, except for her cousin, Hermann, whom Aunt Karolina had not heard from, and her uncle, Franz, whom Aunt Hanna had not heard from. Ilse prayed that both were alive and would one day return home.

CHAPTER TWENTY-THREE

Lucas Landry, September 2017, Sacramento, California—

THE AIRPORT SHUTTLE delivered Lucas to his house in Roseville, then promptly disappeared down the street. With the computer bag strapped over his shoulder, wheeling his suitcases up the sidewalk to the front door, he pulled out his house key, opened the door and called out, "Tawny, Bianca, I'm home." No answer. It was a work day but he knew Tawny wouldn't be at work. If she wasn't here resting, that meant she was still in the hospital.

So much for not worrying. To be sure, he dashed up the stairs. *Nope, not here. Okay, hospital it is.* His brain felt fried after a whirlwind train/subway/airplane journey, followed by waiting to go through customs, and picking up luggage, and completed in a shuttle bus, stuck in traffic for over an hour. After a few moments his head cleared. *Wow, I think I even remember how to get to the hospital.* Maybe jetlag wouldn't be as bad on the return trip as it had been on his arrival in Germany.

He left his luggage in the foyer, made sure he'd locked the door, then entered the garage from the kitchen. Tawny's car was in the garage. *Huh? Oh, that's right. Lani took her to the hospital.*

Twenty minutes later he rushed into the hospital, stopped at the information desk to ask where the maternity ward was, since he couldn't remember, then hightailed it up three flights of stairs, not wanting to wait around an elevator.

In the maternity ward, he snagged a nurse and asked for his wife's room. She gave him the number and pointed him in the right direction.

As he neared the room he heard laughter. He rushed through the open doorway and stopped abruptly, staring. His jaw dropped and he blinked. Tawny was in bed, holding a blue blanket-wrapped bundle in her arms. Next to the bed Lani, Aunt Anna holding Bianca, and Aunt Elsa stared back at him.

What, no. The baby's here already? No. Wait. The aunts are here, too. When did the aunts and Tawny meet each other? . . . The baby is here!

"Lucas! You're here," Tawny said, her voice full of love. All eyes still staring him, he controlled his urge to panic and slowly back out of the room.

"Yeah, I . . . finally made it. When . . . how . . . did all this happen?"

"After I talked to you last, the pains got worse. I called your aunts and they came right over. Aunt Anna filmed the birth for you. Isn't that wonderful?"

"Uh, I'm confused. I never introduced you and my aunts."

"You didn't have to, silly. I called them about a month ago. We've been chatting on the telephone ever since. They're sweet and wonderful. I should be berating you for not introducing us, you know."

Lucas ran his hand through his uncombed hair. *What the hell? They've been talking behind my back.*

Aunt Anna said, "Why didn't you introduce us, Lucas? We kept telling you that we wanted to meet your family. You met ours."

"I . . . ." He stopped talking, the dreaded words sticking in his throat. How could he explain, without insulting anyone? Just because his father and brother were racist, that didn't mean his aunts were, too. "I'm not sure why, exactly. I guess, well, I was afraid."

"Afraid of what?" Tawny asked.

Bianca wiggled in Aunt Anna's arms, attempting to get down, but Anna held her tightly and whispered something to her, something Lucas couldn't hear.

He tried to focus on Tawny's question. Why didn't he introduce them and what was he afraid of? He sighed and sat down on the only empty chair, stalling.

"There's something I never told you, Tawny. About my father and brother." He slowly raked his fingers through his messy hair. *This is bad timing, really bad. Not the way I wanted it to go. How can I say this without . . . oh, hell, just say it. No mincing words.* "They're racist. Dad didn't want to even meet you. That's why he and I went our separate ways."

Tawny gasped. "Oh my God, Lucas. Why didn't you tell me? That explains so much."

"I didn't want to hurt your feelings."

"My feelings?" Tawny said. "That's adorable, but you must surely know that as a thirty year old black woman I've heard mean things all my life. It's hurtful, but I can't let that control my life."

"Wait? You got really upset a few months ago when you lost a patient because he was a racist."

She looked down at the blanket for a moment. "Oh, that." She hesitated several moments. "Well, that wasn't really the problem. I didn't quite tell you everything. My boss was, I think, using that to intimidate me. He was hitting on me. Had hit on me once before, too."

"What?" Lucas stood up and started pacing across the room, again raking his hand through his hair, then clenching his fists.

"He said that my pregnancy didn't bother him, and that it was actually a good thing. Said I could play around without worrying about getting pregnant with another man's baby. Crazy. And this man was in charge of a mental health clinic."

"Did you file a complaint against him?" Lucas asked, anger threatening to burst out of his chest.

"Please sit back down. Try to calm yourself. Please."

Lucas glanced at her, then glanced around, seeing the baby, Bianca, the aunts, and Lani. He strode back over to his chair and plopped down. "Okay. Go on with your story."

"I didn't want to make a big deal out of it. I'm quitting soon anyway. I'll send resumes out and get a job in Sacramento, like we planned."

Lucas didn't know how to respond. A huge part of him wanted to drive over to her clinic and punch out the creep. The logical part of him struggled, telling him to let it go. She wasn't going back to work there, and someone else would turn the guy in sooner or later.

"Yes, I know, the guy is a jerk. I wanted to punch him out myself. But he didn't do anything physical. He just shot off his ignorant mouth like some men do. I'm not saying what he did was okay and I'm not letting him off the hook in my mind, but I don't want to get caught up in a legal battle of 'he said/she said'. All I really want is to be with my family and to get a better job near our new home."

"All right. You're right and it's your decision to make," Lucas conceded, "but if this ever happens to you again, please tell me. Then calm me down again," he smiled sheepishly. "Let's discuss it and figure out how to handle it. We're partners, right?"

"Agreed. And you, too. Please tell me when you have a problem with someone and don't worry about hurting my feelings."

He nodded.

"Now, don't you want to see your son?" Tawny said.

Lucas looked straight at Tawny and the blue bundle. His son. All the remaining anger floated away. He rushed over, kissed Tawny, and then looked down at the sleeping baby, his sleeping son!

"He's adorable, honey." He wiped at a tear that had slid out of the corner of his eye. "I'm so sorry I missed the birth and everything. I tried as hard as I could to get here in time."

"It's okay," Tawny said. "Really. I'm sure lots of men miss the births of their children. Didn't you tell me that Christa's father missed the birth of his son while he was in the war?"

"Yeah," Lucas said. "That was sad. But he had a good reason. I didn't."

"Don't you dare beat yourself up over that, do you hear me. You're a good father and a good husband. If we have another baby, you can be there for that one's birth. In fact, you can give birth to the next baby," she teased. "Just enjoy today. You have a new child. Be happy."

He nodded as she handed him the blue bundle. He knew she was right, that people load guilt onto their own shoulders, even when the people they think they've wronged don't see it that way. He needed to learn to stop loading guilt on himself.

Aunt Elsa said, "I wish our parents were still alive to meet their newest great-grandbaby."

Lucas thought about that. Their parents—yes, they would have been happy, he felt sure. His own parents were another story—well, his mother would have probably been thrilled, but his father wouldn't. That much hadn't changed, even at the end, as far as Lucas knew. Maybe if he'd gotten through to his father and got him off drugs, he might have been able to talk to him about his racist beliefs and could have come to some sort of understanding. If only . . . *stop doing that*, he told himself. *You did the best you could. You promised yourself you wouldn't load up on guilt.*

He sighed. Old habits were hard to break.

Aunt Anna said, "And all their other great-grandchildren and grandchildren. It's a shame Mom and Dad died in that car accident."

"Well, it's good that they didn't know about Seth and Dad," Lucas said, thinking out loud. "I can't imagine they would have been happy with their intolerance."

Aunt Elsa said, "Lucas, they knew about Joseph, your father. They tried to talk to him. Reached out numerous times over the years. Back when you were small."

"That's right," Anna said. "He was stubborn as hell. Our parents finally gave up, but I think they always felt guilty that he'd turned out the way he did. They thought they should have been able to teach him better about being good to his fellow man."

Tawny said, "That wasn't their fault, I'm sure. Look at how you two turned out. You're both kind and caring and tolerant of others."

Aunt Anna said, "You're right about Joseph. They were good parents to him and to us. Joseph was difficult from the beginning, and they did everything they could to steer him on the right path."

Aunt Elsa nodded.

"When Seth came to our house," Aunt Anna said, "we had no idea about the things he believed. That's when we gave him the contact information for our relatives in Germany. The second time he came, he told us about Tawny being black. He also let slip something about Jews. Elsa and I wanted to slap him and tell him the truth, but didn't dare."

Elsa said, "I've wanted to call him up many times and tell him that we're Jewish. That he's got Jewish blood running through his veins. Anna wouldn't let me."

Tawny said, "Probably better you didn't. He might have gone ballistic if you'd told him, and taken out his anger on the two of you. You probably were wise not to tell him."

Lucas didn't say anything. Seth was a problem that wasn't going away, and he wasn't sure what to do about him. Tawny had a point. The guy could be unstable, especially if he learned the truth before he was ready to accept it.

"When are you going to tell us what you found out in Germany?" Aunt Anna said, changing the subject. "We've been dying to hear about your adventures over there. Tawny showed us some of your photos you posted online. Made us want to go back over there for a visit of our own."

"I'll tell you all about it, but first I want to hug my girls, kiss them, and tell them I love them. After that, I want to hear all about what I missed while I was gone. The labor, the birth, everything."

Bianca jumped down from Anna's lap and rushed over to Lucas, standing beside Tawny's bed. Lani stood and took the baby from Lucas's arms, allowing Lucas to reach down, scoop Bianca up into his arms, and smother her with kisses and tickles.

CHAPTER TWENTY-FOUR

Christa Nagel, Oct. 1947-April 1948, Memmingen, Germany—

CHRISTA EXITED SCHOOL for the last time, ecstatic, milling around with her classmates, smiling, laughing and hugging, excited that they'd graduated in spite of all the time they'd lost while the schools were closed during the war. Now they had their whole lives ahead of them. She congratulated two friends on their being accepted to trade schools and a third on his being accepted into an apprenticeship. Their futures were bright.

Now she needed to figure out what she was going to do with her life. Whatever that was, she hoped she could make something good of herself.

For the few first days after, she languished at home, enjoying her newly found freedom and helping Mutti and Aunt Maria with the younger kids. Her head was still floating in the clouds.

A few days later, Aunt Maria said, "Christa, you need to get a job and help support the family, or move out and get your own place. Right, Hanna?"

Mutti was standing next to Aunt Maria, wringing her hands together, her eyes avoiding Christa's. "*Ja*, too many mouths to feed."

"You are an adult now, Christa," Aunt Maria added. "You must start acting like an adult, like your cousin, Ilse."

Christa's excitement suddenly plunged through the floor of her aunt's house. *Right. I am fourteen and out of school. Get to work, Christa. Take care of the kids, Christa. Do the laundry, Christa. Go find your own place, Christa. When did I ever get to be a kid?*

Instead of complaining though, Christa just asked, "How do I get a job?"

Aunt Maria smiled and responded, "Check the bulletin boards, go to the businesses, shops, the factories, and ask if they are hiring. Fill out applications."

"All right, she nodded, resigned. "I will find a job."

She spent the next week checking with every business in Memmingen. It seemed no one wanted to hire a young girl who had just finished school. Searching in other nearby towns might be an option, but she needed a job close enough to home, or else she would have to find an apartment. Only who would rent an apartment to someone her age? And she'd heard that there was still a housing shortage, which meant she would have a slim chance of getting a place of her own.

She sighed as she meandered the streets, meekly kicking stones along the road's edge, trying to decide where else she could look. A group of American soldiers stood outside the café where she'd asked about a job fifteen minutes earlier. That gave her an idea. She could ride her bicycle out to the air base, taking Augsburgerstraße, and see if they were hiring. Maybe they needed someone to help out in one of the offices. She could answer phones and file papers.

An hour later, after rushing home and getting her bicycle, then riding through the residential part of town and into the countryside, she arrived at the air base and stopped to ask a soldier where she could inquire about a job. The guard sent her to a big building with glass double doors. She entered, looked around, then walked over to a desk, where a middle-aged woman sat, dressed in a business suit.

"Excuse me," Christa said in German, hoping the woman would understand her. "I was told this was where I should come to check on employment opportunities."

The woman looked her up and down. "Sorry, we don't have any jobs for you," she said in German with a thick American accent. "Did you look at the bulletin board?" She pointed over to the wall, near the door where Christa had entered.

"Look at the bulletin board?" Christa asked, wondering what good it would do to check their bulletin board, considering the woman had just told her they didn't have any jobs.

"Yes. It's not for official jobs," she smiled. "Our soldiers and their families post help-wanted ads on our bulletin board. You might find something there."

"I will look. *Danke.*"

She trudged over to the board, her shoulders slumping, feeling hopeless and useless. Looking up at the ten or so ads posted, she began reading: Need driver for school aged children. Need handyman for repairs on house. Need math tutor for our teenage son. Need live-in nanny to care for five month old baby. Need . . . wait. Go back. Live-in nanny. She could do that. Mutti wouldn't like her leaving home, but she would appreciate having extra space in the house that her leaving would give them.

She took out a piece of paper and pencil from her handbag and scribbled the phone number, then went back to the desk. "Is there a telephone around here that I could use?"

The woman glanced around, then gave Christa a long look. "I'm not supposed to do this, but if you make it short and it's only one phone call, I guess it'll be all right," she slid her phone over.

Christa dialed the number, her fingers shaking hard enough that she had to start over three times. The phone finally rang.

A woman answered—in English.

Christa felt panic course through her body and she almost hung up. Then she remembered Mutti and Aunt Maria telling her to find a job. She spoke in German, hoping this woman would also understand her.

"Uh, hello, my name is Christa Nagel. I saw your advertisement about a job. A nanny for a baby. I can do that."

"How old are you?" she answered in German. "I'm looking for someone with a lot of experience caring for young children."

"I am fourteen. I finished school early. I am the oldest in my family, and I have six brothers and sisters. I have more experience than you can imagine, changing diapers, feeding, taking care of sick kids, bathing them, everything to help my mother, who had her hands full." She thought about telling her all she had done taking care of the children on their long walk or in the internment camp, but decided against it. "I . . . I even helped deliver my baby brother."

"My goodness. That's a lot for someone so young." The line went quiet and Christa worried she might have hung up the phone. "I was hoping for someone a few years older," the woman added, "but I'm willing to meet you and see if you'll do. Can you come by the house this afternoon? My husband will be at work at the air base, but he's allowing me to choose the nanny."

"I can come now, if you would like."

"*Wunderbar.* Where are you now?"

"At the base," Christa said. "I found your advertisement on a bulletin board."

"Very good. Our house is not far from there."

279

Christa pulled out her pencil again and jotted down the address and directions.

Soon she stood on the street straddling her bicycle and staring at a pretty two-story half-timbered house. She walked her bicycle to the front door, left it slightly hidden behind a bush, and rang the bell.

"You must be Christa," a tall brunette woman said, standing at the screen door. "I'm Helen Robinson. Come in." She held the door open.

Christa stepped inside and wondered how the Americans could afford such luxurious furnishings.

"Please sit. Tell me about yourself. Help yourself to refreshments." She pointed to a tray on the coffee table, a tray holding a teapot, fine china cups and saucers, cookies. "Why do you want to be a nanny?"

Christa took a deep breath, trying to pull together her thoughts and words. This interview was too important to mess up.

She thought back to when she ten. All she'd wanted was to not have to deal with all her brothers and sisters. Changing diapers, wiping runny noses, breaking up fights. How could she have changed so much in a few years?

She licked sandpaper lips and folded her sweat-covered hands together, as she began.

"My family," she said, "like most Germans, suffered greatly during the war. We were luckier than many, although we certainly did not feel lucky at times." Her thoughts felt jumbled, and she shook her head to try to straighten them. She didn't want to go into details, didn't want to tell this stranger about the Sudetenland and their expulsion. Not unless she had to. "I mean, we all survived. I think because we pulled together, protected each other. Bombs dropped around us, soldiers shot at us, we almost starved, and we feared what would happen next. But none of that could break us. We were together, a family, and that made us strong. We are rebuilding our lives now, as the country is rebuilding its cities and towns." She paused.

She'd been staring at the floor without realizing it, and looked up now at the woman.

The woman, Helen, was dabbing tears from her eyes. "Where is your family now?"

"Living in Memmingen with my grandparents, aunt, and cousins. It is a very full house."

"They won't be upset if you live here, with us?"

"It will be an adjustment," Christa said. "We have never been apart. But they really need me to get a job to help with the bills. I expect they will be happy with extra space in the house, too. I will be close enough to visit on my days off. Would I get days off?"

"Of course. Would you like to meet Suzanne? She's our baby girl. Five and a half months old."

Christa nodded and followed Helen up the stairs.

In a beautiful nursery, Helen tiptoed over to the white crib and looked down. "She's awake." She picked up the baby and smiled, then handed her to Christa.

"Does she understand German?" Christa asked.

"No. We speak English in our household. I gather you don't speak English."

"Not yet. I . . . ," she almost said she spoke some Czech, but caught herself, "I am a fast learner and will study hard. English will be good for me to learn."

Helen smiled and nodded.

Christa smiled at the baby, and the baby made adorable cooing sounds. "She is beautiful. I think we will get along well together."

"When can you start?" Helen asked.

"In two days? I just need to pack a few things and finish things at home."

"Wonderful. See you in two days."

Christa rode her bicycle home and made her announcement over dinner. Mutti started to object, but Aunt Maria cut her off, saying, "It is perfect."

OVER THE NEXT few months, Christa made good progress with her English. She listened to English broadcasts on the radio, read English newspapers, and joined in conversations with Helen and her husband, Charles, and sometimes even with their dinner guests.

One day in early November, Charles invited several soldiers from his unit. As their commanding officer, he wanted to get to know his young American soldiers better.

That's when she met Tom, a handsome, dark-haired American soldier. She fell in love with him the moment she saw him. Beautiful blue eyes and perfect features. An Adonis, like she'd read about in one of her library books. She and Tom began seeing each other on her days off. At first, she didn't tell him her age, hoping he would fall in love with her before he discovered how young she was. But he found out at Christmastime, when he came over to the house with the soldiers from his unit for a Christmas celebration. The men were all homesick and couldn't be with their families. That night, in the kitchen he was talking with Helen.

Later that evening, he caught Christa when no one was around. He led her outside onto the front porch.

"We can't see each other anymore," he said, holding her hands in his. "Helen told me you're only fourteen. Why didn't you tell me how young you are?"

"I . . . I was afraid. I'm young in years, but I've been through much because of the war. That makes me older."

"I'm afraid no one will see it that way," he said. "The age difference between us matters."

"How can five years difference between us matter?" she said, staring up at him, pleading.

"If we were in our twenties or thirties, five years wouldn't matter. You're still a child, and that does matter. To me."

She put her hand over her mouth and ran away, into the house and up the stairs to her room, throwing herself onto her bed.

A week later, the beginning of the New Year, they bumped into each other at a café. Looking around to make sure no one they knew was around, they sat together and talked over lunch. Tom finally relented and agreed to see each other again, only he swore her to secrecy, because he was afraid it would get back to his commanding officer and cause trouble for both of them, if she told anyone.

TWO MONTHS LATER, when Christa arrived home to see her family for a weekend, the household was in chaos.

"What is going on?" she asked Fritz.

"Vati. He is home. Got home a few hours ago. Can you believe it?"

Christa said, "Where is he?"

Fritz took her by the arm and led her to the kitchen.

She released a scream of joy and ran into her father's arms.

He told her about his capture by the Red Army, his years in a prisoner of war camp, his eventual release, and his search through the former Sudetenland and Germany for his family.

When it was time to go back to her new home, she reluctantly said goodbye to Vati, but the tears she shed were happy tears.

As she rode her bicycle, she thought about Vati's story and wondered how much Mutti would tell him about their ordeal. She also thought about Ernst. He'd moved out of the house a month ago, which was probably a good thing, now that Vati was back. Petr Jaroslav had helped Ernst get a job at the factory where he worked. A low paying, apprentice job, but a job nonetheless. His flat mate had moved out shortly afterward, so Petr had offered him a room in his apartment. Ernst told her his job was going well and he was happy to have the luxury of a home with only two people in it. He was more excited than she'd ever seen him about anything.

What a wonderful day it had been all around.

As she entered the house, Helen was pacing in the living room, holding Suzanne.

"What's wrong?" Christa asked.

"She's sick. Her temperature is high and we can't reach the doctor."

"Did you try putting her in a bathtub with cold water?" Christa asked. "Mutti does that when we have high fevers. It helps bring the temperature down."

Helen looked at her husband.

He said, "Let's try it."

The bathtub worked, and by morning Suzanne was feeling much better.

Two days later, while Christa was out grocery shopping for the Robinsons, she bumped into Tom.

"Hey, I'm glad you're here," he said. "Can we talk for a few minutes? Do you have time?"

"I guess. Something wrong?"

"I need to tell you something. Your cousin, Ilse, saw us together. She confronted me and told me to stay away from you. I told her to mind her own business, but I thought you should know, in case she tries to make it her business."

"Thank you for telling me. I'll talk to her. I should go."

He touched her elbow as she turned to go. "There's something else. I know I should have told you sooner. At least at Christmas time."

"What is it?"

"I'm Jewish. No one in my unit knows. Not even Captain Robinson. As far as I know, no one knows. It might not matter now that the war is over, but I don't want to advertise it, just in case it does matter."

Christa had wondered why he seemed uncomfortable at the Christmas party but had assumed it was because of their relationship. She'd never suspected this.

"It doesn't matter to me. Not one bit. Your secret is safe with me."

"Thank you. That means a lot to me."

Ilse Seidel, June-July 1948, Memmingen, Germany—

PETR AND ILSE stepped out the French doors at the back of Ilse's family's townhouse and walked along the paved walkway to the edge of the *Stadtbach*, or town brook. It remained Ilse's favorite spot in all of Memmingen. Tonight was no exception. The brook shimmered, reflecting a partial moon off its rippling waters, and stars twinkled overhead like diamonds. *A most romantic setting*, she decided. Petr suddenly stopped, kneeling down in front of Ilse on the sidewalk. Before she could figure out what he was doing, he looked up at her and said, "Ilse Seidel, will you marry me? I know I do not have much to offer, but I love you and want to spend the rest of my life with you."

Ilse stifled a gasp and her eyes became watery with emotion. How long she had waited to hear those few words from his lips, words she had almost given up on. In hindsight, she realized that part of his delay could well have been her failure to really open up to him. He'd asked her many times about her past, about her fears and her dreams and her regrets. He'd told her about his efforts during the war, the men he'd killed, and his work in the internment camp. He'd given her ample opportunity to open up to him and share her secrets.

Now, here she was, hearing those words, finally, and she couldn't say yes. She hadn't told him about Ron and the baby. Good women, the kind of women men wanted to marry, wouldn't behave the way she had with Ron. Would Petr turn away from her if she told him, especially now, after all this time they'd spent together? Would he take back his marriage proposal?

She hesitated, blinking back tears.

After a few moments of silence, he said, "Do you need time to think about it? I don't want to pressure you?"

"Thank you, Petr. I do need to think."

His face drooped, and she wanted to take her words back, toss them into the river and let them float away, but it was too late. "Oh. Well, I guess I should leave now and give you some quiet time to consider."

She reached out to stop him, but he was gone in an instant, quickly walking along the riverway, then turning and disappearing between two buildings out toward the main road. Distraught, Ilse cried for a time before dragging herself back home, then throwing herself onto her bed, crying again into her pillow.

Over the next several days, she tried to call him, deciding to tell him about Ron and the baby, hoping he would understand, only Petr didn't answer his phone. She worried that he'd changed his mind.

As a last resort, she tried contacting him at his workplace, but one of his coworkers told her he hadn't been to work for a few days. Now she was frantic. Had he left town? Gone back to Czechoslovakia?

"What about his friend, Ernst Nagel?" she asked his coworker.

"*Nein*, he is not here, either." Ernst gone, too? Then she remembered that Ernst and his father, Ilse's Uncle Franz, had gone on a trip together, a quick trip to search for Uncle Franz's parents before Franz began his new job as a construction worker. His parents had possibly emigrated from the Sudetenland, as well; if they were still living, that is. Could Petr have gone with them? As soon as she thought it, she dismissed that notion. They had left the day before Petr proposed.

Ilse knew Christa and Petr had a close relationship, sort of like brother and sister, after their time in Theresienstadt. She would talk to Christa. Maybe Petr had confided in her about the proposal. Maybe Christa knew where he was or what was going on.

After work, she talked to Aunt Hanna and got Christa's address, then rode her bicycle to the next town over and knocked on her door.

The woman who answered the door, Christa's employer, told her that Christa was in the back yard with some friends.

Ilse walked around the garden path to the backyard. There was Petr, Christa, and the man Christa had been dating.

"Ilse," Petr said, standing up when he saw her. "What are you doing here?"

"I have been trying to reach you. I could not think where else to look."

Christa said, "We had a long talk. Will you come and join us."

Ilse licked her lips, stalling for time. She wanted to talk to Petr alone, not with Christa and her friend there. Slowly, she walked toward them, stopping near Petr, placing her hands on the back of an old wooden patio chair.

Petr said, "Christa's friend here, Tom Landry, is being recalled to the states. It seems his father has taken ill and asked for Tom to be sent home. The airbase where they are sending him is close to his parents' house. Both Christa and Tom are devastated, both for news of his father, and because they will not be able to see each other again."

Mein Gott! Tom Landry! Brother of Ron! She froze, her emotions exploding, keeping her from breathing. Her insides felt like all the bright lights on the night of the air attack over Memmingen going off all at once. She leaned forward, afraid she might be sick to her stomach.

"Are you all right, Ilse?" Christa said.

"I . . . no, no I am not." She turned and looked straight at Petr. "I have a confession," she said, barely able to stay on her feet. "I did not give you my answer the other night when you proposed. I wanted to say yes, yes, yes, and shout with joy." She stopped talking, wiping tears now streaming down her face.

"I could not say yes to you, because I have not told you my secret."

Tom stood up and said, "I think Christa and I should leave you two alone."

"No," Ilse said. "You need to hear this, too. It affects you, as well."

He sat back down and took hold of Christa's hand.

Petr pulled a chair over and said, "Come sit."

She sat down in the chair beside Petr. "I . . . met Tom Landry's brother, Ron, back in July of 1944. His airplane had been shot down near Memmingen. He parachuted down, survived, but was wounded. I tended to him for weeks, helping his wound heal, but then he developed pneumonia. It took months for him to fully recover."

"You helped my brother?" Tom said. "He's alive? Where is he? Why didn't he ever contact the family?"

"He was alive and stayed hidden in a damaged house in the countryside. Over the months we grew close, eventually we became lovers. I am sorry, Tom, but he died. Petr, I am sorry I didn't tell you. I was afraid."

Tom didn't respond. He sat quietly, still holding Christa's hand.

"It is all right, Ilse," Petr said, glancing momentarily at Tom. "What happened to the American? How did he die?"

"My brother, Johann, was a soldier in the German army. One day he saw and followed me and confronted us. He promised he would not turn us in as long as Ron left in a few days."

Tom gasped.

"Ron and I said our goodbyes that night, and he planned to leave first thing in the morning. But I had to see him one last time so early, before dawn, I went back to see him. Before I got there, I saw my brother and several other soldiers, so I hid. They had Ron and dragged him out of the house. Outside, my brother shot and killed Ron. There was nothing I could do."

"Oh, Ilse, how horrible," Christa said. "I am so sorry for you and for Ron's death. The war has taken too much from everyone."

Petr said, "Ilse, you should have told me. I have told you worse things about what I have seen and had to do. Please do not ever feel you cannot talk to me. I love you."

"*Nein.*" Ilse sucked in her breath and stifled a sob. "You have not heard everything. I gave birth to Ron's baby." She looked over at Tom. "A boy. My aunt Karolina adopted him. I still see him and he is a sweet child."

Petr smiled and squeezed her hand. "I would love to meet him, and your aunt Karolina,"

"My brother has a child? A living child? I need to see him too. He belongs with his grandparents."

"He belongs with his adoptive mother and his birth mother," Ilse said. "I will not have you take him away, where I cannot watch him grow up. I will not have you take him from my aunt, who lost her husband, both her sons, her brother, and her parents in the war. Julian is her lifeline."

"My parents lost their son," Tom said. "That boy is the only thing left of their son."

"They still have you. You have a sister, too, *ja*?"

"I do." He didn't say anything else for a moment. "I would at least like to see the boy and take a photo to show my parents."

"I can arrange that, if you promise you will not try to take him away from us."

"You have my word."

Petr got up and turned to Ilse. Stooping down, he said, "I think we need to go for a walk, you and I, and discuss our future. Do you agree?"

"I do."

CHAPTER TWENTY-FIVE

Lucas Landry, September 2017, Sacramento, California—

LUCAS HAD A ton of work to do to get ready for Tawny and the baby to come home. Luckily he had time, since the hospital was keeping Tawny and the baby a few extra days. The baby was a preemie and Tawny also had minor blood pressure problems they decided to address. That gave him, along with his aunts and mother-in-law, time to get their new home ready. One of his cousins who owned a pick–up truck volunteered to help move furniture.

After looking around Lucas's Roseville house and being told it was going on the market, the cousin told Lucas he wanted to buy it. He and his wife had been looking for a house in the area for almost a year. He said they were even willing to pay full asking price. When Lucas had called Tawny and told her the good news, she was overjoyed and told him now everything was perfect. It would save them the hassle of listing it and the expense of paying realtors.

Lucas finished setting up the crib in their new-old house and took a final look around, proud and feeling satisfied with what they had accomplished, before heading back to the hospital. At the hospital, while they all waited for the doctor to come into Tawny's room and sign her release papers, Lucas turned to his aunts and asked, "Aunt Elsa, did anyone ever tell you who you were named after?"

"No, I don't think so. Why? Do you know?"

"I do. Do you remember me telling you about a second girl in Germany who'd written diaries? Her name was Ilse Seidel."

"I remember you mentioned her. What about Ilse? How does she fit in?"

"Well, Ilse and your uncle, Ron Landry, met during the war. He was a wounded pilot and she nursed him back to health. He was killed, later, but before he died, he fathered a child with her. Your parents named you after Ilse—the more American version of her name, that is."

The aunts exchanged startled looks.

Continuing, Lucas said, "Ilse gave birth to a boy named Julian, and her aunt, Karolina Wagner, adopted and raised him. I got to meet him while I was in Germany."

"What? Wasn't that the name of our baby brother?" Aunt Anna asked.

"Yes. I almost forgot about him."

"Baby brother?" Lucas and Tawny asked in unison, exchanging glances.

Aunt Anna nodded. "Our Julian was born in Biberach, in between Elsa and Joseph. He was what was called a blue baby, because his heart wasn't fully developed. Back in those days, the doctors couldn't do much for blue babies. He only lived a few days. It devastated our parents. We were too young to understand what was happening."

Aunt Elsa said, "Do you think our parents named him after Ron's baby?"

"That's entirely possible," Lucas said. He looked at Tawny. She nodded. "Tawny and I talked the other day about our son's name. We decided he will be named Julian Ronald Landry." Both women broke into tears.

Aunt Anna sniffled and dabbed her eyes dry with a tissue. "Thank you, both of you."

Lucas reached out and touched her arm. "We are honored to be a part of this family. Thank you for being there for us."

After much hugging and the women drying their eyes, Tawny's mother, Lani, handed the swaddled and nearly sleeping baby to Elsa.

Tawny, who had been reading the partially translated diaries and papers Lucas had found and put together, said, "One thing still baffles me. How did the diaries, papers, and all the other stuff from the Sudetenland get here to California? Did I miss something? The family left home with nothing but a suitcase each, and those were left those behind after the first day of walking when they were being expelled. They lost their coats and clothing that had jewels and money sewn inside. So where did all that stuff come from, and how?"

"That's a really good question," Aunt Anna said.

Lucas smiled. "I don't know how much you know about the expulsion of ethnic Germans from the former Sudetenland. I've done quite a lot of research on the topic. At the time, Germans made up about twenty-eight percent of the population of Czechoslovakia. That was almost three and a half million ethnic Germans whose ancestors had called that area home for a thousand years." He paused to recall more of the details.

Aunt Elsa, taking advantage of the pause, said, "So the Germans living in that part of the world hadn't just moved there at the start of the war, when the Reich took it over?"

"That's right. Glad you mentioned that. From what I can surmise, the borders in that region of Europe had been open to migration and settling for at least a thousand years. Ethnic Germans had called Hungary, Yugoslavia, Romania, and Poland home, and likely the other way around, too. Anyway, at the end of the war, all the ethnic Germans, regardless of their political beliefs, were physically and violently expelled from all the Eastern European countries. Somewhere between twelve and fourteen million of them were uprooted, mostly women, children, and the elderly."

All of the women in the room gaped.

Lani said, "Where were they expelled to?"

"Germany. Some were sent to Eastern Germany and lived under communist rule but most ended up in Western Germany. As far as I can tell, none were given a choice."

"I feel bad for them, especially those who were sent to Eastern Germany," Aunt Elsa said. "I can't imagine how horrible it was for them."

Lucas said, "I tell you this, because it's important to understand the extent of what occurred over there. While I was in Germany, I asked Ilse Seidel—now Ilse Jaroslav—how the Nagels got their diaries and other belongings back after their expulsion. She told me that Christa and Tom, and a couple of Christa's siblings were able to travel back to the Sudetenland in the early 1950's. They found their old house in Altstadt and spoke to the people who were living there. They told them who they were and that their family had buried some items, which they hoped they might be allowed to retrieve."

"And they let them?" Tawny asked, wide eyed.

"Yes, but not only that, they let them inside the house and let them take some of their belongings that the Nagels had stored—hidden—under the floorboards. The Nagels took everything they could fit into their vehicles, thanked the family who lived there, and left. They never returned to Altstadt after that. They told Ilse that there was nothing for them there anymore."

"Wow," Tawny said. "That's wonderful they were able to retrieve all that stuff. Didn't Christa's parents or siblings want to keep it?"

"Nope. They wanted Christa to keep it all for safekeeping, in the hopes someday someone would write about their lives. Ilse also gave them some of her things, and so did her husband, Petr Jaroslav."

"Do you think anyone will ever write about them?" Aunt Elsa said. "The part about many millions of Jews being imprisoned, tortured, and killed is widely known, but I doubt most people know about the expulsion and torture of the ethnic Germans."

"Some people still don't believe any of the atrocities really happened—the holocaust or the expulsion. That's why I think I want to write their story," Lucas said. "The Germans and the Jews and the carnages that happened to them are all entwined with my ancestry and my story. My family's story. The American allies who fought alongside soldiers from many other countries to end the Hitler Regime, including my grandfather and my Great-Uncle Ron, and the Resistance fighters, are part of that story, too. Tawny says she'll help me organize everything better, while she's on maternity leave."

"I'm actually excited to help," Tawny said, smiling from her hospital bed.

"I'll be starting my new job and will be busy, but when things settle down, I plan to write our story. It's something I can do on weekends and occasionally in the evenings."

"I'm going to help him with some of the writing, too," Tawny said.

"Yeah, and when the kids are able to travel, I think we'll take a trip to Germany and maybe even to the former Sudetenland for research, but also giving us a chance to see more of our roots."

"Maybe we can help, too," Aunt Anna said. "I used to teach writing in a university. Bet you didn't know that."

He shook his head and grinned. "You're full of surprises."

"Oh, you don't know the half of it."

Aunt Elsa said, "Don't forget that those family roots are spread out in other directions too. Our father's—your grandfather's— family went back to the gold rush days right here in this country."

And Tawny jumped in, "Your mother's family originally came from Ireland, isn't that what you told me? You might have to include Ireland and Great Britain in a future trip."

Lani joined the fray, saying, "Your children's roots also go back to South Africa, don't forget."

Aunt Anna said, "I'm pretty sure our grandfather on Dad's side was in this country for many years, but I'm not sure where our grandmother came from. Dad's mother. I vaguely remember hearing someone say she came from somewhere like Poland or Hungary or someplace like that."

"Yikes. Whoa there, everyone. I'll need to quit my job if I try to go everywhere and research my whole family tree—and Tawny's family tree. Let's just take it one step at a time. I really do feel excited about all of it, though.

Lucas looked around the room at his family and felt comforted. "You have no idea how lonely I felt before my father died. Then, when he died, this incredible guilt hit me. I should have tried to reach him. I should have tried to save him from the drugs. It's too late, but maybe there is still a chance for me to save someone."

"You mean Seth?" Tawny said.

Lucas had finally told her more about Seth's beliefs a couple of days ago, when they were alone in the hospital room. "Yep. I've thought about this a lot. He may be unreachable. If so, I'll leave him be. All I can say is that I have to try. It's time I sit down with him and really talk."

"When will you do it?" Tawny asked.

"After we get you home and settled in, I'll go over to Seth's house and give him copies of everything—the diaries, family tree drawings. I'll leave them with him and plead with him, if I have to, to read them and call me when he's finished." He worried that Seth was far too entrenched in his radical beliefs, and that no one could dig him out of it but, by God, he had to try.

"It's worth a try," Tawny said. "I hope you can reach him. You've been missing your brother for far too long."

Aunt Anna said, "Are you going to tell him that he's half Jewish—ancestry—I mean?"

"Not directly, if I don't have to," Lucas said. "I don't want to set him off by just telling him and having him just dig his heels in." Seth could be a time bomb, but Lucas didn't want to say that out loud and worry his family. "If he reads the materials and figures it out on his own, at a pace that won't shock the crap out of him, I think he might be more willing to re-evaluate his beliefs on his own, you know what I mean?"

"That sounds right," Tawny said. "He might be more willing to accept it if it's not thrown in his face."

"That's the hope anyway," Lucas said. He would be putting himself out there and risking getting hurt again, the way he had when he'd shown up on his father's doorstep with his newborn daughter all those years ago. He was only now getting over that hurt. But if there was a chance he could repair his relationship with his brother, he had to try. At least now he felt stronger, having family support to rely on.

No one spoke for a few minutes.

Aunt Anna, glancing at her sister and then looking at Lucas broke the awkward silence. "We would like to read more of those diaries, if we can."

"Of course you can," Lucas said. "I made extra copies of all that material so that you could have your own copies. I've translated a lot of it into English."

"Thank you," the aunts said in unison.

"Oh, I almost forgot," Lucas continued, "after things calm down a bit, I'd like to have you all over to the house for dinner. I have lots to tell you about the Germany trip and all the family members I met. I finally have all the missing pieces—or at least most of them."

"I can't wait," Aunt Elsa beamed.

Later, as Lucas helped Tawny out of the car in the driveway of his father's—no, their—house, he paused and said, "I didn't know about the baby Julian who died, when I suggested we name our baby Julian. If you want to change his name, it's probably not too late."

"No. I love the name and think it's perfect. I feel like we are now also honoring that poor little soul who never got a chance to live his life."

Lucas kissed her and whispered in her ear, "I love you, Tawny Landry."

Inside the house, Tawny gushed over the way Lucas and the aunts and her mother had redecorated the bedrooms and the living room. "I love it so much," she said. "Everything is exactly the way I imagined. The baby's room and Bianca's room are perfect. Thank you!" She pulled Lucas into a tight embrace and kissed him. "I love you so much."

"I love you, too."

After settling Tawny, the baby, and Bianca in their new house, he went into his new office and picked up the box he'd put together. He said, "I'll see you in a while. Going to drop this stuff off at Seth's."

"Okay. Good luck."

A short time later, after fighting rush hour traffic, he arrived in front of Seth's house. He took a deep breath, trying to work up the nerve to face his brother. *Guess I better do it before his neighbors call the police and report me as suspicious.*

He got out of his Jeep, opened the back door and grabbed the box, then strode up to the door and rang the bell.

Seth opened the door, his eyes showing surprise.

"Didn't expect to see you again."

"Why's that?"

"You got what you came here for, the contact list. Figured you didn't need me anymore."

"Brother, I will always need you, but not in the way you think. I need you precisely because you're my brother. You need me for the same reason."

"Using your psycho-babble on me, huh?"

"What? No. I'm just trying to reach out to you. I brought you something."

"Oh, yeah, what?"

"This box is full of our family history. I've spent months collecting it, putting it all together. These are copies—for you and your family. I'm hoping—you'll read it."

"Why would I want to do that? Maybe you're into all that ancestry crap, but not me. Just go away and leave me alone. Just go, and take that shit with you."

"Seth, wait. I found most of this stuff in Dad's attic. I'm not sure if he ever knew it was up there. I know ancestry isn't your thing. To be honest, it never was mine, either. Not until I started looking at this stuff. There's some fascinating material here. Diaries, poems, old letters. Oh and identity cards. You may have heard of them—officially, they were Ahnenpaß. That translates to 'family tree of Aryan descent'. They were required of all citizens during WWII."

Seth stood up straighter, his attention obvious. "I've heard of them."

"You studied German in school, too, didn't you? I seem to remember you talking about the teacher. Same teacher I had in high school."

"Yeah, I did."

Lucas, hoping against all hope to appeal to his brother, said, "The stuff is mostly in German. I translated some of it and made copies of my translations for you, too, in case I was wrong and you didn't know or remember German. Oh, and some of the diaries are in Czech. I had to get a professor to translate those for me."

"Czech? Why would you have Czech documents?"

"Ever heard of the Czech Resistance fighters?"

"Nope." He inched the door closer to being closed.

Crap, I'm losing him. What can I say to get him interested?

"Did you know we have some Czech ancestry, Seth?"

"What? You're crazy, man. Look, like I said, I'm not interested in that old family history shit. Forget it. Get lost."

No, no, no, that's not the way this was supposed to go. Oh, man, how can I convince a Neo-Nazi to read stuff about his family's history? Wait, I've got it.

"You like guns and wars and Nazi stuff, right?"

Seth nodded, his eyes now showing interest.

"There's lots of stuff about the war. The Red Army. Concentration camps. You'll be hooked. I'm telling you, you've gotta read this. All of it. I've packaged things together in the order you should read."

Seth sighed so loudly it could more accurately be called groaned. He took the box from Lucas. "Fine. I'll read some of it. Not guaranteeing I'll read it all. Like I said, I don't care about family history and I don't want to talk to you about it. Ever. I'm just saying I'll read some to get you to leave."

"Fair enough. When you're done, call me and let's talk. Please promise me you'll call."

"Okay. I'll call. Geez."

Lucas opened his mouth to speak, but Seth shut the door in his face before he got another word out.

CHAPTER TWENTY-SIX

Christa Nagel, July 1948-June 1950, Memmingen, Germany—

CHRISTA AND TOM sat in a church pew, beside Christa's family, watching Ilse and Petr exchange wedding vows. Ilse, her long blonde hair styled in a fancy do, flower wreath atop her head, looked stunning in her long white embroidered gown trimmed in lace. Vati, though only her uncle by marriage, had walked Ilse down the aisle, and Ernst had served as best man. Christa knew that Ilse's brother, Robert, had been disappointed when Petr asked Ernst to be his best man, but he understood that Petr had a connection with all the Nagel siblings.

Completing their vows, husband and wife kissed and everyone cheered. The happy couple turned to face the audience—their families, neighbors, and co-workers. Christa sighed as the bride and groom walked arm in arm, stopping briefly to talk to guests as they meandered down the aisle,. How she wished she were the bride and Tom were the groom. It wasn't to be. Not now, maybe not ever. At fifteen, Christa knew she was too young to marry, which also meant she couldn't ask Tom to take her with him to the states. Once back in California, for the remainder of his three-year tour of duty, Christa worried he would probably find a beautiful woman who would sweep him off his feet, and he would forget about her and Germany.

"Why do you look so glum?" Tom asked when they got outside and stood among the guests, everyone still offering their congratulations and taking photographs.

"You know why," she whispered. "In two days you'll be gone. How else should I feel but glum?"

He wrapped her arm through his. "I'm sorry, Christa. I wish I could go see my father, briefly, make sure he recovers, and then come back here and be with you. I would give anything for that, but I can't."

"I know."

Mutti walked over to them and hugged them both outside the church.

Christa fought back tears. A few days after Ilse's confession, Ilse had taken Christa, Petr, and Tom to Biberach to meet Aunt Karolina and Julian. Tom had cried briefly as he hugged the little boy, whom he said reminded him of his brother, Ron.

"What faith is he being raised in?" Tom had asked Karolina when the boy left to go upstairs and play. "Do you know that his family is Jewish?"

"*Ja*, I know. I am teaching him about both the Jewish and the Protestant faiths," she'd said. "When his is old enough, he can decide for himself."

"Does he know who is biological parents are?"

"He does. I want him to know the truth. No secrets. No lies. No judgments. His surname is Wagner because I have legally adopted him, but he knows who he is and where he came from."

The following day, Christa had known what she had to do. She had taken Tom to her family in Memmingen and told them about their relationship. She didn't know if she would ever see Tom again, after he returned to the United States, but she didn't want to keep secrets from her family. She'd seen how Ilse had suffered, all because of secrets.

To her amazement, no one had judged them. They didn't chastise her, say she was foolish or an idiot for dating an older man, an American, to top it off. They had quietly accepted him and made him feel welcome in their home.

That was Mutti's doing, Christa felt sure. Over the past few years, Christa had discovered a strength and also a wisdom in her mother she hadn't known was there. When Christa was a child, Mutti had seemed to her nothing more than a *hausfrau*, a farm wife, a baby-making machine. Uneducated and simple. The war, the expulsion, and everything done to Mutti and her children, and to friends and neighbors, had forged Mutti into a tough mother, fierce protector, fighter, and morale booster, when that was what was needed. Those traits, Christa suspected, had always been there, hidden from Christa's naive perspective, or perhaps were just lying dormant until called forth. Though forged in dark times, Mutti's caring, nurturing, and accepting non-judgmental nature had remained in the forefront throughout, from the earliest time Christa could remember. That kind nature had remained vigilant even after the war and after the expulsion. Where the horrors of the times had wiped the goodness out of many people, Mutti's innate goodness remained. If anything, Christa noted, those positive personality traits had become even more prominent.

"We should spend every moment together until you leave," Christa said to Tom as they strolled down the street, leaving the festivities, which were going to continue and move to a local restaurant. Ilse's aunt Karolina, such a generous woman, was paying for everything.

"Where should we go? A picnic along the river, maybe?"

Christa recalled Ilse telling them about a damaged house where she had hidden Ron.

"What about the house where your brother stayed? If it's still standing and vacant, we could spend time there." Christa paused, turned, and looked into Tom's eyes. "You could tell me all about your childhood and about your family. I want to hear more, while I still can."

He looked deep in thought for a moment. "I'm not sure that's a good idea. Ron was killed there and a lot of things happened there."

"You think it might be haunted?"

"No, no, not that."

Christa said, "It's also where Julian was conceived."

Tom stared at her. "That's part of the problem. Don't you see? I don't want us to repeat my brother's history. I don't want to leave behind a pregnant girlfriend. I don't want a baby growing up without his or her father."

Christa was struck, devastated. He wasn't planning to come back for her. He didn't love her. She'd been a distraction, a German girl in a country where he was stationed temporarily. It was never meant to be a long-term relationship.

She turned and ran, blind with pain and tears. She couldn't bear to look back.

That evening at the Robinsons' house in her bedroom, she tried to read a book to distract herself, but her mind wouldn't cooperate. Tom's image and words from earlier kept haunting her. *Tom doesn't want me. No, not my Tom. He's going home and he'll never come back.* Her stomach ached and she wanted to die.

Someone knocked at the front door, and she could hear voices trailing up the stairs. Tom? She tiptoed to her door, opened it a crack, and peeked downstairs, straight to the front door.

Not Tom. Another officer, a friend of Captain Robinson. Her shoulders slumped and her legs wobbled, threatening to drop her body down to the floor. Somehow, she managed to drag herself back into her bedroom and close the door. *You fool*, she told herself. *You let yourself belief you were loveable to someone other than your family.*

After that, she knew Tom was gone. His orders had sent him back to the states. Though broken inside for some time, life must go on, she repeated often in her mind. Eventually she convinced herself.

She continued her work with little Suzanne, and when Helen Robinson gave birth to a second child, a girl they named Rosie, Christa devoted herself to the little baby and big sister Suzanne, the way she'd seen her own mother do with all her children.

Christa got to love her parents' new babies, too. Another little boy who they named Stefan had arrived six months earlier. He was Mutti's second new baby after Vati returned from the war. The first, a beautiful girl they named Anna, didn't survive more than a few hours. Each member of the family took their turn holding the tiny doll-like baby before she was placed in a casket. Mutti had been afraid when she found out she was expecting again, six months later. But the healthy boy she'd delivered had thrived, and now Mutti seemed happy and content, being back in the role of making babies. Ilse joined in that role, too, giving birth to a son with Petr.

Petr was the proudest papa Christa had ever seen, and she loved to tease him about it. She would taunt, "Aww . . . look, at the big bad resistance fighter, changing diapers and playing tickle games with his son," and he would just smile from ear to ear, loving every minute.

Time passed. She even dated a boy that Robert, Ilse's brother, knew. That didn't last long. He seemed boring and immature. One day, on one of her jaunts into town to visit family, she stopped for lunch at a café with her brother, Ernst.

"The factory has job openings," he said. "You will be seventeen next month, old enough to find a real job. I can put in a recommendation for you. I am sure they will hire you."

"A real job? I have a real job," she snapped. "I take care of two children, keep house for an important family, and I get paid real money."

"Sorry. I did not meant it as a put-down," he said. "You can make more money working at the factory. That is all I was saying."

"Thanks, but I like what I am doing. At least for now. Maybe someday I will want a change."

He gave her an odd look, shrugged, and let the conversation die.

A week later, as she had just finished putting the kids down for a nap, the doorbell rang. She rushed downstairs, hoping to catch the door before another it rang again. It hadn't been easy getting the kids to sleep, and the last thing she wanted was to wake them and have to start over again.

She grabbed the doorknob and pulled the door open, and almost fainted.

"I was hoping you were still working here," Tom said, smiling, standing tall and broad shouldered and dressed in civilian clothes.

"Oh, my God," she sputtered, in English. Her English had improved vastly since he'd gone home to the states, studying hard, because Suzanne was getting older and talking up a storm in English and Christa needed to keep ahead of her.

"Is that a happy greeting, or are you horrified?"

Shaking, and before thinking, she threw her arms around his shoulders and then restrained herself, kissing him once on the cheek, unsure if a kiss on the lips was appropriate. Was this a dream come true, or a nightmare come to hurt her again?

"What are you doing back in Germany?" she asked, collecting her wits. "Oh, did you come here to the Robinsons' house to talk to the Captain? He isn't home."

"No. I came to see you. I hope that's okay."

She felt her face flush, and opened the door wider to let him inside. "You have to be quiet, the children are napping." She led him into the living room. "Helen is out visiting with friends."

"I wasn't sure if the Captain was still stationed here."

"He may not be for much longer. It's hard to say for sure. I do hope they stay here though. I've grown much attached to the children." She rambled on for several minutes, telling him about the new baby and the things Suzanne was doing.

"What about your parents and siblings?" he asked. "How are they?"

"Very well. Vati is working in construction and loves his work. Would you believe I have a new brother? A baby born six months ago. He's healthy and eats like a horse. Oh, and Ilse and Petr have a son and another baby on the way."

"Wow. Seems like I've missed a lot," Tom said, shaking his head.

"How is your father? I remember he was ill."

"Better. He had heart surgery a few months after I got home. He's tough and hanging in there. My sister, Teresa, got married and she, too, is expecting a baby."

"Did you tell your family about Julian?" Christa asked.

"I did. They were happy and sad at the same time. They have Julian's photo framed and hanging on the wall in Ron's old bedroom."

Christa smiled, suddenly not sure what to talk about.

Neither of them spoke.

The clock on the fireplace mantel ticked and sounded louder than she'd ever heard it.

"Are you seeing anyone?" Tom asked tentatively.

Should she be coy, the way some of the girls in town were when they wanted to keep a boy interested? No, she didn't think she had that ability. Besides, Tom wasn't a boy. He was a grown man. Twenty-two, or nearly that, now.

"I'm not. I've dated a few boys, but nothing serious. I suppose you have a wife back in the states now." She looked down at the floor, afraid to meet his eyes.

"No, I do not. I actually came here in hopes of finding one. That is, if you're still interested in me."

She raised her head and stared at him, feeling shaky again. Had she heard right, or did she hear what she wanted to hear? "What?"

"Will you marry me?"

"I . . . I, what? You want to marry me? After all this time? What if I've changed?"

"You are even more beautiful than ever, Christa. You're taller, more mature-looking, more confident, I think. And I know you. I know your heart. That has not changed. And believe me, Captain Robinson and Helen would not still have you working for them and caring for their children if they didn't see you as an amazing person. Yes, I want you, if you will have me."

She jumped up from her seat on the sofa and ran to him. He stood up too and she fell into his arms.

A MONTH LATER on Christa's seventeenth birthday, Christa and Tom stood in front of a justice of the peace in the town hall. Because of their different religions, and because they'd jointly decided not to tell Christa's family that Tom was Jewish, they'd opted for a simple ceremony, not in a church, but still surrounded by loved ones. After the ceremony Tom called his parents and told them he was married. He'd been afraid they would try to come to the wedding if he'd called them beforehand, and he didn't want them attempting a long trip that could be difficult with his father's medical problems.

Tom had finished his tour-of-duty and left the military before returning to Germany. Having been trained in electronics while in the army, he was able to land a good paying job in a manufacturing company in Biberach. On the down side, the job, meant he and Christa had to move and Christa had to leave her nanny job. She said she didn't mind. Of course she missed Suzanna and Rosie terribly for a while. It helped that they were close to Karolina and Julian and Ilse and her family. Ilse and Petr had moved to Biberach after the birth of their first child. Ilse and Christa finally had time to get to know each other. A few months after the move, a letter from Helen Robinson indicated that her husband had been reassigned to Austria and they were moving.

Before long, Christa was also expecting a baby, her very own, finally. Ilse and Christa had grown close and being pregnant with child drew them even closer. Ilse gave her lots of advice on maternity clothes, shopping for cribs, and even the best methods for cleaning spots out of baby clothes.

Christa finally had her very own family, one that no one could take from her. The war was over and rebuilding was almost complete. She and her loved ones had plenty of food and clothes and heat, they were safe from bombs and soldiers with rifles, and they no longer had to worry about being chased out of their own home and country. They were home in Germany now, not because Germany was where their family had originated. It was home because it was where her family was. The bad times were behind her; behind them all. She was at peace and she couldn't be happier. If she and Tom and their children someday moved to the states to be closer to Tom's family, she believed she would adjust and be just as happy as she was now being close to her parents and siblings. Place didn't matter one bit. The house they lived in didn't matter, as long as they were safe and together.

CHAPTER TWENTY-SEVEN

Lucas Landry, Nov.-Dec. 2017, Sacramento, California—

OVER THE LAST couple months both of Lucas's aunts finished reading all the historical material. The aunts had visited Lucas and Tawny at their house several times and the four of them always enjoyed talking about Germany and the relatives. His aunts would get all animated and laugh and act more like teenagers than seniors, talking about 'the good old days'. Lucas loved it. Bianca also enjoyed their visits, because the aunts always brought her a special presents and cookies, which Tawny said helped her get over her feelings of being 'the second child' to her new baby brother.

The only thing still bothering Lucas now was not hearing from Seth. "Should I call Seth, or maybe stop by his house after work tomorrow? What do you think, Tawny? Am I getting too impatient?"

She looked up from the book she was reading in bed. "Patience. It hasn't been all that long. Give him some space. If he was ready to talk, he would have called you."

"Is that what you would say to your patients?"

"Well, no, but this is different. You dumped a lot of heavy stuff at his doorstep all at once. He needs time to digest it all. That's all I'm saying."

Lucas nodded, but still worried. What if Seth hadn't even read any of what Lucas had given him? He might have tossed it all into the fire, like way Hanna had tossed the parachute her children had found into the fireplace. He'd promised to read it, some of it, anyway. But Seth may have just said that to get rid of his brother. If he actually had started reading it, wouldn't he continue, could he have stopped reading it?

Lucas sat on the edge of the bed, stretched his arms over his head, exercising his shoulders a few times to get the kinks out before getting under the covers. At work he'd led a support group with ten members, two of whom got into a shouting match he finally had to step in and break up. Not his best day.

"Yeah, I guess you're right," he said, pushing thoughts about work out of his head. "But how is it that two old ladies can get through it quickly, while a young guy like Seth is taking forever?"

Tawny, looking incredulous, laughed. "You're forgetting something, dear hubby, those two 'old ladies', as you are labeling your poor aunts, don't have jobs. They don't have a spouse, and they don't have little kids to look after."

"Right, like my brother is too busy being a dad. I find that hard to believe."

She set down her book for a moment and looked at him. "You don't really know what's going on in his life right now, do you?"

"Well, no." He turned off the light on his nightstand. "You're right, goodnight, sweetie," he said, leaning over and kissing Tawny, then rolling over, facing away from Tawny, who was still reading.

Part of him accepted she was right about giving his brother all the time he needed. Another part figured sometimes people needed to be pushed. If he'd really pushed his father and made him understand he needed help, maybe his father would have gone into drug addiction treatment and maybe, just maybe, he'd still be alive.

He smacked his pillow in an effort to make it more comfortable, and closed his eyes, trying to go to sleep. But he couldn't get comfortable and his mind kept going. *What if I go over to Seth's house tomorrow and just ask him how he is doing? No pressure.* Then again, his brother could go into a rage and attack him if he had read the stuff and knew that he wasn't entirely Aryan. That could happen, right? *Maybe I should leave it alone for now. Damned pillow.* He lifted his head and reformed it. *What if I just left him a message? Darn it, go to sleep!*

"What's wrong, Lucas?"

"Huh, what do you mean?"

"You've been ranging around over there. Something still bothering you?"

"Having trouble getting to sleep. Been a busy day."

"Anything I can do?"

The baby started crying, and Tawny reached over and shut off the baby monitor. "I'll get him. It's my turn."

"Nope. I'm the one who can't get to sleep. I'll get him. You can take the next shift, deal?"

"Deal."

The following afternoon, Lucas drove past Seth's house. Seth's wife was carrying bags of groceries into the house. No sign of Seth. Lucas thought about stopping and helping her, but didn't want to make Seth mad if he found out.

He drove around the block a few times, stopped at a fast food restaurant for a soda, then drove back by the house. Seth's car was finally in the driveway.

Lucas parked in front of the house, strode up to the door, and waited, his hands cold and clammy, heart pounding. He recalled feeling that same way when he'd first gone to the house to begin going through his father's belongings. Fear . . . fear of what? Rejection? Failure? Getting yelled at? Bracing himself, determined that fear wasn't going to control him any longer, Lucas took a deep breath and rang the doorbell.

After several minutes, as he was about to leave, the door jerked open.

"What are you doing here? Didn't expect to see you again," Seth said.

"Sorry for just dropping in like this again, but I was wondering how you were doing. Haven't heard anything from you. Is everything okay?"

Seth shrugged. "Like you really care."

"I do care."

"Yeah, right," Seth said in a snarky voice. "Been how long since you came around here? Two months, three?"

"I was actually waiting to hear from you, remember? You were going to call me." He shook his head, making light of it. "Doesn't matter, really. I didn't want to bug you. Wanted to give you a chance to call when you were ready, you know."

Seth didn't answer.

Lucas rubbed his chin, then glanced around the neighborhood and then back at his brother. "I really do want to know how you've been, Seth. Everything okay?"

No response.

"Is that it?" Lucas said. "You don't have anything to say to me? You don't give a crap that I'm trying here, trying to fix our relationship?"

Seth sighed. "Got in an accident a while back. Shortly after you were here. Was laid-up for a while with a bum leg."

"Oh, Seth. I'm sorry to hear that. Why didn't you call? Are you doing okay now?"

"Yeah. I guess so."

He was half leaning on the edge of the door, making Lucas wonder if he was really 'doing okay'. Seth still didn't invite him inside, and Lucas felt an old familiar self-doubt hold him back from pushing his brother.

"Um, well okay. I guess I should head back home," Lucas said. "Don't want to interrupt your dinner or anything." He turned and walked briskly away, feeling disappointed.

Wait a minute. Isn't this what I did with Dad every time I tried to talk to him about going into rehab for his drug addiction? Just walk away and say, oh well, maybe someday he'll come around?

Lucas stopped, turned around, and saw Seth closing the door. He trotted back toward the door and said, "Wait. Gotta a few minutes to talk, Seth?"

"Uh . . . well yeah, I don't have anything going on right now." He held the door open for him, and Lucas entered the house.

Seth cleared some toys and papers off the sofa and motioned for Lucas to sit. "Allison is upstairs with the kids, giving them baths before dinner." He shrugged. "I made the mistake of taking them to the beach this afternoon. Thought I was feeling good enough to go. Damn leg, kept me shut in for too long."

"I hear ya. You know, we each have a son and a daughter now. Tawny gave birth to a boy two months ago."

Seth nodded and kinda smiled.

"We named him Julian." Lucas watched Seth's face, carefully. Would the name mean anything to him?

Nothing. Had Seth even read any of the material Lucas had given him?

Lucas decided to jump right in and say what he'd come here to say. "Uh, the other reason I came by, besides wanting to see

315

how you're doing, was to see what you thought of the stuff I gave you."

Seth sighed and rubbed his hands over his face, hard, the way their father used to do. He suddenly looked exactly like their father, stubble all over his face, a lost look in his eyes.

"Are you taking painkillers?" Lucas asked. "Because of your leg injury?"

"Was. Quit taking them. Didn't want to end up a user."

He sure didn't look like he'd stopped taking them. "Are you doing okay? Maybe find a group to help you stop?"

Seth said, "No. I don't need help. I can do this on my own."

"Seth, that's what Dad used to say, remember? I have a couple groups at the clinic where I'm working right here in Sacramento. Come to one of our meetings. I have one tomorrow night, seven o'clock." He pulled out his wallet, slipped out one of his clinic cards, and handed it to Seth.

"I don't need your help."

"Then someone else. There's nothing wrong with needing help with a problem," Lucas said. "I became a counselor because I want to help people. You don't have to do this alone. Let me help."

"What do you care if I go back to taking pills?"

"You're my brother, first of all. Secondly, I've seen too many people struggling with pain and addiction. I help them with their problems and help them help themselves."

"What will it cost me?"

"Don't worry about the cost. I'll take care of that. Just come, okay?"

"I guess."

"Great."

They sat in silence for a couple minutes. Lucas looked around the living room. It looked shabbier than he remembered, which seemed odd, considering Dad had left both Seth and

Lucas money. Of course, Lucas had no way of knowing what debts or bills Seth and Allison had accumulated.

"What's happening with your job?" Lucas asked. "You still working at the bank? Last I heard you were an assistant manager or something like that."

Seth winced and looked away for a moment. When he looked back at Lucas, he said, "I lost the job. Got laid-off. They cut you loose if you take too much time off. Didn't care that I'd worked my butt off for six years. Didn't matter that I was nearly killed when a wrong-way driver swerved and crashed into me. Hell. What's wrong with people?"

Good grief, his brother was in pain, but not only physical pain. He was in that downward spiral Lucas had seen too many times.

"Oh man, that's terrible. I'm really sorry. I can check around, if you want, see if anyone has a job opening or knows of one. I know a lot of people."

"You'd do that for me?"

Lucas nodded.

"That would help. Thanks."

Lucas's knee started bouncing, a nervous habit he'd tried to break ever since he was a kid. Better try again to talk about the family tree stuff. "Can I ask, did you get a chance to read the diaries and other stuff I brought over?"

Seth closed his eyes, not responding.

Several minutes went by, with Lucas wondering if Seth had fallen asleep. The sound of a clock ticking nearby caught Lucas's attention, and he turned his head to see where it was. The clock was sitting on the fireplace mantel. A memory flashed through Lucas's mind. Mother had given Seth that clock for his birthday shortly before she passed away. She'd told him that it was something he could keep with him to remember her by.

He sat staring at the clock for several moments, thinking about their childhood and their mother. Finally, Lucas started to get up to show himself out. Seth was apparently asleep. As he stood and turned to go, he heard sound coming from Seth. He turned around again and edged closer, leaned down, slightly.

Seth was quietly crying.

Lucas kneeled down in front of his brother and gently placed a hand on Seth's knee. "Seth, what's going on? Talk to me, please. I'm here to help."

Several more minutes passed, as the crying became louder and louder, and then slowly came to an end.

Seth opened his eyes and swiped at his wet face with his shirtsleeve. "Sorry. I don't know what came over me. Never done that before."

"Was it about Dad?"

He shook his head.

"Did it have something to do with our family tree material? I know there was some pretty shocking stuff in there."

He sniffled. "Yeah, you could have warned me. What the hell? We're Jewish. You're married to a black woman. Our grandfather's brother had an illegitimate kid. What other wild creatures do we have in our family forest, huh?"

"Hey, at least we aren't related to Stalin or Ivan the Terrible or some other dictator."

"Not that we know. Yet. I assume you're going to keep digging."

"Yeah, probably. I guess I've got the bug."

"And you just had to go and give it to me, didn't you?"

"Hey, what's family for, right?"

Seth chuckled, then broke out into a full belly laugh. When he finally stopped, he said, "Wow, that crying and laughing felt good. Who would have thought?"

Lucas pulled a footstool over and sat down on it. "Did you read everything? Did you get to the part that I wrote about going to Germany and meeting some of the people who were in the diaries?"

"Yeah. You actually got to meet Ilse and Petr?"

"Yep. And Julian."

"Ron and Ilse's son?"

"Yeah. Julian's in his sixties now and lives in Munich. Real nice guy. He says he wants to visit us here. Maybe in the spring or summer next year."

"Cool." He didn't say anything more for a couple minutes. "Uh, I guess the aunts probably hate me, right?"

"Because of your neo-Nazi beliefs, you mean?"

"Yeah." His face reddened.

"Do you still feel the same way, after learning about your roots?"

Seth shrugged, squirmed and did a sort of eye-roll. "Guess that cat's out of the bag. But just know, I'm not ready to convert to Judaism."

"That's okay, brother, you're making progress, and that's what counts."

Seth smiled and nodded. "Guess there's hope for me yet, huh?"

"Definitely."

Loud noises on the stairs made them both look up. Allison and the kids were on their way down.

Lucas stood up, and said, "I should be getting home. You guys are probably going to eat dinner soon and Tawny's probably wondering where I am and why I'm not there for dinner."

Seth got up and walked Lucas to the door.

Before Lucas left, he turned to face Seth and said, "I'm really glad we talked. I hope to see you tomorrow night at the clinic. Tawny and I are having a cookout on Saturday. Probably the last warm day for one this year. I invited the aunts and I really, really hope you and Allison and the kids will come."

Seth smiled and, surprisingly, gave Lucas a hug. "I wouldn't miss it."

THE COOKOUT AT Lucas and Tawny's house went famously. They drank beer and wine, Lucas cooked hot dogs and burgers on the grill, wearing a chef's hat everyone made fun of. Tawny made a big pot of chili and another of baked beans and put out bags of chips and pretzels (to go with the beer, Lucas attested). Afterward, they cut up and handed out chunks of watermelon and sat around enjoying the company.

Seth and Allison were quiet at first, and Lucas worried about them, but between Tawny and the aunts, the young couple finally relaxed and opened up. Turned out, Allison had never really shared Seth's visions of an Aryan world and while her husband was busy, quietly thanked Lucas for helping Seth change back into the guy she'd fallen in love with back in high school.

Once she said that, a light bulb went off in Lucas's head. Now he remembered the shy girl who had followed the popular football player, Seth, around, always seeming to be ill at ease around his popular friends. However, when alone with Seth and Lucas, she opened up and blossomed like a flower in the sunshine.

Kids always have an easier time, Lucas decided. Put them together in a backyard with a swing set, a few toys, especially the kind you can ride on, and they become instant best friends.

As they sat around the fire pit in the backyard, Seth said to Lucas, "You told me you actually got to meet Ilse and Petr and Ilse's son, Julian."

"Yep."

"Wow, that's cool. I guess you named your boy after him."

"Well, sort of. After him and also after our great-uncle, the first son of our grandparents, Christa and Tom."

"Huh? Wait a minute. I thought they only had one son. Our dad. Joseph."

"Yeah, I didn't know about him, either. After my return, when I told Aunt Anna and Aunt Elsa about Julian, their Uncle Ron's son, they told me about their other brother, Julian. He was born in Biberach, in between Elsa and our dad. He was what was called a blue baby. His heart wasn't fully developed, and he only lived a few days."

"So you named your son after both of them." Seth leaned back and took a swallow of his beer. "That's damn cool, in my opinion."

"Hey, there's something else," Lucas said, "Did you know that our Aunt Anna was also named after Hanna Nagel, Christa's mother, and partly after the baby that Hanna gave birth to after the war. That baby also only lived a few hours. Christa never forgot her precious doll-like baby sister and decided to name her first child after her."

"Oh. What makes you think that?" Seth asked.

"Christa's sister, Giselle, told me. Her mother, Hanna Nagel, is our great-grandmother. Her daughter, Christa Emelie Nagel, married Tom Landry. After they moved here to California Christa began using her middle name, Emelie. That's what threw me at first, when I was told our grandparents were Tom and Emelie Landry. Well, you've probably already figured all that out." Lucas shrugged, trying to remember how much he'd written down and put in that box. "Anyway, Aunt Anna and Aunt Elsa didn't know. They were really young when they came to the U.S. They actually met their grandmother, Hanna, while they lived in Biberach, but they knew her only as Oma, not as Hanna Nagel. Their cousins, Giselle, Fritz, and some of the other siblings, as well as some of their children, told me some of that history."

They sat for a time, drinking beer, watching their kids play together, tending the fire and just enjoying the afternoon sun. The aunts walked over to the fire pit and sat in lawn chairs nearby, drinking wine coolers. Anna and Elsa talked to each other a few minutes while they watched the kids play. Then they moved their chairs closer and began telling Seth and Lucas what it had been like for them, living in Germany when they were little. They talked about winter festivities around the town, sledding on the hills, and ice skating when they were kids. Oh, they said they had great fun as youngsters in Germany.

By the time everyone went home, they'd all agreed to meet again for another family party at the aunts' house in a few weeks. Seth and Allison and their kids would get to meet the rest of the family that lived in Northern California—the aunts' kids and grandkids and great-grandkids.

A MONTH LATER, on Christmas Eve, in the old German traditional celebration of Christmas, Lucas and his family and Seth and his immediate family gathered together at Lucas's home in the Victorian house where the two men had lived with their parents. The adults drank a warm German spice wine that Tawny had found the recipe for online.

Lucas and Tawny sat on the sofa, near their Christmas tree, watching as the kids played with the presents Santa had brought. Tawny leaned her head on Lucas's shoulder, while baby Julian slept in her arms.

Tawny's mother, Lani, and her new boyfriend, Earl, an Australian who had a thing about wearing hats all the time— everywhere—sat on the loveseat, holding hands, watching the kids and sharing smiles with each other. Tonight Earl had switched it up, wearing a Santa hat instead of his outback hunter's hat that he said he'd gotten after he'd caught a crocodile. Lucas had a hard time knowing when Earl was kidding and when he was being serious.

Allison kneeled on the floor shining a laser light around, exercising the cat.

Seth stood in front of the fireplace, holding the family photo taken at Christmastime, years ago. This was the same photo Lucas had felt sad to look at after their father died but was now very grateful to have. It was funny, he thought, how time and perspective could change feelings and attitude.

"Do you think Mom and Dad are watching us from Heaven?" Seth asked, looking over at Lucas.

"I hope so. I picture them smiling and looking fondly at the family they created while they were here on earth. Where they are now, I expect they probably know everything that we were all too blind to see before. The more we learn about history and the world and how things are connected, the more likely it is we can understand that everyone makes mistakes, and that we can learn from them, and that we don't have to hold onto guilt feelings forever. Just grow and do better in the future."

Seth smiled. "I like that idea." He hesitated a moment, setting the frame back on the mantel. "I'll add to your comment. I now believe that our mistakes and struggles make us stronger and better able to face whatever challenges come our way."

"I couldn't agree more," Lucas said.

After a few moments, Seth added, "I think Dad was actually a decent father. A little screwed up, like we all are, but not as bad as I remembered when I was angry with him."

"Yeah, I think we didn't get to know Dad the way I wish we had. But you know, we actually did have some good times as a family, didn't we? And this house wasn't a bad place to grow up, either."

CAST LIST

Landry family in Sacramento, California in 2017—
Parents: Joseph Landry (born 1959) and Jennifer Landry (born 1961). Both deceased. Oldest child: Lucas Landry (born 1989), psychologist who specializes in drug addiction.
Wife of Lucas: Tawny Landry (born 1987), also a psychologist.
Child of Lucas and Tawny: Bianca Landry (born 2014).
Brother of Lucas: Seth Landry (born 1992).
Wife of Seth: Allison (Ally) Landry.
Children of Seth and Allison: Skyler Landry (born 2014), Benny Landry (born 2016).
Aunts of Lucas and Seth: Anna Marshall (born 1951) and Elsa Cartwright (born 1953).
Mother of Tawny: Lindelani (Lani) Theron

Nagel family in Altstadt in the Sudetenland—
Parents: Franz Nagel (Vati) and Hannelore (Hanna) Nagel (Mutti).
Oldest child is Christa (born July 1933). She is ten when the story begins.
Christa's Siblings: Ernst (born 1934), Julia (born 1935), Fritz (born in 1936), Giselle (born 1939), Andreas (born 1942), and Dirk (born March 1945).

Seidel family in Memmingen, Germany—
Parents: Bernhard Seidel (Vater) and Maria Seidel (Mutter).
Oldest child is Ilse (born August 1928). She is fifteen when the story begins.
Ilse's Siblings: Johann (born February 1930), Robert (born 1936), and Ursula (born March 1932). Grandparents: Klauss Fischer (Opa) and Anna Fischer (Oma).

Jaroslav family in Czechoslovakia—
Parents: Olexa Jaroslav (Otec) and Jolanta Jaroslavova (Máma).
Son: Petr Jaroslav (born April 1928). He is fifteen when the story begins.

Petr's Older Siblings: Antonin (born 1925) and Josef Jaroslav (born 1926). One is three years old than Petr and one is two years older than Petr.

Petr's Younger Siblings: Kamila (born 1936) and Milena (born 1940), Gabriel (born in 1942), and Vera, (born 1933).

Antonin's girlfriend: Rebeka is Jewish and she and her family—close friends of the Jaroslav family—are taken away to Terezin/Theresienstadt concentration camp.

Landry family in Sacramento, California in 1944—

Parents: William and Rachel Landry.

Oldest child: Ronald Landry (born 1924).

Ron's siblings: Thomas (born 1927), and Teresa (born 1937)

ABOUT THE AUTHOR

Besides her story telling, Susan Finlay's passions include photography, hiking, and traveling. Susan has two grown functional offspring who, having left the nest, are making their own success in the world. Susan resides in the Phoenix, Arizona metro area with her husband and their three pampered cats (though whether they own the cats or the cats own them remains another unsolved mystery in its own right).

Before becoming an author, Susan earned a degree in business, worked for some years as a Bank Auditor and later under the Bank Secrecy Act performed suspicious activities investigations.

To date, she has nine published novels and more stories yet to tell. This novel represents the first book in her Tangled Roots historical mystery series. She has written four books so far in her Outsiders mystery series, *In the Shadows*, *Where Secrets Reside*, *Winter Tears*, and *The Forgotten Tomb*. She has two books so far in her Bavarian Woods time travel mystery series, *Inherit the Past* and *Tanglewood Grotto*, and has initial novels in two other series, *Liars' Games* in her Project Chameleon suspense series and *The Handyman* in her Chambre Noir mystery series.

Susan began blogging in October 2013. You can read articles by Susan and her guests, on various topics, on her blog. You can also find her on Facebook and on Twitter.

https://susansbooks37.wordpress.com/
https://www.facebook.com/pages/Susan-Finlay-Author/108287392652815?ref=hl
https://twitter.com/SusanFinlay4

Please leave a review, for this book and her other books, on Amazon.com. Reviews provide the author and other potential readers with useful feedback.